For the Love of Ethan

A novel

Marjorie Reynolds

PUBLISHED BY WINDSTORM PRESS
Portland, Oregon"

ISBN-13: 978-1547229314
ISBN-10: 1547229314

NOVELS BY

MARJORIE REYNOLDS

The Starlite Drive-in

The Civil Wars of Jonah Moran

Ideal Beach

In memory of my sons,
David and Matthew Shoemaker

Chapter 1

I am an ordinary woman.

I have never rescued anyone from a burning building. I have never painted a picture, written a poem, or composed a piece of music that would live beyond me. I can recognize an eighteenth-century sampler in a box of old linens, but otherwise I possess no uncommon talents or skills. Giving birth to my son Ethan is the only truly important thing I have ever done.

If you had asked me a year ago if life was good, I would have said it was. I had a devoted husband, a sweetheart of a son, and a charming vintage home with two mortgages that would be paid off in a hundred years. We'd had our problems, but through them all I'd careened along, taking little time for self-examination or introspection. It never occurred to me to feel dissatisfied with my limitations.

Should I have made better choices? Probably. Did I do everything possible to avoid what happened? No mother could ever answer that she did.5

Winter eased into a neon spring with fourteen straight days of sun, a Seattle miracle. A few weeks of this kind of weather and a person almost forgets the gloom that invades the Northwest much of the year.

I went to an estate sale that May morning at a capacious, rundown white elephant of a home on Seattle's Capitol Hill. The whole place smelled musty. A few dozen people elbowed each other to examine the displays of china, glassware, silverware, and curios — a good crowd for a Monday morning. I perused the first floor, ending up in the parlor, which was dominated by an impressive staircase and a diving brass fish shooting up from the baluster. Its mouth held a white globe bulb.

A woman with perfectly coifed blond hair, tailored navy blue dress, and black-rimmed reading glasses pored over some paperwork at a small secretary desk in the corner. She'd probably been hired to manage the sale.

I glanced around. Nothing much here. I turned and started toward the door, but then I felt a familiar tingle in my sinuses. My friend, Liz, used to say it was the dust from all that old junk clogging my nose, but I argued it was a sign. I couldn't explain it, but like a water witch with a divining rod, I knew when I was near a treasure.

My gaze landed on a lamp set back under a table. With its muddy green, orange, and brown, flower-patterned glass shade, it nearly faded into the home's dark woodwork. I bent over and examined it. It had a few long scratches on the tarnished brass base but no serious damage — and no price tag.

I strolled over to the saleswoman, who offered a practiced smile.

I gave her a restrained one in return. It had taken me years to control my excitement at moments like this. "How much is that lamp over there?"

She eyed it across the room. "It should have a sticker on it."

"I didn't see one."

She walked over to the lamp, extracted it from its place under the table, and set it on a marble-topped sideboard nearby.

I looked it over. "It is pretty ugly, isn't it?"

"Well, I wasn't going to say anything since you seemed interested in it." She pulled out her inventory list and ran her pale pink fingernail down it.

"I've always been fascinated by old lamps," I said, "especially ones that are so ugly they're charming. Do you ever wonder about the history of the pieces you sell?"

She looked up from the list. "Oh, yes. In some cases, they come with documentation."

"I wasn't thinking of that. Those are just pieces of paper. I was thinking of what this lamp has seen. The Christmases and birthdays and family arguments. Even deaths. There was a time, you know, when the deceased was laid out in the parlor, and I can see this lamp lighting the room."

"Hmm," she said.

I wiggled the switch. "This is loose, and the base has some scratches on it. Can't be more than fifteen dollars."

"Oh, here it is. Thirty-five dollars. No documentation, unfortunately."

"Thirty-five for an ugly flowered lamp? How about twenty?"

She didn't reply. She was studying the lamp further, taking off her glasses, peering under the glass shade, and frowning. From the corner of my eye, I saw an elderly gray-haired woman watching us. She wore baggy jeans, a heavy turtleneck sweater, and a knowing smile. Her face was a wrinkled map. I rested a proprietary hand on the lamp and shifted my position so I blocked the saleswoman's view of her.

"I guess thirty-five is okay," I said in a low voice.

She hesitated, and I knew she was questioning the price. I could have offered her more. That's what a less experienced collector might do, but it would only have fueled her suspicions. I smiled at the saleswoman. The doubt passed from her face, and she reached for her receipt book.

On the way out, I whispered to the woman who had been watching us, "Pairpoint."

Her shoulders fell in disappointment. "Thought it might be. An even uglier one than that sold last winter at an auction in Concord, Massachusetts, for two thousand. I'll pay you that much right now. You would make a terrific profit."

I touched my fingertips to the glass shade and felt the electric charge between us.

"Oh, no. I couldn't part with it. It's really quite a beauty." I smiled. "Besides, I remember reading about that auction. The Pairpoint sold for four thousand."

I was still feeling the glow as I walked toward my car.

My cell phone rang. I pulled it out of my purse and looked at the display. Betsy Saffle, the nurse from my son's school, Kimichee Elementary.

"Ethan's complaining of a stomachache, Mrs. Franklin," she

said in a voice so high she sounded like one of the students. "Could be genuine. His teacher doesn't have any tests scheduled today."

Sick to his stomach? More likely sick of school. He had been struggling with fourth grade math all year. I assured the nurse I would be there in ten minutes.

Kimichee Elementary perched on the north slope of Queen Anne Hill. As I headed in that direction, winding my car around traffic circles and through streets narrowed by parked vehicles, I considered how I should deal with this so-called stomachache. It didn't take a psychologist to see the parallel between it and the onset of fractions. Not that his father would agree.

The week before, as we were trudging up the stairs to bed, Joel had said, "Delainie, Ethan doesn't seem himself lately."

"And who else would he be?" I said. "A creature from outer space? Or one of those gory monsters he builds in his bedroom?"

"He looks tired and spacey. Maybe he's got some bug or a low-grade infection."

Men, I thought. They see only what's on the surface. I waved away his comment. "Ethan's fine. He's stressed out about school. It'll be over in two months, and he'll perk right up."

If we could just get him though the next few weeks with decent grades. I couldn't think of anything worse than his flunking fourth grade. He would be mortified. I pulled into the school parking lot and nosed my twelve-year-old Buick into a lone, cramped space between a Mercedes sedan and a Miata convertible.

The sun hovered over the school's stylized cupola, backlighting a white-faced clock that actually displayed the correct time, two minutes after noon, while twenty yards away, a string of kindergartners with Barbie and Noisy Dinosaurs book bags hooked over their shoulders boarded a yellow bus. Decked out in every primary color in the spectrum, they were as cute as lollipops.

Inside the school, Miss Saffle, looking old enough to be a

candy-striper but not a school nurse, greeted me at the sick-room door with an effusive smile and ushered me into the tiny room that resembled the one where I used to hang out in elementary school: white square sink, shelf with Band-Aid boxes, tongue depressors, spare blankets, a fold-up bed. Ethan, wan and forlorn, lay stretched out on it, a brown wool blanket pulled up to his chin.

He stared up at me with glazed eyes. "Hi, Mom."

I dropped onto the chair next to the cot and pressed my hand to his forehead. Seemed cool enough. "Bad tummy, huh, Ethan Skywalker?"

Usually, he grinned when I called him a "Star Wars" or comic book name. This time, he looked at me and nodded. As I gave him a cursory inspection, I felt a rush of love. He reminded me of my father — not a blessing when it came to his appearance — because Dad was a true block of a man with short arms and legs, a square jaw, and ears that could serve as fans on a hot summer day. Ethan was short for his age, but I wasn't worried. His pediatrician said kids grow at different rates. He and my father both had generous smiles and cotton-soft hearts, but some people couldn't see those.

I remember my mother-in-law watching Ethan demolish a slice of chocolate cake on his third birthday.

"So homely he's cute," she had said in a make-the-best-of-it tone.

"Shhh," I'd hissed, not caring if I offended her. I hadn't liked her before and, after that, I liked her even less.

Ethan struggled to a sitting position on the cot and emitted a tight groan. I studied him, trying to decide whether it was genuine or manufactured. "Is this the flu, young man, or an allergic reaction to math?"

Without a word, he hunched his shoulders and with impeccable aim vomited onto my favorite beige wool slacks.

I thrust my hands under his chin to catch the rest of the orange-tinged Cheerios and toast chunks that tumbled out. "Oh, Batman."

A sour odor wafted upward.

"Oops," said Miss Saffle in a chirpy voice.

She yanked a few paper towels from the wall dispenser, and held them out. I emptied the contents of my hands, then scrubbed at the mess, leaving a nubby, orange residue on the fabric. My goodness, he really was sick.

He looked stricken.

"No harm done." I rose from the chair and deposited the paper towels in a black, flip-top waste can. "Luckily, we've got an excellent dry cleaner, haven't we, Batman?"

Pushing back a strand of her brown hair, Miss Saffle frowned. "Those dry-cleaning chemicals aren't healthy for any of us. I myself wear hemp. It's washable and sturdy."

I wanted to say I preferred to smoke it, but instead I ran my gaze over her rough-textured jumper and said, "Uh-huh."

"Does your son eat meat, Mrs. Franklin?" She had one of those pale faces that have never seen the stain of wanton cosmetics.

"Only McDonald's bacon burgers. Why do you ask?"

She bristled. Apparently she disapproved of McDonald's.

"His color looks off. I've seen people who eat meat get that sallow look."

It was my turn to bristle. "We're not vegetarians, Miss Saffle, but I can assure you Ethan has a healthy diet..." I turned away and added under my breath, "with the exception of a few dozen foods."

"I hate vegetables," Ethan murmured helpfully.

Miss Saffle looked down her nose at him. "That's probably because you weren't introduced to them properly. Too many children grow up with food coated in salt or sugar."

"Uh-huh," he said.

"They think nothing tastes good without it."

Never mind that, to tempt him, I had prepared vegetables in every possible way, from crispy raw to puréed.

I had offered him a nickel for every pea he ate and, when that didn't work, deprived him of his favorite foods and sent him to bed hungry.

The only option left was to force feed him, which I couldn't bring myself to do. It was obvious this school nurse had never run into a colossally stubborn child. She leaned over and peered into his eyes, apparently examining the size of his pupils. I confess I wouldn't have minded if, at that moment, Ethan had suffered another bout of projectile vomiting.

Before she could criticize me because he wore dirty jeans or because I washed his clothes in phosphates, I bundled him off to the car. Outside, in the sunlight, Ethan's naturally tawny skin did look yellowish.

I gave him a quick hug. "You poor kid. You really do feel awful, don't you?"

He slouched into his most pathetic pose, which involved a tilt of his head, a pronounced droop at the corners of his mouth, and a settling of both eyelids at half-mast.

A little too pitiable, I thought, my maternal skepto-meter kicking in again. "Either that or your pizza and potato chips diet has finally caught up with you."

Looking queasy, he took a few steps, bent over, and expelled what little was left in his stomach. Whether it was luck or planning on his part, he stood directly over a grated drain.

Feeling guilty, I reached toward him. "Maybe we should stop at the drugstore and get something to calm your insides."

"No-o-o," he moaned. I opened the car door, and he crawled onto the worn velour seat, snapped on his seatbelt, and leaned back wearily. "I just want to go home."

Chapter 2

My gourmet group was meeting at my house that evening. I decided not to cancel but to sequester Ethan in his bedroom with a children's book of biographies on famous men, including Albert Einstein, who failed math in school. My friend Jaya usually brought her son Krishna to hang out with Ethan whenever we cooked at my house, but I called to tell her Ethan was ill.

"Oh, Delainie, I hope it's not serious."

"I'm sure it isn't, but I don't want to expose Krishna to anything. If Ethan isn't better by tomorrow, I'll call the doctor."

Jaya Stern was the most nurturing woman I knew, and as the only other mother in our gourmet group, we talked ad nauseam about our two boys. She and the others in the group, Cappy Fiorito and Liz Wylie, were my best friends, the kind you pledge your undying loyalty to in high school and hope to have as roommates in the nursing home. Only I couldn't stand the girls in high school and I didn't meet this trio until long after Doc Martens, big hair and stirrup pants were unfortunate memories.

Cappy had posted a three-by-five card on the community bulletin board at Safeway. "LOOKING FOR OTHER LOUSY COOKS LIKE ME," it read.

There were replies penned in the white space.

"You mean there's life beyond tuna casserole?" Jaya had written, using a rounded script with little circles to dot the "i's." "If so, count me in."

Liz's message read, "Will this help me get a man or merely indigestion?"

I knew before I met them I would like these women.

In the beginning, fourteen years ago, there were seven of us in our cooking group. We began with earnest optimism, shifting each month from house to house, packing our specialty pans and thirty-ingredient recipes from *Bon Appetit*, *Gourmet*, and some French culinary magazine that Diane, one of the original members, subscribed to. A few of us found the meetings much more fun when we tapped into the cooking wine.

One evening, Katrina, a bank executive, swept her gaze over Liz, Cappy, Jaya, and me. "You're not taking this seriously,"

"And you drink too much," said Charlene, a prissy little store manager.

Staring at the Medallions of Buffalo in Wild Mushroom Puree, looking as unpalatable as cow pies poached by the sun, we collapsed into laughter.

"These aren't gourmet dinners," Liz hooted. "These are animal sacrifices."

The others never saw the humor. After that, they stopped coming. We—the remaining four—continued meeting once a month, sometimes more often, simply because we liked each other. Gone were the cow pies and the Cold Paupiettes of Halibut with White Pepper Mousse coalescing like lumps of wallpaper paste on Jaya's gold-rimmed plates. Instead, when we felt ambitious, we boiled pasta and slopped a little marinara sauce over it. More importantly, we talked and listened — and then talked some more.

That evening after I'd picked up Ethan from school, Cappy, Jaya, and I were seated around my dining room table, enjoying Ritz crackers, Alouette cheese, a lovely Washington cabernet (we had become more discriminating about our wine), and a box of fine chocolates, when Liz breezed through the front door. She dropped her designer handbag next to my antique porcelain umbrella stand and headed straight for the chocolates.

"Oh, my God, let me at them." She swept a stack of newspapers and magazines off a chair and sank onto it. "I have had the worst week. People think television production is glamorous, but I work like a mad woman and they pay me shit."

She bit into a large truffle. "On top of that, I've gained five pounds, and I haven't had a date in eight months."

Liz, who actually worked out, was leaner than the rest of us. Jaya cupped her hand around her ear. "Anyone else notice a nasal whine in the air?"

"Hey, I deserve sympathy, not ridicule."

"I deserve a smaller butt, but that doesn't mean I'll get one," I said.

At that, Jaya and Liz laughed and nodded in agreement.

Cappy registered a faint smile but didn't join in the banter since she was diagnosed with multiple sclerosis.

We were at her side in the doctor's office two years ago when he told her she had the progressive variety: a slow, unremitting demyelination of the central nervous system, marked by increasing loss of muscular control and the onset of other disabilities. First, a cane, then a walker, possibly a wheelchair. There was no cure for MS and she never complained, but her quick, dry wit fell through a crack and hadn't yet resurfaced.

Liz plucked another piece of candy. "Do you realize if chocolate gave you power, women would rule?"

We silently pondered the wisdom of that for a few moments.

Liz glanced around. "It's too quiet in here. Where are Ethan and Krishna?"

I was updating her when Ethan shuffled into the dining room, his skin murky, his features pinched tight. Before he could open his mouth, I dashed into the kitchen, grabbed a plastic bowl, ran back into the dining room, and thrust it under his chin.

He stared at it for a moment, then pushed it away. "I wondered why everyone had stopped laughing."

He looked so forsaken that all I could say was, "Oh, Ethan Skywalker."

Jaya scooted back her chair. "Come sit on my lap. We'll be laughing again soon, you wait and see." As she scooped Ethan into her embrace, the light from the candles — we never neglected ambience — caught the shine of her black hair and the deep rose color in her warm brown skin.

"He might be contagious," I said.

She hugged him. "I have a terrific immune system."

A few years back, Joel took a snapshot of the gang. I propped it on the kitchen windowsill, intending to frame it, but it still sits there, sun-faded and water-stained. We look like stair steps: Jaya, a round-on-the edges, black-eyed East Indian beauty, is the shortest. Next in height is Cappy, a widowed computer analyst, her gray-streaked, coco15a-colored hair in its usual muss, a crooked half-smile on her face. Next to Cappy was Liz, a divorcee with blond hair cut into a feathery cap, small eyes, no boobs, but a sense of humor that could put her on a Las Vegas stage. And there I am in the photo at the far right, slouchy tall with blond-streaked brown hair, my mother's thin nose, and a waistline that looks small only because of the sturdy pedestal it rests on. We range in age from thirty-five to forty-five, although Liz is strangely circumspect about where she falls within that span. The others and I speculate she's had a facelift, but we've never come right out and asked her. Liz wears contacts. The rest of us wear glasses when we feel the urge to see.

Cappy came to our last meeting leaning on a cane. Before then, she had relied on kitchen counters, tables, the backs of chairs, and whatever else it took to get around. Liz tried to make light of Cappy's new appendage, suggesting we all carve our names in the wood the way people used to write on a friend's cast. Cappy didn't look amused.

When Ethan sat on Jaya's lap, Cappy, who I knew had a quiet but strong affection for him, merely glanced at him. Then she roused herself, cocked her head, and studied him intently for several seconds, finally, leaning over and pushing a hank of hair back from his forehead. "Been eating a lot of carrots lately, Ethan?"

"I hate carrots, Aunt Cappy," he said.

Having grown up with my group, Ethan called all of them his aunties. He was closer to them than he'd ever been to my twin brothers, Douglas and Donald.

Cappy rested her hand on Ethan's shoulder. "How about a bowl of ice cream? Think that might make you feel better?"

"I knew we were missing someone at the table," I said. "We forgot Ben and Jerry."

Liz went to the kitchen and brought back a dish of Chunky Monkey for Ethan. She set it in front of him, then turned to me. "Did you pay real money for that lamp in the kitchen?"

"It's worth four thousand dollars."

"My God," Jaya said.

"Only if you can bring yourself to sell it," Liz murmured, surveying the antiques in our cluttered dining room.

"I'll sell it when I get my shop." In my mind, I could see that cubbyhole of a store tucked inside an old brick building in Seattle's Pioneer Square, crammed with collectibles, and smelling of polish, weathered wood, and pleasant memories.

Ethan gobbled down the ice cream with more enthusiasm than he'd shown all day. Well, there, I thought, he'd be back to normal by morning.

After a few more minutes, his eyes began to droop and he shuffled down the hall to his room.

Cappy turned to me and raised her eyebrows with a sense of importance. "He should see a doctor, Delainie."

Cappy didn't have any children. Otherwise, she would have known they hop from one infectious illness to another. I gave her my mother-knows-best smile. "It's only the flu."

"He looks jaundiced, Delainie,"

I waved my hand at the chandelier dangling overhead, casting its dim saffron glow over us. "It's the crummy lighting."

"I don't think so. Unless he's using a fake tanning cream, a child who has gone through our sunless winter shouldn't have the tawny complexion he does."

I felt a chilly tickle along my hairline. "What do you think might cause that?"

"I don't want to speculate. He needs to have a doctor look at him."

Immediately after the group left, I hurried upstairs to the office Joel and I shared. Sitting at the computer, I shakily punched the word jaundice into an Internet search engine that led me to a list of diseases that included yellowing of the skin among their symptoms. After I ruled out alcohol-induced cirrhosis and drug-induced liver failure, I was left with a choice of about thirty others, including hepatitis B and C, liver tumors, and two with the jaw-breaking names of hemangioendothelioma and familial hypercholesterolemia. I rubbed at the growing tightness in the back of my neck. I'd always believed the more difficult an illness was to pronounce, the more deadly it must be.

Finally, I came upon the diagnosis I was looking for, although I had no idea beforehand that it existed: Gilbert's syndrome, according to the medical dictionary, created mild jaundice during stress, a hereditary condition requiring no treatment.

Once the crisis had passed, it would disappear like a summer tan. My shoulders collapsed in relief. Of course, that's what it was. He was worried about school.

He was failing fourth grade math. That was plenty of stress for a ten year old. And what had I done? I'd made him read biographies of famous men, as if he wasn't good enough just the way he was.

There was something else about this minor condition that I found appealing. Because my father's first name was Gilbert, the coincidence seemed a favorable omen.

By the time Joel walked in a few minutes later, my hands had stopped trembling. He looked so exhausted I decided not to mention what I'd been doing. He and his partner, Yoo Jin Lee, another former Boeing engineer, designed high-end websites with video streaming, clanging bells and multiple whistles, a business that required twelve to sixteen-hour workdays. I missed Joel but understood the investment it required. Every few weeks, he assured me things were going well, although I wondered which of us he was trying to convince.

When Ethan was born, we agreed I would stay home with him as long as possible while I built up an inventory for the antique shop I planned to open. Our four-bedroom, craftsman-style home cost more than we'd planned to spend, but the moment we saw it we had to have it.

If it were located two streets farther south, we would have a view of Mount Rainier, Lake Union, and the Space Needle, and the price would have been far beyond our means. As it was, we looked at the backside of an Emerald City Pizza sign.

Joel shed his suit jacket and laid it over a chair.

Even when he was tired, he looked perfectly put together. His weight was the same as it had been when we'd married.

He had fine-grained skin and hair so deeply black I had always wondered if he was part Indian (his mother insisted he wasn't). I thought he was handsome, but when I looked at him objectively I wasn't sure. His features seemed too irregular for that, and his intensity had ground a groove between his eyebrows. But after fifteen years of marriage his face was so familiar I might as well have been staring at my own.

I closed the laptop and stood.

"I assume the ugly lamp downstairs in the kitchen is worth more than it looks."

"Four thousand dollars," I said cheerfully, "or thereabouts. How about that?"

Joel stretched his arms over his head, then gave an exaggerated yawn.

"What? Four thousand dollars doesn't impress you?"

"Honey, it would if I thought you'd be able to part with that lamp someday."

"Of course I will. It's an investment."

"They're not investments if you never sell them."

I pursed my lips in mock disdain. "Well, I will when I have my shop."

He walked over, wrapped his big arms around me, and kissed the curve of my neck. "You smell good."

"That's PAM. I accidentally sprayed myself with it this morning while I was fixing Ethan a pancake."

He laughed. "That's why you taste so buttery. Dinner in the oven?"

"There's chicken, but it's probably dry as a potato chip."

He released the knot on his tie and unhooked the top button of his shirt. "I'll get it in a minute. So, how's the big guy?"

"I had to pick him up at school around noon. He was throwing up."

Joel was suddenly alert. "How is he now?"

"Much better. He had a low-grade fever a few hours ago, but he ate a bowl of ice cream, crawled into bed and immediately fell asleep. I'll see how he is tomorrow morning." I hesitated. "Cappy thinks I should take him to the doctor."

"I agree."

"It's no big deal, though. It's what happens when kids are in school. They pass those germs around like valentines."

Ethan's orange cat, Oscar, ambled in, leaped onto the arm of the swaybacked sofa, and prodded my hand with his nose, purring like a vacuum cleaner.

Joel didn't say anything for a few seconds. Oscar headed toward him, and Joel absentmindedly scratched between the cat's ears. "Delainie, I know you don't like doctors, but I would feel better if he got checked out. Seems like he just got over a cold, and now he has the flu."

I took a deep breath. "That clinic is depressing. He'd probably catch something just walking through the door. I don't like that place."

"They've remodeled it. When was the last time you were there?"

"I don't know. Before they changed it, I guess."

I hated all things medical. A person might go to the doctor's office with some minor ailment and the next thing she knew they'd stuck her in the hospital, jabbed her full of holes, and anchored her to the bed. Then she really got sick.

My grandmother's illness began with a sore throat.

I remember seeing her in the hospital. I was ten at the time. Her arms were strapped to the bed rails so she wouldn't yank out the tubes that ran into her arm, neck, and nose, and the one that trailed from under her bed covers and emptied yellow liquid into a bulging plastic bag.She mumbled incoherently. My grandfather, crying openly, wished aloud that he had never taken her to the doctor in the first place.

"She started going downhill the minute she got here," he said.

Joel looked at me shrewdly. "I know what you're thinking, but this has nothing to do with your grandmother. You would only be taking Ethan in for a checkup."

I felt something twist in my chest. "Do you think something's seriously wrong with him?"

"I don't know, but it won't hurt to find out."

Oh, yes, it could. It might hurt very much.

"All right," I said. "I'll call the pediatrician tomorrow."

"Good. Then we'll all feel better."

Chapter 3

At nine o'clock the next morning, Ethan and I huddled in the clinic's antiseptic-scented examining room as he perched on the end of the high, paper-draped, exam table, dangling his jeans-clad legs over the pullout step and crossing his arms protectively over his buttoned plaid shirt. He'd refused to wear the Bugs Bunny gown the nurse gave him.

"Stupid," he said in a small voice.

I sat on a chair, staring at him, wondering how I could not have noticed that his skin looked like paper left out in the sun.

He grimaced. "I'm going to get a shot, right?"

"I don't think so. The doctor is going to make sure this flu isn't anything serious. She'll probably thump on your back, listen to your heart — things like that."

"Why do I have to have a lady doctor? Why can't my doctor be a man?"

"Because you've seen Dr. Snyder since you were tiny, and she's a nice person."

"Well, I'm not a baby anymore."

He ran his fingers through his sandy hair until strands of it stood on end, giving him a slightly wild appearance. I glanced in the mirror over the sink and decided we both looked like cornered animals.

"I'll bet she gives me a shot," he muttered. "She does that every time I come here. Tell her no shots, Mom. Okay? No shots!"

"But it's for your own good, Superman."

I sounded so phony.

He gave me a distraught look that said he expected in a pinch I would betray him.

Dr. Sally Snyder, a trim, fiftyish woman with strawberry blond hair and blue-rimmed glasses, walked in, clutching Ethan's medical records. "Hello there, young man. It's been a while since I've seen you," she said cheerily. "I think the last time was for your third grade physical."

Ethan's lips tightened and he murmured, "Yeah, I remember."

I gave him my stern, don't-embarrass-me look, and he pinned his gaze on the maroon-and-gray pattern of the industrial carpet.

She glanced at the chart. A nurse had already checked his blood pressure and taken his temperature. "Let's see now. When did you come down with this flu?"

"Yesterday." His voice was low. "I threw up at school."

"I see." She moved closer to him and palpated his neck with her fingers. "So how is school these days, Ethan?"

"It's okay." He added under his breath, "except for math."

"Math?" She slipped her hand under his chin, lifted his head, and examined his eyes.

If she saw anything unusual about them, she didn't say.

"Fractions," Ethan said.

She nodded sympathetically. "I had problems with them too. Then one day they all made sense. I bet that'll happen to you."

Ethan looked morose. "I don't think so."

I tried to give him my most reassuring smile.

Dr. Snyder checked his mouth, nose, and ears. She stepped back and studied him for several moments. Normally the upbeat, vibrant type, she was frowning so of course I began to worry.

"Any other symptoms you've noticed, Mom?"

I hated being called Mom by people other than my son, but I answered politely, "Well, his skin color seems a bit off."

"Yes, it is. When did you first notice the jaundice?"

"Actually, I didn't. My friend pointed it out yesterday. Could it be...?" I lowered my voice. "Could it be Gilbert's disease?"

"Excuse me?"

I took her aside.

"Gilbert's," I whispered. "I read about it. It comes from having a mother who makes her son read biographies about successful people he can never hope to be. It's not terribly serious, though. Once she stops doing things like that, the jaundice goes away."

"Hmm," she said.

She walked back over to Ethan and used one of her little flashlight tools to look into his nose again.

"Had any nosebleeds lately?"

I thought she was asking me, so I said, "Not since last summer when he ran into a cedar tree in our yard."

I shifted uneasily. There had been those specks of blood on his pillow the last time I changed his sheets, little dark red dots like grains of dirt flung against the fabric. They didn't constitute a real nosebleed, though.

"Has your nose been bleeding, Ethan?" Dr. Snyder asked.

He gave me a guilty look as if he were snitching on me. "Yeah. Sometimes."

"Let's have you take off your shirt."

He looked embarrassed but wiggled out of his plaid shirt and the Spiderman T-shirt under it. I shot up from the chair with a gasp. Two bruises the size of fists colored his flesh. One had already turned yellow, looking as if it might have been there a while.

I rushed over to him. "My God, what hap-happened?"

"Nothing," he murmured.

"Ethan," Dr. Snyder said, "could you take off your jeans so I can look at your tummy?"

He turned tomato red but after giving me an accusing glance that said I had obviously joined the enemy, he complied. A long thin bruise, flecked with red-and-blue pinpoints, ran along his waistline. Several other marks like sooty smudges mottled his belly.

I hugged his squared-off shoulders. "Did you get into a fight at school?"

23

"No." He wouldn't look at me.

During his toddler-hood, I knew every scratch and mark on his perfect little body.

But when he turned the age of seven or eight I was no longer allowed to look.

"Did you fall, then?" I asked.

"I guess."

"I'll bet you didn't really get these in a fall, did you, Ethan?" Dr. Snyder said.

He eyed her. "I guess not."

My heart began thudding. "My God, how did you get them then?"

He shrugged, tears welling in his eyes.

I said, "Ethan, I want you to tell me."

"Let's have Mom wait outside for a few minutes," Dr. Snyder said gently.

I stood there, blinking. My son had bruises all over his body, and she wanted me to go outside. What kind of mother would leave her child at a time like this?

It came to me in a flash. She thought I'd hit him. She thought Joel or I had beaten our child.

"No, look," I said, "I don't know how he got those bruises. I didn't even realize they were there."

Ethan's eyes looked big as eggs.

She opened the door. "For only a few minutes, Mrs. Franklin,"

Already feeling like a condemned mother, I slunk into the hall. She closed the door, and I pressed my shoulder against the wall, too stunned to cry. She was questioning him now. Does your mother ever knock you around? How about your father? You can tell me. You're safe here.

He would protest, of course. No one hit him. His parents were kind to him, especially his dad.

He'd been spanked only twice, and that was because his mother totally lost her patience. She'd regretted it ever since.

Dr. Snyder had to understand something was terribly wrong with him. Either someone else was hitting him, or he had a terrible illness.

She opened the door, stepped out, and closed it behind her.

"I swear we've never abused Ethan," I said immediately. "Something else must have caused those bruises. You have to find out how he got them."

She put her hand on my shoulder. "I knew you didn't hit him, but Ethan needed for you to calm down. He's scared enough as it is. I'm going to schedule some tests for him at Children's Memorial. I would like you to take him directly there and check him in."

"To the hospital? Right now?"

"They can do a more extensive examination than I can here."

"But why do we need to rush right over there?" I felt caught in a current. "Couldn't I wait until my husband comes home?"

"It would be better if you had him meet you at Children's Memorial. I'll phone the hospital and make arrangements. They'll be expecting you."

I stared at her, trying to absorb what she was saying. "I know he's not feeling well, but he doesn't seem that sick."

"Do you know where Children's Memorial is located?" she asked.

I nodded. "Over on Pill Hill." There were a half dozen or so hospitals bunched in a five-mile-square area east of downtown Seattle.

"All right. Let me give you some paperwork."

She opened the door to the examining room and gestured me in. I knew I should ask more questions, but I couldn't think straight.

Ethan, his jeans cinched tight, his shirt buttoned right to the top, bounded off the table. He looked frightened and wary, and I ached for him. I wrapped my arm protectively around his shoulders, and he leaned against me the way he did when he was younger.

"It's okay, Ethan Skywalker."

He looked up at me. I managed a smile, but I didn't know how to keep the fear out of my eyes.

25

Chapter 4

I have mixed feelings about worrying.

When I was twenty-three years old, having decided the things you agonize over don't happen and the worst catastrophes tend to blindside you, I promised myself I would never worry again. I adopted this philosophy—at least temporarily—after spending most of my childhood in a state of panic over my father.

Dad worked for a large trucking company that assigned him to a new region every few years. When we moved, we didn't even take our beds, although you would think he could have found a truck to haul them in.

"We'll buy furniture when we get to the new place," he would say with undue cheer. "It's good to start fresh, pumpkin. Then, we can see what we really need." As it turned out, the place was never new and the shabby furniture we bought at garage sales had already run through many uncaring hands. I knew better than to latch onto something that wasn't portable. What few items I treasured, mainly an old porcelain-faced doll I'd found at a garage sale (I knew quality even then), three or four favorite books, and my diary, I carted from house to house. I felt like the child of nomads.

Through the years, I'd convinced myself Dad was in imminent danger when he wasn't in my sight, and I had good reason to feel that way because, as well-meaning and good-natured as he was, every step he took was a tightrope walk over disaster. Through the years, he had inadvertently set fire to our garage, nearly asphyxiated our entire family when he tried to fix the gas furnace, and once almost killed one of my brothers by attaching a chain from a rotted porch post to our car and yanking it out before he'd braced the porch and told Douglas to get off it. Doug ended up with a concussion.

Dad routinely dislocated his nose, and, on one occasion that will continue to haunt my nightmares until my death, he reared back with a scythe he was using to cut weeds and carved an unintentional, unattractive cleft on his already rugged chin. He persuaded a veterinarian friend to sew it up.

I sincerely believed that, some dark night, while driving his big rig across Arizona, he would fall asleep at the wheel, veer off the highway and pitch into the Grand Canyon. When I tried to convey this entirely reasonable fear to my father, he laughed, affectionately scrubbed my head with his big knuckles, and went back to packing his battered duffel bag for the road.

To this day, I have not seen that spectacular chasm, but in my visions it's filled with all sorts of vehicles, from motorcycles to eighteen-wheelers, a kind of mass grave for the sleepy, ill-fated traveler. As long as my father was on the road, my mother's safety seemed secure.

She never took chances, and yet there was nothing she couldn't do. In addition to working full-time, she cleaned house, fixed meals, washed clothes, and doted on my ungrateful brothers and me. I seldom concerned myself with them, except to fear they wouldn't pass out of my life soon enough.

When I was twenty-one and living across town in the Capitol Hill neighborhood of Seattle, Dad announced he was taking Mom to Hawaii for their first vacation ever.

He had seen everything he wanted to see in the lower forty-eight states, and then some. In another year, he would retire.

He would be done forever with trucks, he said, and from that time on he would take a plane, train, or cab.

I drove them to the airport through rain as thick as a beaded curtain. With grins stretching their mouths like rubber bands, they tossed me their raincoats, then trotted toward the terminal gate in their sandals, shorts, and matching Seattle Mariners T-shirts while I smiled indulgently. They could have been a couple of kids dashing off to the end-of-school party. After too many rocky teenage years, I was just starting to like them again.

Halfway between Seattle and Honolulu, the plane plummeted into the Pacific Ocean. Their bodies were never recovered.

I went through eighteen stages of grief, although some therapist along the way told me there were supposed to be only five. I thought I deserved double credit for losing both parents.

By then, my twin brothers were living in Boston and Atlanta respectively, where they had married and proceeded to produce a half dozen miniature replicas of themselves.

Alone, struggling with college and a new career as a Quik Stop clerk, I actually found myself missing my siblings.

When the numbness and pain of my parents' deaths finally lifted, I decided worrying about much of anything was fruitless. I thought about all those years I had wasted, gnawing at possibilities, priming myself for disaster, completely misjudging the real threats. My dad died falling out of a damned plane — not driving his truck into the Grand Canyon, not toppling off the roof, not decapitating himself with a scythe. How could I possibly have guessed he and Mom would leave me that way? I told myself I would never try to predict or agonize over the future again.

I kept that pledge for the next ten years — through a series of roller-coaster romances and a tilt-a-whirl job cycle — until I met and married Joel and our son came along. The moment Ethan was born I started to worry again.

I worried I wouldn't have enough milk to feed him or I wouldn't hear him when he woke up at night. I firmly believed he would cry all the time and dry up like a little prune from hunger and dehydration.

Fortunately, none of those things happened. He was slow to talk and walk so I feared he had damaged his brain that time he'd banged his head on the coffee table.

Finally, he began to toddle and speak. When he began to screech and run at the same time, I desperately wanted those quiet times back.

I worried he would never be potty-trained and he would go off to kindergarten in a diaper.

Until recently, he grew right on schedule, but now he was short compared to his classmates.

I worried he would get cancer from his vegetable-free diet, that the other kids in school would tease him because he couldn't throw a ball straight, that he would never get into college because of his terrible math grades and, worst of all, the girls wouldn't think he was handsome enough to love.

I learned quickly that motherhood was a conspiracy. It sucked you in with powdery, sweet-smelling babies of friends, then gave you your own heart-wrenchingly beautiful child to tend, without any of the most necessary warnings. Someone should tell you that you will love him so much it will hurt, that you will feel his pain more than he will, that the older he gets the less you can protect him. A new car comes with more safety warnings than a baby does.

Chapter 5

Ethan and I drifted through the maze of hospital corridors, trying to find the main lobby. Despite the map at the entrance, I'd somehow managed to come in the wrong door. Somewhere in this mammoth building Joel was waiting for Ethan and me.

The hospital wings were named for Mother Goose characters. Everywhere we turned, wooden cutouts of bluebirds, sunbursts, barn animals, and storybook figures danced across the walls. We wandered around until a kindly nurse directed us to take the Jack Sprat elevator to the Tommy Tucker wing, then turn left, where we would find a yellow brick road leading us to the lobby. Seemed to me they were mixing their metaphors, and in my fear and frustration I found that intolerable.

Nurses in white uniforms, blue-jacketed nurses' aides, and parents and children in all colors crowded the wide halls, but Ethan and I were the only ones in the Jack Sprat elevator.

Ethan studied a painted depiction of Jack and his plump wife on the wall. "I don't like this place. It's for dorky little kids, not ten year olds."

I didn't like it either, but for a totally different reason. We were slipping into the black hole of medical chaos.

We found Joel in the main lobby, seated on a blue-and-green, vinyl-covered bench shaped like a cumulus cloud. He jumped up and embraced both of us, and I could feel the tremor in his strong arms.

"You all right?" he whispered.

I nodded. "Got lost."

He bent down to Ethan's level and gripped his shoulders, giving them a reassuring little shake. "It's going to be okay, son.

30

You'll be out of here in no time."

Ethan didn't look convinced but he said, "Yeah, I guess."

People streamed through the lobby. A woman wearing a purple sari pushed a child in a wheelchair. An elderly man guided a blind boy around the clusters of people. A gray-haired receptionist, dressed in a yellow cotton pantsuit, directed us toward an admissions desk occupied by a middle-aged woman with bright red hair and an aggressive perfume.

She ran through a number of basic questions, typing our answers into a computer. "Who's your insurance carrier?" She sounded polite but mechanized.

"Pacific Health," Joel said.

He turned away but not before I caught the concern in his expression.

He'd had excellent benefits at Boeing, but they had disappeared with that job.

As we left the admitting office, he grabbed hold of Ethan's shoulders again. "It's going to be okay."

I took Joel aside and whispered, "Don't grab hold of him. His body is covered with bruises."

Joel's face turned chalk white.

As we went through the rest of the day, nurses measured Ethan's heartbeat and his blood pressure and drew as much blood as they could from him until it seemed he'd lost all color in his face.

Hours went by. Medical personnel came and went. Finally, Dr. Snyder entered Ethan's room, said a few reassuring words to him, then took Joel and me aside.

"Ethan's liver function tests aren't what they should be. He has an elevated white count and an increased protime level. Protime is a measure of how long it takes his blood to clot."

"But what does that mean?" Joel asked.

She looked at him sympathetically. "He appears to have liver damage, but we don't know yet what caused it."

"His liver is damaged?" I echoed, bewildered.

"I'm afraid he's going to be here for a while," she said.

They assigned him to a sixth floor room directly in the

crook of the seven-story, X-shaped building, its breath-stopping view of downtown Seattle, Puget Sound, and the Space Needle a jarring contrast to our dismal prospects inside.

The parade of doctors, nurses, and technicians continued. We were told we could spend the night on chairs that unfolded into cots.

Joel looked stunned. He kept telling Ethan that things were going to be okay, but they obviously weren't. Couldn't he see that? Could he not see the doctors' grim faces as they examined Ethan?

I stared at the strip of white gauze on Ethan's arm where a nurse had poked another needle. It was ten o'clock in the morning, and we'd been in the hospital almost twenty-four hours. I quickly refolded the cots into chairs as soon as we rose that morning. I didn't like the idea of settling in.

An hour later, Ethan was transferred to a room in the Bo Peep wing, which he found mortifying.

"It's for girls," he said in disgust.

Reclining in an adjustable bed with a backdrop of machines and monitors, he looked all eyes, two enormous hazel eyes in that tawny face, his freckles standing out in bas-relief. I was still clinging to the fantasy there had been a terrible mistake. He'd had the flu and that's why he looked so peaked. He'd fallen off the climbing bars at school and didn't realize he'd been bruised.

Although his new room looked clean and Ethan was the only patient, it smelled of overripe bananas. I had no idea why, and to tell the truth I didn't want to find out. It made me sick to my stomach.

Joel said he couldn't smell any strange odor. "You're imagining it."

"No," I insisted but I couldn't identify its source.

A nurse came and took Ethan down the hall for an x-ray. Joel went with them, and I was suddenly alone in the smelly room, with all its monitors and the big hospital bed that had made Ethan look like a peanut in a shell.

I dug my cell phone out of my purse, called Cappy, and gave

her a quick summary of the past twenty-four hours.

"Do you have a diagnosis yet?"

"No, but they're talking about some kind of liver problem. That's what you were thinking when you said he was jaundiced, right?"

"Yes, but I've never wanted more to be wrong."

"He doesn't seem that sick, but they're giving him all kinds of tests. He's scared, of course. We all are, even Joel, who's always calm and in control." I sank onto the edge of Ethan's empty bed. "How could I have not seen it, Cappy? I spend more time with him than anyone else, and yet I was the last to notice."

"But that's precisely why you couldn't see it. The jaundice came on gradually, not overnight."

"Joel insisted he wasn't well."

She sighed. "If you want me to confirm that you're a flawed, negligent mother, I refuse to do it. I've watched your life revolve around Ethan ever since he was born, and no one could have taken better care of him. Whatever he has, it's not your fault, Delainie."

Whatever he has, I thought. Not a passing stomachache, not a touch of the flu, but something I might not be able to do anything about.

After I ended the call, Ethan returned, with Joel's arm hooked around him and a nurse walking alongside. Joel tucked him back into bed and poured him a glass of water.

Shortly after, a doctor came in, with a young woman trailing him. He identified himself as Charles Baxter, chief of gastroenterology, and introduced the female resident, whose name quickly escaped me. Tall and rangy, Dr. Baxter reminded me of Abraham Lincoln without the beard.

He had black bushy eyebrows and a firm jaw that suggested confidence and focused determination. He checked Ethan's chart, then went through the same routine all the other doctors had gone through. He examined Ethan's mouth and eyes, palpated his belly, and asked him if things hurt.

"When are you going to tell me what's wrong with me?" Ethan asked in a small voice.

Dr. Baxter pulled the starched sheet up to Ethan's chest. "We're not sure yet, but we're working on it. Is it all right with you if I talk with your mom and dad out in the hall?"

Ethan nodded. Joel and I exchanged a quick anxious glance, then followed the doctor out of the room.

In the hall, Dr. Baxter turned to face us. "You have a very sick little boy." He eyed me. "But you knew that, didn't you?"

Joel moved closer to him, and drew himself up as if his own sheer size might intimidate the man. "Exactly what does he have?"

Dr. Baxter stayed where he was. When he turned his face toward Joel, I saw his long, angular profile, looking even more like the man on the side of a copper penny. "I'm not sure yet. We need to do more tests."

"What are the possibilities?" Joel asked.

Dr. Baxter crossed his arms and took in a deep breath.

"A lot of diseases can cause liver damage," he said. "Could be hepatitis. Could be a genetic disease that's now showing up. Could be cancer."

All I heard was the word cancer. I might as well have been one of those spindly, three-legged stools that a sudden jostle knocks off its pins.

My legs buckled, and I found myself crumpling to the hall floor. Both Joel and the woman resident grabbed me by the arms and pulled me to my feet.

"You okay?" Joel asked, holding me against him for support.

I nodded, although I wasn't, of course.

Dr. Baxter remained expressionless, as if he had women dropping to the floor on a regular basis. And perhaps he did.

The muscles in Joel's jaw worked repeatedly. "You're saying we have a life-threatening situation here, aren't you?" His voice sounded ragged.

Dr. Baxter nodded. "Oh, yes. No question about that."

Joel sat on the cot in Ethan's room and looked at me. "Go home. You need some rest, and there's no point in both of us being here as long as he's sleeping."

I was running on adrenaline, past exhaustion but with little hope of sleep. I lifted my head and looked out the window. The sun, suddenly a common fixture in Seattle, bloomed with afternoon brightness and the buds on the cherry trees had opened into a festive pink. I could almost hear the birds twittering. Everything looked numbingly serene.

"I can't leave," I whispered. "You heard the doctor say this illness is life-threatening. What if Ethan should die while I'm gone?"

In an instant he was standing over me, his face so close to mine I could feel his breath, thick and overly warm.

"Don't say that." His voice was low, charged with anger. "Don't even think it."

He looked far different from the man I'd married. In fact, he didn't even resemble the one I'd known a week ago. I had never seen this kind of anger in him.

My eyes burned with tears. "But we can't pretend any longer he's going to be fine."

"Oh, God, he has to be." He turned and gazed at Ethan, who lay in motionless sleep under the white sheets, only his small, round, buttery face visible. "Look at him," Joel said. "He's a sturdy kid. If he was as sick as they say, he would be losing weight."

"I didn't like the way Dr. Baxter tossed out the word cancer as if it were a case of chicken pox. Didn't he realize how that would make us feel?"

"He's pretty cold." He turned toward me, the lemony light from the window transforming him into a gray silhouette. "Whatever he comes up with, we'll get a second opinion."

We were barreling down a mountain and I knew — absolutely knew — if we stayed this course, we would shoot right off a cliff.

"Let's take Ethan home," I blurted. "If he hangs around here he'll get sicker."

Joel looked at me as if I had suggested we rob a store.

"We can't leave him in this hospital," I said. "There's so

much pain here. Please, let's take him home while we still can."
I rose from my chair and walked over to him, trying to find the
consent in his eyes.

"You know we can't do that."

I didn't speak or move for several seconds. I looked out
the window and wished it would rain. Rain would feel so familiar, so comforting.

"Go home for a while." His tone had softened. "It will help to
get out and clear your head."

"Okay." I didn't move, though.

He looked up. "Maybe you can bring back some toys — his
fidget spinner or his monster books, something to distract
him."

I liked that idea. If I could, I would bring him a space ship
that would transport him to a safer planet far, far away.

Chapter 6

I never entered Ethan's cramped bedroom without caution, having known the pain of treading on a Lego in the middle of the night. I looked around, trying to decide what items I could take back to him. His iron-framed daybed that I'd picked up at a yard sale squatted in one corner. I sat on it and laid my head on his pillow. I could smell the fragrance of his hair shampoo. He never seemed to rinse all of it out.

I wanted to stay on his pillow but I didn't want to sleep. I wanted to get back to Ethan, but my eyes closed as though I had no control over them.

I awoke about two hours later. I was just as tired as I had been when I laid down.

I shook myself to clear my head and surveyed the room. The floor was a minefield of sharp-edged toys and treasured rocks under a camouflage of dirty clothes and homework pages. It had a slightly gamey smell. His forties-style dresser papered with NASCAR stickers hunched next to the bed. A workbench that Joel had built out of a door and two sawhorses rested against the wall. In the center of it sat an old football helmet Ethan had found in a dumpster. He was covering it with papier-mâché, turning it into an alien fly. When it was finished, it would have giant, bumpy eyes, broom-straw feelers, and a red wound of a mouth. I looked affectionately at the work in progress. What artistic talent he had.

Ethan's goal in life was to become a special effects artist. He bought magazines on the subject and ordered latex masks, severed rubber appendages, and fake blood by the pint through the mail. He learned the names of special effects artists who had gained fame in the movies and sent them letters expressing his admiration and asking their advice. They didn't answer, but he continued writing them.

I never knew when or where one of his grisly creatures might turn up. A visitor strolling up our front walk could stumble across a bloody dummy, posed among the rhododendrons like a misplaced corpse from a funeral home.

It became a challenge for Ethan to catch me by surprise. I might open a door and get smacked in the forehead by a dangling shrunken skull, or collecting laundry from the dryer, I would find half a dozen black plastic spiders, each the size of my fist, perched atop a nest of freshly dried clothes.

Ethan would be lurking nearby, shaking with glee. "Did that scare you, Mom?"

I would clasp my hand to my heart and release a trembling breath. "My goodness, I almost fainted on the spot."

He'd bounce around like a pogo stick, then run off to his room to see what he could come up with next. Jaya said it took a special mother to live with Ethan, but I disagreed. I was the ordinary one. He had a creative streak I couldn't begin to match. For his birthday, he asked for a poster of the movie, "Texas Chainsaw Massacre." I found one at a movie memorabilia store. Thrilled with the present, he taped it to his bedroom door.

"You're raising a mass-murderer," my brother Don once said during a visit. "Do you realize that, Delainie?"

"That is cruel and not true." I considered punching him, but I knew from childhood fights he'd hit back—harder.

Some of Ethan's creations were pretty gruesome, but I had plenty of evidence to prove Donald wrong. He didn't fight with the other kids at school; in fact, he was reasonably well behaved, except for the time he threw a firecracker from the school bus and got suspended for a day.

It was the safe-and-sane variety so no one was hurt.

He was never malevolent, only mischievous. He never speared flies or tortured cats.

In fact, he found Oscar shut in the crawl space of an abandoned house, suffering from dehydration. He freed him, brought him home, and fed him his vegetables.

"Your brother is criticizing our son?" Joel said. "This is the man whose teenaged daughter recently got suspended from high school for doing drugs?"

We rarely saw my brothers after that.

Joel completely indulged Ethan, telling him he had a unique gift. Before he got so tied up with his new business, he spent Saturday mornings with him, knee-deep in fake body parts.

When it came to real blood, Ethan nearly passed out at the sight. Once, while slicing open a watermelon, I put a deep gash in my palm. As I reached for a towel on the counter across from me, the blood oozed from my hand and puddled on the floor. Ethan, who was eating a peanut butter sandwich, jumped off the chair at the kitchen table, his face leaking color like bleached cloth.

"I'll call 911," he said in a strangled voice.

I shook my head, pressing the dishtowel to my throbbing palm. "It's not that bad. I just have to stop the bleeding."

As the green-and-white checkered fabric turned crimson, his eyes grew larger. "But the blood's running out of you," he said in a choked voice. "You'll die."

I managed to staunch the wound, but it took a hug and a frozen Snickers bar to revive Ethan. He was a little boy, not a mass-murderer in the making.

Only once did I think he had gone too far. I had called a repairman named Bob, a good-looking, thirty-something guy my neighbor had recommended, to fix our erratic water-heater.

As I led him toward the basement, I ticked off the problems we were having with it. "Sometimes, we can take three showers. Other times, it runs out of water in two minutes."

"Sorry, but the overhead light's burnt out here and I haven't replaced it yet. I have a flashlight, though, and—"

Bob followed me down the stairs, past my wall-to-wall stash of antiques, to a dim corner of the cellar.

I flicked on the torch, took one look at the water heater, and literally fell into Bob's arms. A full-sized, severed, papier-mâché head, its golf-ball eyes dripping some sort of black goo, its mouth a gaping red trench, stared back at me.

"Whoa," Bob said, releasing me the way he would a hot pan. "I appreciate the offer, Mrs. Franklin," he said stiffly, "but I'm engaged to be married."

"Oh, no, it's not what you think." I aimed the torch at the top of the water heater, its yellow glow capturing Ethan's newest creation in all its bloody glory.

He jumped back. "Jesus Christ."

"My son did that, but it's fake, of course."

"Right," he said cautiously, retreating another step. "I'm afraid you have a bigger problem than I can help you with."

For that one, I grounded Ethan two weeks.

I walked past the workbench to his bed, where the cat lay curled like a potato bug amid the rumpled comforter, the pillows, and a scattering of Transformer action figures.

I grabbed a few of them, his iPad, a fat Harry Potter book, a book titled *Monsters and Vampires* and dropped them into a plastic grocery bag.

There was something else I wanted to take to the hospital. I rummaged through the bottom drawer of his dresser until I found it: the remnant of a blue baby blanket with a frayed satin edge. His binky, he called it. Only about twelve ragged square inches of it remained. Maybe it would help to soothe him. As I fingered its love-worn fabric, an entire movie reel of memories unspooled in my head.

I shoved his tattered blanket into the grocery bag and lugged it into the kitchen. Oscar ambled in, circled his empty food dish, and meowed until I shook some dry O-shaped nuggets into it. He rubbed against my leg in gratitude and then nudged a sagging carton of linens I'd bought at a garage sale. The box had a suspicious yellow streak on its side. I looked at the cat. "You didn't have to get spiteful, Oscar. It wasn't like we abandoned you."

The kitchen was as I'd left it yesterday morning: the sink filled with dirty dishes, spilled sugar on the counter, Ethan's cereal bowl still on the table with parched Cheerios clinging to its rim. *The New York Times* lay open near Joel's plate, a balled-up, dirty paper napkin partially covering the political cartoon. A fly danced across a splotch of jam on a saucer. It looked like one of those dioramas you see in a museum, with everything perfectly preserved. Well, no sense cleaning it up now.

I parked in the garage across from the hospital entrance and took the elevator to the sixth floor.

A lovely, middle-aged Asian woman stood in the doorway of the room next to Ethan's, her slender fingers massaging the muscles of her throat as if she might be working a lump out of it. She wore a neatly pressed, black tunic over tan slacks and several gold rings. She gave me a weak smile. Over her shoulder, I could see a thin ridge on the bed and hear a hacking cough that might have come from an old man — except we were in a children's hospital.

In Ethan's room, which still smelled like overripe bananas, I found Joel sitting near the window, watching the April light seep from the sky. Ethan's bed was empty, the covers thrown back. The skin around Joel's eyes looked bruised as if he'd been crying.

I took that to mean something had happened to Ethan, and I panicked. "Where is he?"

Joel turned and stared at me with unfocused eyes. "What?"

"Where's Ethan?"

"They took him to radiology for another test. I would have gone with him, but he didn't want me to."

Dark stubble had surfaced on his jaw, and by the looks of his wrinkled blue dress shirt and gray slacks he had spent the last several hours tossing around on his narrow cot.

I sank onto the chair next to him, dropping the grocery bag on the floor near my feet. "I'm sorry. I thought something had happened to him."

I leaned over and kissed him. His cheek was cold, and he didn't respond. Because of Ethan, I thought. He probably

41

couldn't think of anything else.

I rummaged through my bag and withdrew a wrapped sandwich I'd bought on the way to the hospital. It was a little squished on one corner, but I held it out. "Ham on rye, sweet hot mustard, no mayo." He hated mayonnaise, and through the years I had come to dislike it myself.

"I'm not hungry."

"You have to be. When was the last time you ate?"

"I said I'm not hungry."

"It's from the Upper Crust. You know how you like their sandwiches." I couldn't seem to let the subject go.

"You eat it then."

I tucked the sandwich back into my bag, not wanting to admit that I had wolfed one in the car while stuck in traffic. I didn't want to speculate on what kind of mother could swallow even a morsel of food when her son was desperately ill.

"Look, I know you're angry," I said to Joel, "but you don't have to take it out on me."

"I don't need any lectures on..." He stopped and shook his head, as if deciding he had better not say anymore.

"What are we going to do, Joel?"

"Do?" His voice sharpened again. "We're going to sit here until they tell us exactly what's wrong with our son."

I wanted to say, but what will we do after that? How do people in these circumstances cope?

He rested his elbows on his knees and massaged his forehead with his fingertips. "I called Jin and got the phone number of the agent who sold us our insurance plan. I wasn't involved in choosing it. Jin handled that."

As if we didn't have enough to worry about, there was the money. But I trusted that Joel's business partner, a close friend and a genius with numbers, had made the best possible choice.

"And," I prompted Joel.

"Good policies cost companies a lot. It's what we could afford."

I hesitated. "How much does it pay?"

"Eighty percent."

My mathematically-challenged mind reeled. Eighty percent of what? A thousand a day? Two thousand? I looked around Ethan's private room with its elaborate monitoring equipment and its adjustable bed and pristine white sheets. I had no idea how much all this cost, but it had to be far more expensive than a room at The Four Seasons. Then, there were the doctors, the nurses, the tests, the x-rays, the magnetic resonance imaging, and these appalling cots they gave us to sleep on. I wondered if they charged extra for them, like hotels did for rollaway beds.

Our money was tied up in two places: our home and Joel's business. We'd cashed in our mutual funds for the latter and mortgaged ourselves to the earlobes for the former. We were managing, but barely. I thought of our little emergency account of two thousand dollars. Enough to cover repairs on a car or a water heater — but not on a child.

I didn't care what it took. We would sell our cars and the house, abandon Joel's business, live in a cardboard box under the viaduct, go on welfare, do whatever was required to save Ethan. I didn't mention all that to Joel because he couldn't see clearly right now.

His usually calm nerves were raw, his steadiness shaken. We would have to take turns at being strong.

They brought Ethan back, his sturdy little legs poking out of his Hickory Dickory Dock hospital gown, and he crawled into bed.

Joel tucked the sheet and covers around him. "How was it, buddy?"

"Okay. I had to lie completely still, but I could do that."

I pulled his baby blanket remnant from the grocery bag and laid it next to his hand.

He made a face and pushed it away. "Jeez, Mom, I don't need that."

Didn't need it? Why, when he was five, he accidentally left it on one of those plastic swivel seats at McDonald's during a vacation to the Oregon beaches. We had to drive thirty-five miles back to Astoria to retrieve it, Joel swearing under his breath, Ethan crying the whole way.

Someone, not recognizing its value, had thrown the blanket in the trash — although it was larger then and, from my irritable point of view, obviously some child's cherished possession. With the help of an eager-to-please teenager (she led the way to the dumpster), I fished through the garbage, and I do mean "fished through." I found it smeared with tartar sauce and rank with a fishy odor.

I washed it out in the McDonald's restroom and carried it dripping to the car. Ethan clung to that damp rag all the way to Cannon Beach. And now he didn't need it?

I fingered the blanket's worn, soft fabric, wondering how I'd missed the moment when he'd left his babyhood behind.

Ethan looked at my shopping bag. "Did you bring my *Monsters and Vampires* book?"

I reached into the bag. "Right here next to Harry Potter."

"Okay, thanks." He slumped against the pillow, his eyelids drooping. "I guess I'll look at it later."

"That's fine. Rest a while."

He looked so peaceful, his head tilted to the side, his stubby fingers (so full of promise) clutching the bed sheet. He'd been with us only ten years, and look how much he'd changed our lives. Before he was born, we'd said that after we had a child we would still go out on dates, take backpacking trips, stay up late, do all the things we'd done before. We wouldn't be myopic young parents whose children dominated their days and nights.

Then Ethan came after a heroic struggle on my part one rainy night and altered everything forever. We rarely went to movies or restaurants. He might cry. Besides we didn't need any other form of entertainment now.

Our backpacking gear gathered dust. We didn't want to expose him to the damp wilderness.

We didn't want to stay up late anymore not after rising at midnight, two A.M., and four A.M., and tucking him into bed with us at daybreak. That last part was the best, the three of us snuggled together like a litter of puppies.

Without Ethan, we wouldn't know how to act. We couldn't

go back to being just a couple, two married people staring at each other across the table at a Chinese restaurant. What would we talk about?

Ethan's eyes blinked open. "You won't leave, will you?"

"No, Superman, we'll stay right here, in case you need anything."

His grin flared for a moment. "Hey, that's what you can bring next time, Mom. My rubber spiders. I bet they would really scare the nurses and doctors."

I smiled back. "Good idea. We'll have some fun then, won't we?"

Any kind of fun one could have in a hospital seemed tempting. I had visions of Ethan opening his mouth, a black rubber spider skittering out, Dr. Baxter leaping skyward.

When I looked at him again, he was asleep. I gripped his baby blanket for dear life.

Chapter 7

It was eight-thirty in the evening, and Ethan was sleeping. Joel had gone to the cafeteria for coffee. Outside, the moon rose over the Tommy Tucker wing, round and waxen as a pearl. The hospital was silent except for the wracking cough of the girl in the next room. I didn't ask the nurse what was wrong with her (I didn't want to know), but she sounded as if she were bringing up her lungs every few minutes.

The next noises I heard were not the child's coughs, not the nurses' quiet tones, but a repeated thunk against the vinyl floor followed by whispers, giggling and the jangle of metal against metal. From Ethan's door, they were about five yards away, Jaya and Liz on either side of Cappy, offering support. She was using her cane, and it was the soft thud of the rubber cap hitting the floor that I'd heard. The clinking came from the gold and silver bangles circling Jaya's wrist.

"You're here," I breathed.

Liz grabbed my hand. "Well, of course, we're here."

Jaya embraced me, holding me tight against her so that I smelled her sweet perfume. After she released me, Cappy gave me a one-armed hug.

"How is he?" she asked.

I choked on my words. Standing in the hall outside Ethan's door, I sobbed my way through what little Joel and I knew about his illness. Like a magician extracting silk scarves, Jaya yanked pink tissue after pink tissue out of her purse and stuffed them into my clenched hands.

Liz gestured toward the open door. "Can we see him, Delainie?"

"Sure. He doesn't look sick, but he's really tired and he's got

46

a little fever."

Jaya clutched my hand. "Tell us what you need."

"Need?" I said, thinking in terms of medical miracles.

Liz moved to the other side of me. "You want us to water the plants, collect your mail, clean the house? Simply say the word and we'll do it."

I thought of the Cheerios congealing in Ethan's bowl on the kitchen table, of Oscar probably dying of thirst. I had forgotten to fill his water dish.

"The cat," I said. "If you wouldn't mind putting out some water for him and...." I started to say, "and clean the litter box." No, I couldn't ask them to change the cat litter, even though I knew they would do it without a second thought.

They didn't think less of me because I wasn't the best housekeeper, but I did. The seeds of my supermom complex were sown long ago. My mother kept a clean home and raised three kids while holding down a nine-to-five job as a saleswoman in a fabric store. I never managed to live up to those standards.

Given the choice of helping Ethan with his helmet project or mopping the floor, I dug into the papier-mâché and paints every time.

Liz squeezed my hand affectionately. "Key still in that fake rock in the planter?"

I looked at her blankly for a moment. "Yes, but you don't have to do anything other than set out water for the cat. I'm sure we'll be taking Ethan home soon."

"Well, then, everything will be fine," Cappy said.

"That's right," I said. "Just fine."

They didn't stay long. They hovered over Ethan's bed and whispered endearments to him. He opened his eyes briefly and smiled a loopy smile as if he might be incorporating them into his dream.

Shortly after they left, Joel came back into the room, toting two cups: coffee for him, hot chocolate for me.

"You missed the gang," I said.

"Saw them in the elevator." He handed me the chocolate.

"They asked where we kept the cat litter. I assume you know what that means."

"I'm afraid I do." I warmed my hands on the paper cup. "You must have gone all the way to the market for this."

"There's a coffee shop across the street."

"What took you so long then?"

He folded himself onto the chair, looking as tired as I've ever seen him, and stared at Ethan's motionless form.

He said, "We had a message from my parents. They want to fly out here."

I abruptly set the cup on the windowsill. "Oh, no, please say you didn't agree to that."

"I had to. He's their only grandchild. They love him too."

"But it's so pleasant in Ohio at this time of year."

He looked at me as if there couldn't possibly be a logical response to such a remark.

I thought again of the dead Cheerios and sticky kitchen floor. "But where would they stay?"

"At our house, of course. We've got room."

"Barely."

"I know they'll do whatever they can to help."

His mother had visited shortly after Ethan was born, to care for her new grandson and, ostensibly, to help me. We lived in a smaller home then, a two-bedroom, World War II bungalow with no washer or dryer and a stove that had only two functioning burners. I remember when Joel brought Barbara from the airport. I heard them enter the back door, just as I was staggering down the hall to our only bathroom.

I'd had an awful pregnancy, punctuated by severe bouts of morning sickness all nine months. My delivery, twenty-two hours after my water broke, was a harrowing, psychedelic experience. Two days later, my bottom still hurt, my breasts ached, my insides curdled and churned.

"Well, look at this," I heard Barbara say in a disapproving tone.

I knew she was surveying the kitchen with its sink full of dishes and a floor that hadn't been scrubbed since before

Ethan's conception.

"This could be a very nice house once it's fixed up," she said.

A little clunk sounded as Joel dropped her suitcase on the floor. "Yes, we think so."

There was a deadly silence and then her puzzled voice. "Do you suppose she was raised this way?"

I didn't wait to hear Joel's answer. I shuffled as rapidly as I could to our bedroom and slammed the door. Later, he swore to me he'd told her I was the best wife a man could have.

I stared at him now across the hospital room. "Joel, I don't think I can handle having Ethan in the hospital and your parents in our home."

"What would you have me do?"

"Ask them to stay in a hotel."

"They don't stay in hotels, Delainie. They think they're a waste of money."

His parents' other claim to fame was that they'd never had a babysitter for Joel. He was always under their doting care.

"But this time is different," I said, as calmly as I could manage. "Maybe, considering the circumstances, they could make an exception."

I was looking forward to returning to the cozy privacy of our home. I didn't want any houseguests, much less my in-laws. I would have suggested we pay for other accommodations, but we couldn't afford it. Besides, I knew they saved more money in one year than we spent.

"You should treat them with more respect, Delainie."

I lost it. My voice rose. "I'll do that when they treat me with respect. May I remind you I overheard your mother asking your father, 'What possessed him to marry her? He could have done better.' His respectful response was 'I never thought the marriage would last.'"

Joel phoned his parents and asked them to delay their visit until we knew more about Ethan's prognosis. They said they would wait a few more days. I'd been hoping for a few more months.

The days and nights wove themselves into a tangle.

I felt caught up in it, disoriented, disconnected from the outside world. We'd been in the hospital five days. We must have resembled prisoners of war— haggard, scared, sleep-deprived, ready to agree to almost anything to end the nightmare. The nurses and doctors came in with their clipboards and charts, asking question after question.

When they began to repeat ones from the day before, Joel lost patience. "We already gave that same information to someone else."

The young intern or resident or whoever he was dipped his head apologetically. "Sorry, Mr. Franklin, but that was Oncology. I'm from Radiology."

"Well, can't you people compare notes?"

On the fifth evening of Ethan's hospitalization, Joel and I were alone in the room, waiting for the nurse to bring him back from yet another test. The bullet lamp cast a yellow glow over Ethan's empty bed.

Joel sat about five feet from me, his legs stretched out, his dark hair pressed against the wall behind his chair. He sighed heavily. "I have to go back to work tomorrow."

He'd dropped by his office for short periods over the last few days, but now he was talking of returning full-time. I wanted to argue him out of it, to protest that Ethan was more important, that when he came back here he would probably find me curled like a dust bunny under Ethan's bed, but I couldn't complain. He needed to keep his business going.

"We've hired a computer whiz away from Microsoft." His tone came across as slightly odd, almost as if he were revealing a secret.

"When did that happen?"

"A week ago yesterday."

He meant before we brought Ethan to the hospital, I realized. Up to now, the company had consisted of only five people. A new employee was an event, and I wondered why he hadn't mentioned it before. "Ex-Microsoft, huh? How did you persuade him to take the pay cut?"

"He's a she, and she's excited about what we're doing. She

says she loves the challenge of building a new company."

"What's her name?"

"Milena Soracco."

"One of those twenty-year-old prodigies with straight brown hair, thick glasses, and Birkenstocks?"

He gave a low laugh. "Not exactly. She is in her twenties though."

His face was in the shadows, but I knew by his voice that she was also pretty, or at least attractive. I didn't ask any more about her. I'm not a jealous woman. Through our fifteen-year marriage Joel had never given me reason to be.

Ethan was staying in bed most of the time. He didn't have much energy, but the nurses said it would be good for him to walk around.

There was a lounge designated for teenagers, but he didn't meet the minimum age of thirteen.

He and I strolled down the hall to the hospital playroom, where he stared at the blocks, the wooden train, the easy-reader books.

"These are for babies," he said, almost accusingly.

"Sorry," I murmured.

We went back to his room.

"I want to go home," he said to every nurse and doctor who came to see him.

Dr. Baxter ruffled his hair. "We're trying to get you there, young man."

After the doctor left, Ethan asked, "What's going to happen to me, Mom?"

"You're going to get well, Ethan Batman, and then we'll all go home and live happily ever after." My heart ached for that fantasy.

Looking glum, he slid down under the covers. "I don't know. I just don't know."

I didn't either, but I couldn't tell him that. Hearing the dejection in his voice, I thought my heart would crack.

Chapter 8

On the sixth day of Ethan's hospital stay, I went home for a shower and a change of clothes. As soon as I opened the front door, I smelled a blast of Pine Sol and furniture polish. Our two overstuffed chairs had been moved closer to the fireplace, giving the living room more balance. Previously, I'd scattered the knickknacks around the room, not through any sense of design but because that's where I'd happened to leave them. Now they were displayed in little groups on a long library table that rested against one wall. The magazines, newspapers, and junk mail that had covered nearly every flat surface had been sorted and stored under the table.

But where were my antiques? I thought of the spare room that housed only a threadbare sofa. When I opened the door, the antiques were there, mostly covered with clean sheets. They probably had dusted them first. Everything smelled like Pledge.

I walked through the recently vacuumed, freshly polished living room into the kitchen. The table there had been cleared, the countertops tidied, and the stove wiped clean. The scrubbed linoleum squeaked as I crossed it.

A bouquet of daffodils on the table caught my attention. Joel might have made an attempt at vacuuming and dusting, but flowers were not his style.

I pulled out one of the chairs and sank onto it, clasping my hands and resting them on the table, staring at the one bright patch of yellow in this otherwise bleak day.

I thought of my friends, dressed in old jeans and sweatshirts, debating where to stow all the clutter and who would dust the antiques. Cappy, staggering defiantly with her cane, would insist on running the vacuum cleaner, and Jaya, her hair twisted into a knot at the nape of her neck, would assail my bathroom tiles with bleach and a toothbrush. Born with an entire set of silver spoons in her mouth, she liked to demonstrate she wasn't above manual labor.

Liz would be the one who flitted around, rearranging furniture, brandishing the feather duster, and complaining I had too much junk. She would call Joel a saint for putting up with all this.

Knowing them, I figured they turned the work into fun and finished the day with glasses of wine. I wished I could have been here with them.

On Ethan's seventh day of hospitalization, Dr. Baxter came to his room and called Joel and me into the hall. Once again, we huddled under the white lights with the lanky gastroenterologist and his resident sidekick.

He scratched the side of his bony nose. "We want to biopsy your son's liver."

This time I was ready for him. I grabbed Joel's arm for support. "You can't do that. He's a little boy, not a guinea pig. You can't cut chunks out of him until you find something wrong with him. You've already drained him of half his blood—"

"We'll be using a needle, Mrs. Franklin, not a scalpel."

"But you've had him for seven days," Joel said. "I would have thought by now you would have a diagnosis." A tremble lay under his voice.

Dr. Baxter's expression didn't flinch, and it occurred to me he was accustomed to dealing with angry, anxious parents. "We need to do this biopsy so we can be sure of our diagnosis."

"What do you expect to find?" Joel asked.

"Cirrhosis, substantial damage. I would be surprised if he has much liver function left." His voice was flat, emotionless.

"Look, Dr. Baxter," Joel said, his shoulders so rigid they looked wooden. "I know you do this all the time, but this is our son, our only child. We would appreciate a little more sensitivity here."

The doctor regarded him thoughtfully for several seconds. "I'm not insensitive, Mr. Franklin. Sometimes I go home at night and agonize over what I've done and what I have to do. I'm fully aware of how my decisions affect your child and others. If I had any more sensitivity, I couldn't do this job."

Well, it wouldn't hurt to show it, I thought.

"All right then," Joel said. "Do your biopsy."

A few minutes later, we were flanking Ethan's bed, with Dr. Baxter explaining the surgical procedure to him.

He pulled back Ethan's gown and pressed his fingers to his abdomen. "We'll extract a few cells, nothing to worry about."

With each word, Ethan's eyes grew larger, and I knew that, despite all the fake blood he'd spilled during his fantasy play, he was terrified of anyone tapping into his own organs.

"It'll hurt, won't it?" His voice sounded small.

Dr. Baxter shook his head.

"It will be a little sore afterward, but you won't feel much while we're doing the biopsy. You'll be awake, but we're going to give you what we call our goofy medicine. It'll make you feel like Goofy in the cartoons? Do you know who he is?"

Ethan nodded.

Dr. Baxter folded his gown back over him. "Do you have any other questions?"

"Can my mom and dad come into the operating room with me?"

Dr. Baxter's mouth stretched in a sympathetic smile. "I'm sorry but we don't allow that. We have to keep everything extremely clean so we can't have any more people than necessary."

Ethan chewed on his lower lip. "Can I go home after that?"

"It won't be much longer now," he said, but I knew that wasn't true.

It's difficult to be a person who doesn't believe in God. In times of crisis I feel so completely alone.

Having been raised by a staunch atheist father, who maintained that most of the planet's atrocities were committed in the name of religion, and a compliant mother, who hid her Holy Bible deep in her lingerie drawer, I leaned more toward my father's noisy position.

As a teenager, I occasionally tried to adopt my mother's quiet piety. I attended church with friends and marveled at the beauty of Christmas Eve services. I watched the parishioners sing the hymns and pray with bowed heads.

I mimicked the motions, but nothing happened. I felt no connection at all.

Jaya, Cappy and Liz called me their "little heathen."

Joel and I didn't attend church, and our approach with Ethan was laissez faire. A fallen Episcopalian, Joel believed in God but didn't like the idea of others telling him how to worship. I had the feeling his parents had done plenty of that. If he prayed now, he kept it private.

On the evening before Ethan's biopsy, I walked down the hall to the empty, dimly lit hospital lounge and sat in a corner. Although it didn't seem right to ask favors from a God I'd never believed in, I prayed the biopsy results would show he was fundamentally healthy. Fulfilling my wish would require only a small gesture on God's part. No burning bushes, no split seas, no dramatic resurrections, just a slight wave of the hand to cure an innocent little boy. In return, I would give my endless gratitude and devotion, or so I said under my breath in what I assume was a prayer. The problem was I couldn't tell if anyone was listening.

That same evening, Joel went home for a shower and a change of clothes.

Ethan sat in bed and waged battles with his action figures, but he didn't have his usual enthusiasm. I sat in the chair, a book on liver disease resting upside down on my lap, my eyelids fluttering as I attempted to stay awake. I'd bought the paperback at the hospital pharmacy. It was written for laymen, but there seemed so many variations of liver disease with such an array of symptoms that I couldn't manage to match Ethan's to any of them.

I heard Ethan make a little noise across the room, a fusion of a murmur and a whimper, and because he often added sound effects to his play, I didn't think much about it. A minute later, I heard him again and realized he was quietly sobbing.

I leapt from my chair, rushed to his bed, and enfolded him in my arms, knocking over his neatly arranged space warriors. "Oh, sweetheart, are you scared about the biopsy?"

He shook his head.

I gripped him tighter. "If you are, that's okay."

His small shoulders trembled. "I don't want to be like Goofy." I pulled back and stared into his red-rimmed eyes.

"You mean the cartoon character, Goofy?

He nodded.

I tried to make the connection in my fuzzy head. "I don't understand."

He tilted his face toward me so that the overhead light caught the silver in his tears. "People knock him around, and he bounces off the walls. What if they do that to me? You and Dad won't even be there to stop them."

A lump the size of a boulder formed in my throat. I couldn't cry, not while he watched, but I wanted to. I bit my lip and rubbed my hand over his, trying to dredge up some composure. He still retained some of his baby pudginess, reminding me he was only a little boy. I swallowed hard. "It's not going to be like that at all."

I explained the procedure again, as best as I could remember, reassuring him that the "goofy medicine" wouldn't hurt him or make him do anything he wouldn't ordinarily do.

I told him it would prevent any pain. We gathered up his action figures and dropped them into their paper bag, and I sat on the edge of his bed and held his hand until he fell asleep. Then I went out into the hall, turned my face to the wall, and cried.

"Are you okay?" asked a male voice behind me.

Without looking at him, I pressed the wadded tissue to my nose with one hand and waved him away with my other.

"Well, of course, you're not okay," he said. "If you were, you wouldn't be standing here crying."

I hated to be seen weeping in public, and I probably would have slunk away if I hadn't turned and caught sight of his gentle smile.

He gestured toward the open door. "That's your son in there, isn't it?"

I nodded.

"I'm one of the doctors who examined him a few days ago."

I ran my gaze over him, taking in his receding hairline backed by dense brown curls, his wire-rimmed glasses, intelligent eyes, and full lips nearly enveloped by a mustache and a curly beard. His cheeks were smooth and ruddy. The ubiquitous stethoscope poked from the pocket of his white lab coat.

I thought of the parade of doctors and nurses who had hovered over Ethan, but he didn't look familiar. "I'm sorry, but I don't remember you."

"You weren't here. I talked with your husband."

"You examined Ethan?"

He nodded and extended his hand. "I'm Dr. Alan Sidon."

I did something then that I would never have done if I'd had any sanity left. I seized his hand and held on. "Please, tell me my son is going to live."

He seemed to consider his reply, or perhaps he was simply planning his escape.

I tightened my grip. "I know I'm not supposed to say he might die, much less think it, but I'm so scared." His hand felt warm and substantial, and I thought if I could hold onto it as long as I needed, I might be able to draw some strength from him. "I won't be able to watch Ethan in pain. And, I don't think I can survive if he doesn't."

I shifted my position slightly and a wave of dizziness rushed over me. I'd felt that sensation before when I'd drunk a few glasses of wine and then closed my eyes. In fact, I did shut my eyes, and I felt myself sucked into a vast, hostile darkness where I couldn't see a thing: no shadows, no movement, not even a pinprick of light. I got the cold jitters. How would I know which way to turn or where to step?

The world tipped a little, and I grabbed Dr. Sidon's arm for support. If he had pulled back in horror, I wouldn't have blamed him. He didn't, though. We huddled in an odd, slightly distant embrace. He was no taller than I was, but he had a comforting sturdiness about him and I didn't think I could stand on my own.

"I don't know what to do," I said, shivering.

"Would you like to walk down to the cafeteria and get some coffee? I could ask one of our social workers to join us."

"I don't think I can do this."

He gave me a puzzled look. "You mean you can't drink coffee?"

"No, sit out in the waiting room while they poke long needles into Ethan. I'll be thinking about what he was like when he was only a few days old, and then when he was four and five."

I tried to smile. "Those are such wonderful ages. Did you know that? Some people consider ten-year-old boys a menace, but no one is sweeter than Ethan. He makes these strange, gory dummies, but he isn't the least bit violent or mean. He's scared now too, and I'm supposed to be brave for him and I'm nothing but a sniveling fraud."

I saw a glimpse of white from the corner of my eye and realized a nurse had walked by. Even so, Dr. Sidon didn't retreat.

"I wish..." I stopped and looked at him.

"What do you wish?" He seemed to give me permission to admit to any sort of lunacy. He wouldn't judge me.

"I wished I could take his place." I uttered the words in an awful croak. "I wish I were in that bed instead of my son. I wish I were the one in danger."

"I would feel the same way."

"Do you have a child?"

"No, but I can imagine how it might be." He drew back a little but held onto my hand.

What a good person, I thought.

After two straight days with only a sponge bath in Ethan's bathroom, I felt sticky and disheveled. I hadn't even brushed my teeth that morning. The fact that he was willing to touch me at all seemed amazingly kind.

"Your bedside manner is so much better than Dr. Baxter's. Do you think you could take care of Ethan instead?"

He smiled. "You won't find a better gastroenterologist than Dr. Baxter."

"But I'm sure you're an excellent doctor too."

I released him then. I dug a worn shredded tissue from my wrinkled black slacks and blew my nose on it.

"I'm sorry. You probably have better things to do — anything other than holding a deranged woman's hand in the hospital hall."

"No, it's just that I'm not very good at it. I might unintentionally make you feel worse. We have a whole staff of social workers who are far better trained at their jobs than I am."

"I don't want a social worker. I want a miracle worker."

He gave me a long steady look. "Yes, don't we all?"

Chapter 9

Ethan, clutching the mask the doctor had used to administer the anesthesia, was back in his room. He smiled woozily. "The doctor said I get to keep it. I can take it home with me."

Joel stroked Ethan's forehead. "How are you feeling?"

"Okay. That medicine didn't really make me goofy. I don't even remember much — only bright lights and a machine beeping." He lifted his head and gazed in the direction of his belly. "I wanted to have a scar but I guess I don't."

I kept my voice as upbeat as I could manage. "It's still impressive, sweetheart. Your friends will think you're a brave warrior."

Ethan's head swiveled from me to Joel. "Does that mean I can go home now?"

Joel's eyes brimmed with tears. "It won't be long."

That phrase had become our mantra.

When the biopsy results came back, Dr. Baxter called us into a small conference office near Ethan's room. What day was it? Tuesday, I thought wearily. Ethan had been in the hospital nine days.

Dr. Baxter directed us toward chairs at the oval wooden table. Clutching Ethan's chart, he peered at Joel and me over his reading glasses. "How are you two doing?"

"All right," Joel said, when it must have been ridiculously clear we were not." Well, I wish I could have better news for you." He cleared his throat in what seemed an attempt to compose himself.

"A liver should be soft and pink and spongy," he said. "Biopsying your son's liver was like poking a needle into a chunk of wood."

I felt every breath leave my lungs. He looked at me, wondering, I suppose, if I would topple off the chair. I concentrated all my efforts on staying upright while a watery glaze filmed Joel's eyes. His mouth twisted slightly, and I could see he was struggling. I didn't bother to hide my deluge of tears.

Dr. Baxter shifted uncomfortably and transferred his attention to his paperwork. "We also did a blood test that measures serum copper and ceruloplasmin. Your son has a genetic disorder called Wilson's disease that causes excessive copper build-up in the liver."

"You're saying he got this from us?" Joel asked.

"Well, we occasionally run across someone who gets the disease because of a spontaneous mutation in a gene, but it's more likely you're both carriers. That means you each have an abnormal gene. We'll want to do some tests on you to confirm that — nothing invasive, just urine and blood."

Joel brushed his nose with his sleeve. "I've never heard of Wilson's disease. No one in my family has ever had it." He looked at me. "How about you?"

I shook my head.

"That's not unusual," Dr. Baxter said. "Many Wilson's patients have no family history of it, and carriers with one defective gene don't become ill."

The words "defective gene" seemed to be all I could hear. Ethan was sick because we were flawed. We gave our son a terrible disease.

Joel rose from his chair and paced the room. "He will get better, won't he?"

"If it's left untreated, Wilson's disease is fatal. We can give him Penicillamine to remove the copper and forestall further toxic accumulations, but that's a stopgap measure. I'm afraid his liver may already be too damaged to recover."

If this was God's answer to my prayer, he'd hit me directly in the heart. There could be no God, I decided — certainly not one I would wish to worship. I had been praying only to myself.

Joel stopped his pacing and rested his palms on Dr. Baxter's desk, the tendons in his arms twisting. "Could you please explain why it has taken you nine days to figure out our son has a fatal disease?"

Dr. Baxter drew a deep breath. "It's a fairly rare condition. Ethan was difficult to diagnose because he was missing some significant symptoms we look for. One of them is Kayser-Fleischer rings, which are discolorations around the irises. Your son doesn't have those, at least not yet, but then not all Wilson's patients do."

He paused and glanced at the papers in front of him. "And his fingernails aren't particularly rounded but that's probably something you'll notice as time goes along."

As time went along? Did he mean 'as we watched our son die'?

He turned to look at me. "The only option for Ethan is a liver transplant. In fact, he should have a complete work-up so that we can get him on the list as soon as possible."

"A liver transplant? But he's only ten years old."

"We often transplant organs into children much younger."

"I want a second opinion," Joel said sharply.

Dr. Baxter stood and gathered the paperwork into Ethan's folder. "Of course. That's certainly your right." He gave us a look that said he'd heard this reaction before. "We can provide you with the names of other liver specialists to consult, but I would suggest we begin your son's medical treatment right away. It's not something that can wait."

He explained that they could use medication to reduce the copper in his system, at least temporarily, because without it the copper would build up and poison him, causing confusion, slurred speech, tremors, loss of muscular control, abdominal cramping, psychiatric disorders, and recurrent internal bleeding. They sounded like the symptoms from some medieval plague.

I was swimming in water that was too deep. I couldn't grasp the thought that death could be so imminent that a single day or a week mattered. I thought of Ethan in his room down the hall.

When we'd left him, he was sitting in a chair, looking better than he had in days. He didn't have any of the symptoms Dr. Baxter talked about.

He didn't act confused. His words weren't slurred, and he certainly wasn't clutching his midsection in pain. His eyes were bright, his expression alert.

"When do we get to go home?" he'd asked.

I lowered my head into my hands for a few seconds. When I lifted it, my gaze met Joel's and I saw my fear mirrored in his eyes.

Dr. Baxter stood, gathered the paperwork into Ethan's folder, and told us he'd arrange for immediate treatment. We didn't ask all the questions we should have. We couldn't even think of what they might be. We left the room so stunned and bewildered we could hardly walk.

Joel held Ethan's hand, repeatedly running his fingers over Ethan's pudgy knuckles. I knew from memory the grainy little warts that had latched onto his fingers like barnacles.

"Dr. Baxter thinks you've got a bum liver," Joel said.

Ethan's eyes widened. "Can he fix it?"

I noticed Joel didn't look him in the eyes.

"We're not so sure Dr. Baxter's right. We're going to consult another doctor."

Ethan seemed to think about it. "Yeah, that's a good idea."

Joel said he had to go to his office for a few hours, and he left without another word to either of us. We'd always had that sweet little ritual of kissing each other goodbye. It seemed a precaution against a fatal accident on the road or some other dire event, and we violated it only when we were so angry we couldn't bear to touch.

I was confused. When had the rules changed? I spent the afternoon playing with Ethan — fighting a mock battle with his action figures (He was Batman; I was the Joker), listening to him read from the book, *Monsters and Vampires*, and debating whether Harry Potter should be added to the school history books.

At times I felt like a ten year old arguing my position with all the passion and skewed beliefs a child might have. I choked on my tears.

Ethan eyed me suspiciously. "You okay?"

I grabbed a tissue and dabbed at my nose, not meeting his gaze.

"Allergies, I think." I slid off the edge of the bed. "I'll go down the hall and get a cup of hot tea. Maybe that'll make me feel better."

Outside Ethan's room, a nurse pushed a girl in a wheelchair toward the room next door. This was the person I had heard coughing like an old man. She was thin but extraordinarily pretty with exotic dark eyes, soft brown hair, and an exquisitely shaped mouth. She had an aura of weary gentleness.

The elegant Asian woman I had seen before, a tall man of European descent (presumably the girl's father), and a young boy stood by the door. They made a handsome family.

The mother smiled at me. "She's feeling better."

"That's wonderful. When will she go home?"

The mother's smile flickered, then faded. "Soon, we hope."

I regretted my lack of hospital manners. In a place where some children might never be healthy enough to return home, I had reminded her of that possibility.

Joel returned to the hospital around six o'clock that evening, looking as exhausted as he had when he'd left. Ethan was a few steps away in the bathroom, so I kept my voice low. "How was it?"

He slumped onto a chair. "Bad. Too much not getting done."

"You would think someone else could do the work at a time like this."

He stood abruptly and walked across the room. "There is no one else. Jin can't do it. He can't run the office and round up business at the same time."

"But you hired that new person."

"She's a computer expert, not a businesswoman."

"Well, you would think she could help out in an emergency."

"Damn it, Delainie, you make it sound easy. It isn't. They need me there. I need to be here. What do you suggest I do?"

"I'm surprised there's any question."

The veins in his neck pulsed. "Go home for a while. We're getting on each other's nerves."

It was true, but there was no one else we could attack. The enemy was untouchable.

Chapter 10

The next two days brought a sandstorm of conferences, each one leaving us more overwhelmed and frightened than before. We met first with Taylor Buchanan, the liver transplant coordinator whose job it was to guide us through Ethan's medical treatment.

Tall and slender with milk chocolate skin and tight black curls, she shook my hand with a firm grasp. "Call me Taylor. We'll get to know each other pretty well over the next several months."

Joel gave her a curt greeting, and I heard the tension in his voice and felt it in his stride as we followed her past a string of cubicles to her office with its single, narrow window overlooking an outdoor playground populated by red, yellow, and blue climbing toys and life-sized wooden cutouts of barnyard animals. A modular gray desk and files ran the length of one wall.

Taylor arranged two chairs for us and slipped into her own with graceful athleticism.

As she passed by me, a breeze of cologne, a light floral fragrance, unfamiliar but lovely, sweetened the air. On a bulletin board behind her, children — little survivors, I assumed — smiled from photographs.

I sat down but Joel remained standing. Taylor gestured at a row of numbered names on her computer, each bearing a red paper dot beside it. "Those are our successful liver transplants." Her voice held a note of pride.

I zeroed in on "successful," feeling a surge of optimism. I'd become a human thermometer that climbed or dropped at the slightest hint of good or bad news.

She opened another document on her computer, these with yellow dots. She nodded toward them with a maternal smile. "And these are the patients who are waiting."

I quickly scanned the numbered names. Too many. My heart plunged.

She closed her desk drawer and faced us, all business now. "I will be your liaison with all the departments in this medical center, whether it's cardiology, radiology, anesthesiology, nephrology, or any of the others. And I will try to answer the hundreds of questions that will come up as we go along."

I shook my head in puzzlement. "Cardiology? Ethan's problem is his liver, not his heart."

"Yes, but we need to know his other organs are functioning properly so that he can be in the best possible condition for a transplant."

Joel leaned forward, resting his palms on his knees, invading her space. "As I told Dr. Baxter, I want a second opinion on his diagnosis."

Taylor didn't retreat. "Sure. We can provide the names of other specialists in the field, if you like."

"I have my own," he said tersely.

I wondered where he'd managed to acquire one so quickly. I felt embarrassed, caught in the middle. He might be frightened about Ethan's illness and exasperated with the process, but he didn't have to be rude to Taylor.

She gave him a clear, direct look. "No problem. But, in the meantime, we'll operate on the basis that your son will need a transplant. You'll find that time is a major consideration."

"It's difficult to accept all this because Ethan doesn't seem very ill," I said.

"He doesn't right now but that's not unusual. Some Wilson's patients have few symptoms in the beginning."

"Maybe the medicine will work and he won't need a transplant."

"We'll do what we can with medication, but Dr. Baxter's concerned that his liver is already too damaged. Let's assume he'll need a transplant."

They were probably trained to repeat the same information over and over until a parent finally accepted it.

She leaned forward in a gesture of understanding. "We have more people waiting for livers than we have donors. By the time one becomes available for him he may be quite ill."

I closed my eyes, unwilling to consider that possibility.

"I'm sorry." Her voice softened to the consistency of butter. "I don't mean to sound harsh, but that could happen. I promise you that throughout this process I will always tell you the truth — at least to the extent that I know it."

Joel wasn't looking at either of us. He was staring out the window, his jaw rigid, the shadows under his dark eyes a dusky purple.

Taylor pulled out a pencil and a pad of yellow paper and positioned them to the right of her computer. She referred to some notes on them. "Let me start with the basic information. A new patient is put on a computerized list of transplant recipients maintained by the United Network for Organ Sharing — UNOS. It's a national organization that assigns each patient a status, depending on how sick he is.

"Someone who is likely to die within a week without a transplant is Status 1. Status 2 means very ill but not close to death, and Status 3 means a patient is healthy enough to wait a while. Ethan is Status 3. When a liver becomes available, UNOS checks the Status 1 group to see who's the best match according to blood type, weight, and size. They send the liver to the person at the top of that list."

Joel asked. "Are you telling me my son can't get a transplant until he's within a week of dying?"

"We try to save the sickest first."

Joel's fists were clenched so tight I was afraid the tendons in them might snap. "What kind of sick system is this that lets kids nearly die before they can get well?"

His anger filled the room. Taylor didn't appear to react, but I felt as if my body were too large for my skin. Any more of this and I would rip apart.

"That's it?" I said in as calm a tone as I could manage. "There's no other way except to put Ethan on this UNOS list?"

"Actually, there is," she said. "Because of the organ shortage, we're getting more living donors, usually a parent or an adult sibling whose blood type matches the patient."

Joel's blood type was A positive. Mine was B, the same as Ethan's.

"I could be a donor," I said, awash with hope. "I could give Ethan my liver."

Joel's gaze shot toward Taylor.

She smiled. "You wouldn't have to give him the whole thing, just part of it. The great thing about the liver is that it can regenerate. And the advantage of having a living donor is that the transplant could be done before your son becomes critically ill. But I have to caution you. The donor requirements are stringent, and the surgery puts both of you at risk. Doctors don't like to operate on healthy people if there's another way."

"I don't care if doctors don't like doing it," I said. "Ethan is not their son."

She smiled gently. "We can run some tests on you and see if it's a possibility. You would have to be in excellent health."

Joel's shoulder muscles eased, and I realized that he too was seeing some light in this frightening darkness. "Delainie is in perfect health. She's never sick."

It was true I rarely caught a cold or the flu and I had no chronic medical problems, but I wasn't sure that meant I was sound at the core.

Taylor raised her fingers to her cheek, a gesture that seemed to indicate restraint. "I don't want to give you false hopes. The sad truth is that most donor livers come from people who have died."

68

"Well, we're not going to wait that long," I said firmly.

"That's it," I said to Joel as we walked down the hall. "I'll give him part of my liver and he'll be okay."

He squinted doubtfully. "I would like to think it'll be that easy, but so far nothing else has been."

Exasperated, I stopped and looked at him. "It's hope, Joel. It's the most hope we've had yet. Can't you be a little more optimistic?"

At that moment, I decided I was going to change. No more crying, no more complaining about our bad luck, no more fear that Ethan will die. If God wasn't going to help, I would try hope. I would be positive, uplifting, maybe even cheerful. I would give Ethan every ounce of strength and hope I could. If I believed Ethan would get well, maybe he would, too.

We were standing outside the office of the hospital's financial assessment coordinator, who was going to help sort out the quagmire of hospital bills, insurance coverage, and personal assets. Amy Stankowski invited us in with a no-nonsense smile. Waves of salt-streaked black hair swept off her oval face. She looked about forty pounds overweight but sturdy, not soft. Every corner of her office held tidy little stacks of papers and books and, for some reason, I immediately decided she had a good grasp of numbers.

Joel dodged a low hanging mobile of silver stars and a gold-foil planet and sat down. Hunched like a walrus, he seemed to fill the small office with his tension. I knew he was scared we wouldn't have enough money to give Ethan the best care. I was too, but it wouldn't help to alienate these message-bearers.

She eyed Joel. "I suppose you're worried you'll lose your house."

"Is that what it's going to take?" His voice was controlled but edgy as a razor.

"Everyone comes in here thinking that." She bent toward him. "We will work with you, Mr. Franklin, to prevent that from happening."

I noticed, though, that she didn't promise it wouldn't. She explained our medical insurance placed a lifetime cap of two hundred thousand dollars on organ transplants and follow-up care. That seemed adequate until she gave us the costs. One hundred and seventy thousand for a liver transplant without complications (a few weeks spent in intensive care could double or triple that).

If I were the donor, there would be the additional cost of my surgery.

If the donor was a cadaver, there might be organ acquisition fees of about twenty-five thousand dollars (not a charge for the liver itself — that would be illegal — but the cost of surgical removal and transportation). I sat there dazed, barely able to comprehend the numbers.

She ran down the rest of the list: Eight hundred dollars a month for the drugs and blood tests Ethan would need during the waiting period, and then, if the transplant was successful, a thousand dollars a month for the immunosuppressive drugs he would take daily to prevent his body from rejecting his new liver — drugs he would need for the rest of his life. The insurance company would cover some, but not all, of these expenses.

Even my battered mind grasped the enormity of her words.

If we sold both cars and every single antique my friends had stashed in the spare room, we might come up with fifty or sixty thousand in cash to add to our meager savings account.

We had a few maxed-out credit cards and a vacation to Disneyland we were still paying off.

Joel was looking at her through slitted eyes. "And the part the insurance doesn't cover? How do other people pay for that?"

"We've seen some excellent examples of families raising funds in the community. Bake sales, walkathons, events like that. We can give you the names of organizations that offer guidance in setting them up."

"Begging for money." His lips drew back in contempt, and for a moment I thought *I don't know this man.*

Amy didn't blink. "Other people won't see it that way. They'll see a family that needs help, and their generosity will surprise you."

I thought of the little containers at the grocery store, requesting money for Wounded Warriors, March of Dimes and Shriners. I always threw in a few dollars.

Taylor leaned forward, keeping her sharp blue eyes on Joel. "This hospital does not turn away sick children, Mr. Franklin. If all other resources are exhausted, we can turn to Medicaid."

Joel's sharp intake of breath sounded like the hissing of a gas flame. "Welfare, you mean."

"Government assistance, but I assume you will want to do whatever is necessary for your son."

Joel stood, his head smacking the silver stars and knocking them out of orbit. Without another word, he strode out of the room.

I caught up with Joel at the Bo Peep elevator. The door opened, and we stepped into the empty cubicle. He reached toward the panel of buttons.

I intercepted his hand. "No, let's go down and take a walk outside. I need some fresh air and sunlight."

"Well, I don't." He punched the button for Ethan's floor.

I stared at the brightly painted, wooden Little Bo Peep on the wall opposite me, at the dark lashes fringing her bright blue eyes and the mouth curled into a little pink O. She carried a gold shepherd's crook in one hand and a limp woolly lamb in the other.

I leaned against the elevator wall. "I'm in some unreal place, Joel, like Dorothy in Oz. I was tooling along in a straight line when this storm picked me up and tossed me sideways and now here I am, contemplating these ridiculous Mother Goose characters, which I know are supposed to cheer me up but instead make me want to draw mustaches on them."

He looked at me but didn't say anything. When the door opened, he stepped out without waiting for me.

I ran after him and grabbed his shirtsleeve. "We have to talk, and we can't do it in front of Ethan. We have to think positively."

The space between his eyebrows drew into a hard ridge. He pulled away, the sleeve of his blue dress shirt slipping through my fingers. "What is there to say? You heard those numbers. We're talking a minimum of two hundred thousand, and it will likely be closer to three. Even if we sell everything we own, we won't be able to come up with the twenty percent the insurance won't pay."

"We can sell the house."

He gave me a disgusted look. "We have a second mortgage on it or did you forget?"

I had, and the weight of those costs crashed down on me. I tried to find that shred of hope I'd felt earlier.

"So, is there anything else you want to know?" Joel said.

"Yeah," I whispered. "Are we going to fight this together or separately?"

"Well, of course we're going to fight it together, but that's not exactly the point right now, is it?"

"It's very much the point if we're going to make it through."

He looked at me for several interminable seconds. "Oh, Delainie," he said in one long breath.

I took two steps toward him and pressed my head against his chest, feeling a shirt button press into my cheek, feeling his body radiate a reassuring heat through the layers of our clothing, and eventually his arms encircling me. I wished he would have hugged tighter, but I didn't want to ask.

The next morning, we met with Eleanor Villardi, the Children's Memorial social worker who was supposed to help us get through "this difficult time."

Eleanor was a soft-around-the-edges, fortyish woman whose office decor of lacy, heart-shaped pillows, silk flowers, and kitten figurines didn't inspire my confidence. I could imagine what Joel thought. She tried to coax him into saying something —anything— but he trained his gaze on the dust motes tangoing in a streak of light from the window. I didn't have complete faith in the value of "talking out" one's problems, but Joel was rabid about it.

If a person couldn't fix things himself, it was because   he was indecisive, incompetent, or weak, and the additional unspoken opinion was that no self-respecting man would admit to such inadequacies.

"Right now, Ethan is our only concern," I said.

Eleanor said, "Of course, that alone can bring up a whole new set of issues. It's possible your marriage will suffer from the stress."

"Oh, our marriage is quite solid," I blurted. "Isn't it, Joel?"

He murmured his agreement—if I heard him correctly.

"I'm sure it is." She gave me an indulgent smile. "We can talk about all this as we go along. In the meanwhile, phone me with any concerns you have."

Joel's flat expression told me he wouldn't be making that call anytime soon.

Chapter 11

We took Ethan home the next day, packing pills to reduce the accumulated copper in his liver and lower his blood pressure, a steroid to decrease inflammation, a diuretic, assorted vitamins, and other medicines that would alleviate the side effects of the first ones. Despite his frequent requests to leave, he'd looked distressed and apprehensive when the time came.

Dr. Baxter said he could return to school on a limited basis, that it would be wise to restore our lives to normality as much as possible, but Ethan said he didn't want to go back to school. I knew he had visions of tedious assignments and harrowing math tests to make up.

But that wasn't all that was bothering him.

"The kids will call me a pumpkin and ask if it's true I'm going to die."

"Well, we'll show them," I said as cheerfully as I could. "They should be so lucky as to skip school without getting into trouble. There will be plenty of time for classes after you're well."

By the time we left the hospital it was five in the afternoon. After a week of sunshine that we saw mainly from the windows of the Bo Peep wing, a spring downpour pummeled the hospital's circular driveway and it seemed as if Mother Nature had been waiting for us. Joel dashed to our car and pulled up to the entrance. We bundled Ethan into it.

As we rode down Broadway, Joel suggested we stop at Dick's Drive-in, locally famous for its burgers and shakes.

"I don't think Ethan should eat that kind of food," I said. "He's supposed to be on a low sodium diet."

"One meal won't hurt him."

"Jeez, Mom. I'm ten years old."

I don't know that had to do with it, but not wanting to be the bad guy on his first day home, I gave up my protest and turned to gaze out the window at Capitol Hill, a flashy section of the city, a carnival of ethnic restaurants, art film theaters, funky shops, and alternative lifestyles.

As I stared at a young couple with matching yellow-and-purple-striped spiked hair and leather collars, Ethan asked, "Mom, can I dye my hair like that?"

"When you're eighteen." I had given him my standard line without thinking. Now, I shivered at the possible irony in it.

"Look, Dad, there's Dick's," Ethan yelled. "We're going to stop, aren't we?"

I sighed but didn't say anything. Joel turned left, nearly colliding with a Starving Students moving van, and pulled into the burger stand's packed parking lot.

The only available spot was behind the small building, where a vent spewed out fat-laden cooking odors. Joel dashed through the rain to the take-out window, returning several minutes later, completely soaked, with our burgers, chocolate shakes, and grease-soaked French fries. After we ate our food, Ethan sighed with satisfaction. I regretted I'd wanted to deprive him of this.

The old Buick held us like a cocoon. We huddled in there and fogged the windows with our breath, smiling cozily and pretending Ethan was fine, that life was the way it had been before.

Joel beamed at Ethan. "Tastes better than that hospital food, doesn't it, bud?"

Ethan's head bobbed in agreement, while his tongue shot out and caught a smear of mustard from the corner of his mouth. Joel reached across the back of the driver's seat and mussed up his hair.

The moment was perfect. If I could have captured it in time and sealed us in that big, safe car forever, I would have.

But it was over too soon. A few minutes later, as Joel was driving up Queen Anne Avenue toward home, Ethan slumped down, bending slightly at the middle.

I eyed him from the front passenger seat. "You okay?"

He gave a little burp. "Uh-huh."

"Tummy upset?"

"Not really."

I didn't believe him.

Joel parked in front of our house, where a banner WEL-COME HOME, ETHAN stretched above the front door.

The slanted rain had splashed the red-and-blue poster paints, streaking them and obliterating some of the letters, but Ethan was delighted anyway. I was sure Cappy, Jaya and Liz had put the banner there.

Inside, Oscar sauntered down the hall to greet us. He nuzzled Ethan's pants leg, hunching his back into an arc of orange fur. The house still smelled of Pine Sol and furniture polish.

Ethan walked around the living room, studying the photos on the mantel, our one-hundred-year-old, flower-patterned love seat, the Morris chairs, the old sailing trunk usually cluttered with magazines. He frowned. "Everything looks different — kind of smaller, like it shrunk."

"Your aunties gave it a good cleaning," I said, "but otherwise it's the same."

He looked around again. "That's probably it. It'll feel better when it's dirty."

Joel made a face, but I laughed. This was how it was supposed to be, the three of us at home together. I followed Ethan into his room.

He switched on the light and glanced around, his gaze stopping on the papier-mâché fly monster on his worktable. "Whew! I was afraid you might throw it away."

"Ethan," I said, genuinely shocked, "what would make you think such a crazy thing?"

He ran his hand over his irrepressible cowlicks. "Well, some moms are like that."

I started to protest that I wasn't one of those moms, when I saw his eyes narrow and his mouth twist into a little grimace.

"Your stomach hurts, doesn't it?"

"No-o."

"I was right. You shouldn't have had that burger and fries."

He groaned. I didn't know if he was expressing his exasperation or his physical distress, but what had I been thinking? We had a sick child, and we were still trying to pretend he wasn't, as if fast food and a little family bonding were going to make our lives the way they used to be.

I yanked his pajamas from a bureau drawer. "That's it! Into bed."

"Do you think I could have some Pepto-Bismol first?"

"I was right. You do have a stomachache."

"Jeez, Mom, it's not a contest."

"Yes, it is. That's what motherhood is — a constant, no-holds-barred, never-ending contest. And you know what, Ethan? I'm going to win it for both of us."

"Does that mean I can't have the Pepto-Bismol?" he moaned.

I tried to recall the various instructions we'd received with his medications. "I think they gave us some liquid medicine for tummy aches. Let me check."

Joel had already stored the bottle in the refrigerator. I found it nestled between a bag of green salad and a tuna noodle casserole my friends had prepared. It's an understatement to say I have the sweetest, most caring friends ever. We could have had the casserole for dinner instead of the artery-clogging fare we'd eaten.

An hour later, Ethan lay curled into a ball, his knees doubled against his chest, his face a pasty yellow. I was trying my hardest not to give Joel my told-you-so look. "Maybe I should call the hospital."

He eased onto the edge of Ethan's bed and felt his forehead. "He doesn't seem to have a fever."

Ethan glanced from one of us to the other, his eyes registering turmoil. "I'm feeling better." He stretched his legs straight. "The stomachache is going away. I'm sure I'm getting better."

An hour later, he did seem to have recovered. After he'd fallen asleep, I plodded upstairs and found Joel in our bedroom, setting the alarm clock for the next morning.

I dropped onto the blue-and-yellow patterned chair across from him.

"Now he feels guilty," I said. "He feels responsible for being sick when it's our fault for feeding him junk food to begin with."

"We don't know it was the hamburger —"

"No, it was probably the greasy fries."

"All right, Delainie. I got the message."

"Well, you won't be the one getting up in the middle of the night with him. I will. I always have."

"Then I must have been sleepwalking all those years he was a baby." He tugged off his slacks and tossed them several feet toward the other chair. They slid down the blue-and-white striped arm and puddled on the floor. He yanked off his pullover shirt, balled it up, and tossed it in the same direction. It landed square on the seat.

"Well, that's certainly grown-up," I said, charging toward the bathroom.

I brushed my teeth and changed into a ratty old nightshirt labeled SORRY IF I LOOK INTERESTED. I'M NOT. By the time I walked back in, Joel was hunched under the covers, facing the wall, but I knew he wasn't asleep. After fifteen years, I'd internalized the pattern of his night breathing. I crawled between the sheets, and he shifted closer to the edge.

Joel and I met at the True Value Hardware store five years after my parents died. I was looking for something to hang a heavy, framed mirror on the wall. I stared at the bewildering selection of screws and hooks, then picked up a round-headed screw that was about an inch long. I put it back and reached for one with attached metal wings that flipped out. It seemed sturdier, but I wondered how you managed to pop open the wings once you got it on the other side of the wall. I examined it a little longer, then turned to the tall man standing next to me. "Could you help me? I need a screw, but I'm not sure this is the right one."

He studied me for a moment, while I zeroed right in on his eyes, the exact color of his muddy brown T-shirt. A sheaf of

4>fort>8fort>8

ht hair fell over his forehead. I immediately found him endearing.

He tried to suppress a smile. "Is that a pickup line? Because if it is, it's the best one I've ever heard."

I think for the first time in a decade I actually blushed. I dropped the screw into its bin and retreated a pace. I was tired of men who thought they were so cute. I should have made some flippant comeback — it's how I would have handled anyone else and then thought myself so clever. Instead, I turned and started back down the aisle.

"That's called a molly screw," he said, raising his voice slightly, sounding truly repentant. "It's probably what you would want if you're hanging something on plasterboard."

I stopped and turned. I walked toward him.

He reached over, picked up the winged fastener, and held it on his palm. I immediately fell in love with the shape of his wrist and his big hands with their thickly callused fingers because a man could look like Bob Frankenstein if he had sturdy arms and powerful hands. I knew that if I laid my arm next to his, his skin, coppered by the sun, would be the darker of the two; mine would look pale, almost delicate. It was a primal thing.

"I have an antique mirror I want to hang," I said. "It's in a huge, ornate frame."

"This is what you need then, unless you use a stud. Have you looked for one?"

I almost said I'd had mixed results in that area, but then I would have had no right to criticize him.

"I remember my dad had some sort of sensor device to find studs. Do I need to buy one of those?"

"You could try thumping on the wall, the way you would a watermelon."

His youthful features made me think he was younger than I was, by maybe by a decade or two, but he was big enough to know what he was doing. If I stood close against him, he could probably rest his chin on my head, and as short as I am, that possibility offered reassurance.

79

"And if it sounds hollow, then what?"

His face registered surprise. "You don't know much about construction, do you?"

"No, but I spell really well."

"I'll hang your mirror for you," he offered.

I thought about letting this stranger into my apartment and decided I must be crazy. "I don't know you. You could be a serial killer. Ted Bundy used to fake an injured arm and lure women into helping him load his boat onto his VW bug."

"I can't be Ted Bundy because my name is Joel Franklin. I don't think serial killers give out their names, by the way, and in case you've forgotten, you spoke to me first. How do I know you're not a serial killer?"

I held out my hand, palm up. "I want to see your driver's license."

He exhumed a creased, flattened wallet from his back pocket and flipped it open. There he was — the same youthful face staring at me from the laminated permit with the name he'd given me, and an address only six blocks from my apartment building. I noticed he was a year younger than I was.

I handed back his wallet. "Don't think you can get away with killing me. While you're hanging the mirror, I'm going to write your name and address on strips of paper and hide them all over my apartment."

"Okay. I'll give you my phone number so you can add that."

He came home with me, hung my mirror, and left. Already, I missed him.

He came back and, during the next several days, repaired the leaky faucet in my bathroom, installed a dead bolt on my door, fixed the flat on my bicycle, removed the metal corn pick from my jammed garbage disposal, and changed the oil in my car. I suppose it was his way of saying he was interested.

On our first real date, we talked all night. I still recall the excitement of finding someone who wanted the same simple life I did. We didn't make love right away, but we did something better.

We hiked a rocky beach on Puget Sound at six in the morning, inhaling the tang of salt air and shellfish and watching the sun rise over the Cascades, Washington's mountainous spine, and ate huckleberry pancakes and sausages at a tiny restaurant on Alki Point.

And we talked nonstop. We asked each other every question we could think of — and never seemed to run out of them.

I liked his steadiness, his intelligence, his complete and total devotion to me. I was the flag that waved in the wind. He was the post that anchored me. He used to say he would always be there for me, and I believed him. We agreed on all the big things: values, money, and goals. He was loosely religious, and I could live with that. He wanted his own business someday and so did I. He said that what a person did was more important than what he owned. I was stunned by his profundity.

Two weeks after we met, we were sleeping together.

And, now, after a forced separation on hospital cots, we slept together again — but did little else. There was a time when we marked life's meaningful moments by making long, sweet love, but now I couldn't recall when we'd last had sex. I finally remembered it was about three weeks ago, before Ethan got sick.

Chapter 12

B enumbed and bewildered, we compensated by pretending everything was   fine, and that was easy to do because the medicine seemed to help Ethan. His stomach cramps were gone. He was more energetic than he'd been at the hospital, but he also seemed spacier, not the boy he was six months ago.

Joel contacted a liver specialist at a Chicago hospital and arranged to have Ethan's records and tests sent to him for a second opinion.

"Maybe it will turn out he has something more treatable," Joel said.

Frightened by the lack of hope in his eyes, I clamped down on whatever optimism I could find. Children's Memorial had sent us home with an initial bill, and the following afternoon, I found Joel upstairs in the office, checking over the numbers, his eyes rimmed by gray-tinged skin.

"Damned hospital," he muttered. "Do you remember a dietitian visiting Ethan?"

I recalled a middle-aged woman with gray-flecked brown hair, spine-straight posture, and a plastic smile. "She came on one of those days you were at work."

"How long did she stay?"

"Five minutes. Ten at the most. Why?"

He slapped his pen down on the itemized bill. "Because that little visit cost us three hundred dollars."

"That can't be right. All she did was ask him what foods he liked and recommend he eat more vegetables and cut down on salt. I could have told him that. Oh, and she gave him a pamphlet with one of those pyramid food charts surrounded by dancing strawberries and asparaguses in sailor hats."

I felt like marching right down to the hospital and throwing her silly chart at her.

He had pulled up our financial files on the computer and was scribbling figures on a yellow notepad. "I'll tell them we won't pay it."

"Can we do that?"

"We can try." The muscles in his face went slack. "Won't make much difference anyway. Three hundred dollars is beginning to look like a drip of water in the Pacific."

I sank onto a chair. "What will they do to us, Joel?"

"Do to us when?"

"When we can't pay the bills. I'm thinking about the cost for Ethan's transplant, his visits to the hospital, and all that medication."

"I don't know."

"We've always paid our bills. Not necessarily on time but eventually."

"I said I don't know."

I saw the expression in his eyes before he turned away. He looked trapped.

I had hoped that Ethan could return to school right away, but he had a series of outpatient visits scheduled at the hospital over the next two weeks. A complete work-up would assess his suitability for a liver transplant. Once that was done, I could be tested to determine my compatibility as a donor. I thought it was a good sign that Ethan felt well enough to see his friends, so on the Saturday after he came home from the hospital, I called Jaya and invited her and Krishna over for the afternoon.

They arrived, shaking the rain from their jackets and kicking off their shoes at the front door. When I protested that the floor was dirtier than their shoes, Jaya merely laughed and gave me a hug.

She looked like a businesswoman in a cranberry-colored blazer that brought out the pink in her cheeks and a paisley scarf that cinched her satin-black hair. If I had been the jealous type, I would have envied her soft beauty.

Krishna, who was small, wiry, and serious, wore his black ninja costume and carried a light saber. He surveyed Ethan with curiosity. "You got a scar?"

Ethan shook his head in disappointment. "Just a little spot where they stuck the needle in."

"That's still pretty cool. Maybe we could smear fake blood on it."

Ethan's eyes brightened. "Yeah, that's a good idea."

They headed for Ethan's bedroom, while Jaya and I moved into the kitchen.

I gestured toward the small table against the wall and she slid onto the chair next to it. Ethan's plastic medicine bottles sat in a row on the wooden surface. Before she arrived, I'd been distributing pills into a wallet-sized plastic case with individual compartments for days of the week and coming to grips with the realization that they filled the entire container. I pushed the pill bottles aside.

Jaya propped her elbows on the tabletop. "How are you doing?"

"I don't know. I'm trying to think positively and convey that to Ethan, but then I consider what could happen to him and..." I stopped and made a gesture of futility, my eyes drowning in tears once again.

She was next to me in an instant, rubbing my back and murmuring reassurances. "What can we do for you, Delainie? Run errands, fix meals, drive Ethan to some of his appointments? We'll do anything you need."

I smiled through my tears. "I sort of figured that when you changed the kitty litter and cleaned my house."

She released me. "You want me to come over and stay with Ethan one day this week so you can get out, maybe go to an antique auction or an estate sale?"

I missed my antique trips. Between the hospital and our home, I was feeling confined and desperate to get out and continue my search for the one perfect treasure that would fetch a few hundred thousand dollars, providing the money that would give Ethan everything he needed.

I suppose I was like the gambler who thought "One more time and I'll hit it big." But I couldn't do it.

My lower lip trembled. "I'm scared to leave him."

"Oh, honey," she said, gripping my wrist.

"I want you to come over once in a while and talk with me."

"Anytime. How's Joel holding up?"

I thought about how I had found him behind the garage that morning, lighting a cigarette. Dark clouds of sleeplessness had gathered under his eyes. As far as I knew, he hadn't smoked in ten years. He quit after Ethan was born because he didn't want his son to see him smoking.

He flicked his wrist, extinguishing the match and tossing it in the dirt in one quick gesture. "What are you doing? Checking up on me?"

I lifted the grocery sack I was carrying so that he could see it. "Taking out the garbage." I removed the lid from the trashcan next to him, dropped in the bag, then replaced the lid with a clang. "You don't have to hide from me. I'm not your mother."

I walked away before he could answer.

I looked at Jaya's inquiring face. "Joel's fine."

Later, I wondered why I didn't tell her the truth — that it was bad enough to have a sick child without tossing in a moody, angry husband. Jaya was one of my closest friends, and I should have been able to confide in her. I knew the private details of her complicated life.

She'd inherited a truckload of money, which — out of irrational guilt, I believed — she spent on everyone but herself.

Her husband Rob, a Boeing attorney, was usually able to tease the seriousness and self-penance out of her, but a few years ago he launched a brief but steamy affair with an elementary school teacher, and for three agonizing months, Jaya came to our meetings with red-rimmed eyes and a sob lodged in her throat. We all suffered with her.

Maybe I didn't tell her the truth because I couldn't shake the feeling that, while it was acceptable and eminently deserving of sympathy to have an ailing child, serious discord with your husband was a waste of precious time.

Our loving, unbreakable marriage was a point of pride for me, and I didn't want to admit I was seeing cracks.

Chapter 13

I was walking into the kitchen when I heard Joel say, "Would you recommend some other kind of treatment?" He leaned against the counter, the phone to his ear, his face turned so that I couldn't see his expression. "Okay. Yes, we will. Thank you."

I held my breath.

He hung up the receiver and rose from his seat. When he caught sight of me, his businessman's mask slipped off, revealing an expression of despair.

"The liver specialist from Chicago?" I asked.

He nodded.

"What did he say?"

"He said..." He paused and exhaled slowly. "He said Ethan has Wilson's Disease, and his liver is damaged to the extent that he'll need a transplant within a year."

"Maybe we could get a third opinion. Maybe we could send him to the Mayo Clinic or some place like that. I mean, we can't —"

"How many opinions will it take, Delainie? This doctor in Chicago is one of the top-rated liver specialists in the country."

I wanted to protest that it had been his idea to consult someone else, but I swallowed my words. No sense turning it into another argument. The specialist's report cast a gloom over the already rainy day. We were into the second week of May and still having cool temperatures and prolonged drizzle.

Later that day, I threaded the car through Seattle's crowded streets to Children's Memorial for an appointment with a cardiologist. Ethan wore his Seahawks cap (wheat-like wisps of hair jutting from its edges), a baggy navy blue windbreaker, crisp new jeans, and white athletic shoes that made his feet look like pontoons. He sat slumped on the passenger seat, quiet most of the way. The windshield wipers slapped from side to side. The car's heating and dehumidifying system wasn't working properly, so our breaths fogged up the windows and the interior smelled like dirty socks. Ethan shifted uncomfortably.

"Are you having cramps?" I asked.

He looked away. "What are they going to do to me today?"

I used my sleeve to clear a spot on the windshield. "I'm not sure. Maybe they'll listen to your heart while you run on a treadmill."

When we passed a sporting goods store, he gestured toward it. "Let's go there instead."

"You know we can't. We don't have time. Your appointment is in fifteen minutes in the Miss Muffet wing, and I haven't been in that part of the hospital before."

"What if we don't go at all?" His voice sounded hopeful.

"You want to get well, don't you?"

He seemed to think about that. "If I don't get well, I die. That's what the doctor in Chicago said, didn't he?"

I felt a jolt of panic. "We're not going to even think like that. Both doctors said you would be a good candidate for a transplant, and I'll give you part of my liver. Of course you'll get well, but we have to work at it."

"I don't know why I have to work so much harder than other kids do." He crossed his arms, pulling them tight against him, bear-like. "Krishna doesn't do a thing, and he never gets sick."

That had been the highlight of his weekend, seeing Krishna. I could have given him my "life isn't fair" speech, but I never liked it when my parents recited it to me.

"Lots of people have transplants," I said, although I personally didn't know one.

"Well, I spent nine days in the hospital, and they still didn't fix me." He sounded petulant. "They kept poking me with needles, which weren't supposed to hurt but did anyway. And they sucked out a piece of my liver, and that didn't help. Now they want to do more stuff, and what if that doesn't work?" He was in full whine now, punching up some of his words. "Then it will all be for nothing."

I stopped at a red light. "We have to do it, Ethan."

"Why?"

"Because your father and I can't live without you."

He sat up straighter and stared at me. "But you lived before you had me."

"That's true, but we didn't know what we were missing. If we had known, we would have wanted you to be born sooner."

He settled back into his seat, pondering my answer. "Yeah, that makes sense." After a few silent moments, he turned to look at me. "Do you promise if I really work at it I won't die?"

The light changed, but I froze. I thought about our need to think positively and how doctors say the attitude makes a huge difference.

Still, I hesitated. "Yes, you'll get well. Maybe later you'll become a surgeon yourself. Look at how good you are at creating severed arms and bloody leg stumps."

"Yeah, but that's fake blood. I don't like real blood."

I shifted my gaze to the row of shops along Broadway. "Oh, look, there's a martial arts store. Do you suppose they have a Ninja outfit like Krishna's?"

His head looked out the window. "Can we stop there?"

"On the way back," I said, tension seeping from me like air from a balloon.

The cardiology examination took about an hour.

"Did I pass the tests?" Ethan asked as we left.

I patted his back. "You did fine. These aren't the kind you get graded on."

I thought we were walking to the Miss Muffet elevator, but somehow we wandered into the Bo Peep wing of the hospital. Ethan looked around, almost fondly. "Hasn't changed much."

"It's been only six days."

When a nurse passed us with a warm hello, Ethan beamed. "Do you suppose she remembers me?"

"I'm sure she does, Spider-man. How could she forget a radioactive insect?"

"Spiders aren't insects, Mom." His long exhalation of breath showed he was trying to be patient. "They're Arachnids."

"Right. I knew that."

The mother of the girl who had occupied the room next to Ethan's emerged from the visitor's lounge, carrying a cup of coffee. She stopped when she saw us and smiled at Ethan. "I thought you'd gone home."

"I did, but I have to keep coming back for tests." He gave me a meaningful look, happy that she'd recognized him.

I extended my hand. "I'm Delainie Franklin. I've seen you here so often I feel as if I know you."

She shifted the coffee cup to her left hand and grasped my fingers with a firm touch. "I'm Alice Spenser." Her starkly tailored black dress called attention to her pale face and tired expression. She glanced toward the lounge. "Do you have time to talk?"

"Mom, you said —"

"We'll stop at the martial arts store, Ethan, I promise. But I want to visit with Alice for a few minutes first."

Because we were in the Bo Peep wing, the lounge's round benches were covered with fake fleece, and tail-wagging sheep cavorted across a mural on the wall. I made myself a cup of tea. Alice refilled her coffee cup, and we sat at a table. She paused for a moment, watching Ethan head for the table that held a communal jigsaw puzzle.

"He looks well," she said in a low voice.

I thought I detected a hint of resentment in her tone.

"He seems better," I said, "but the doctors say it won't last. He's going to need a liver transplant."

"My daughter's waiting for one now."

"How long has it been?"

The corners of her mouth flattened. "Eleven months."

"Eleven months," I said incredulously. "Why has it taken so long?"

"Didn't anyone tell you there are more than thirteen thousand people in this country waiting for new livers at this very moment?"

"Well, I know there's a shortage, but—"

"Only a few hundred will get them this year."

"Yes, but children have priority, don't they?"

She looked at me. "Where did you get that idea?"

"I assumed children would go to the top of the list. They have so much more life to live."

She gave me a pitying look. "You really don't know how this works, do you?"

I felt like a little girl who had said something stupid on her first day of school.

Alice leaned forward, wrapping her hands around her cup. "Let me run through some information for you. You do know about the United Network for Organ Sharing, don't you?"

I nodded.

"Well," she said, "there are more adults than children on the UNOS waiting list, so most pediatric livers go to adults."

I stared at her. "Are you saying that some seventy-year-old man could get a liver before my son does?"

"If he's sick enough. They match blood type and size. They don't care about the recipient's age." Her lips, carefully sculpted by lipstick, curled with bitterness. "Haven't you ever wondered how some old ballplayer who destroyed his liver with alcohol can get a new one?"

"I've never thought about it before."

She gave a sharp laugh. "Rickety old politicians and rock stars get transplants while children die. They'll tell you they waited a long time for their chances like everyone else, and you're supposed to believe that."

I must have looked shocked, because she said, "You wait until your son has been sick for almost a year, then tell me money and power have nothing to do with it."

I glanced at Ethan across the room. "The doctors wouldn't allow that."

"The doctors?" She sniffed derisively. "You'll find out the doctors play God. If they decide they don't want to give your son a liver, they won't. They can say he's too sick or he's not sick enough. But then, they transplant somebody who's so far gone he dies anyway. They can do what they want. They can even waste it if they want. You'll see how they are — these holy doctors."

I shifted uncomfortably on my chair. "They have difficult jobs. I'm sure they're doing the best they can." I sounded sanctimonious and I knew it.

She looked away and a few seconds of awkward silence followed.

I studied Alice. How could I know what she had done? Maybe she'd handled her daughter's situation poorly.

Maybe she'd complained too loudly and too often, offending all the doctors and the staff. I knew people like that, people who believed they were always the victims, who thought they could get more by yelling and demanding. The hospital had rules — reasonable rules — and she wasn't following them. That was it, I decided. I wasn't going to take everything she said as the complete truth.

"How old is your daughter?" I asked.

"Fifteen."

I tried not to show my surprise. She had looked so small under her hospital blanket that I would have guessed she was closer to Ethan's age.

"They moved her into intensive care," Alice said. "She has a lot of fluid buildup in her abdomen and her protime level is rising."

Protime level? I remembered Dr. Baxter said that was a measure of how fast a person's blood clotted.

But everyone was different, I told myself. I shouldn't assume what was happening to her daughter would happen to Ethan. I managed a smile. "I'm sure your daughter will get her new liver soon."

Alice made a dry, bitter sound. "Sarah has a rare blood type. They don't get too many type B donors."

I felt my throat constrict. "That's Ethan's blood type," I whispered.

She glanced across the room at him. "I'm sorry to hear that."

I firmly reminded myself Ethan's situation was different.

"But I'm going to give Ethan part of my liver," I said. "Can't you or your husband do that with your daughter?"

Her eyes looked empty. "I'm not a match, and my husband has heart problems. Our four-year-old son has the right blood type, but he's too young. Even if he could do it, we can't risk it. We could lose both of them."

It seemed grotesque that a parent would have to make that choice, that she would have to measure her daughter's life against her son's. Alice tapped her middle finger on the laminated tabletop, the way a child seeks comfort in repetition.

"Isn't there anyone else in your family who could help?"

"It's not as easy as you might think to find a living donor. Who wants to take the chance he might die while giving forty percent of his liver to someone else?"

What if I couldn't be Ethan's donor? I didn't even want to think about that.

Alice said, "We'll have to wait for the right person — someone we don't even know—to die." She looked at me. "Sounds terrible, doesn't it? But that's how it is. Even if a liver does become available, she may be too sick for the operation. She might have a secondary infection like pneumonia. In that case, they would transplant the organ into someone else."

"Maybe she'll get better. Maybe she won't need a transplant after all." My words sounded lame.

Alice gave me a scathing look. "People with diseased livers don't get better. It's not like a broken bone. They only get worse."

"Well, yes, but..." Once again, I felt foolish. I couldn't offer anything but platitudes.

Alice's lips trembled, and her eyes took on a shine. "Sarah can't get much worse. If she does, they'll move her to Status 1."

I remembered Status 1 meant she would die within a week unless she got a new liver.

"You'll see," Alice said in that knowing voice a mother uses to tell a pregnant friend about the pain that lies ahead. "That's the way the UNOS system works. Your child can't get a transplant until she's close to death, so you don't know whether to wish for her to get sicker or temporarily better."

I looked down at my hands, which had taken on a life of their own. They were quaking, rattling the cup, the tea slopping over the brim and splashing pale brown spots onto the table.

Alice put her hand on my wrist. "I'm sorry. Honestly, I didn't mean to frighten you."

I nodded and stood. Across the room, Ethan was fitting tiny pieces into the puzzle, humming "We Are the Champions" under his breath.

I stood and hurried toward him, intending to grab him and run down the hospital corridor past the puffy clouds, singing bluebirds, and smiling sunbursts, into the Jack Sprat elevator, down to the first floor, and out the lobby door. I would guide him from the hospital the way I might rush him from a burning building. Because Alice was clearly that kind of threat. She and her daughter were as dangerous as an inferno at my heels.

That night, I dreamed of my father.

My first memory is of him falling off the roof, the sort of thing that makes an impression on a three-year-old. I have no idea what he was doing up there — replacing shingles, maybe, or fixing the chimney. He was always repairing something. The thud of him hitting the ground and the image of his crumpled body are caught up in a single, stark moment, like a snapshot. That's all I remember. The rest I heard later from Mom and Dad.

"You cried like a banshee," Dad said with a laugh. "I didn't break any bones, but I sure was sore. And here you are screaming your head off and your mom comes running out, thinking I must have landed on you. And the twins are shouting they saw the whole thing and I looked like Superman flying off the roof and 'Gee, Dad, could you do it again?'"

But he had scared me so much I had wet my pants. Mom said that was probably half the reason I was crying. I hadn't been toilet trained all that long, and I was proud of the fact that

I got to wear big girl underpants. But that part I don't remember. I have this noisy picture in my head of Dad smacking the ground like a downed airliner. Come to think of it, that was an omen and I didn't recognize it. I wondered about how many others I'd missed.

Chapter 14

Joel looked at me warily. "They're arriving on Wednesday morning."

I leaned against the sink and focused my attention on scrubbing glutinous oatmeal from Ethan's cereal bowl.

"Did you hear me?" he said.

Of course I'd heard him. I set down the crockery bowl with a clunk. "I have to take Ethan to the hospital at ten o'clock that day for the last of his tests."

Joel jammed a slice of bread into the toaster, then raised his hands in exasperation. "What do you want me to do, Delainie? They're my parents, for God's sake, the only ones we've got."

I felt as if he were blaming me, as if I had been the one who had reached out that awful afternoon, plucked my mother and father's airplane from the drizzly sky, and snapped it in two.

I resented the comparison, his parents to mine. His descended on us once a year, advising us on our son, our jobs, our house, our lives in general, while my parents remained in their watery graves.

"I don't know why they're coming now," I said. "Ethan will probably go back to school next week."

"You said yourself he should start out with half days." He opened the refrigerator and reached for the tub of soft margarine. "You can get out a bit and Mom can be here when Ethan gets home. She'll fix dinners and spruce up the house."

I surveyed the kitchen, registering the clutter that had already gathered since my group had cleaned. I stood, walked over to the counter near the stove, and picked up the cookbook that lay open to the page for banana bread.

It had been sitting there for a week, next to three slowly rotting bananas. Maybe that was why I smelled bananas at the hospital. I thought there must be some profound connection, something more than mere coincidence, but that's as far as I got. I snapped the cookbook shut and set it on a shelf, then lifted the bananas from the basket and headed across the room.

"What are you doing?" Joel asked.

I opened the door to the cabinet under the sink and dropped them into the garbage. "I'm putting them out of their misery."

I straightened and looked at the food crumbs that speckled the counters, at the dozen or so perfect cat paw prints that pranced across our beige, fake-tile linoleum, the newspapers, bills and assorted invitations that offered us the opportunity to sink deeper into credit card debt than we already were, the dirty dishes, and other detritus that covered nearly every flat space of our kitchen. I had been so busy ferrying Ethan back and forth to the hospital and so focused on him that I hadn't even thought about the house.

"They want to see Ethan and they want to help as much as they can," Joel said, reaching for a table knife from the drawer. "My parents know we're under a lot of stress and they'll try to make things easier for us." He cut the toast in two.

"Right," I said. I had put up with their annual invasions and his mother's strong opinions through the years, but now he was pushing it. I had the horrible feeling they would stay for months.

Joel vigorously buttered his toast, spattering more crumbs over the counter. "Maybe we can even go out to a movie while they look after Ethan."

"Uh-huh."

"Come on, Delainie. Give them a chance."

"You'll have to pick them up at the airport. I can't do it."

"No problem."

He sounded excited and I wondered why the danger of marrying an only son hadn't occurred to me fifteen years ago. All that parental energy focused on one egg in one basket. I stopped. Oh my God. Maybe, someday, Ethan's wife would have that same thought, but then I would be thrilled and grateful, simply for my son to grow up, for him to *have* a wife and children.

Joel poured himself a glass of juice. "It's too bad, though, that you and Ethan can't go with me to the airport. They're really looking forward to seeing you."

"Uh-huh."

He gave a little grunt, slapped his toast onto a paper napkin, grabbed the glass of juice and strode out, the newspaper clutched under his arm.

I surveyed the kitchen.

Ethan had another appointment at the hospital tomorrow, and if past history was any indication we would spend most of the day waiting. When would I have time to clean this place up? I couldn't allow my friends to do it, and I couldn't afford to hire it done. Feeling frustrated and overwhelmed, I walked over and brushed the crumbs onto the floor. There, what a good idea. Just slop everything onto the linoleum and bulldoze it out the back door.

———

"Hello, Delainie."

My mother-in-law's voluminous nylon raincoat swished through the front door, bringing with it the scent of soap and a dripping umbrella.

"Hello, Barbara." I gave her cool cheek a peck.

She was a tall, thick-boned woman with small, sharp eyes and gray hair parted down the middle so that it gripped her head like a clamshell. She wore a pink flowered cotton blouse and a loose-fitting gray corduroy jumper. She sewed most of her own clothes.

She and Hal were both in their sixties, but several decades older in attitude. Joel was a late arrival.

Hal gave me a bear hug. He was a big man, an inch or so taller than Joel, with a chest like a refrigerator, skinny legs, bushy eyebrows that were darker than his pewter gray hair. I liked him because he was adept at ignoring the elephant in the room.

I was going to be as nice as I could because Joel needed his parents right now and I'd been less than understanding. I had to remind myself these two people produced the man I'd married.

"Where is the little fellow?" Hal asked.

"Ethan," I called.

He came out of his room and walked down the hall toward us. He'd lost a few pounds and looked peaked.

"Well, there he is." Hal said, giving Ethan a hug that nearly enveloped him.

I smiled. "Isn't it nice to see your grandparents?"

"Uh-huh." He turned toward Barbara, "Hi, Grandma."

Barbara reached out her arms and hugged him briefly, as if he might be contagious.

"He looks fine," Hal boomed. "Are you sure he's sick?"

"That's what the doctors say," Joel said.

The skin between Barbara's eyes pinched into a crease. "You can't always trust them, Joel. You got a second opinion, right?"

"Yes, Mother, we did."

Ethan's eyes widened and I knew he felt awkward being discussed.

"I had a friend," Hal began. "A fellow named Smitty. You probably remember him, Joel. Anyhow, he slipped on the ice two winters ago." He looked at Barbara. "Was that two years or three?"

"Three."

"Lord, it don't seem that long."

"It was the winter the truck broke down."

"Was it?" He thought for a moment, then raked his fingers through his hair. "I guess you're right. Anyhow, Smitty broke his leg. So he goes into the hospital to get it set. Next thing he knows they're telling him he's got bone cancer, and they're running all kinds of tests on him and saying he's going to need chemotherapy and radiation and who knows what all. So he goes home, thinking he's gonna die in a few months and they just aren't telling him. Then, a couple days later, the hospital calls and it turns out there wasn't nothing wrong except his leg was broke. They probably figured they could make some extra money on him with all those x-rays and tests."

"I know just what you mean," I said, shifting my gaze toward Joel.

"We'll be careful," he said.

Barbara turned toward me. "Well, now." Her distant expression told me she was wondering for the umpteenth time how her son could have chosen someone so...so unsubstantial?

I gestured toward the kitchen. "Would you like some coffee, Barbara? I'll make a fresh pot. I would have done that earlier, but we just got home. I suppose Joel told you Ethan had a doctor's appointment, so we couldn't go to the airport to pick you up. It wasn't that we didn't want to be there. We couldn't."

"Yes, he did mention that."

"I'll get the luggage," Hal said.

When they returned with the bulging suitcases, Hal jiggled the front door handle. "You oughta replace this thing, son. It's loose and tarnished."

"It's supposed to be tarnished," Joel said. "It's an antique."

"Well, I could replace it for you. Wouldn't cost much."

As I walked into the kitchen, I heard Joel say, "Hey, Dad, I want you to look at this back porch. It's a nice big one for this style of house, but some damn fool painted it years ago and now it's peeling. What do you think I should use on it?"

"First, it needs to be sanded down to bare wood."

Their voices faded. Joel had promised he would keep his energetic father busy and out of my path. The last time Hal visited, he became so bored he alphabetized my soup cans. Chicken Noodle, Cream of Mushroom, French Onion and a five-year-old can of Consommé. I know he meant well, but it drove me crazy maneuvering around him — and then crazier after he left.

I felt some obligation to keep up the organization, so I dutifully alphabetized for the next two months. Then a bottle of homemade root beer that a friend gave Joel blew up in the cabinet, shooting caramel-colored sugar water all over the inside of it. While cleaning up the mess, I was so annoyed that I tossed the cans back in any order they landed, half of them missing their root-beer soaked labels.

Now that his parents were here again, I told Joel under no circumstances did I want his father touching my soup cans.

Joel looked puzzled. "Your soup cans?"

I sighed. "Oh, never mind."

Ethan had followed Joel and Hal out to the back porch. Barbara trailed me into the kitchen, and I motioned her toward the small wooden table. "Make yourself at home."

I was opening the package of coffee when she whooped, "Oh, good Lord in Heaven! What is that?"

I dropped the bag, spraying a fine brown dust across the counter that I'd spent an hour cleaning the night before. I ran over to her.

She was staring at the chair seat, her eyes rapidly blinking. "It's something dead."

What looked to be a black shriveled cat, its emaciated legs splayed outward, stretched from one side of the seat to the other. Its mouth gaped, as if it had been tortured.

Barbara clamped her hand to her chest. "Oh, my heart! It's skipping beats."

I picked up the creature by one stiff paw and held it out for her to see. "It's not real, Barbara. It's just a coat hanger."

It was bent into the appropriate shape of a cat, padded with rags, bound with masking tape and spray-painted black.

"Wh-where did it ca-come from?" Her words tripped across one long, shallow breath.

I looked over my shoulder. "Ethan!"

He stood in the doorway, his skin more gray than yellow, his eyes as round as buttons. "I didn't mean to."

I shook the creature so that flecks of black paint fluttered to the linoleum, which I'd also cleaned the night before. "This wasn't funny."

Tears rolled down Ethan's cheeks. "I thought you'd sit there, not Grandma."

Joel and Hal hovered behind him. The smell of coffee perfumed the air.

"What is that thing?" Hal asked.

"It's not real," I said. "It's something Ethan made. Here, Barbara, you can sit down now."

Joel jabbed his finger in the direction of the hall. "Go to your room, young man."

"I didn't know Grandma would sit on it."

Hal hummed under his breath, as if he'd shifted his thoughts to other things.

Barbara wrinkled her forehead. "That's an awful thing to do to anybody. I don't know if my heart will ever calm down."

She was flushed and trembling, her hand clutching a wad of fabric from her jumper. I had a difficult time feeling sympathetic. It seemed to me she was overreacting. Ethan stood frozen, the tears still rolling.

"That's totally unacceptable, Ethan," Joel repeated. "Go to your room."

Ethan looked at me as if to say, "But tell them, it's just a game we play." Then, he turned and shuffled down the hall, his heels treading on the hems of his baggy cargo pants.

Barbara's lips pruned up. "What kind of child would do something like that?"

"Our child," Joel said.

I don't think I had ever loved him more.

———

Shortly after we bought our house, we had turned the main floor parlor into a bedroom. It had my grandparents' brass bed that I had managed to snatch from my parents before they had the chance to sell it.

Usually, Joel and I slept in that double bed, which required a closeness some couples loved. Upstairs, we had a spare room mostly stuffed with antiques. I stood in the doorway watching Joel pump air into a blow-up bed. I bit back complaints. His parents could be sleeping in a hotel room. We shouldn't be relegated to the blow-up on the floor. But it wouldn't help to accuse Joel. He was caught in the middle.

That evening, as I crawled into bed, I bumped my hip against his. "I'm sorry things didn't start out well."

He rested his head on his clasped hands and stared up at the ceiling. Moonlight spilled through the window, illuminating his face. "I don't like scolding Ethan, especially now, but he has to be more careful about scaring people. My mother has a heart problem. Who knows what might have happened?"

"He feels awful about it."

"I know he does. I told him we want him to keep right on making his creatures, but he needs to be respectful of his grandparents."

I rubbed my hand across his bare chest, tangling my fingers in tendrils of hair. "I'll be glad when we're back in our own beds."

"Yeah, me too."

I wound my legs around him and shifted my weight on top of him, pressing my hips against his and nuzzling the hollow below his breastbone. I laid a line of kisses along his arm, tasting the salt on his warm skin.

"Come on, Delainie, you know we can't do that." He turned on his side so that I tumbled gently off of him.

I blinked. "Why not?"

"For God's sakes, they're in the room right below us."

"We'll be quiet. They won't hear."

"This blow-up bed squeaks like an old sow."

"Well, that's a lovely comparison." I flopped back to my side of the bed with a little snap of my hips. I flipped over and burrowed my face into the pillow, saying in a muffled voice, "I thought you would want it too."

"What?"

"Oh, nothing." I rose up on my elbows and looked over at him. "How long are they going to stay?"

He murmured something.

"How long?"

"I said I don't know."

"Well, two weeks, a month?"

He didn't answer.

"My God, it can't be any longer than that."

"Quiet down, will you?"

"I am not going without sex for a month." My voice rose. "And if you can do without it that long, I would like to know why."

"Shut the fuck up, Delainie!"

"So that's how it is. You don't mind if your parents hear you swearing at me, but God forbid they should hear you screwing me."

He abruptly sat up and got out of bed. "I'm going outside to have a cigarette."

"Does your mother know you smoke? What do you suppose she would think about her son having a dirty habit like that?"

What was wrong with me? I was losing it. I was digging the hole deeper.

He strode to the armoire, yanked open the door, and grabbed his robe. The wire hanger banged back and forth, smacking the inside of the wardrobe.

"And what about Ethan?" I hated every word coming from my mouth, but I couldn't seem to stop. "If he sees you smoking, what kind of lesson is that for him? Especially if you get cancer."

But Joel was already out the bedroom door.

I grabbed the pillow and squeezed it tight. A whole month. We used to rush home from our jobs and skid into bed. Now that part of our lives was changing too.

Chapter 15

E than was feeling well enough to return to school for half days. He was apprehensive about the math he'd missed, but we told him not to worry. There would be plenty of time to catch up once he was well. We should have crossed our fingers when we said things like that.

Joel went off to work, telling his parents he couldn't shirk the demands of a startup company. His father said he understood, but Barbara sighed noisily.

I discovered Hal had a unique way of tuning out the conflict. Wearing a tool belt that encircled his hips like a cowboy holster, he set about stripping and sanding the back porch, raising a dust storm that found its way through vents and cracks into our home. While he was working, Hal was the happiest man I'd ever seen, shrilly whistling tunes from "Showboat," "Paint Your Wagon," and "Oklahoma!"

He didn't even seem to mind when Barbara clucked at him for tracking in dirt.

She fussed around with a T-shirt rag and a bottle of lemon polish, restoring the furniture to a bright shine every day. If they'd heard my argument with Joel the night before, they didn't show it.

I had a medical appointment that morning, beginning the lengthy procedure of donating part of my liver to Ethan. The clinic visit took longer than I'd expected. I provided a sample of every bodily fluid I possessed, measurements of my heart and lung functions, and visual scans of all my organs.

By the time I left, it was after one o'clock. I walked out into the gray, misty afternoon, feeling buoyant and relieved. The clinic would have the results in a few days, and then I could move to the next stage, passing the new tests like a skilled student. I was confident of the outcome. I had given Ethan life before and I would give him life again.

From the car, I called Barbara on my phone to let her know I was on my way.

She answered immediately.

"Well," she said, as if I had caught her in mid-conversation. "It's a good thing you told the school we could pick up Ethan."

I went cold. "What's wrong?"

"Nothing really. I think they were making a bigger fuss than they needed to—"

"What happened, Barbara?"

"Well, he seems all right to me."

I had to bite my tongue to keep from yelling at her. "Is his nose bleeding?"

"No."

"Is he at home with you now?"

"He's in the bedroom resting."

Someone said something in the background, but I couldn't make out the words.

"No, Hal." Barbara's voice drifted as she turned away from the phone. "She doesn't need to know that."

"I'll be there in five minutes." I would have to speed.

"Oh, there's no reason to rush home now."

"Five minutes." I switched off my phone with a poke and tossed it onto the passenger seat.

I wove the car through traffic and turned onto Queen Anne Avenue. What could I have been thinking, allowing my in-laws to look after Ethan? They didn't seem to realize how ill he was, and I wasn't sure Barbara even had a mother's normal instincts. Joel must have been born so put-together and self-sufficient that he raised himself.

I found her in the kitchen, digging petrified food out of the crevices of my stove with a wooden toothpick. Ammonia and oven cleaner permeated the room. With the exhaust fan running, she didn't hear me enter.

I set my purse on the counter with a thud, and Barbara leaped half a foot in the air.

"Oh, goodness, you startled me."

I swept past her and hurried down the hall to Ethan's room. The door was open, and I could see him on the bed, lying on his back, breathing easily, peacefully, his arms flung over his head in what I called his Jesus Christ sleeping position.

I sagged against the doorjamb, a little prayer slipping unbidden into my thoughts. I would give up everything if he could live. I wouldn't care anymore about Pairpoint lamps or a shop to put them in. I would devote myself to my family. I would become the most religious person on earth, if only....

I leaned over and lightly kissed his forehead, feeling his cool flesh on my lips. He seemed to breathe normally.

I returned to the kitchen. "What exactly happened?"

"Well..." Barbara carefully peeled off her rubber gloves, flipped them yellow side out, and laid them with maddening slowness on the rim of the sink. "It was nothing more than a stitch in his side. The school nurse was all worried but it stopped the minute I got there. Kids get those all the time, but I suppose she's too young to know that. He's fine now. You really didn't have to rush home."

"A stitch in his side?"

"Well, you know, the kind you get from running too fast."

"Did the nurse say she'd taken his temperature?"

She dabbed at a spot on the stovetop with the dishrag. "Not that I recall." She looked up. "Do you have an old toothbrush?"

"A toothbrush?" I was trying to think what that had to do with Ethan.

"For cleaning the cracks." She gave me a look that said anybody with any sense should know that. "What do you use?"

"I don't use anything," I snapped. "I wait for the crud to build up. Then I scrape it off and serve it over our salads for dinner. It has a nice little crunch to it."

Her eyes blinked rapidly several times.

I leaned back against the counter.

"Barbara, what you call a stitch in his side is probably a

cramp. That's a symptom of Ethan's illness, and the school nurse should be concerned. He could be bleeding internally. He seems to be comfortable now so we'll see how he is when he wakes up."

I started to say more, but my anxiety had left me so parched that the words stuck to the roof of my mouth. I opened the refrigerator to get a can of soda. On the shelves, each item — the carton of milk, the ketchup bottle, the tub of margarine, the Tupperware container with last night's leftovers — rested on white paper towels, neatly folded to catch any drips. I gazed at it for a few moments, then closed the door without removing anything.

Barbara didn't seem to notice.

"Well," she sniffed, "if you treat him like a sick child, he's going to act like one. That's something a mother learns with experience."

I turned around to face her. "He *is* sick. This is not some kid faking illness to get out of school. He is deathly sick and his symptoms will get worse as time goes along. I don't see why you can't understand that. Don't you have a heart, for God's sake?"

She went rigid, her mouth closed tight as a fist. Then, I realized she was looking at something over my shoulder. I turned toward the doorway, where Ethan stood, his irises so dilated his eyes had no color other than black. He stared at me accusingly.

I couldn't talk. I couldn't breathe.

He turned and ran down the hallway.

Too late, I whispered, "No, Ethan, I didn't mean it."

Barbara's eyes blinked rapidly. "I have a heart. Of course, I do. That's a terrible thing to say to your husband's mother."

I gritted my teeth. "If you did have a heart, you would realize what has happened."

"The doctor says mine beats too fast and I should take it easy."

I left her standing there, stuck on that point, and rushed after Ethan. As I passed the dining room, I caught a glimpse of

Hal on the back porch, his hammer poised over a board he was replacing.

The back door was open and I had the feeling he knew I was there, but he didn't look up. A shrill whistle pierced the air as he hit a high note in "Oklahoma," which is where he probably wanted to be right then. Wood dust danced over his head in a beam of sunlight.

I heard the bathroom door slam and the lock click.

When I reached the door, I rested my head against it. "Hey, Superman."

He didn't answer.

"Oh, Lord of the Rings, speak to me."

Nothing.

"Ethan, sweetheart, I swear I didn't mean it."

"You lied to me," came his muffled voice.

"No, I didn't. I just wanted your grandmother to understand your illness is serious, that you're not pretending."

"You promised if I worked at it I'd get better. Now you're saying even if I do that, it's not going to make any difference. I'll still get worse."

I pressed my ear against the door. "No, that's not what I meant."

How could I explain I was worried he'd give up if he thought he was going to die?

The cat soft-stepped down the hall and rubbed against my ankle, his innards reverberating like a car engine. "Oscar is out here. He wants to see you."

"That's not true. He doesn't care about me any more than you do." His voice was clearer. He sounded closer.

"Oh my God, Ethan, how can you say that? I love you more than anything else in the world."

I backed against the opposite wall and slid to the floor, skimming the wall like a flattened ribbon.

"What was that noise?" he asked. "Where are you?"

"I'm sitting down." My legs jutted across the width of the hall, the tips of my shoes nudging the baseboard.

"Why are you doing that?"

"I seem to have problems staying on my feet these days."

The lock clicked and he cautiously opened the door. He looked down at me, his chin trembling, his cheeks glazed with tears. "You shouldn't have said that stuff to Grandma."

"You're right." I swallowed the rock in my throat. "I was very, very wrong, but I promise to do better."

My commitment to improving my mother-in-law relationship had lasted exactly three days.

"I bet you hurt her feelings too."

"I'll apologize. Honest I will."

He slid down beside me, his bare heels squeaking on the hardwood floor that Barbara had shined to a high gloss, and curled against me. "I'm sorry you fell, Mommy."

He hadn't called me Mommy in two or three years. Usually, it was Mom in a tone that said: You're ridiculous and embarrassing, but I'm still willing to acknowledge we're related. I took him in my arms. He felt as warm as if he'd been a stuffed teddy bear left out in the sun.

I rocked him the way I used to when he was a little guy, and we sat there together, his face pressed against my chest, swaying to a wordless lullaby.

―――――――

"I can't believe you told my mother she has no heart," Joel said coldly. "What is wrong with you, Delainie?"

"I apologized to her twice. I really am sorry about saying that, and I'll apologize again if you want me too." I did feel genuine remorse.

We were sitting on wicker chairs on our newly renovated porch, staring up at the few stars the clouds hadn't blotted out, breathing the pungent odor of the linseed oil Hal had used on the wood along with the clean, earthy fragrances of the cedars and firs that dotted our backyard. He had done a terrific job. The porch was brighter and cleaner than it was when we bought the place, but unfortunately it now looked too new and modern to go with the house. I missed its rustic shabbiness.

Joel ran his hand along the railing, testing the smoothness of the wood, I suppose. "You can't just take back what you said with a quick apology,"

It was too dark to see his face. "Well, what should I do?"

"You need to think before you speak. You have a habit of saying whatever pops into your head," he said. " You did that before Ethan was born when you told my mother to butt out of our marriage, that three was more than a crowd, it was a fucking conflagration."

"I said that? I meant congregation."

"It was Christmas and you'd had a lot to drink."

"Not enough. Your mother had made some crack in front of your entire extended family."

"What crack?"

"Oh, I don't know," I said, my good intentions for improving relations barely a memory. "One of the usual ones that contained her thinly veiled, eternally hopeful agenda of breaking us up. Never mind that we'd been married four years and I was one month pregnant at the time."

"She didn't know you were pregnant. Hell, you didn't even know you were pregnant or you wouldn't have been drinking. And she wasn't trying to split us up. She had certain expectations."

"And I didn't meet them." I rose from the porch chair. "I don't know what to do, Joel. I don't know what to say or do that will make anything better."

I turned, intending to walk back into the house, but Hal had moved the newly painted wooden planter from one side of the porch to the other and I smacked right into it, scraping my shin. I yelped and grabbed my leg. "I want my porch the way it was. I want the peeling paint and the moss and the mildew back on it." I jabbed my finger at the darkness. "And I want you to move that planter in a spot over there."

He didn't answer.

"I also want you and me and Ethan back the way we were too."

He looked up at me. "So do I, but it's not going to happen."

"Well, can't you at least pretend it will?"

"No."

The rawness of his voice drained me of anger. I folded myself onto the chair and, curled like a leaf, I slipped dejectedly into thought. He was right. Our lives would never be normal again. In the material Taylor had given us, I read about the aftermath of a liver transplant.

They would have the tests for my liver back in just a few days. His body wouldn't reject the soft, pinkish-brown lump of new life that I would give him.

Once he got well, I would work two hours everyday with him on math. I would teach him calculus if I could figure out what that was. I looked it up in the dictionary. It said calculus was a "branch of mathematics that deals with the finding and properties of derivatives and integrals of functions, by methods originally based on the summation of infinitesimal differences."

What the hell did that mean?

Ethan would need scholarships to go to college. He was a smart child, of course, but I wasn't sure if they gave money to special effects artists.

I shifted my thoughts to my marriage. Joel was sitting on the porch chair, massaging his temples. We seemed to be chipping away at our relationship, knocking off several fragments at a time and grinding them into the ground. By the end of all this, we could be looking at a handful of sand.

I broke the night quiet. "We never used to fight like this, not even when you decided to go back to school and we lived in that dingy studio apartment with the creaky pipes and the lukewarm water and the people who banged on the ceiling whenever we made love."

Joel nodded. "We couldn't get angry at each other because the room wasn't big enough for it. That was the best apartment we ever had."

"We had no money."

"We didn't need any." He stretched out his legs and clasped his hands behind his head. I knew that pose. He was loosening up, letting the cool stillness slip into him. The night air did that for him the way it did for me.

I propped my ankle on my knee and massaged my throbbing shinbone. "That apartment was so drafty and damp I snif-fled all the time and had to wear fifteen layers of clothing."

"You were the one who insisted on renting it because it had hardwood floors and leaded glass windows."

"Those are hard to find."

He smiled. "I thought you looked spiffy in that gargantuan gray wool sweater and those bright pink mittens that matched your nose."

"Spiffy? What kind of spinster-aunt word is that?"

He didn't answer, but I heard a low laugh.

I gave a martyred sigh. "I knit that sweater for you, but you wouldn't wear it."

"I wasn't cold."

As the clouds parted, I gazed up at the moon, a thin circle of rice paper rising between the evergreens. "That apartment had a terrific roof, though."Where else in town could you get such a good view of the Fourth of July fireworks, drink cheap wine, smoke a little grass and make love at the same time?"

"In the rain."

"It wasn't rain. It was a heavy mist. At least when it rained you couldn't smell the garbage in the alley."

"Sometimes I think I liked that apartment better than this house." He sounded wistful.

I knew why he liked living there. Everything was ahead of us then, and there was a certain excitement to that, being young and wild and intoxicated with each other. We had prob-lems but nothing we couldn't manage. We weren't responsible for anyone but the two of us, and we were easy.

The moon moved hypnotically through the trees, glazing our newly refinished porch with a pale light. It was already the middle of May, and the night air was mild. I looked across our yard at the inviting pond-shaped patch of grass and at the trees with sturdy trunks.

I reached my hand across the space that separated our chairs and took Joel's hand, weaving my fingers between his.

I tugged on him. "Let's go."

"Where?"

"To that bed of grass over there."

"What for? It rained last night and —" He stopped, and I knew he was tripping over my thoughts. "Oh no, Delainie." He pulled his hand away.

"I could get a blanket."

"No."

"There was a time when you would have."

"But that was before."

Shrubs that looked like stooped old women in a church pew edged our yard, and I was counting on them to shelter us from the neighbors. "No one will see. Your parents' window is on the other side."

"My parents have nothing to do with it."

I should have given up then, but I wanted so much to make it the way it used to be, to reassure myself that when Ethan's illness was over we would still be us? I surveyed the rest of our property and the alley, my gaze landing on the place where he parked the Buick. I stood and yanked on his hand. "Come with me."

Moonlight caught the glint of suspicion in his eye. "Where?"

"Trust me."

It was a code phrase we'd used jokingly in our younger days.

He hesitated but I pulled him from the chair and we crossed the spongy grass.

When he realized where we were headed, he stopped. "The shed?" he said in an oh-no tone.

"Well, look at that. What a snug little place," I said.

I opened the door. Dust motes danced in a streak of moonlight, spiders with bodies the size of bats stitched tapestries, and I heard what I would have sworn was the scurrying of tiny feet. The place smelled like an old shed that had sat out in the rain for fifty years — which it was.

"Delainie," he said sharply.

"Well, okay." I closed the door.

I turned toward the Buick. "It has a big back seat."

"Jesus, Delainie, we're not kids anymore."

"Well, let's try to be. Do you have the car keys?"

He shook his head.

I smiled. "I'll go get them."

"Shit," he said and pulled the keys from his pocket.

I grabbed them, opened the car door and glided onto the back seat. "Hey, it's nice in here."

He held back for several moments. Finally, he slid in next to me.

I tried to tease him into passion, to touch him where I knew he liked to be touched.

He performed without desire while I listened to the rhythmic slosh of gasoline in the Buick's cavernous tank and felt my own hollowness inside.

Afterward, Joel climbed back into his pants, buckled his belt in a gesture of efficient finality and went back into the house. I sat in the car and cried for both of us.

Chapter 16

"It's a party my friend Jaya and her husband host every Memorial Day," I told Barbara. "Rob is an attorney at Boeing, so some of the people there will be friends Joel used to work with."

"Well, of course you should go," Barbara said. "Hal and I can stay with Ethan."

We were cordial again. She was pressing my only tablecloth, the blue one she had given me for my birthday, on a rickety ironing board that she'd found holding up cobwebs in a corner of the basement.

"Ethan seems to be stable now," I told Barbara, "and if you need us we'll be only ten minutes away."

"Oh, heavens, he'll be fine."

"We'd really appreciate this," I said, although I was scared as hell. "We'd never feel comfortable leaving him with a sitter."

"He's an easy child. He practically takes care of himself. Joel was like that too." The board jiggled as she bore down on the iron, little puffs of steam rising from the fabric. "You really should get a new ironing board."

"Hmm." As a matter of principle, I didn't believe in ironing cloth. It was simply one more method of subjugating women. I have distinct memories of my mother bent over that steaming hot triangle of metal, her hands marked with red welts from accidental burns, her face shiny with perspiration. Shortly after marrying, I decided that if a blouse or a shirt couldn't be fluffed free of wrinkles in the dryer, it shouldn't be manufactured and it certainly shouldn't be purchased.

"It will do you and Joel good to get out and have some fun,"

Barbara said, without breaking rhythm with the iron. "I'm sure it's been a while."

I thought of our laborious efforts the night before and heard the car's slowly creaking springs in my mind. She was right. It had been a long while.

———

"What do you mean you don't want to go?" I said.

"Keep your voice down."

We were standing upstairs in our little office. I could hear Barbara clanking pans in the kitchen and Hal fixing whatever was left in the house to work on. Fortunately, he would never run out of projects.

I strode across the wood floor, my steps landing a little harder than usual. "I'm tired of keeping quiet. This is my house and I don't care who hears me. Why won't you go to the party?"

Joel walked to the door and shut it. "I'm not in the mood."

I wanted to say, "Seems to me you're not in the mood for much of anything," but I held back.

He turned sharply and walked to the desk. Although he'd taken a nap after he came home from work, his face looked tight.

I dropped onto an overstuffed chair. "I know you're worried, but we'll be just a few miles away."

He rubbed his forehead.

I sighed. "We have gone to Jaya and Rob's house every Memorial Day for the last ten years. It will be fun to see every-one."

He sat down and hunched his big shoulders over the computer keyboard. "It's not ever going to be the same. Can't you understand that?"

"Of course, it won't be, but that doesn't mean we can't enjoy ourselves a little bit."

He didn't answer.

"Joel, talk to me."

He gave me an impassive look. "Go by yourself. You don't need me."

"How can you say that? Of course I need you." My voice dropped to a whisper. "We're a couple. Couples do things together."

"You're getting overwrought."

"Overwrought?" I bit off the word. "Is that all you can do these days? Find fault with me?"

He shifted his gaze, fixing it on some indeterminate spot a few feet over my shoulder, while I stared at him, wondering if this was how it would be until Ethan was well again.

"Joel, sweetheart, I need this right now. I think we both desperately need it."

A flash of pain crossed his face. Then it became expressionless again. "All right, Delainie, if that's what you want."

"It starts a little later this year," I said. "It's at five o'clock."

I walked out of the room, stood at the top of the stairs and drew in a deep breath. Why on earth would he think I didn't need him?

———

Joel drove along Lake Washington Boulevard. If the day had been clear, we would have had a sweeping view of the mountains, but rain landed on the windshield in noisy plops. Lead-gray clouds darkened the sky. I didn't mind. It was usually like this on Memorial Day.

Joel fiddled with the heater and air conditioner switches to clear the condensation off the glass. He seemed on automatic pilot, his thoughts elsewhere. I was back thinking of Ethan. He had looked so good today. I couldn't see any jaundice in his skin at all, and he was up and around, fashioning a severed arm out of a cardboard tube, papier-mâché, and a gallon of fresh, fake blood.

The medicine was working better than we'd expected. Maybe, he could just keep taking it for the rest of his life. When I told Dr. Baxter we were thrilled with Ethan's improvement, he warned me that it was only a stopgap measure. All right, I thought, but miracles do happen.

118

I didn't want to be the Pollyanna my in-laws were and, above all, I didn't want to second-guess the gods, but if Ethan were suddenly healthy again, I would fall on the ground in gratitude. I wouldn't complain about all the anxiety we'd already suffered. I wouldn't curse the doctors or anyone else for mucking things up. I would have Ethan back, liver and all, and that was all that mattered.

Joel turned off Lake Washington Boulevard and eased the car down the Sterns' long, winding, tree-flanked drive. Halfway down the hill, we came upon a line of cars that rimmed the right shoulder of the road. Because of the narrow drive, parking would be more limited the farther we went. Joel edged into a spot behind a gray Land Cruiser, set the emergency brake, and switched off the key. "I don't want to stay long. We'll make an appearance and leave."

I grabbed the umbrella and opened the car door. "Let's see how it goes. It's been a long time since we've gone to a party."

At the end of the steep road, the windows of the Stern's home glowed through the evergreens.

Two of Jaya and Rob's dogs came lumbering up the hill. One was a cross between a malamute and a German shepherd, while the other had no discernible parentage. You had to like dogs if you visited Rob and Jaya. Having five of them, they probably owned about three more than the law allowed, and all of them were big, a reflection of their owners' over-sized hearts. Unlike most people I knew who shut their animals away during a party, they allowed theirs to run free, begging food from guests, and drooling on their shoes. They had a love-me, love-my-pets policy.

The two dogs moved toward us at crotch level. Their fur smelled a bit rank.

"Sit, Jack," Joel ordered, and both flattened their sizable rumps on the wet blacktop, grinned at us, and swept their generous tails from side to side.

"Good boys — or girls," I crooned.

Rob named all his dogs, male or female, with the same name, on the theory that he could say "Stay, Jack" or "Heel,

Jack" and they would all snap into position. What they did when he told them to heel, I don't know. Two human feet weren't enough to go around. We moved along, my two-inch heels clip clopping on the steep road. Joel, who had more traction, walked a few steps ahead of me.

I surveyed the line of cars at the edge of the road. "Must be quite a party this year. There are more cars than usual."

"Rob invited the new people from our company," Joel said over his shoulder.

I stopped for a moment. "Well, that will be interesting."

When I had called ahead to ask Jaya if she needed any help, she hadn't mentioned the employees from Joel and Jin's new company.

A retriever-collie mix lay splayed on a burlap bed under the overhang at the front door. He had serious hip problems, so when he tried to rise, I pointed my finger at him. "Down, Jack."

He sank like a sack of cement. I turned to Joel with a grin. "You know it really is handy to have the same name for them. If we have any more children, we should call them all Ethan."

He looked at me as if I had uttered some unaccountably sick remark.

"I didn't meant to suggest he might be replaceable or even duplicable in any way," I said.

"Delainie, you need to think before you say things." He turned and resumed his stride.
Where was the man I had married, the one with the great sense of humor, strength, and devotion to Ethan and me? Of course, Ethan's illness had devastated him, but we should have glommed onto each other.

We should have been kind and supportive. I'll admit I was cranky now too, but we didn't usually bicker so much. We didn't have the distance, the chasm between us.

———————

Moss-dappled, brown cedar shake siding cloaked Jaya and Rob's rambling home in cushioned silence and a lush cedar smell. With its low, sloped roof, multi-paneled windows, and dark niches, it was the sort of place Edgar Allen Poe might have lived in.

When I mentioned that once to Jaya, she said she'd heard someone pacing the halls at night, muttering to himself in a deep, singsong voice.

"Quoth the raven nevermore," I intoned.

Although the property measured almost an acre, the house itself was modest. Jaya had probably inherited enough money to buy and furnish twenty waterfront homes, but they lived within reason, spending much of it on educational charities and orphanages in India. Whenever I was around them, I felt as if I hadn't done enough for the world.

From the front porch, I could see people milling around inside. There was a red-haired young woman standing near the living room window, a champagne flute in her hand. She wore silver, lamé jumpsuit and a shiny black painter's hat, the sort of outfit you might see on "Star Trek." She was holding a cigarette between her fingers and talking to Jin. I didn't know there were still people who smoked in other people's homes.

I paused on the front step. "Who's that?"

"Where?"

How could he have missed her? She looked like a space alien in a crowd of earthlings.

"The woman in silver."

"Oh, that's Milena." He didn't even glance her way.

"Milena, the computer whiz? Where's her pocket protector?"

Without answering, he opened the front door and waved me through it. I folded the umbrella, shook the rain off it, and left it outside.

Joel found Rob on the deck with four other electrical engineer types, all staring at the clay-colored lake swathed in woolly clouds and complaining about Boeing's current management. I poured myself a glass of wine and walked across the living room, stopping to talk with Susan Donner, a friend I hadn't seen in months. She'd sent me a card expressing her concern about Ethan.

She put her hand on my arm. "I didn't want to bother you with phone calls so I've been getting reports from Jaya. She said you planned to give Ethan part of your liver."

I took a sip of wine. "I've gone through all the tests and I'm just waiting for the results. I should know within a few days."

"Let me know if there's anything I can do."

"Thank you, Susan." I looked around the living room. "Where is Jaya?"

She gestured toward the kitchen. "She hasn't come out of there yet. You know Jaya—always worried about the food."

I found her hovering over a platter of salmon-topped bread triangles, removing the plastic wrap and sniffing at them like a rabbit.

I slid my arm across her back. "Hi, sweetie, lovely party. It's great to see everyone."

A line creased the space between her eyes. "Sniff this, will you? I think the salmon smells off."

I leaned over the platter and inhaled deeply. "It smells wonderful. You ordered it from Chez Provence, didn't you?"

She nodded, her black hair flashing under the can lights that studded her kitchen ceiling. "But if it poisons people, I'll be the one responsible."

I sipped my wine. "No, you won't. Tell anyone who survives to sue Chez Provence. Rob's a lawyer. He can represent you."

She squinted at them doubtfully and I knew she didn't get my joke.

"My grandmother was regarded as one of Delhi's best cooks," she said. "She made chapatis and curries and mattar paneer to die for, and she whisked them out of the kitchen like she was buttering toast." She sighed at length. "I can't cook like that. I blame my mother. She served us white bread and canned fruit cocktail to Americanize us."

Jaya could easily have hired a staff to cook and serve the food on the spot, but she once told me she thought that was ostentatious. In truth, I think she wanted her guests to believe she'd prepared it herself.

She moved down the counter to another tray of carrots, green beans, yellow tomatoes, and radishes sculpted to resemble a bouquet of flowers with green onion stems.

"Have you met the new woman from Joel and Jin's office?" I asked.

"The receptionist?"

She was dodging the question.

"No, Milena Soracco, the computer person." I glanced toward the door to make sure we were alone. "She certainly is striking, isn't she?"

"Oh, I don't know," Jaya said. "She looks like an over-dressed auto mechanic."

"I can't believe she's rude enough to smoke in your house."

"I don't mind. It covers the smell of the dogs."

"You're too generous, Jaya. I'm tempted to grab that cigarette right out of her hand and drown it in her champagne."

She looked at me with mild surprise in her bright, dark eyes. "You're under a lot of stress."

"Right." I wondered how long I could use that excuse. I finished the wine.

For God's sake, I didn't even know the woman, but it bothered me that Joel hadn't mentioned her. In fact, he didn't talk about his work the way he used to. When he and Jin started their business, he came home each evening spilling over with enthusiasm, eager to tell me about the progress they'd made that day.

They interviewed new employees by the dozens, believing their superior staff would be their best sales tool. When he couldn't decide which person to hire, he ran through the pros and cons with me. Although I rarely did more than listen, he invariably made up his mind by the end of our conversation. Of course, that was before Ethan's illness.

I held up my wineglass and said to Jaya, "Guess I'll get a refill."

She took the plastic wrap off a platter of fruit. "I'll be out there in a few minutes."

I drifted toward the bar set up in the dining room and

poured myself another glass of wine. I could justify a second dose because it was my favorite, a cabernet I couldn't afford and because it slid down my throat like honey. I felt it warming my insides. At the table lined with food, Jaya's guests gobbled down the fishy triangles at a frightening rate. Several people hovered around the over-sized rock fireplace with its blazing wood.

The room was so noisy I didn't hear Jin until he was standing at my elbow. The most eligible bachelor in the room, if not the city, he was the best-looking man I knew and, although he wasn't much taller than I was, he carried himself with a bearing most men could only hope to emulate.

The sleeve of his sweater, which I didn't have to touch to know was cashmere, rode up his wrist just enough to reveal a titanium watch that looked consequential enough to be linked to a station on Mars.

He gave me a one-armed hug and a buss on the cheek. "How's Ethan?"

"He looked really good today, but the doctor is still saying he'll need a transplant within the year." I shrugged, gulping the wine. "Oh, I don't know, Jin. I don't seem to know anything anymore."

He squeezed my shoulders sympathetically. "The doctors at Children's Memorial are the best. They'll find him a new liver."

I looked at him in surprise. "Didn't Joel tell you? I'm going to give him part of mine."

He lifted his eyebrows in surprise. "No, I didn't know. That's good news."

Strange that Joel hadn't mentioned our one great hope for Ethan. Jin was his best friend, someone he'd known since elementary school. We moved to a corner of the living room, where our voices wouldn't be over-shouted by the others. Jin set his empty glass on a nearby table.

"How does Joel seem at work these days?" I reached for the bottle of cabernet.

"The company is doing even better than we projected at this point."

"Yes, he told me that. But how is Joel?"

He looked down at his Italian shoes, the kind with those decorative little tassels. "He's having trouble concentrating on work, because of Ethan, of course."

"Yes, but does he seem angry or distant to you? I mean, I realize Ethan's illness has changed things, but I feel...." I tried to come up with the right words. Until then, I hadn't even strung them together in my head. "We've always been so close, but now I feel I can't quite reach him, that each day he takes another step away from me. You've known him for a century. What do you think?"

He shifted uncomfortably. "Well, you can't really know someone else."

I stared at him. "Good Lord, Jin, what kind of platitude is that?"

His eyes wavered and he turned slightly. At first, I thought he was avoiding an answer.

Then I followed his gaze and in the window glass saw the dripping trees outside and the reflected image of a woman in silver breaking away from the group near the fireplace, moving toward us like a splash of glittering water. I slugged my wine.

Quickly forming the third point in our triangle, she leaned toward Jin, resting her hand on his arm. "Awesome party, isn't it?"

"Jaya's a good cook," Jin said, not really looking at her.

Milena had that duality that's found in some women: a face with contours of youthful innocence but shrewd, street-savvy eyes. She couldn't have been more than twenty-five.

Jin turned to me. "Have you met Milena Soracco?"

There are moments when you know the situation is more than it seems. I felt a gust of air, cold and briny, and it wasn't because Edgar Allen Poe had walked through the door.

I shook my head. Milena set down her champagne flute and thrust out her hand, her fingers cool to the touch.

"This is Delainie, Joel's wife," Jin murmured.

She feigned surprise. "Of course! I should have recognized you from the picture on his desk. He's told me a lot about you."

125

I couldn't bring myself to ask how Joel had described me.

Her long twist of hair was an apple red that hadn't come off of any dye chart I'd ever used. It reminded me of the counter-top in our downstairs bathroom. She had green eyes that also had no parallel in nature, an expertly outlined fuchsia pout, and squared-off, pearled white nails that could have lacerated computer keys. She also had a roundness that would later turn to fat, and I felt petty as hell for thinking that.

If she had any interest in me, she didn't show it. Her eyes darted around the room. "Have you seen Joel?"

Jin shook his head.

"I want to talk with him about the platform we're setting up. Well, I'll find him." She flashed me a smile. "Nice meeting you, Delainie."

And she was gone, heading for the deck. If she had left a luminescent   streak the way a meteor does, I wouldn't have been surprised. I felt as if one had hit me.

"She's brilliant," Jin said, as if that explanation served all purposes.

"Is that right? Who hired her?"

"I didn't."

I looked at him in astonishment, then turned to see where Milena had gone. She'd tracked down Joel, and I saw them through the open French doors, standing close and talking. He gave her a smile I hadn't seen in years. The back of her hand brushed his. He didn't move away. They maintained that slight, sensuous connection, and I knew — although I had no tangible evidence — that he was sleeping with her, or at least wanted to.

I closed my eyes and whispered, "Why her?"

The floor tilted and I must have listed, because Jin's hand cupped my elbow. "Let's get you some food to go along with that wine."

"No, I couldn't eat a thing." My eyes flashed back to the deck. "I just remembered there's something I have to tell Joel." Before Jin could reply, I rushed off, drinking my wine along the way.

I had her in my sights as I crossed the room. Joel had his back turned so he didn't see me until I slid in next to him and rested a proprietary hand on his arm. I managed to smile at Milena. She smiled back. It had to be her mind that appealed to him. I could see how a man like Joel would prefer a woman who grasped numbers and exalted concepts. I swigged the rest of my wine.

Dan Adams, a Boeing pilot who stood across from us, said to Milena, "Microsoft, huh? So how did you get along with Bill?"

Joel murmured something about the restroom and took a step back, unsteadying me. He headed toward the hall, leaving me with Milena and the three men who were ogling her. If Joel thought he'd picked a faithful mistress, he was wrong.

I left the circle, sailed toward the wine table and poured myself another glass. I wasn't sure if it was my fourth or fifth. Jin, kind man that he was, was soon hovering at my side.

"Should I tell Joel you want to go home?" His voice was so soft-spoken I had to lean against him to hear it.

"Oh, I don't know. Maybe not." I wanted to cry.

He propped me against the nearby wall. "You wait here."

I swallowed the cabernet. "No, I don't think so," I said, but he was already walking toward the hall.

I shuffled into the kitchen, where I came upon Jaya frantically popping Kalamata olives onto crackers spread with Rondelé cheese, her standard emergency hors d'oeuvre.

"I didn't realize so many people would come," she whispered.

They were clustered all over the room so I had to whisper. "Joel's having an affair."

Her eyes widened like a fawn's. "Don't be silly."

"I'm not silly. I'm s-serious." I might have had more credibility if I hadn't slurred my words.

Her gaze fixed itself on something over my shoulder. "And here's Joel right now."

"Wonderful party, Jaya." His arm slid around my waist, more for support than affection, I thought. "Terrific food. Wish we could stay longer but Ethan's with my parents and, well—we should get home."

"Oh, darn," I said, "just when I was starting to feel better." I gulped the wine.

Joel cleared his throat in embarrassment.

Jaya glanced from me to Joel. "I hope everything's okay."

"I'm sure it is." He rotated me in the direction of the front door, spinning my world.

I looked back over my shoulder at Jaya and mouthed the words, "I'll call you."

Her head bobbed vigorously.

Outside, the rain had stopped, but a mist loomed in the night-blackened evergreens and maples. Strategically placed spotlights illuminated the driveway, which was slick with runoff and fallen leaves.

I lurched to the point where the drive met the narrow, winding road and stared up the steep slope. "I'm not walking up there."

Maybe it was the shadows but his face suddenly seemed darker. "I don't know how else you think you're going to get to the car."

The few times in the past I'd drunk too much, I'd been obnoxiously cheerful but at that moment I felt mean enough to bite. "Drive it down here."

"I am not going to do that. For one thing, there's no place to turn around and, for another, you're perfectly capable of walking up this hill." He tramped ahead a few feet and turned back to look at me. "Come on, Delainie."

I tried to glare at him and might have pulled it off if I hadn't lost control of my eyes. "Where's your sympathy? For that matter, where's your loyalty?"

"What's gotten into you?"

One of the Jacks lumbered alongside me and leaned against my leg until I wasn't sure who was propping up whom. I reached down and rested my hand on his broad back. He was the one with some malamute in him. His coarse, damp, brown-and-black outer coat felt like horsehair over a spongy cushion of down.

Even though he had a rank, wet doggy odor, I had the urge to accompany Jack back to his burlap-and-cedar-chip bed and curl up with him. I certainly had no desire to sleep anywhere near my husband that night.

I did my best to fix my gaze on him. "I can't do this alone, Joel. I cannot climb this hill alone."

"If you hadn't drunk so much, you wouldn't have this problem."

"That's me, silly and irresponsible. Is that what you think?"

"No, of course not, but sometimes...well, never mind."

"Sometimes what?"

"Well, you don't seem like you're all in one piece. One part's here..." His hand punctuated the air in a kind of three-pointed gesture. "Another part's there, and your brain is in some other time zone altogether."

There must be something about adrenaline that counteracts alcohol, because my vision suddenly cleared and I straightened, moving the leg that was supporting Jack. The poor dog stumbled, then regained his footing.

I was shaking but not from the wine. "And when was it you decided I'm the flaky one in this marriage, leaving you to carry most of the burden?"

"I didn't say you weren't carrying your share of the burden. I meant you're a little scattered at times."

"Is that right?" I wanted to say I wasn't so scattered or dense that I didn't notice him and his computer whizette, but I couldn't bring myself to accuse him directly. I don't know if I was holding out hope that I was wrong or if I simply lacked the courage to drop an atomic bomb.

"You've never mentioned this before," I said, "so should I assume it's something new."

He gave a heavy sigh. "Look, I don't want to pick a fight. Things are already bad enough."

"Answer me."

He raised his hands in a gesture of resignation. "You've always been a bit that way. I don't mind — except when it causes problems."

" 'A bit that way' meaning flaky."

"All right, if you want to call it that."

"Give me an example."

"Come on, Delainie."

"Just one." I clenched my jaw. "Any example will do."

"All right. Here's one. How about your gourmet group?"

"What's wrong with it?"

"You've been going to these meetings once a month for what? Twelve years?"

"Fourteen."

"Yeah, well, I like your friends, but look at how much good it's done. Your idea of fixing a fancy dinner is piping twin ribbons of mustard on a foot-long hotdog."

"That's a bad example. You know we don't get together for that reason."

"Then why call it a gourmet group?"

"Because it sounds better than the Let's-Bitch-About-Our-Husbands group."

"Uh-huh, except that Liz and Cappy don't have husbands anymore."

"Yeah, but they have long memories."

He stared at me for several seconds. "If we're going to make this a male-bashing session, let's at least do it in the privacy of our bedroom, instead of under a patch of dripping trees."

"I'm not bashing anyone. I'm making a point."

"Which is?"

"I am fiercely loyal. You won't find a better friend. I'm like Jack here—" I patted the clumped fur on Jaya's dog. "Only better."

"We're not talking about loyalty."

"Oh, yes, we are." Say it, I told myself. Say exactly what you mean. Instead, I executed a verbal right turn. "And you know what else? I'm a terrific mother and a good wife, and if that's not enough for you, if I'm not enough for you—"

A cone of light from a fixture attached to a cedar lit up his face enough for me to see his eyes shift.

"You're drunk," he whispered, as if he thought someone might hear him.

I looked over my shoulder. People were still milling around

in the bright glow behind the windows of the house.

I turned back to him. "Unfortunately, I'm not. I'm suddenly more sober than I was before I started drinking. In fact, I'm thinking clearer than I have for weeks."

The Stern's front door opened and the cheery jangle of party conversation floated toward us.

"Goodbye," someone called.

The door closed, and two pairs of shoes began the gritty click-click on the pavement. Jack, faithful dog that he was, plodded toward the new sound.

Joel still stood several paces ahead of me.

"Come on. Let's go. It's starting to rain." He was straining to keep his voice low.

I'd left my umbrella at the house but I wasn't going back for it. I didn't care if I got soaking wet. I planted my size seven shoes a short distance apart. "You help me up this hill or I'm staying right here."

"Don't do this, Delainie."

I heard a murmur of voices behind me but couldn't make out the words. As I started to turn, a hand clamped my wrist, and remembering that game where you fall back and hope he doesn't let go, I leaned away from him. He didn't let go, and in my desperation I took that as a solid connection between us.

I held onto his arm and he pulled me up the hill. Tracy and Cam Sorenson caught up with us.

"Hey," Cam boomed, "looks like Joel's running a tow rope on the ski slope. Maybe we should get in line."

"Heh-heh-heh," Joel wheezed. He wasn't amused.

Tracy's hand squeezed my free hand. "I didn't get a chance to ask you earlier. How's Ethan?"

"Well, actually—"

I suppose, after fifteen years of marriage, Joel could recognize when I'd lost all inhibition because he flashed me a warning look.

"Ethan's feeling better, thank you," he interjected, giving me another tug.

I refused to move. "Joel's not being completely truthful.

Ethan does seem better at the moment, but he needs a liver transplant. If I can't give him part of my liver, he'll die. In other words, our whole world is falling apart."

Tracy blinked against the bright light from the fixture on another tree. "Oh, my goodness, I'm sorry."

Cam gave a little cough. "I had no idea he was that sick."

"Yes, and who knows how things will turn out. These operations are delicate and Joel could lose both of us. Or maybe Ethan would live, but I wouldn't make it. Then Joel would have to find another wife, but that might not be so bad for him. I'll bet someone would turn up."

Horror and consternation sprang to Tracy's face. Cam's eyes focused on the trees as if they held some mysterious message.

I let out a long sigh. "I want Joel to help me up this hill, but he's not being very cooperative."

Glancing at Joel, I was struck by the fury in his eyes, and yet I suppose it was exactly what I wanted.

"That's just about enough," he hissed in my ear. He grabbed my wrist and hauled me up the hill.

I looked over my shoulder. Tracy and Cam stayed where they were, apparently too stunned to move. Jack, not the malamute-German shepherd mix but the plain brown mongrel, nosed his way between them and dropped onto his haunches. It was the oddest sight: two people and a dog, all in a row, as stiff as one of those public bronze statues you see scattered around Seattle.

Once we'd made it to the car, which was beaded with moisture, Joel steered me around to the passenger side, bumping the thick rhododendrons that rimmed the road and sending a shower of raindrops over both of us. Huffing with a combination of exasperation and exertion, he unlocked the door and unceremoniously shoved me onto the velour seat. I wanted to be drunk again, but I was completely sober. I pulled my knees against my chest, bent my head, and curled into a ball.

The sky opened up and rain fell like a cascade of beads. They pounded on the car top and in my head.

Chapter 17

Cappy leaned against the counter, rinsing an apple under the faucet spray. "I don't see how you can accuse him of anything on the basis of a smile."

I folded a white paper napkin and set it on the stack. "It wasn't only the smile. It was the way they looked at each other." I picked up the napkin and dabbed at my eyes. "And their hands touched."

"Sounds like enough evidence to me," Liz said. She and Jaya were setting the table with Cappy's brown earthenware plates.

"Well, I think you're judging him too quickly," Cappy said. "People flirt at parties. Big deal."

"But Joel's not the type to do that," I said. "I know him. Doesn't that count for something?"

Cappy was hosting our dinner meeting on her box-shaped houseboat on Lake Union. The living, dining, and kitchen areas were all one room separated only by a peninsula that jutted from the kitchen wall. The bedroom, cubbyhole office, and bathroom were located at the back. The whole floating home made up for its lack of size with prime moorage at the end of a skinny, swaying wooden dock and its Chamber of Commerce view of the Space Needle and downtown Seattle.

Jaya took the napkins I'd folded, minus my crying towel, and set them next to the plates. "What did he say on the way home in the car?"

"Not a thing until we got a block from the house. Then he stopped at the stop sign, looked at me, and said, 'I'm going to take into account you had too much to drink and we're both under a lot of stress. Once we're in the house we won't mention it again.'"

"And what did you say?" Liz asked.

"I said, 'Bullshit, you're just worried I'll make a scene in front of your parents.'"

Jaya's mouth gaped. "You didn't?"

"Sure, I did. I wasn't in the mood for fighting fair."

"Men don't follow the rules," Liz said. "Why should you?"

She had been divorced for thirteen years and never spoke about her husband without bitterness. He left her for a sleek, model-thin French artist, the kind who actually wore a black beret and a long scarf around her neck. Because he and his new wife both worked in television, Liz ran into them more frequently than she could bear. I think what bothered her most was that they were happily married, and she was left with the belief that any man, given the opportunity, would betray his wife in a heartbeat and get away with it.

"I had to say something. Jaya, you must have seen the way he was looking at that woman."

"Actually, I hardly left the kitchen. That was the worst catered dinner I've ever had. I am not going back to Chez Provence again."

Cappy opened the oven door to check on our tuna casserole with the potato chips on top. It smelled great, like one of my childhood dinners.

"So what happened after that, Delainie?" Cappy asked.

"I can't remember exactly. He said something sarcastic. Then I said something snotty. Oh, and then he said something about my being a prima donna."

Jaya stopped with a clutch of silverware in mid-air. "I have never once thought of you that way."

"See, that's a man for you," Liz said. "If all the attention's not on him, you're a prima donna."

I set the salt and pepper shakers on the table. "Oh, and you know what else he said? He said we may be under a lot of stress because of Ethan but you don't see him losing control."

Jaya rolled her eyes. "Joel and his precious control."

She surprised me. Jaya rarely criticized anyone, not even

Rob when he was in the throes of his affair. She had blamed herself until three years of expensive therapy convinced her otherwise.

Liz perked up. "That's when you should have said something about that woman. You should have asked him right then if he thought fucking her gave him a sense of control."

Jaya shook her head. "He would have denied it. They always do in the beginning." She laid down a fork on the table with such precision that I knew she was trying to keep a tether on her emotions.

"What bothers me so much isn't that he's screwing her," I said. "It's the betrayal." I got that burning sensation in my nose and eyes that comes before tears. "No, that's not true. I hate it that he's screwing her."

Jaya reached over and pulled me into an embrace. "Stop blaming yourself."

I laid my cheek against her warm neck and sobbed while Cappy pressed a fresh paper napkin into my hand and Liz patted my back soothingly.

"I feel stupid," I said. "I honestly thought we had a good marriage. I must have been delusional."

"No, you were not," Jaya said.

I blew my nose on the napkin. "After Ethan was born, I kept having the same terrible anxiety dream. In it, Joel and Ethan are swimming in a lake, paddling around in circles fifty yards apart, and they both suddenly dipped below the water and flailed their arms. I stare at them, paralyzed. I didn't know who to save. Should I zigzag between them and try to rescue both? Maybe, if I were skilled in crisis management, I could have concentrated on one at a time. But, I would be taking the chance the other would drown. And, yet, if I did nothing, I would lose both of them. That dream made me crazy, because I couldn't imagine choosing between them. Now, I know exactly who I would choose."

"That's a perfectly normal anxiety dream," Liz said. "I get them all the time."

"But questions like that scare me witless. My mind goes

blank the way it did in junior high math whenever I saw one of those convoluted story problems on a test. If a train travels forty miles an hour to a distant planet — Jupiter, let's say — and a boat sails to Mars at the same rate, which will arrive first? How much fuel will they use? And will I be on either one? If I couldn't solve a problem like that, how can I figure out how to save my son or my marriage?"

"Well," Liz said, "if it turns out Joel's having an affair, I think you should ditch him."

Cappy frowned and Jaya looked shocked.

But Liz blustered on. "Kick him out and file for divorce. Any man who has an affair at a time like this deserves it."

Kick Joel out? Carry on alone? That thought hadn't occurred to me. Just considering it, I heard the grinding, shrieking collision of a train and a boat south of Jupiter, and I felt a big chunk drop out of my life.

———

Some people believe that children don't have the intelligence or the experience to understand the complexities of adult relationships and that may be true. I believe they may not understand them, but they feel them. They're like little barometers measuring the tension in the air. Ethan continually wore a worried expression and more than once I caught him looking surreptitiously at Joel and me.

Barbara obviously sensed the strain between us. She gave us sideways glances and went so far as to scrub the basement's concrete floor.

Ever since the party, we'd been cautious with each other. At night, you could have driven a truck down the center of our blow-up bed.

He was spending more time at the office, and when he was home, he was either devoting his attention to Ethan or upstairs sorting through our stack of medical bills. He struggled over them as if they were a crossword puzzle, and he agonized over every dollar we spent on our daily needs, as if we were taking it directly from Ethan.

I knew how much he valued his self-reliance and our ability

to manage debt, but I had a much more fatalistic attitude. If we couldn't pay our creditors, we'd have to declare bankruptcy and then worry about it after Ethan was well. I didn't say that aloud though.

I became the worst kind of wife. I went through his pockets, even his wallet, while he was showering. I found a State Farm insurance card, an assortment of personal and company credit cards, three neatly folded gasoline receipts, twenty-eight dollars, and one lone photo of Ethan and me. I saw the picture as a good sign. In his pockets I found only loose change, Tic Tacs, and lint. Nothing incriminating. I guiltily stuffed it all back. I had never rifled through his possessions before, and my snooping only left me more depressed.

On a Tuesday evening, he announced he was leaving Thursday for Chicago on a three-day business trip. I was sure she would accompany him on his business trip, if that's what it was.

I got a phone call on Thursday afternoon from Amy Stankowski, the financial assessment coordinator at Children's Memorial.

"I'm getting some contradictory information from your medical insurer," she said. "Could you look through your files and see if there might be an addendum to your policy that you and Joel didn't give me?"

I told her I would check our files and call her back. I went upstairs to our office and searched Joel's desk drawer but didn't find anything we'd missed. I even dug below the files, thinking something might have slipped down. I didn't find any insurance papers, but I came across a few pages of technical material with a yellow stickie on which Joel had written: "M, tell me what you think of this."

I couldn't make any sense of the tech stuff, but I decided it might be some important information he was missing. I'd mention it when he returned.

When I laid it on his desk, I noticed a reply had been written on the back: "This is old stuff. I can fill you in on the latest encryption programs. We're getting together after work tonight, aren't we? Need I say I'm looking forward to it?"

I gripped the edge of the desk. I saw him crawling into a heart-shaped, silk-sheeted bed with a sheer drape around it, and I hated both of them.

I removed the sheet of paper with her reply, folded it into a square the size of one of those notes we passed in high school, and carried it in my pocket. I would keep it with me in case I wanted to present it as evidence to Joel, but I planned to put it out of my mind for the meantime. I would concentrate totally on Ethan, who was bored and restless from staying inside. It had rained the entire first two weeks of June, but the day after Joel left we got a break in the weather. Ethan wanted to ride bikes after school with his friends, but I wouldn't let him. What if he crashed and injured himself? He couldn't afford to lose any more organs.

"If I can't play with my friends, I might as well die," he said on Friday afternoon.

"That's not funny, Ethan."

He kicked the baseboard with the toe of his sneaker. "I wasn't trying to be funny."

"You can invite your friends over. I just don't want you getting tired out."

I dug in my pocket for a tissue. My hand touched the folded paper. What had made me think I wouldn't dwell on it?

I wondered if they were sitting next to each other at a meeting with a venture capitalist, her hand touching his leg under the mahogany conference table. Or maybe his hand was touching her. I wanted to scream.

I fingered the sharp corner of the note. What if I'd read it wrong? What if "getting together" referred to some routine meeting they'd planned? But, no, I couldn't have misinterpreted the "looking forward to it" part.

"If we can't do anything?" Ethan said.

I blinked at him. "What?"

"I said what fun is it if we can't do anything."

Out the window, I saw Hal hammering a nail into a shingle on the moss-encrusted roof of our tilting, ivy-trimmed shed.

He'd wanted to demolish the entire shed and rebuild it from the slab up. I don't know whether it was my look of horror or my insistence that Joel wouldn't approve that stopped him, but he finally settled for replacing the chipped window and patching holes. He was working on it now, whistling his show tunes at a decibel that sent the neighborhood dogs running.

"Why don't you go out and help Grandpa?" I said to Ethan. "Maybe you can hand him his tools."

"I don't like to clean and fix things."

There was something in his voice that made me turn and look at him. He moved away but not before I saw his eyes fill with tears.

"Ethan, what's wrong?"

"Nothing." His hunched shoulders belied that.

"Do you feel sick?"

"No," he murmured in a tone that meant yes.

I walked over to him, slipped my fingers under his chin, and lifted his face so that I could see his eyes. "What is it, Ethan Skywalker?"

He wriggled away and edged toward the counter. "Can I have some cookies?"

"May you have some cookies? Yes, you may if you drink some milk and take your pills."

"They taste bad," he said irritably as he scooted onto a chair at the table.

I took his large plastic pillbox from the cupboard. Normally I would have kept it within easy reach on the counter, but Barbara had taken to storing things out of sight. I was seeing tile countertops that hadn't been visible since we'd moved in. I opened Friday PM and shook out the tablets. Resting his elbow on the tabletop and his chin on his hand, Ethan stared into space. I poured a glass of milk, then fished out three Chips Ahoy cookies from a bag in the cupboard. Of course, it was the friction between Joel and me that was causing his moodiness. As guilt set in, I placed milk, cookies and pills in front of him and waited.

He poked his finger at the pills. "Mom, when you were in

fourth grade, did any of the kids ever say you were a freak?"

So that was it.

"Only every other day. Fourth grade was tough."

He popped a whole cookie into his mouth. "Kendra... munch, munch... called me...munch, munch...a freak and a... munch, munch."

Oh, my God, a girl had said something cruel. But I didn't catch the last word. "What did Kendra call you?"

"A pumpkin head."

Apparently that bothered him more than "a freak." I suddenly disliked ten-year-old females with the fury that only a mother of a son could feel. I swept my hand through the air, wishing I could brush Kendra aside that easily. "Well, I hope you ignored her. Children who call other people names tend to feel bad about themselves, and—"

"She said that because I have orange skin."

"No, you do not." In fact, I thought his color had improved.

"Jeez, Mom, yes I do. You should look at me more often."

"Look at you? I don't even like to let you out of my sight."

I studied his face. Okay, maybe the jaundice wasn't completely gone, but it didn't look any worse than it had before he'd been diagnosed. I told him he could stay home if he wanted. He didn't have to go to school. Surely his mental health at a time like this was as important as his physical health.

His chair scraped the hardwood floor as he slid away from the table. "I didn't say I wanted to stay home. It's not like I can't cope."

Cope? Where had he learned that word?

From me and the group, of course. We must have used it a dozen times whenever we got together. "I can't cope with this job...this man...this stress." "My shrink's giving me Zoloft to help me cope."

I reached for Ethan and pulled him into a hug. "I didn't mean you couldn't handle it, sweetheart. It's just that I would love to have you at home. So would your grandparents."

He avoided my gaze. "I can't talk with Grandma and Grandpa. They don't even know how to use a computer. And, besides,

Grandma thinks I'm weird."

I looked around. Where was Barbara now? Probably out buying cleaning supplies.

"Your grandma doesn't think you're weird. She's just not used to being around little boys anymore."

As he wriggled out of my grasp, I realized I had committed the unpardonable offense of calling him a little boy.

"How is the Fly coming along?" I was trying to make amends.

"Okay."

"Aren't you still excited about it?"

"Yeah, but I'm tired." He turned toward the doorway to the hall. "I'm going to take a nap."

He hadn't taken naps voluntarily since preschool, but I couldn't deny that he looked weary. I didn't want to believe the medicine wasn't working. I didn't want to believe the doctors when they said he would only get sicker.

I heard him step into the hall bathroom and close the door. A few minutes passed while I stood there, trying to decide if I should go after him. Maybe I should call Ethan's teacher and have her talk to Kendra and his other classmates. It might be a good time for her to teach these fourth graders about diseases and organ transplants, about how hard an illness like this is on a child and his family. I carried Ethan's plate and glass to the sink.

What did he mean when he said I should look at him more often? Didn't he know that for years, long before his illness, I left my bed in the middle of the night and went to his room just to watch him breathe?

The toilet flushed, the door opened, and his shoes squeaked on the hardwood floor. Poor kid. He wasn't sulking; he needed to go to the bathroom.

The door to his bedroom closed.

I walked down the hall to close the toilet lid, something the men in my family rarely did. For Joel I suppose, it was a small gesture of rebellion. Nobody but Barbara cared about such things. I certainly didn't, but now that my housekeeping habits were being seriously challenged, I was taking the offensive. Barbara regarded the porcelain bowls as cesspools of germs — which they probably were — but I believed exposure to germs was necessary to health, to build up your defenses, and any mother who sent her child into the world without that inoculation could expect only trouble.

I switched on the light and reached for the lid. I lowered it halfway when I happened to glance at the seat. Two little drops of brownish blood speckled the white enamel. With shaking hands, I yanked off a length of toilet paper and wiped them off, then flushed it away.

I hurtled toward Ethan's room, the hall tilting so precariously that I had to stretch out my arms for balance. I rapped on his closed door and, when he didn't answer, I said, "I'm coming in."

He lay on the bed, reading *20,000 Leagues under the Sea.*

"Didn't you hear me?"

"I was just getting to the good part."

"I thought you were going to take a nap."

"I changed my mind."

"Why was there blood on the toilet seat?"

"I don't know." He turned away.

"Ethan, look at me!" My voice was shaking. "I want you to tell me what happened."

"Nothing." He tossed the book aside, flopped onto his stomach, and tunneled under his pillow.

"You should have said something, honey. You should have told me."

"I didn't want you to know." His voice was muffled. "I don't want anyone to know I'm pooping blood."

I grabbed the edge of his dresser. "Oh, Ethan."

I phoned Taylor at Children's Memorial. "What should I do? Should I bring him in?"

Her husky voice came over the line. "How long has this been

going on?"

"Several days. But he said he doesn't always have it."

"How many times a day? Two, three?"

"I don't know."

"Does he have any cramping or abdominal pain?"

I recalled his relaxed position on the bed. "I don't think so. He hasn't complained of any lately."

"What about a fever?"

I hesitated, embarrassed to admit that taking his temperature hadn't occurred to me. "I'll check." I carried the phone down the hall toward Ethan's bedroom. "The blood, though — it has to be a bad sign."

"But we talked about variceal bleeding, don't you remember?" Her tone was patient, soothing. "The walls of his blood vessels are weak in spots."

"I know you talked about it, but I really didn't think it would happen so soon. Maybe in a year, if he really got sick, but not now.   The medicine seemed to be working so well that I thought he might actually be improving—" I choked on the words. "That he might not need a transplant at all."

"That's not going to happen, Delainie." Her voice sounded like butter. "The damage to his liver can't be reversed."

"I know you said that, but I thought he would be a —" I wanted to say he would be a miracle child, that he would be spared. But how could I — a wishy-washy agnostic, too lazy to be an atheist — speak of divine intervention? I hadn't seen any sign of it yet.

"I thought he would be different," I finished lamely.

"Yes," she said, and I could almost see her sympathetic smile. "That would be nice, wouldn't it?"

My God, I wanted to strangle Joel for taking off when I needed him. Ethan's door was cracked open. I gave it a little push. He lay under the blankets, his mouth slightly open, his pale lashes feathering his freckled cheeks. Oscar's orange body coiled atop his head like a turban.

"I'm in his bedroom, but he's asleep."

"Don't wake him then. When is his next appointment with

Dr. Kittredge?"

"Tomorrow at one o'clock."

"If he has any pain or excessive bleeding before then, bring him in."

Ethan rolled onto his stomach and splayed his limbs, nudging the cat into a new spot.

"He looks so peaceful now."

"You get some rest too, Delainie."

Tears burned my eyes. "I'm not sure I know how to do that anymore."

Chapter 18

Dr. Kittredge said the variceal bleeding was to be expected and that we would need to watch Ethan more closely now.

I stared at the doctor. "Watch him what? Bleed to death?"

"If he's losing a lot of blood, we'll give him transfusions."

"What about the tests on my liver? Why hasn't anyone told me I can be the donor?"

He exhaled a long breath. "These things take time. We'll let you know as soon as we find out."

"But it's been more than…"

I didn't finish my sentence because at that moment Ethan and the nurse walked back in.

Dr. Kittredge jotted something on his paperwork, then looked up. "I want you to stop by Nutritional Management before you leave the hospital. The nutritionist has prepared an individually-tailored diet for Ethan."

A diet? Ethan needed more than a diet. He needed part of my liver right now.

We left the doctor's office and headed for the Nutritional Management Office. I'd been there once before, so I thought I knew the way.

I reached over and slipped my arm around Ethan. His shoulders seemed smaller. "How are you doing, sweetheart?"

"Okay."

I bent over and pulled him closer. "I have this good feeling that things are going to get better soon."

That wasn't the least bit true, but it couldn't hurt to say it. I had read about cancer victims who had managed to get better by thinking positively.

After we'd wandered the hospital corridors for ten minutes, I stared at double doors ahead of us that said INTENSIVE CARE.

"This is supposed to be Nutritional Management."

People were walking up and down the corridor, but none of them appeared to be hospital staff.

Well, this was definitely the end. I wasn't running this maze any longer. I told Ethan to wait right where he was while I poked my head into Intensive Care and asked them why they weren't Nutritional Management. I charged through the double doors.

Individual, glass-walled rooms with beds and monitors rimmed a large open space. Two nurses sat at a central desk. One was on the phone, and the other, who had her back to me, was filing something in a cabinet. While I waited for one of them to notice me, I looked around. The beds in all the small rooms were filled, and I could hear the steady beeps of monitors and the hushed conversations of nurses, doctors, and family members. In a room about twenty feet from me, Alice Spencer, the woman I'd met a few weeks ago in the Bo Peep wing, sat on a chair near a hospital bed, her head bent. I didn't want to go in there. I swear to God I didn't, but I crossed the short distance between us and said hello.

She looked up but didn't answer. Her eyes were rubbed raw.

"I'm sorry. I didn't mean to disturb you." I was backing from the room when I saw her lips move. I thought for a moment she was praying, but then I realized she was speaking to me.

"Sarah's dying." Her face looked numb, her expression frozen. "Maybe tomorrow, maybe in a few days."

Her daughter thrashed and moaned, kicking her covers off. Her skin was gray with a yellow tinge, and her exposed legs, thin as toothpicks, seemed caught in a tremor. In contrast to her bony limbs, her abdomen was swollen to the size of a basketball.

"She has ascites," Alice said. "Her belly's filled with fluid, and she's bleeding inside."

Sarah flailed at the tube that ran down her throat, but instead her hand landed on her faded brown hair, so thin I could see her scalp. A loose bandage covered one small section of it.

"Yesterday, they put a bolt in her head to relieve the pressure on her brain, but it doesn't seem to be helping."

I couldn't speak. My breath was coming in hard, fast pants.

The nurse who'd been on the phone was now standing beside me. "Excuse me, but—"

I didn't stop to talk with her. I ran out of the room.

In the hall, Ethan stood where I'd left him. I grabbed his hand. "We're going home."

He stumbled along behind me. "Why?"

"To save your life."

———————

By the time we arrived home, I was shivering all over. It was late June, but I felt the cold deep in my marrow as I brushed past Barbara, guided Ethan to his room, and pulled back the covers on his bed. "Rest. Lie down here and sleep for a while."

His eyes shone with tears. "Are you mad at me?"

"No, sweetheart." I encircled him with my arms. "I'm not the least bit angry. I'm just..."

I wanted to tell him I was scared, that I'd seen the most horrible sight in my life, that I knew I would dream about it forever and, in those wrenching nightmares, he would take the place of the child in the bed. But I couldn't say any of those things.

"I'm just tired, honey."

"Is that why you're shaking?"

"Yes. I'm sure I'll feel better after I have a nap." I rose to my feet, then thought of Sarah's scrawny limbs and the nutritional consultation we'd missed. "I'll make a sandwich for you first."

"I'm not hungry."

"Ethan, you have to eat! You're supposed to have fruit that has potassium in it, like bananas."

"Okay," he said agreeably. "I'll eat some later."

He laid his head on his pillow and closed his eyes. I clasped my arms tight around me to hold myself together. He was too agreeable; he hated bananas.

Hunched over the phone in our bedroom, I called Joel on his cell phone in Chicago. He answered on the first ring.

"I need to talk to you."

"Is Ethan all right?" he asked in a low, tight voice.

"He's looks the same as he did yesterday."

He sighed with relief.

"Couldn't this wait then? I'm in a meeting with the company president."

"I still need to talk with you."

"Okay, Delainie." His tone was crisp. "Hold on."

I heard him exchange words with some other people in the room.

After several seconds, he came back to the phone. "I'm out in the hall now."

"Come home, Joel."

"I'm sorry but I can't. We're close to making a deal here. This guy would be our biggest client."

I sucked in a deep breath and told him about seeing Sarah Spencer, about her bloated stomach, her patchy hair, and the tube that ran down her throat.

"And they drilled a bolt in her head, Joel. They did that because her brain is swelling, and they had to release the pressure."

"That is not going to happen to Ethan." He sounded like he was speaking through clenched teeth.

"How do you know?" A new wave of coldness swept through me, causing my teeth to chatter. "You can't promise anything."

"Stop it, Delainie. Don't do this."

"What should I do then? Pretend Ethan isn't getting worse? Pretend I didn't see Sarah Spencer?"

"You're not thinking clearly. Ethan's situation isn't the same as hers. You're going to give him part of your liver."

"What if I can't?"

"You have to be able to," he said, desperation rising in his own voice, "because there has to be a limit to bad luck happening to one family."

I gripped the phone. "I need you here, Joel."

"I'll be home tomorrow evening."

"Please come now. I can't stop shaking."

"I have to get back to the meeting. I'll call you later."

And he was gone. I had never felt so alone in my life.

With my teeth still clicking, I took off my slacks and blouse and crawled gingerly under the bed covers. Afraid that if I moved too quickly my bones would snap like icicles, I lay still for what seemed like hours, replaying the image of Sarah Spencer over and over in my head.

I might have stayed in bed longer, if I hadn't heard a solid knock on the bedroom door. I pulled on my peach-colored chenille robe and opened it. Barbara was standing there, her sharp eyes surveying me.

"Dinner's ready."

As I cinched the ties of my robe tighter, I had the feeling that sleeping or wearing bedclothes while it was still light outside violated her code of behavior.

"That's nice of you to fix something," I said, "but I'm not hungry. I want to stay in my room a while longer."

Glancing at the unmade bed, she drew her lips together. "Are you sick?"

"No, I'm just tired."

I wanted her to leave so I could hide in the darkness under the covers, but her sensible brown shoes seemed anchored to the floor.

"Ethan and Hal are downstairs at the table, waiting for you."

I almost snapped, *Look, Barbara, you are not my mother*, but her piercing stare stopped me.

"Your son is not feeling well," she said, "but he came to dinner anyway. What reason should I give him for your staying up here?"

I wanted to shout, *You didn't see Sarah Spencer today. If you had, you would be crawling under the covers too.* But I looked into her steady eyes and knew I was wrong about that. She was a strong woman who did what needed to be done, and I thought of Ethan sitting at the dining room table, waiting expectantly.

"I'll put on my clothes and be down in a minute," I said in as firm a voice as I could manage.

She nodded her approval.

Chapter 19

Joel came home at seven o'clock the following evening. I felt like one of those single mothers whose ex-husbands turn up only when a crisis is over. He gave me a perfunctory homecoming kiss and spent the next hour with Ethan, who greeted him more enthusiastically than I had.

Later, when he came into the kitchen, I said, "Ethan has blood in his stool."

I had saved the announcement to shock him, I suppose. Maybe, if he realized how sick Ethan was, he would lose interest in Milena.

"Jesus, why didn't you tell me?"

"I thought you had enough on your mind with your work and all."

"You took him to the emergency room, didn't you?"

I wanted to say, *what happened to the "we" in this equation?*

"It's not like he was hemorrhaging, and he already had an appointment with Dr. Kittredge yesterday morning."

"How can you be so cavalier about this?"

Cavalier? My emotions could not have been more volatile.

"Dr. Kittredge said a little bleeding is to be expected," I said as calmly as possible. "Don't you remember?"

"Yes, but I didn't think it would happen this soon. Makes me wonder if the staff there is taking Ethan's case seriously enough. One of the things I've learned in business is the person who makes the most noise gets the most attention."

"And runs the risk of alienating the only people who can help. Look, if you don't like the way I'm handling it, then you do it."

He rubbed the back of his hand across his eyes. "I'm capable of doing only so much, Delainie."

"So am I," I said, and strode out of the room.

Somehow, he was managing to find time for her.

———

Joel was still at work when I got a call from Taylor late the following afternoon.

"I have the results on your work-up." Her voice gave no clue as to what they might be.

"And?" I whispered.

"How about you and Joel coming in tomorrow morning so we can talk about them?"

"Tell me now, please."

"It's better to discuss these things in person."

"I can't wait that long."

"Sure you can. We'll meet at nine o'clock."

I leaned against the counter and closed my eyes. "All right."

This process was teaching me patience. I called Joel at his office, but the receptionist said he'd already left for home. I was in the kitchen fixing dinner when he arrived. I was missing sour cream from my recipe so his parents had gone to the grocery to fetch it. I was tired of the bland meals his mother had been fixing.

Joel, his blue shirt wrinkled and his tie askew, looked drained, almost empty, but I was feeling the excitement of Taylor's phone call.

"Taylor will give us my test results tomorrow morning at the hospital."

"That's terrific but I can't go with you." His voice was low. "I have to catch a flight to San Francisco at eight A.M."

"What? You just got home. You didn't tell me you had another business trip coming up."

"I didn't know until this afternoon."

"Joel, you have to be here. We may have to sign papers for my surgery. I want to have it as soon as possible."

He pressed the heels of his hands to his eyes. "Believe me, I wish I could, but this trip is important."

"And your family isn't?" I said, snipping each word close to the edge.

"I'm doing this for my family."

I turned to the window and saw only dreariness. Rain thrummed on the roof, adding to the disturbance in the room.

Is she going with you? I wanted to ask but didn't.

He walked over the refrigerator and opened it.

"We're meeting Max Wells, the billionaire investor Jin has been wooing for months." He took out a carton of milk and poured himself a glass. "The guy called yesterday and said, 'You fellows come on down, bring all your numbers, and run through your dog-and-pony show. If it sounds good, I'll sign on.' His money is going to make a huge difference. It will take the company to the next level. Some good things are finally starting to happen."

I prodded the sizzling strips of steak I was frying for stroganoff, inhaling the meaty aroma. "How long will you be gone this time?"

"Tomorrow and Wednesday."

"Two days?"

"I believe that's how it adds up," he said dryly.

"Who's going with you?"

"Jin, of course."

I searched his face for signs of betrayal. "That's it? Just the two of you?"

He stared at his glass of milk, as if it required close scrutiny. "And Milena."

"I see."

If I hadn't asked, he wouldn't have mentioned her. I took in a deep breath, trying to steady my voice. "Why do you have to go then? It sounds like they'll have it covered."

"We're a team and that's how we want to present ourselves. Jin handles the finances. I'm the tech guy with the vision. Milena's the whiz kid who can carry out our plan." His eyes took on a radiance. "We want to show this guy that we've got new ideas and all the right people to make this company take off."

I ground some fresh pepper over the meat. "Did she go with

you to Chicago?"

"No, and Jin didn't either. It wasn't that kind of trip."

That stopped me for a moment.

Maybe I was crazy, stress causing my imagination to run amuck. I reached in my pocket and touched the note. Why not come right out and ask him? Say the words. I found this piece of paper. Are you having an affair? Don't be accusatory. Don't let your voice crack. Keep your tone even, as if you were asking how much money this big-time investor could provide.

But, of course he would deny it, as Jaya had predicted. He would pause long enough to let my words echo, and then he would laugh, shake his head in wonder, and say, "What am I going to do with you, Delainie?"

No, he would more likely be furious, giving me his famous hard stare. "Here I am, working my tail off to get this company going, killing myself with sixteen-hour days so that we can afford Ethan's transplant — and what are you doing? Accusing me of sleeping with my co-worker. That's really helpful, Delainie."

Worst case scenario. He admits it. "I'll stay with you until Ethan has the surgery, but then it's over. It's not that I don't love you. It's just that I'm not in love with you anymore. And Milena? I know she dresses like a teenager, but we have these great conversations about higher concepts like bytes and bits and bauds. She's spontaneous and exciting. Actually, Delainie, she reminds me of how you used to be."

I grabbed the salt and shook it furiously over the pan.

Chapter 20

I sat in Taylor's sunny office. "I have defective vasculature?" She must be right because my hands felt numb.

"No, I wouldn't call it that," Taylor said, her tone low and soothing. I'd come to realize it turned softer in direct proportion to the severity of the bad news she was delivering. "Your blood vessels work fine for you. That's not the problem. In a living donor transplant, the portal vein has to be positioned just right. Unfortunately, yours isn't."

I tilted up my chin, trying to keep the tears from spilling. "Who will it hurt if I give him part of my liver, Ethan or me?"

She leaned toward me and laid her hand on my arm. "It doesn't make any difference. The transplant surgeons won't do it."

"Maybe they can stitch together some vessels from another part of my body."

She shook her head.

I lowered my voice to begging level. "But don't you see? I'll do anything to save him, even if it means living with mangled blood vessels or only one arm or one leg."

She straightened as if to fortify herself. "I'm so sorry."

Tears swamped my eyes. "He's my only child. He's the only thing I have right now. Isn't there anything I can do?"

Her habitually calm eyes dulled, and a wet sheen slid over them. "I don't make these decisions. I can help you try to understand them, but I can't change them."

"It's not that I don't understand them. It's just that I was counting on this. What will happen now?"

He would go on the UNOS transplant list, she explained,

putting him in line for a liver from a dying person who had the same blood type and probably had to fulfill a hundred other requirements. It was hard to say how long that would take, a few months perhaps, more likely a year but, in the meantime, the doctors would try to control his symptoms as much as possible.

"How much sicker will he have to get?"

"I honestly can't tell you. We'll try to keep him as stable as we can."

I stood, teetering on my shaky legs. "Has Sarah Spencer received her new liver yet?"

I looked at Taylor, who had risen from her chair. She seemed to stop breathing for a moment.

Finally, she said, "I wish your husband could have been here. You need his support right now."

"You don't want to tell me she died, do you?"

Her lips trembled. "We did all we could for her, but she didn't get a liver in time. Delainie, that doesn't mean —"

"No, I'm sure it doesn't."

"I can't let you go home like this."

"I'm okay."

"Is there someone you can call?"

I thought of Jaya, Cappy and Liz. Any one of them would have rushed to my side and accompanied me to the hospital if I had asked. Why didn't I? I bit my lower lip, not wanting to admit to my answer, which was embarrassingly childish. If Joel was going to desert me, then I would show him I didn't need him or anyone else. I could do it alone.

"I'm fine, really," I told Taylor. "My in-laws are staying with us. They'll be home when I get there, and of course I'll talk to Joel by phone."

I tightened the belt on my raincoat and dug in my purse for my keys. It tipped sideways so that my wallet, a comb missing three teeth, some coins, and a wad of used tissue tumbled onto the carpet. Taylor and I scrambled for the debris, stuffing it back into my limp handbag.

She handed me two stray dimes. "I want you to see the social worker before you leave."

"Oh, I don't think so." I tried to instill some cheer into my voice. "Not unless she's got a cure for clumsiness."

Taylor didn't speak, but her expression said she wasn't retreating from her position. I reached for the doorknob, my hand so cold the metal felt warm to my touch. I might have been a blind mouse in a maze as I bent my head and charged through the hospital corridors, finally finding the main lobby and the automatic exit doors.

Outside, people gathered under the overhang, waiting for a break in the crashing downpour. I didn't care how wet I got, but I couldn't remember if I had parked in the Jack Spratt or Bo Peep garage.

Dodging SUVs and collecting raindrops, I dashed across the road to the Bo Peep garage, a river was coursing down my neck by the time I reached cover. I walked along the rows, my frustration increasing. I had parked on the ground level (that much I recalled), but if the car was here, it was hiding behind a semi.

Braving the rain again, I ran a half block to the Jack Spratt garage, where I traipsed up and down its rows until I thought I might collapse into a puddle on the concrete floor. Over a lost car, a stupid lost car. Then I spotted the Buick, looking grimy and forlorn in a far corner, and felt a sweet relief.

But I couldn't find my keys in my handbag. I tossed the purse on the hood of the car and jammed my hands in my raincoat pockets, poking around until I found my key ring under a cheap, stretchy black glove I'd bought a week ago at Target. I'd already lost the mate.

Inside the car, I leaned back against the seat, slowly sucking in the cold, damp air, feeling as if the garage's metal beams and thick concrete ceiling were settling down on me, crushing me. Once again, the supreme forces of life — the word God now seemed much too humane and cozy — had ignored my plea. It was clear I was left to fight this battle on my own.

I switched on the ignition and listened to the engine turn over — and over and over. It ground like a blender, working strenuously but not quite catching. The broken strands of my worn straw seat pad dug into the back of my knees.

A glance in the rearview mirror revealed my hair was a damp mop and my face looked like a fright mask. When I tried the engine again, it rasped and shivered but failed to connect. I slammed my fist against the steering wheel. I don't know how long I sat there, shaking with anger and helplessness, but when I turned my head, Dr. Alan Sidon's kind face was staring at me through the window.

He mouthed, "Are you okay?"

Oh, God, could I look any worse? I quickly patted my hair and opened the car door. "Once this wreck starts, I'll be fine."

To his credit, he didn't laugh. I recalled how kind he'd been to me those first few days in the hospital.

"Let me try it." As I was crawling out, he asked. "How is your son?"

I collapsed against the side of the car, tears rising like a tidal pool. Frantically, I dug in my coat pocket, hauled out the lone black glove, and pressed it against my nose.

"Would you like to walk back to the hospital?" he said gently.

I shook my head. "Got to go home."

I felt his hand on my shoulder, his fingers lightly touching the skin on my neck. His warmth rushed through me, and I closed my eyes.

"Do you think—" I began.

"Yes?"

"Do you think you could hold me?"

As he pulled me into the snug cave of his chest, I didn't look at him. I was as tall as he was, but he managed to enfold me completely with his soft-edged body.

I pressed my temple to his, burrowing against his mass of wiry hair, his thick dark beard tickling my face.

"I don't have anyone to hold me anymore," I whispered.

"You got some bad news, didn't you?"

My tears dampened the small patch of skin where our faces touched. "I was going to give Ethan part of my liver, but they said I couldn't. I have inadequate vasculature, and right now that's the way I feel — inadequate. And then I found out that Sarah Spencer died, and I'm so scared that Ethan will—" I couldn't finish.

He gripped tighter, and his heat and strength seeped through layers of clothing into me. "No two patients are alike. She had different problems than Ethan does. His prognosis is better."

I pulled back and looked at him. "Is it really?"

"Yes," he said softly.

I wanted to tell him I loved him, but I had the good sense not to do that. During the several minutes he embraced me, he never drew back, not even when a man feigned a cough and entered a car across the aisle. I wanted to crawl inside him, to pull him around me like a cocoon. I clung to his sturdy body and, to my horror, felt a stirring that was more carnal than gratefully loving. And, yet, I held on.

At that point he released me. "How about going back into the hospital with me? I think you should talk with a social worker."

I shook my head vehemently. "I want to go home."

He studied me for several seconds, while I tried to look like the sane woman I wasn't.

"All right," he said. "Let's see if we can get your car to start."

I handed him the keys and he lowered himself onto the driver's seat, working his middle behind the steering wheel. He adjusted the seat back and stuck the key in the ignition. A little twist, a surge of gas, and the old Buick churned to life, the kind of inexplicable resurrection you expect to happen only in a mechanic's garage. The engine rumbled and, after a few seconds, eased into a low hum.

I attempted a smile. "That was a small demonstration of a miracle, wasn't it?"

He wriggled from behind the wheel, bringing the woven seat pad with him. "Your engine was flooded." He stuffed the pad back into place.

I almost blurted, "My life is flooded," but I was afraid he would call for restraints.

I slid onto the driver's seat. "Thanks for fixing the car."

He stood over me, his hands pressed against the car roof. "Any time."

He reached for my shoulder, probably nothing more than a comforting gesture, but in my desperation I wanted it to be something else.

He drew back before he made contact. "Take care of yourself. You need that now."

I nodded, caught in an eddy of conflicting emotions. Was this what anguish and anxiety and carnal love did to a woman? While my son was dying, I wanted sex.

After he shut the door, I snapped on my seatbelt and shifted the transmission into reverse. If he had touched me, I wouldn't have resisted. If he had asked me to go somewhere away from the hospital with him, I would have gone, without guilt or regret.

As it was, I simply drove away.

Chapter 21

When I returned home, Barbara was standing inside the door, a spray bottle of Lysol in one hand, a pristine swatch of towel in the other. She gave me a questioning look, and I had the feeling she had been waiting for my report.

"They won't let me do it," I said brusquely. I turned toward the hall closet to hang up my raincoat.

When I looked back, she was standing in the same place. Was that reproach that I saw on her face, in those tightly pinched lips and narrowed eyes?

"Why not?" she asked.

"A vein that isn't positioned in the right place for transplantation — something like that. Nothing serious for me."

"Well, at least that's good news. We don't need another catastrophic medical problem right now but, of course, Ethan's out of luck."

I briefly closed my eyes. Did she ever listen to what she was saying? I shut the closet door with a nudge of my hip.

She was still staring at me. "What will we do now?"

We? Up to now, she'd done nothing but wash clothes, scrub every surface in the house seventeen times, and annoy me with her stony, faultfinding presence. Ever since she arrived, she had been my conscience, censuring me with unsaid words.

"We'll have to find a donor for him," I said. "The UNOS program won't give him a liver until he's close to death. And we certainly don't want to wait for that, do we?" That was the reality and she might as well know it.

She didn't answer but all color drained from her face, leaving it as white and rigid as marble. Feeling too weary to deal with her, I walked into the kitchen with her trailing me. I pulled my cell phone from my purse and turned it on. I had shut it off while I was with Taylor so we wouldn't be interrupted, but I saw now no one had called, no one had left a message. Maybe he had contacted his mother.

"How many times has Joel phoned?" I asked.

She looked confused. "I don't know."

"He hasn't called at all, has he?"

She shook her head.

I sniffed. "Well, that's just great. He knew the appointment was three-and-a-half hours ago. You would think he would be concerned about his son, if not me."

"Of course, he's concerned about *Ethan*."

Unbelievable. Had she no checker in that blood-starved brain? "Why hasn't he phoned then?"

"He's probably in meetings."

"Right. Some very, very private meetings." I looked to see what effect that had on her.

She seemed puzzled. "Private meetings?"

"With his colleague, Milena Soracco" I took a glass from the cabinet and ran water into it.

"Why don't you call him?" she asked. "He's got one of those phones you carry in your pocket."

"Well, gosh, I certainly wouldn't want to bother him at a time like that, now, would I?" I swigged half of the water and set the glass down with a thump. A section the size of an extra-large egg fell out, and the remaining water spread across the counter.

In two seconds, Barbara was beside me, her big, bony, out-stretched hand brandishing the rag.

I grabbed at the swatch of white cloth. "I can do it!"

She held on. "No, I've got it."

I tugged. "I can clean up my own mess."

She gripped harder, making a low guttural sound. I had trespassed into her territory. What childishness! I gave the hunk of towel a yank and it flew from her hand. She tried to snatch it back, and we tussled over it the way two women

162

might fight over a sweater at a department store sale.

A wire, strung too taut, broke inside me. Along with the release came an upsurge of power. If there had been a car in my kitchen I could have lifted it off the ground by its bumper. I jerked on the rag, but Barbara matched me, tug-for-tug. After a few seconds, it came to me that I was wrestling my mother-in-law for control of a square of cloth. I should have stopped then, but I kept it up until Hal walked into the kitchen, took one wide-eyed look at us, and retreated, shrilly whistling "They Call the Wind Mariah."

I released the rag and stepped back.

Barbara clutched it to her midriff, panting slightly. "I'll take care of that spill now."

No anger. Not even the show of triumph I'd expected. She blinked several times and patted the counter with her folded cloth, intent on soaking up the puddle.

I stayed where I was, watching her and thinking I couldn't handle Ethan's illness and Joel's parents at the same time. "Uh, Barbara, you don't need to—"

She waved my words away. Then, with her head bent, she scrubbed frantically as her tears splashed on the countertop.

I left the kitchen and climbed the stairs to my makeshift bedroom. I perched on the edge of my blow-up bed and lowered my head into my hands, but I didn't cry. I had moved into barren territory that drew all the moisture from me.

I wouldn't become Alice Spencer, waiting and wishing for someone to die so my son could live, pleading with the doctors, complaining to anyone who would listen, aching with futility, slowly dying inside as I watched my child's life fade away.

I would do something. I didn't know what that was yet, but I would find some way to save my son. I wouldn't stand by quietly waiting. I would howl at the moon if that was what it took.

The cell phone in my pocket rang. I considered not answering it but decided it might be Ethan's school. Maybe he was throwing up, maybe he had the bleeds, as the doctors called them. We were acquiring a whole new lexicon, the lingo of illness and hospitals.

The screen said "Joel." I punched the accept button.

"Why didn't you call?" he asked.

"I figured if you were interested, you would contact me."

"Interested?" His voice shook. "Jesus, Delainie, what's wrong with you?"

Ten minutes earlier, I had fought over a hank of rag. Now I couldn't muster any anger at all. He grumbled that he had skipped part of a meeting, expecting I would call from the hospital. Finally, he phoned Taylor.

"What did she say?" I asked.

"She said that basically you failed the tests."

Failed the tests? He made it sound like they were college finals.

"You were counting on this too much," he said.

"Yes, and you weren't?"

"Maybe you should wait until I get there to tell Ethan."

"He knew I was seeing Taylor this morning."

"I suppose you'll have to tell him alone then, but try to hold yourself together. It won't help him if you fall apart."

"Oh, I won't fall apart. I've become amazingly strong these days."

He asked if I had told his parents yet, and I said his mother knew.

"How did she handle it?"

"All right." Once she had her cleaning rag back in her hand.

"Have them with you when you tell Ethan, okay?"

"Of course."

He was silent, as if amazed I had agreed with him.

"Oh, by the way," I said, "Sarah Spencer died."

The only sound for several seconds was the hum on the phone line. Finally, he said, "Delainie, don't do this."

"I'm not doing anything. I'm just conveying some information."

"We're not going to let this happen to Ethan. Have you called your brothers yet?"

"No. I was waiting to hear about my chances first. I'll call them, but I don't think they have the right blood type." I felt bad about asking them if Ethan could have a slice of one of their livers, considering I rarely contacted them at all. "Are you coming back tomorrow?"

"I can't."

No surprise in that.

"It's Wells. His lawyers are reviewing the contract tomorrow. He says that if it passes their inspection, he'll sign it on Thursday morning."

"Good."

"Jin says we can't leave until we've got his signature on paper. He's that kind of guy."

"Makes sense."

"We're having another meeting this afternoon and then dinner with Wells, but I'll call you after I get back to the hotel tonight."

"Okay."

"Are you going to be all right? Because you don't sound like you are."

"I'm fine."

"How about asking Jaya or Cappy to come over and stay with you this evening?"

"I'll think about it."

There was a brief, awkward moment.

"Well, goodbye," he said.

I hung up the phone and would have punched the wall if I hadn't seen Ethan standing in the doorway, just back from school. He was wearing his oversized Seahawks jacket and his baggy cargo pants with the frayed edges. His hair, damp from the rain, lay against his head like molded plastic. Maybe it was the hair that made his face stand out in stark relief or maybe it was the light from the nightstand lamp, but his skin looked preternaturally golden, deceptively healthy.

"You should have worn a hat."

He shrugged.

"How was school?"

He screwed up his face. "It's the last day, don't you remember?"

I searched the jumbled inventory of my memory but came up blank. "I guess not."

"I brought home the announcement about the fun run and ice cream last week. I laid it right in front of you." His tone was accusatory.

"I'm sorry. I'm terribly forgetful."

"Doesn't make any difference. I couldn't run anyway, and the ice cream didn't taste good." He turned to leave.

"Ethan, don't you want to know about my meeting with Taylor?"

He looked down at his stocking feet. "She said you couldn't do it."

"Did your grandmother tell you that?"

"Nope. She didn't have to. If Taylor said it was okay, you wouldn't be hiding up here. You'd be downstairs dancing on the dining room table."

When did he get to be so smart?

He eyed me. "You aren't really sick or anything, are you?"

"There's nothing wrong with me except some misplaced blood vessels."

We sounded so perfunctory, as if our absent leader had given us "buck-up" orders.

Ethan dug at the rug with his toe. "Well, I figured it wouldn't work out anyway."

"Why not?" Had I been the only foolish one to cling to that hope?

He lifted his head and fastened his gaze directly on me. "I know you like having things easy, Mom, but life isn't that way."

I was too stunned to answer. He turned and shuffled out of the room.

I called my brother Douglas, who offered copious sympathy and support but no body parts. Besides, he didn't have a compatible blood type. There was no point in contacting his identical twin.

The next time I looked in on Ethan, he was curled on his bed, taking one of his afternoon naps that had recently become routine. He slept at least two hours, sometimes three. I didn't want to invite Jaya or Cappy over, but I wanted to get away from the house and my in-laws, so I told Barbara I was leaving.

I dug into my oversized purse for my car keys and finally found them under Ethan's binky. I took it out and fingered its soft fabric. I could have taken the little ragged blanket into the house but instead I stuffed it back into my purse and drove the few miles to Cappy's houseboat on Lake Union.

The rain had moved east, but the sky remained a mottled gray. I parked in the area reserved for houseboat owners and their guests and walked toward the floating dock, thinking how much I needed a glimpse of the sun at that moment.

It was the third week in June, but as the old saying goes, summer doesn't begin in Seattle until July fifth. The air smelled fresh, though, the fragrance of blossoming plants and new growth defeating the stale smell of weeds and debris that had collected near the dock.

At the end of the wooden pier, I stepped over the foot of watery space to Cappy's houseboat. How did she manage crossing it? Her multiple sclerosis made her unsteady.

She had one of those doorbells that doubled as the belly button on a green-tinged, brass frog, but her dog, Port, signaled my arrival a second before I pressed it.

I heard Cappy say, "Quiet," and then the intermittent thumps of her cane and the five unsteady legs they had between them, shuffling toward the door. As a pup, Port had lost a leg chasing a car.

Cappy opened the door, looked at me, and said, "You had bad news at the hospital, didn't you?"

"I don't have the right vasculature."

Reaching across the space between us, Cappy pulled me inside.

She wasn't the hugging type, but she held onto me. "You should have let me go with you. You shouldn't have heard that alone."

With Port spinning ragged circles around us, we staggered toward the living room, each providing a crutch for the other, and collapsed onto the sofa. The houseboat smelled like a combination of wood smoke and wet dog.

Cappy, looking frumpy in baggy corduroy pants and a pilled brown wool sweater, arranged her legs in front of her, lifting and moving and positioning them as if they were a pair of sticks. Although she never complained, I knew enough about MS to recognize she no longer had any sensation in them.

Port slumped to the floor so that his haunch rested against her foot. Sometimes I wondered if he was trying to tell her, it's all right. We're all crippled in some way.

"I want to help Ethan," Cappy said.

I fingered some loose threads on the sofa arm. "Um, that's really sweet of you but—"

With an annoyed look, she abruptly struggled to her feet. "Want some tea?"

Port raised his head.

"Green, black, or herbal?"

"Uh, green."

She gripped her cane and stumped across the carpeted floor. I heard the gush of water as she filled the kettle, then the click of the gas stove igniter. After giving Port an extra fondle, I walked to the peninsula that divided the kitchen and dining spaces.

I cleared my throat to speak.

She waved her hand to stop me. "I know what you're going to say, and you don't have to be tactful about it. We both know I have MS. You don't have to pretend a giant pink elephant isn't squatting in the middle of the room."

"I wasn't trying to—"

"Of course you were." She gave a wry smile. "The irony is that I have the same blood type Ethan has. Jaya's raising money but we need to do more."

I must have looked uncomfortable because she said, "Oh, stop. If you don't like your friends helping you, go find some who won't. "

"I know you want to help, but frankly I don't know what you can do. I've run out of ideas." I turned my gaze to the window and watched a sailboat split the water between the houseboats

168

and pass like a slowly unfurling mural. "Cappy, I'm fighting with my mother-in-law and my husband, and today Ethan lectured me on the perils of life. I feel like the clown punching bag my brothers had when we were kids. I've been clobbered but I swear I'm going to pop back up."

"Good. I knew you would. I'm calling Jaya and Liz, and we're meeting at your house tonight."

I sighed. "I don't have the energy to cook."

"We're not coming over to eat."

That evening, they arrived on my doorstep as a group.

Ethan was waiting to see them before he went off to bed. Despite Barbara and Hal's protests, I'd managed to send them off to the local movie theatre. They said they found most movies offensive, but I recommended the new Disney film that was playing. That should be safe enough.

Liz ruffled Ethan's hair. "So Mom can't give you a piece of her liver, huh? Ain't that a crock of poop?"

He grinned and ran his hand across his cowlicks in an attempt to smooth them down again.

"Well, your aunties are going to take care of this problem," Cappy told him.

His eyes brightened. I envied his simple faith.

Liz grasped his pajama-clad shoulders and propelled him toward the hall. "Let's get you to bed, so this cabal can plan its offensive."

"What's a cabal, Aunt Liz?"

"It's a sisterhood of the smartest women in the world, like our gourmet group is. Most men don't know this, but cabals of women actually control everything — trade, politics, computers, the high seas, even the television networks — and they let all the men work for them. You need to learn this early and always treat women with respect, because they secretly rule over everybody, even the United States President and Congressmen, those fools." Her voice trailed off.

By the time she returned, we had settled at the dining room table, where I laid out saltine crackers and a tub of Alouette. I offered diet soft drinks, but Jaya had brought a bottle of wine.

Liz slid onto a chair. "That boy just might grow up to be one of the few decent men in this world." She looked around. "Where are your in-laws?"

"At the movies."

"I didn't see Joel's car outside. Is he still at the office?"

I methodically spread a clump of cheese on my cracker. "He's in San Francisco, supposedly on a business trip with Milena Soracco,"

Jaya's brown eyes widened. "Do you think he's sleeping with her?"

"No, I think he's having sex with her," I said. When I realized how snippy I sounded, I gave her a wobbly smile. "Sorry. I seem to be overly touchy these days."

Liz muttered something under her breath.

I turned to her. "What?"

"Nothing."

I knew she had called Joel a son-of-a-bitch, a fucking slime ball, or another one of her favorite epithets when it came to men, but she wouldn't say it very loud. We had a long-standing, unwritten pact. We might criticize our own husbands or significant others, and the rest of our group could vehemently agree, but they were careful not to condemn them so strongly that they couldn't reverse their opinions when we took the jerks back.

Cappy shook her head in disgust. "Now that we've passed judgment on Joel, let's figure out what we can do for Ethan. Unfortunately, Jaya and Liz can't be donors."

"I'm AB," Liz said, "although I've occasionally been accused of having no blood at all."

"And I'm A positive," Jaya said, disappointment in her tone.

I shrugged. I wasn't surprised. It would have been too easy if one of them had been a match.

Jaya rested her arms on the table. "Maybe we could contact every person we know, asking if anyone with the same blood type would offer to become the donor."

"I like that," I said. "We can do it easily on Facebook."

Liz was chewing absentmindedly on her thumbnail.

Cappy studied her. "What are you thinking?"

"I'm thinking we take it one step further and put them on television."

"Put who on television?" Jaya asked.

"Why, Joel, Delainie and Ethan," Liz said.

"Do you think your station would do that?" I asked. If hearts could soar, mine was doing its best.

"Sure, the story's got pathos written all over it. A poignant family tableau, a plea for someone to donate part of his liver to Ethan. Anyone with a child will want to help. We'll run it during the five o'clock hour when mothers are fixing dinner. They'll be crying in their spaghetti sauce. I'll pitch it to the executive producer this week."

Jaya wrinkled her nose. "Do you think you could be a little less crass about it?"

"I'm not being crass. It's the business. Every profession does that. Doctors joke in surgery. Cops make raunchy cracks. The important thing is that a television appearance could have all kinds of benefits. At best, we'll get a donor for Ethan. At the very least, it'll draw attention to the need for more organ donors. What's so wrong with that?"

Nothing except the mere thought of going on television set me quaking. I could already see that big camera targeting me like Cyclops, freezing me with its hard stare.

My reaction was almost phobic. It wasn't something I could overcome with practice. Ever since the first time in high school when I had to give a book report, I panicked as all eyes shifted to me. I remembered exactly how it felt. Heat rose to my face until I thought I might spontaneously combust, while cold sweat flowed from my armpits and saturated my blouse. Every coherent thought dropped from my brain and, when I opened my mouth to speak, the words bumped into each other like a string of rear-end collisions. I'd have to persuade Joel to do the talking.

My gaze strayed to Ethan's third grade photo, which I had propped on the ledge of the china cabinet, intending to paste it in an album someday. It had sat there for a year. His grin was lopsided, his shirt collar was crooked, and his eyelids were lowered to half-blink. It was your typical school picture, but what I saw was the most handsome child on Earth.

When I looked back, the others were staring at me.

"So what do you think?" Cappy asked.

I straightened. "Absolutely. Let's do it."

Chapter 22

I sat in bed, my back pressed against the massive carved head board, my knees drawn to my chest, and stared at the clock. It was past ten and Joel still hadn't phoned from San Francisco. On a business trip, he usually called after dinner. Of course, I could phone him and insist he come home immediately.

I remembered Taylor saying a medical crisis doesn't create a rift in a relationship. It only makes the problems that existed worse. I looked back over the last year, trying to understand the descent of our marriage, and trying to find the tiny cracks that had opened into chasms. We must have been like two people, walking side by side but always turning our heads to look at something else. He was consumed with building his new company. I was absorbed with my child, my friends, and my antiques. We both doted on Ethan but not on each other. We talked, but mostly about the mundane. Maybe he had given me clues indicating he was unhappy, but I'd had the sand-clouded insight of an ostrich.

Was that what had happened? I didn't know, but I'd become obsessed with figuring it out.

Outside, a heavy summer rain battered the roof, drowning out the ticking of the clock as it passed eleven. Lightning flashed a warning, and I counted the seconds until the boom followed. At eleven-thirty, I called the San Francisco Four Seasons to ask for Joel Franklin. Then I had an idea, one that could deliver a devastating answer but would eliminate any question.

I asked the clerk, "Could you tell me if Jin Lee and Milena Soracco are still registered there?"

After a few seconds, he said, "Mr. Lee has checked out.

Would you like me to ring Ms. Soracco?"

"No, thank you."

I hung up, breathing hard. I leaned forward, grabbed my knees, and hugged them, wanting desperately to cry, but the tears didn't come. I'd moved into a new stage of tearless weeping.

He would claim to have good reasons for staying. The investor still hadn't signed the paperwork. He wanted more information. A few details had to be worked out. But Jin could have stayed, not Joel with the sick child and the distraught wife at home. Jin would have agreed that Joel should be the one to return. I knew he would have. He cared about us.

I fumbled for the phone, finally gripping the handset with fingers that were so slippery wet they slid all over the buttons. I had to punch in the numbers three times before I got them right.

I pressed the receiver to my ear and heard Jaya's sleepy hello.

"It's Delainie. I woke you up, didn't I?"

"Don't worry about it." She was suddenly alert. "What's wrong?"

I told her about calling the hotel. On the phone line, my teeth must have sounded like castanets. Outside, the rain hammered the windows, the noise echoing through the room.

"I'll be right over," she said.

"That's not a good idea. The streets must be flooded."

"I'll call you in a few minutes from the car."

"No, Jaya—"

She had hung up.

I shouldn't have called her. She'd already had to listen to my grim description of Sarah Spencer and comfort me. She was a kind and loyal friend, but she had her own life to live, clearly a much better one than I had.

Within a few minutes, my cell phone rang. Joel, probably. But the display said Jaya.

I answered it. "You can turn around now, sweetie. I'm already feeling better."

I could hear the growl of the engine and the slosh of windshield wipers in the background.

"No, you're not. And there's a reason why you called me."

"Well, yes, but it's over now."

"No, I mean why you wanted to talk with me instead of Liz or Cappy."

I hesitated. "I couldn't ask for better friends, but Liz is so jaded about men and—"

"And you knew I would understand exactly how you feel."

I walked to the window and faced the watery blackness.

"How did I manage to screw up my marriage, Jaya? I know it sounds trite, but I swear I didn't realize we were in trouble."

"Now, wait a minute. Joel's responsible for his own choices. My God, I sound like a shrink. Anyway, I'm pulling up to your house."

My legs wobbled as I walked down the stairs to the front door. She stood on the porch, wearing a damp sweatshirt over her nightgown. Behind her, the rain clattered against the sidewalk.

I shook my head. "You shouldn't have come out in this."

She stepped inside, gave me a long, moist hug, and closed the door behind her. Without asking, she pulled Joel's ski jacket from the coat closet and wrapped it around her. Then, she took my hand, guided me into the dark living room, and sat me down on the sofa.

"If Joel really is having an affair, I can guarantee it has more to do with Ethan than with you."

"You're telling me he's in San Francisco with another woman because our son is dying?"

She put her hand on my arm. "He's feeling powerless, maybe even impotent. What else can he do to remind himself he still has some control over something?"

I rolled my eyes, although she probably didn't see me in the faint light. "I'm having real trouble feeling any sympathy."

"Believe me, I'm not excusing him."

"Did he think I wouldn't notice?"

"He didn't intend for you to find out. She's an escape for

him, Delainie. I saw her. She doesn't look like she has the makings of a serious relationship."

"Well, if he was looking for an escape, he should have gone to Disneyland."

"But then he couldn't blame you, could he? He couldn't punish you for reminding him daily he's helpless in a real crisis."

I sat there stunned.

"We're women, Delainie. We can't believe that something isn't our fault."

"I'm not putting up with it," I said sharply, "even if it's not personal."

"No one says you should. You're way ahead of where I was when Rob had his affair. It took me three years and big doses of therapy to figure out I wasn't the unattractive, inadequate woman I thought I was and that I hadn't done anything wrong."

"But I feel so dense not to have seen it. Maybe this doesn't have anything to do with Ethan. He hired her before Ethan got sick. He didn't tell me until afterward. Maybe they hopped into bed right after they met."

"Are you completely sure he's even having an affair."

I dug the folded note out of my jeans pocket and handed it to her.

She read it and her eyes filled. "This is the way I found out about Rob, remember? I was looking in his car for a button from my winter coat."

I nodded. "I'm sorry I've brought all this back for you."

Her moist eyes widened in surprise. "Why would you think I'd ever forget it?"

"I suppose it will be like that for me too, won't it? Whenever I try to remember something that happened, I'll be thinking to myself, 'Now, was that before Joel's affair, or was it after Ethan's illness?"

"You will get through this, Delainie. If I could, you will. You're stronger than I am."

I hugged her. "I can't afford a psychiatrist. Will you be my shrink?"

She brushed away her tears. "I'm pretty busy. I'm organizing a benefit drive for my best friend's little boy, but I think I can fit you in."

I managed a smile.

The next morning, Joel came directly from the airport, or so he said. He was carrying extra baggage — puffy, dark half circles under his eyes. He didn't kiss me as he usually did when he arrived but then I didn't care.

Ethan was still in bed. He no longer bounced up in the morning. He no longer ran outside to ride bikes or shoot baskets with the neighborhood kids. Fatigue had become his persistent companion.

Joel stretched his arms across the back of the sofa, dominating our small office. "You want to put Ethan on television?"

"With you and me."

"And the point of this is?"

"To find someone who'll help."

"Someone who'll give us a liver for Ethan? You don't really expect some stranger to take a risk like that."

"Well, we're asking for a little chunk, not the whole thing. If nothing else, maybe they'll send us money."

"Why not hang a banner from the house? CHILD DYING. DONATIONS ACCEPTED."

"I would, if it would help. People beg for far less important things."

He waved his hand in resignation. "Put Ethan on TV if you want, but don't expect me to get involved."

I felt the panic rise to my throat. "You have to make the appeal, Joel. You're used to giving speeches and presentations. If they turn a camera on me, my brain might shut down."

He shook his head. "This isn't a sideshow. I am not going on television, Delainie. That's final."

As I stared at him, every insecurity I'd ever felt flooded me, and it wasn't just the prospect of a TV interview. I wasn't sure that I could function without him. Since the beginning of our marriage, he had been my captain, my anchor. His chief role was to point me in the right direction and rescue me when I fell off the boat. Now, he too was flawed, perhaps more imperfect than I was. If I couldn't rely on him, I would have to trust myself. I'd had little experience with that, but with my son at stake, I could do it.

He stood and picked up his jacket.

I moved between him and the door. "I can tell you right now that I won't let what happened to Sarah Spencer happen to our son. I will not watch him die slowly and do nothing."

The tendons in his neck tightened. "And that's what you think I'm doing? I may not be willing to walk around with a tin cup in my hand, but I don't plan to sit on my ass. I'm going to talk to Ethan's doctors and demand they take his case more seriously. They're the people who can do something."

"Fine, whatever you want then."

I walked toward the door. He probably thought I was leaving, but when I got there I closed it and turned back toward him, my heart thudding.

"You said you aren't going to sit on your ass," I said. "Speaking of your anatomy, I don't like the idea of your fucking Milena Soracco, but I'm setting my self-respect aside right now for more important things."

To say his jaw dropped wouldn't be doing his reaction justice. His face went slack and bloodless, and I could almost hear the gears grinding and shifting in his head as he tried to figure out how I knew.

He opened his mouth to speak, but I waved him away. "Don't insult me with denials or rationalizations. My time is more valuable than that."

I left the room, pausing for a moment at the top of the stairs. My hands trembled like two frightened birds, but I had done it. I didn't think I could be brave enough but, by God, I had done it and on my own terms.

Barbara stood at the base of the steps, a stack of folded laundry in her hands, her gray hair looking more flyaway each day as little spikes rebelled against their bobby pins. I said good morning as I passed her.

She must have known something was amiss because she eyed the upstairs with uncertainty. "I have your clothes."

"Thanks. I'll carry them up later."

I took the stack from her and laid it on the wooden stair step. She looked at it as if I'd set it in a mud puddle, as if the floor weren't as spotless now as our kitchen counters. I smiled cheerfully and walked into the kitchen.

Joel must have been close behind because I heard him say, "Hello, Mother."

I busied myself searching for a Diet Pepsi in the refrigerator, finally locating one in the new pop can holder, stacked alphabetically behind Diet Mug root beer.

Joel's footsteps stopped behind me. "I want to talk to you."

I popped open the can and took a hefty swig. "So talk."

"Not here."

"Yes, here." I was giddy with my newfound power.

"I'm not going to deny it but—"

I felt something drop out of my heart. I realized that, despite the note and despite my intuition, I had been nursing hope I was wrong.

"But it's not an affair," he said.

"What is it then?" I asked softly. "Because whatever it is, I'm feeling like I've been hit in the side of the head by a flying rock."

"It was...an accident, I guess." His face looked contorted, as if he might actually be in pain.

"No, no, no. An accident is where you run a stop sign you never saw and crash into another car. Are you telling me that when you were about to do this you didn't see a red stoplight?"

"I don't know, Delainie. It wasn't like that?"

"How many times?"

I didn't think he'd answer, but after a long pause he said, "Twice."

A coldness came over me. "Okay. You call it a two-night stand, and I'll call it an affair. Do you plan to end it?"

"Yes," he said, his voice low. "I already have."

My throat was as dry as sand. Barbara had slipped away but I hoped she was around the corner hearing this. Her perfect son wasn't perfect. I tipped the pop can toward my mouth and took a swallow.

"I can't understand how you could do this, Joel, especially now. We should be concentrating on Ethan. We should be circling our wagons, joining forces, conserving our ammunition, and doing whatever else people do when times are rough and they need each other. Do you know how many couples with a seriously sick child break up? A pamphlet that social worker gave us said it's about eighty percent. Now, maybe they don't do it right away. Maybe they wait until after the kid's better or worse, but that's how it ends. Is that what you want? We save our son but lose our marriage? Because, right now, it's a real possibility."

He looked up at the ceiling. "That's not what I want."

I poured the rest of the soda into the kitchen sink, opened the broom closet, and tossed the empty can into the recycling bin. "I don't know what I'm going to do. I don't have a contingency plan for an affair. I was foolish enough to think I wouldn't need one."

He didn't say anything, and I didn't want to know what they'd done or where it had happened. Any details and I might lose what little control of my emotions I had left. I put my hand in my pocket and touched the note, my strongest piece of evidence. Having no reason to carry it around anymore, I opened the door under the sink and threw it in the trash.

"Well, then," I said, grabbing the kitchen towel from the counter and wiping off my hands, "I don't think we have anything else to talk about—other than where you're going to sleep tonight."

"I don't want to leave here." His words were barely audible.

I could force him out. I could get a court order or whatever it is people do when they want to get rid of their spouses, but I knew he would go to jail before he'd leave his son and any separation would devastate Ethan. I wanted to yell and cry and swear at him, but I couldn't do that either because Ethan was just down the hall in his bedroom.

I raised my voice slightly. "I think the sofa in our office will be appropriately uncomfortable until we figure out what we're going to do."

He glanced at the doorway. "Don't talk so loud."

"Why? Is there something you're ashamed of?"

"Yes."

He turned and walked out of the kitchen.

———

Joel moved into our office that evening, transferring his clothes to the closet in there and stretching out a sleeping bag on the sunken sofa. He said he would use the bathroom downstairs.

I closed the bedroom door and looked at our vintage double bed that came from an antebellum southern plantation, thinking of the number of times I'd complained he took his share out of the middle. It barely had room for two people of normal size, much less a six-foot, four-inch man and his not-too-tiny wife, but when we snuggled up close we could fit. I peeled back the covers, fluffed up the two pillows and piled them on top of each other.

Thirty seconds after I laid down my head, I realized my face was pressed against the one he'd used. I could smell his scent embedded in the blue ticking and in the worn rosebud pillowcase.

I cried until the pillow was soaking wet, and then I threw it at a nearby chair. That night, I had more room than I'd had in fifteen years, but I was cold and uncomfortable and incapable of sleep. I was surprised by how much he had warmed the bed.

———

The next day I drifted from room to room like a cast member from "Night of the Living Dead." Barbara clearly knew what was going on because she left our clean laundry in a basket at the bottom of the stairs.

At one point, I walked past the living room and saw her sitting on the sofa, with her back to me and her spine as straight as a ruler. Being a chronic slouch myself, I had to admire her posture. I was about to move on when I noticed the top of a head of spiky, sand-colored hair just east of her shoulder and heard Ethan's voice.

"But why didn't Friday think the footprints were his own?"

"Well, I'm not sure," Barbara said.

"Maybe we find out in the next chapter."

"I'll bet you're right."

His head tipped against her shoulder. I heard the rustle of the page followed by her nasal monotone.

Barbara read, "'All this while I sat upon the ground, very much terrified and dejected....'"

I stood there for several seconds, feeling a big thaw in that small segment of my heart labeled mother-in-law.

———

Liz called later that day. "I've pitched the idea to the station, and we're going to discuss it at our two o'clock staff meeting tomorrow afternoon. Can you come to the station around three so that I can introduce you to Jordana Baker, our anchor-woman?"

Eager for the distraction, I said I would. I cleared my throat. "Uh, Liz, I asked Joel if he was having an affair."

"Good girl! And he denied it, right?"

"No. He admitted it immediately."

"Oh." She sounded deflated, as if she'd expected less from him. "I suppose then he said it was over and you believed him."

I let that remark hang in the telephone air for a moment.

"I know you think I should hate him," I said, "but I can't seem to do that."

"I'm not saying you should hate him, but you can't let him get away with this, Delainie. You are angry, aren't you?"

"I'm beyond furious."

Strangely, I didn't sound furious, even to myself. I sounded depleted, too body-worn to wreak revenge on anyone.

"Don't let him get away with it," Liz said again. "He needs to recognize the damage he's doing to you and Ethan."

Did he recognize the extent of it? I wondered.

He came home for dinner that evening, and for the first time in a long while we ate together as a family. Barbara had laid out the blue tablecloth and lined up the matching napkins she must have found in the bottom of the china cabinet drawer. I hadn't seen them in years.

Ethan stared at the one next to his plate. "Are we supposed to wipe our mouths on these?"

"Of course," his grandmother said, "why not?"

"Well, because it's not paper."

I gave him a weak smile. "People use cloth napkins for special occasions, honey."

"Oh." He laid it back on the table.

I looked across at Joel, at his stiffly composed face. He picked up the basket of rolls and handed it to his father. Joel asked Ethan if he'd had a good day and smiled at his description of the Fly. He told me his company was going to be featured in an industry magazine article about their new innovations in video streaming, and I said, "That's great."

I wondered if he felt as crumpled inside as I did.

Midway through dinner, he announced, choosing his words carefully, that he would have to return to the office for a few hours to finish some paperwork. He didn't look my way.

I felt a twist of pain. He'd said it was over, but of course this was how it would be now. Whenever he left during the evening or stayed late at the office, I would question whether he might be meeting her. I could hear Liz saying, "And you believed him," marveling at my gullibility.

The following afternoon, I put on my navy blue dress and stared at the mirror, at the softly draped folds where there used to be bulges. Finally, I'd found a no-fail weight reduction formula, although the price was astronomical. I transferred the contents of my battered brown purse into my one decent handbag and set out for Channel 3 in Seattle. A brilliant July sun shone directly in my eyes as I drove...no, crept through heavy traffic at the base of Queen Anne Hill.

Near the television station, I parked on a side street and walked the three blocks to the shiny new glass-and-concrete building that overlooked Puget Sound. A breeze brought in the briny scent of saltwater.

In the lobby, a receptionist signed me in and issued me a guest badge, and I took the elevator to the second floor. Two painters worked atop a scaffold in the hall. Inside the newsroom, emergency band radios squawked, computer printers clacked, phones rang, and people shouted information back and forth.

Several television monitors suspended high on the walls broadcast Channel 3's programming as well as the competition's, and a dozen or so cubicles rimmed the large open area where most of the activity was happening. The place smelled of coffee and doughnuts. I passed a long lateral file, its top littered with brown-stained paper cups and a cardboard box containing a few sugary remains.

A few yards away, Liz leaned against one of the dividers with her back to me, talking to a sharp-faced blonde with heavy but carefully applied makeup.

"This is political. Martin has it in for me, doesn't he?" Liz asked.

"Martin has it in for everybody. It's nothing personal."

"Well, something is going on."

"Think about it for a moment. What's the problem with this story?"

Liz snorted. "According to Martin, Cassie, and Robert, everything. It's been done before. Time is limited. I should be devoting my attention to that story on Indian fishing rights. But if Martin had okayed it, the others would have gone along. The only one who liked it was Jordana."

"Jordana's looking for an Emmy. She thinks tearjerkers lead to the holy grail." She looked down her nose at Liz. "If you weren't so personally involved in this story, you would know what the problem is. The kid's homely. He's built like a stump, and his ears stick out like Ping-Pong paddles. Unfortunately, he's not ugly enough to be cute, though. Now Martin isn't going to come right out and say those things, so he feeds you these other reasons. But that's what he meant when he said, 'Maybe if you can find a kid who's better looking and more ethnic, maybe Hispanic or African-American.'"

"That callous son-of-a-bitch. Did he tell you that?"

"He didn't have to. Come on, Liz, this isn't radio. Appearance trumps all." She turned slightly and, glancing over Liz's shoulder, caught sight of me. "Can I help you?"

I was already backing up. Even if I had wanted to, I couldn't have spoken.

Liz turned around. "Oh God, Delainie."

I waved her away, then turned, and bolted out of the newsroom.

Liz caught up with me at the elevator, her plum-colored lipstick and thick mascara looking garish against her blanched skin. "Kate wasn't even talking about Ethan, sweetie. She was babbling about another show we're working on that—"

"Please, don't."

She stopped. "She's jealous she didn't get the story."

"It's okay, Liz."

"No, it's not." She reached out and clasped her arms around me.

I couldn't lift my arms to hug her back. The paint fumes in the hall were closing in on me. "I have to go, really I do."

She shook her head so vigorously that her hair swished against my temple.

I covered my mouth and my nose with my hand. "That paint's making me sick."

The workmen were staring at us.

Liz pushed the elevator button. "Let's go downstairs. We can get something to drink in the cafeteria."

"I have to go outside."

She grabbed my hand. "That's right. We should go outside." In the elevator, she punched the lobby button. "They liked the pitch I made for Ethan's story. We just have to work out some of the kinks."

I leaned against the elevator wall and closed my eyes. "Okay."

"Jordana Baker is ready to do it. She loves the idea." She was getting that frazzled look that came when her Ativan wore off.

I took off the guest badge and handed it to her. "I need to go home."

"Sure. Where did you park? I'll walk you there."

"You don't have to, Liz."

She shifted nervously from one foot to the other. "Shit, Delainie, I don't want you to—"

"I'll be okay once I get outside." I turned and hurried out the towering glass doors.

Standing on the sidewalk, I gulped in the salty air. The kid's homely. He's built like a stump, and his ears stick out like Ping-Pong paddles. I would never forget those words.

Chapter 23

My cell phone was ringing inside my purse as I walked in the door. I set my keys on the kitchen counter. It was probably Liz, and I didn't want to hear her repeated apologies and reassurances that Ethan was adorable and everyone would love him as much as we did if only they knew him.

But then it could be the hospital. I dug into my purse and extracted it. It was Cappy.

"I want you to come to my house tonight," she said without preliminaries.

"Oh, gosh." I tried to muster the semblance of a normal tone. "I've got some things I really should do."

"No is not an option. Be at my place at seven o'clock."

I started to protest again, but she'd hung up. Obviously, Liz had been quick to send out the alarm.

"It was awful," she must have told Cappy. "We didn't know she was standing there."

Despite Cappy's command, I wouldn't go tonight. I sighed because, then, they would show up at my door — Liz subdued by repentance, Jaya brimming with concern, Cappy determined to make things happen. They would crowd around me, telling me to forget those shallow fools at the television station. It's a heartless business. Ethan is handsome in his own way. Barbara would stand in the doorway of my kitchen, wondering what had caused all this chaos, and Hal would whistle the entire score of "My Fair Lady." Joel wouldn't say anything but he'd be thinking I should have known the TV thing was too good to be true.

It would be easier to go to Cappy's house.

I decided at that moment I needed to see Ethan, and I needed to put my arms around him.

I found him in his bedroom working on the Fly, testing to make sure the gooey paper he'd layered over the helmet was dry. He was spending more and more time there, too fatigued to play outside with his friends.

He didn't seem to hear me, so I stayed in the doorway for several seconds, studying him. He wasn't built like a stump—in fact, he'd lost weight since that school picture I'd given Liz was taken — and he certainly wasn't homely.

Look at the freckles that fell like pepper across his nose and at that adorable shank of hair that flopped across his forehead the way Joel's did. What about that solid, square jaw? No one thought it was unattractive on John Wayne. The fury rose inside me. Those television people couldn't recognize beauty unless it came in a glossy package.

Ethan had dappled the Fly with gummy lesions and now he was preparing to paint it. There were five small plates from my everyday dishes on his workbench, each splotched with a different color of paint. When he'd used up all of my plates, I would come collect them and carry them to the dishwasher. It was like a search-and-rescue mission because I found them everywhere: under his bed, beneath a stack of clean clothes, stuck to his dirty socks. Once, I discovered Oscar splayed across a plate of blue paint. He stood, stretched, and sauntered off, a vibrant new color added to his orange fur.

"Hello, Ethan Skywalker." I reached over and hugged him as tightly as I could.

"Hi."

I peered over his shoulder at the Fly. "How's it coming?"

"Okay, I guess." He tapped a spot on its head with his finger. "Krishna says I should put a tumor here, but I don't know. I don't want too much stuff on it."

"I agree with you. Less is more."

He turned and gave me a blank look.

"A tumor would be overkill," I explained.

"Yeah, that's what I think," he said in a satisfied tone. Then, his expression turned to annoyance. "Do you suppose you can keep Grandma from coming in here?"

I scanned the room, which looked only slightly tidier than its natural state. "Has she been cleaning it up?"

"Yeah, and I can't find anything. So I have to put everything back the way it was, and that takes time."

"She has good intentions. That was so nice of her to read to you yesterday."

He picked up a tube of black paint and took off the cap. "I think Grandma's sad a lot."

"Why do you suppose that is?" I'd learned questions like this were the psychologically acceptable way to encourage discussion.

"Well, she never gets to do anything exciting. All she does is clean, clean, clean."

He rummaged under the wads of spattered paper towels on his workbench, looking irritated. "Some of my plates are gone. She must have tooken them."

"Taken," I said automatically. He wasn't too sick to learn grammar. "I'll get you another one from the kitchen."

"No." He stood there looking at the jumble, his lower lip stuck out like a shelf. "I don't want to do this anymore. It's stupid, stupid, stupid."

I looked at him in surprise. He was speaking of what had always been his favorite activity. His eyes were glazed, and his mind didn't seem to be tracking the way it usually did. Then I remembered what Taylor had said. We would notice increasing confusion and irritability because his body wasn't metabolizing ammonia as it was supposed to. It was building up in his system, intoxicating his brain. The medication was supposed to prevent that, but clearly it wasn't working as well as it had when he'd first started taking it. Taylor had warned us, but she didn't say how terrible it would be to watch, how it would make my very soul ache.

I wanted my little boy back. I wanted the funny, bright-eyed, mischievous child who played tricks on me. I wanted him to drop plastic scorpions into my congealing Jell-O, hide severed latex hands in my laundry basket, conceal spring-loaded plastic eyeballs so that they popped out of cookie tins. It had been too long since he'd played any pranks or laughed at my jokes. He was the only one who had ever understood them. I missed all of that, and I missed him.

I rubbed his back. "What would you like to have, sweetheart? A bowl of ice cream? A Hershey bar? A Toyota Land Cruiser?"

He gave me a puzzled look, then wriggled away, complaining, "Mo-om."

I spread my hands. "Sorry. I couldn't help myself."

He crawled onto the bed and flopped onto his stomach. "I want to watch TV."

I walked over and switched on his nineteen-inch television.

A big-screen, one that would fill the wall, would make him ecstatic. That's what I would buy him — if only we could afford it. When a "SpongeBob SquarePants" cartoon popped into view, Ethan sat up to watch it, his eyes filming over.

I eased onto the bed next to him, kneaded his small shoulders, and felt him melt beneath my hands. "Does that feel good?"

"Uh-huh."

"Do you remember watching television with me when you were a little boy and couldn't sleep?"

He thought for a moment, then shook his head. "How old was I?"

"About four. You said there were monsters under your bed."

"Guess I didn't like monsters then, huh?"

"We told you they were good, not scary, but you went too far the other direction." I found my hands slipping to the sides of his head, pressing his ears flat. When I realized what I was doing, I jerked back, ashamed.

"We watched late night movies on TV, didn't we?" Ethan said. "Sometimes you fell asleep and snored."

"I did not. That was your dad."

He frowned in thought. "I can't remember what movies we saw."

"There were so many. 'Wuthering Heights,' 'Forever Amber,'

'Casablanca." That's how you learned to give me movie kisses."

He made a face. "Movie kisses?"

"You pressed your lips against my cheek and turned your head the way they did in the movies. We thought that was the cutest thing in the world." I felt a sudden swelling in my throat. "We thought you were the cutest boy in the world."

"Yeah, I remember that."

Chapter 24

I stood in the center of Cappy's living room. "I'm not upset. I'm just saying it's obvious the TV program won't work."

Cappy patted the space beside her on the sofa. "Come on, Delainie. Sit down for a few minutes. Liz says she knows how she can do it."

I plopped down beside Cappy. "Look, it's not right to force my family tragedy on other people."

Liz clasped her hands in a prayerful pose. "We're not forcing anything on anybody. It's a good story and people will want to see it."

"Except for the people at Channel 3." I regretted the words the moment I uttered them.

"I'll say it for the tenth time. I am so sorry you heard that conversation. Kate's a mean-spirited bitch that likes to pretend she knows everything that goes on at the station. Believe me, she doesn't."

I tried to keep my voice neutral; I didn't want to sound accusatory. "Liz, your boss doesn't want you to do it. He must have had some reason."

She gave me a supplicating look. "It's office politics. I swear it has nothing to do with you or Ethan."

Cappy leaned forward in her chair. "I think we can trust Liz's judgment, don't you, Delainie?"

I looked down at the floor. The whole houseboat was swaying to the rhythm of the water. "Yes, of course."

Cappy rubbed her hands together. "Good, that's settled. Now sit down, Delainie, and Liz will explain what she's going to do."

It turned out she planned to write and produce the program on her own time. She had a camera person lined up, and Jordana Baker had already offered to do the interview."

"You know, I'm actually starting to like that woman," Liz said, "and, to tell the truth, this is a much better way to do it. Once they see the finished product, they'll back it completely."

"And if they don't?" I asked.

She grinned. "We'll show them. We'll take it elsewhere."

"How soon can you tape it?" Jaya asked.

Liz looked at me, the same question in her expression.

I wondered what I would be putting Ethan through, if there would be others out there who would see only his protruding ears.

But what was pride under these circumstances?

I grinned at Liz. "You tell me."

She grinned back at me. "I've got studio time at two o'clock on July twentieth. It'll be nice and quiet, just you, me, Ethan, Jordana, and the cameraman. And who knows, maybe Joel will reconsider."

———

The next evening, Ethan walked into the kitchen, clutching his hand to his nose, blood oozing between his splayed fingers, his eyes wide with panic.

I grabbed a dishtowel and clapped it over his nose.

"Barbara!" I yelled. I could see her in the dining room, gripping a stack of plates in her shaking hands. I heard them rattle.

"Tilt your head back, sweetheart," I told Ethan, amazed at the calm in my voice.

It was Tuesday evening around six-thirty. Joel was still at the office, and Hal had gone for a walk. I lifted the towel for a moment and bright red blood gushed from Ethan's nose and mouth.

I pressed the cloth against his nose again, watching the blood seep through it, course down the sides of his face, and splatter the floor. He'd had a few minor nosebleeds in the last few weeks but nothing like this. I pinched his nose. The seconds seemed like minutes. The blood was still flowing.

"I can't get it to stop." I turned to Barbara. "Call 911."

She stood there unmoving, her eyes blinking rapidly.

"Call 911, please!" I said sharply.

She grabbed the phone and, as if from a distance, I heard her give the dispatcher our address. Ethan was looking scared and woozy. After I managed to get him onto the floor, Barbara grabbed a handful of folded kitchen towels from a nearby drawer, and I slipped them under his head. It wasn't until I heard the sirens approaching that the bleeding slowed.

Barbara met the medics at the door, and two men came rushing in. One carried an emergency case that he set on the floor and snapped open. I moved aside. Ethan lay in a pool of blood.

"He...he's got liver disease," I stammered. I was having trouble breathing and forming sentences at the same time.

One medic was taking Ethan's blood pressure while the other packed absorbent material into Ethan's nose. His face was stone gray.

The next few minutes blurred.

Soon he was in the emergency van, sirens sounding and lights whirling against the dark sky. They were taking him to Children's Memorial. I wanted to ride with him, but the medics asked me to follow in my car.

"He's going to be all right," one of them said.

"He's going to be all right," I murmured over and over to myself.

By the time Barbara and I arrived the hospital, Ethan was in the emergency room. We waited in a lounge, staring fixedly at the candy-colored fish in the lighted tank. I was shaking all over, apparently a delayed reaction. Finally, a lean, young doctor came out.

"Mrs. Franklin, I'm Dr. Terry Ervin. We've managed to stop Ethan's bleeding. He's a bit weak, but—"

"He's got Wilson's disease. He needs a transplant."

"Yes, I saw that on his chart."

"I couldn't get the bleeding to stop."

It wasn't my fault, he assured me. It was the illness, causing the tiny blood vessels to burst inside him.

Barbara and I went into the hospital room to see him. His face was pasty white, and his eyes looked as big as coat buttons. A bag of blood hung on a hook on the pole beside the bed. He looked like he had fifteen tubes running in and out of him. Dr. Ervin wanted to keep him for the night so they could do an endoscopy of his esophagus and stomach to determine exactly where the bleeding originated.

I leaned over Ethan. "I'm going to call your father. Grandma will stay here with you, okay?"

"Uh-huh." His eyelids drooped.

I left Barbara there while I called Joel's office from my cell. It rang four times, then switched to voice mail. I tried reaching him at home but got the same result. I called his cell phone number, and his voice, measured and professional, asked me to leave a message. My hands shook almost as much as they did while we were waiting in the lounge for the doctor, but this time I was angry. I left a curt message.

I went back to Ethan's room, where a nurse was tucking him in.

"He'll sleep until morning now," she said with a reassuring smile. "Why don't you go home for a while and get some rest. We'll take good care of him."

I turned to Barbara, who sat on a molded plastic chair like an alabaster sculpture, her hands folded in her lap. Blood splattered her lilac jersey pants and embroidered pullover. I looked down at the patches of blood on my jeans and light blue T-shirt. Even my hands and arms were sticky with it.

I sank onto the chair next to her. "I don't know where Joel is. He said he was going to stay at his office until ten o'clock, and it's only nine. He's not answering his cell phone either."

I was satisfied to see a guilty look flicker across her face. For some perverse reason, I wanted to hold her responsible for her son's behavior. If she had trained him better, he would be standing by my side. In fact, at that moment, I wanted to blame everything on her: Ethan's illness, Joel's tumble off our marital wagon, even the rainstorm that was in our forecast.

"I'm sorry," she murmured, although I hadn't spoken those charges aloud.

I looked at her. What was wrong with me? Poor woman. None of this was her fault.

"I should be the one who's sorry, Barbara." I laid my hand on her arm. "I'm so glad you were with me. I couldn't have taken care of him alone. Thank you for helping."

"He's my grandson," she murmured.

"And you're a wonderful grandmother." I dug my keys out of my handbag. "I'll drive you home. Then I'll come back and stay the night with Ethan."

"All right." She appeared exhausted enough to agree to anything.

———

When Barbara and I walked into the house, Joel was kneeling on the kitchen floor, scrubbing at it with a wet, pink-stained cloth. He looked up with a shell-shocked expression. Hal was standing at the sink, rinsing out an old, tattered pair of my cotton underpants that I used as a rag, squeezing the water out of them with broad hands tanned the color of a leather wallet.

Joel rose to his feet. "What happened?"

"Ethan had a nosebleed that took forever to stop. The medics took him to the hospital."

"How is he?"

"He's getting a transfusion. The doctor wants to keep him for the night. He's going to have an endoscopy tomorrow morning."

"You shouldn't have left him alone, even if he was sleeping."

"Excuse me, but your mother was exhausted, and you were nowhere to be found."

"I was at my office."

"Not when I called." Nothing he did would be above suspicion now.

"I'd probably just gone out to get some coffee."

"You didn't answer your cell phone either."

"I guess I left it on my desk."

There was something about the way he stood there, holding that rag as if he should be wearing rubber gloves to avoid contamination, reminding me of Barbara, and with his dark eyes and long, bony nose, he even looked like her. I'd spent many a minute staring at the mirror, searching for some resemblance to my own mother as I aged, but it never occurred to me that my husband might turn into his mother.

He tossed the rag in the sink and washed his hands like a surgeon suiting up. "I'm going to the hospital to spend the night with him."

"Well, fine. At least I'll know where you are." I regretted the words as soon as I uttered them. I had to stop this nastiness. It would destroy us.

I showered and put on clean clothes, but I could still smell the metallic odor of blood, as if it were in my nose and would remain there for years.

By the time Joel and I drove back to Children's Memorial, Ethan was asleep so Joel and I unfolded cots and stretched out on them. I pulled the hospital blanket over my head. That night, I dreamed blood was gushing from Ethan with no end to the quantity. Nearby, my parents' dismembered bodies bobbed in the Pacific Ocean. Then, I saw all of us — Ethan, Joel, my parents, my in-laws, me — flailing in a red pool, trying to keep our heads above the bloody water.

Ethan and I awoke at about the same time the next morning. To my surprise, the clock on the windowsill said ten o'clock. Joel had already left for the office, taking a cab, but he'd written a note for Ethan, telling him he loved him and would return as soon as possible. He wrote they would work on the Fly when they got home, and he praised Ethan's artistic abilities. He may have failed as a husband but there could be no better father.

Fortunately, I was decent when Dr. Alan Sidon came into Ethan's room, wearing a snow-white doctor's coat and a stethoscope around his neck. His hair and beard were so bushy he might have come straight from the shower. Just looking at him, I felt an adolescent tingle. I'll confess I looked at his right hand. No ring but then some men don't wear one.

He smiled at me. "Couldn't stay away, huh?"

"Not with these five-star accommodations."

He studied Ethan's chart. "Hear you had a pretty bad nose-bleed, pal. How are you feeling now?"

"Okay." Ethan, his face a grayish yellow, lay motionless on the bed, as if he feared any movement might trigger another nosebleed.

Dr. Sidon glanced my way. "And how are you doing?"

There are times when people speak words that have no meaning beyond their surface. His held the weight of some-thing more, although I couldn't have said what it was. I decided he was afraid I might leap at him again and he would have to push me away, embarrassing us both.

I stood straighter. "I'm all right, thank you."

And I realized I was. Hadn't I been calm in the face of Ethan's crisis?

"Good," Dr. Sidon said.

He gave me a long look then. People talk about their hearts missing a beat. Mine skipped an entire measure. Maybe I was fooling myself, but for a moment he seemed to look at me as a woman, not as some young patient's struggling mother. The heat rose to my face.

Finally, he cleared his throat and shifted his attention back to Ethan. He examined him with skilled, gentle hands, while Ethan eyed him warily, an unusual response since he wasn't carrying a needle. Dr. Sidon told him about the endoscopy he would have and said they would try to make him as comfort-able as possible during the procedure.

He wrote a few notes on the chart, then turned to me. "Let me know if you need anything."

I need you right now, I wanted to say. I need you to hold me and reassure me — and, yes, to kiss me and love me. I promise I won't care how guilty that makes me feel. But he was already striding down the hall, a man in complete control of his sturdy frame.

After he left, Ethan stared at the door for several seconds, as if worried he might walk back in.

"Something wrong?" I asked.

"No."

Which meant, of course, I had to guess. "You don't like Dr. Sidon, do you?"

"He's okay."

"What bothers you about him?"

"He's got that fuzzy beard. It looks like a blackberry vine without the leaves."

"I didn't know you were anti-beard."

"I am sometimes."

I used to say that while a few people had six senses, Ethan had at least a dozen. He could sniff out a chocolate chip cookie from fifty yards, not to mention pizza, Christmas presents, and dog-do, which he invariably stepped in. When it came to animals, he was a pied piper, insisting it wasn't his fault they followed him home. He could predict changes in the weather, and his judgments of people tended to be uncannily accurate. Looking at him now, I saw the mistrust in his eyes, as if he had sensed a new threat to his well-being.

———

Ethan had his endoscopy. Around four in the afternoon Joel returned to the hospital, and we had a brief consultation with Dr. Baxter in the hall outside Ethan's room.

"I'm afraid you're going to see more of these bleeds," he said. "The illness is weakening his blood vessels."

"Can't you give him more medicine?" I asked.

"That won't help. The best we can do is give him a transfusion if he loses too much blood."

To our surprise, he released Ethan with instructions to rush him to the hospital if he started bleeding again.

Joel tucked Ethan under a blanket in the back seat of the car. Then he and I climbed in the front and sat like stone statues during the ride home. The problems of our marriage would have to wait.

For the Love of Ethan

Chapter 25

Although Ethan still felt weak, he looked so much better the following day that I began to breathe normally again. Even so, whenever he reached for his nose, I felt a cold hand settle between my shoulder blades.

That evening, I went into our office for a piece of paper, intending to write myself a reminder to pick up refills of Ethan's medicines at the pharmacy. When I heard a cough, I turned and saw Joel standing in the doorway.

I nodded toward the sofa. "I suppose you want to go to bed."

"Not yet."

I tore a slip of paper from the notepad and grabbed a pen. "Well, I'm out of here."

He stepped into the room and closed the door behind him. "Stay for a minute, will you?"

I gazed at a spot on the plastered ceiling. "If you want to talk about something other than Ethan, I'm not sure I can do that without getting angry."

"We have to straighten this out."

"Straighten this out? Now, see, right there it felt like you ran your fingernails down a chalkboard. This isn't something you can realign like a couple of twisted wires and expect it to be fixed on the spot."

"What do you want me to do?"

"I don't know."

I was being honest. I wasn't sure what I wanted from him, or whether it was even possible for him to give it.

"I want our relationship to go back to the way it was before Ethan got sick," he said.

I raised my eyebrows. "Well, that's really surprising because whatever we had then wasn't enough to stop you from having this affair."

"It was never really an affair, Delainie. It was never that serious. She was there and available, and it just happened."

I sat down hard on the edge of the desk. "My God, that is such a lame excuse. In fact, it makes everything worse. You were willing to risk our marriage and our family for something that wasn't even serious."

I thought of how miserable and alone I'd felt that terrible evening at the Stern's party. I thought of how all this tension and anger must be affecting Ethan.

"I'm not trying to defend myself," Joel said.

I turned away. "Only a lovely distraction, huh?" The most pure form of rage I'd ever felt rose inside me. "That's interesting, because Jaya had a different theory. She said you felt impotent because—"

"Impotent?" His face went a deep red. "Christ, have you been talking to your friends about this?"

"Of course. Who else will give me the advice and support I need?"

He strode across the room. "I can't believe you're blabbing everything to your gourmet group. You have no right to—"

"I have no right? I believe we have things turned around here."

"What else do you tell them?" His voice sounded like the hull of a boat scraping on rocks.

"Do you discuss our sex life?"

I gave him an innocent look. "What sex life?"

"Well, great. I would say we've talked long enough."

"No, we haven't." I felt totally calm, even dispassionate. "After Ethan has his transplant, I want a divorce."

"A divorce?" he echoed in disbelief.

I'll admit I'd surprised myself. It was one of those surreal moments when the words that came out of my mouth sounded like someone else speaking. And, yet, they seemed quite sensible, possibly even inevitable.

Maybe marriages are like appliances. They wear out. They break down and can't be repaired. They've outlived their usefulness and it would be foolish to invest anything more in them.

Joel paced the room. "A divorce? It never occurred to me you'd want that."

"What did you expect? Did you think I would bend my head, bite my lip, and soldier on like a good little wife? Or did you think at all?"

"You wouldn't get a divorce. You wouldn't do that to Ethan."

"No, I would do it to you." I opened the door and walked out.

———

In our bedroom, I kicked off my shoes with a fury, and they tumbled onto the floor next to the chest of drawers. He never saw it as anything serious, I muttered under my breath.

Did he really believe that would make me feel better?

I scrubbed every vestige of makeup off my face and brushed my teeth until the toothpaste foamed pink. I shed my clothes and left them in a pile on the bathroom floor. As I reached for my robe in the closet, I caught sight at my unclothed image in the long mirror on the door. For a moment, I wasn't sure it was me. I turned and looked over my shoulder. A rearview vision of my body usually sent me in immediate despair to the freezer for ice cream, but this time I didn't even cringe.

My clothes felt looser but I always wore baggy blouses and pants. I hadn't weighed myself in months, but judging by my reflection I'd lost about twenty pounds. Aside from the plum-colored shadows under my eyes, I looked better than I had in years — maybe, even good enough to attract another man. I pulled on my faded pink cotton nightgown with the hole in the sleeve and lay down directly in the middle of the bed. I couldn't believe he thought a show of repentance and a reasonably sincere apology were all it would take.

He looked shocked when he learned it wasn't. Couldn't I see Milena had snared him with her youth and flashy ways? Didn't I understand how tempting she was? Nothing to worry about, though. He'd always planned to come back to his boring but reliable wife.

Well, I didn't intend to be boring or reliable.

I got out of bed and rummaged through a bureau drawer for a I'd bought it when I was single as part of an emergency kit in case a man stayed over. Once I was married, I'd put it away, thinking it was too pretty to wear and, besides, I didn't have to worry about emergencies anymore.

I found it and held it up.

It was as I had remembered it, the softest pale blue silk I'd ever touched. I used to hope that if my emergency man ever ran his hand over it he might think it was my skin.

Even now, it held a dusky seductiveness. I wriggled out of my cotton nightgown and pulled it on instead. I the onto bed again and lay on my stomach, the silk a glossy film between my body and the sheets. I thought of Alan Sidon then, of what might happen if he were beside me — if he were inside me.

I felt the scrub of his wiry beard, the soft fullness of his mouth and his breath warm on my cheek. I felt his naked body, not smooth like Joel's but furred with hair. He felt damp, as if he'd just toweled himself dry.

He rubbed his fingers across my nightgown and then slid them under the silk. I believe the hands of a doctor are special. They're soft and smooth and trained to feel the body's secrets. I loved the way they grazed my thighs and moved inward.

The heat rose between my legs, until I could no longer lie still. I gripped him hard and jammed my hips against his. He looked at me in surprise, as if he hadn't expected such behavior. I hadn't either.

His eyes grew dark and ferocious. Good, I thought. I wanted him to be a worthy lover. I would be one too. We pawed and scrabbled at each other, and we kissed until my mouth hurt. At one point, I even bit him on the shoulder. I was that passionate, or maybe just angry.

He whispered my name and said all the things I wanted him to say.

I didn't talk and I tried very hard not to think.

Otherwise, I would debate whether what I was doing was

wrong. I don't mean the self-gratification. When I was a teenager, I'd figured out that wouldn't cause my eyes to turn black and fall out of my head. It was the disloyalty to Joel that bothered me. I have an exceptionally low guilt threshold.

And, yet, it had been years since Joel had made love with any enthusiasm, and I'd been naïve enough to believe his lack of desire had nothing to do with me. He was consumed with building his new company. Once his business caught hold, once Ethan got through grade school, once the cost of our modest lifestyle didn't suck us dry, we would have more time for each other. I didn't even see Milena coming.

So, if Alan Sidon or some other man wanted me, I might as well sleep with him. Why not? I had been the good little girl since forever, and look where it had landed me. I'd done all the right things and, still, I had a straying husband and a dying child. What difference would it make if I did some wrong things now? I gripped harder.

Seconds later, the orgasm swept through me, but to my surprise it felt incomplete and ultimately unsatisfying. Somehow I'd lost that pleasure too. I spread my arms across the empty bed and wept a truckload of tears, feeling more hollowed out and abandoned than I had before.

Ethan watched the back door each evening, waiting for Joel to return, maybe worrying that some night he might not. He must have noticed the rolled-up sleeping bag in the corner of the office.

When Joel was home, Ethan latched onto him and held tight. No longer shooting basketball hoops or tossing the football or even working together on the Fly, they spent most nights watching TV from the sofa in the office upstairs. Ethan didn't have the energy for anything else. He nestled under Joel's arm, content to have him near.

I spoke to Joel only when I needed to. He seemed to watch me carefully, probably waiting for me to change my mind. His parents tiptoed around the house.

Chapter 26

I became consumed with the television interview. It was coming up in three days, and every time I thought about it, I trembled. My one salvation, I decided, would be to memorize every fact and figure I could about organ transplantation.

I called Taylor and asked her for information. She gave me what she had and suggested I contact the United Network for Organ Sharing in Richmond, Virginia, for more. Donning my best business voice, I talked to a man there who rattled off horrifying statistics that I wrote on my big pad of yellow paper. But the number that made me weep tears the size of pennies onto the yellow paper was the thirteen hundred who had died waiting for liver transplants during the previous year.

I laid the pencil down on the kitchen table and covered my face with my hands. I would never be able to say that number on television. I would think of Ethan, and I would fall apart. I would forget everything I wanted to say about dying children.

I picked up the phone and dialed Liz's number.

When she came on the line, I said, "Can I use notes?"

"Notes?" She seemed to have trouble picking up the thread of the conversation.

"Crib notes. I'm never going to remember all these statistics about liver transplants. I have a brain like a sieve."

"Don't worry about it, Delainie. You don't need a lot of numbers and, no, you can't use notes. We don't want it to look staged."

"Oh, God, I don't know if I can do this," I said.

"Yes, you can," she said and hung up the phone.

I envisioned the television camera, jeering and taunting me

like a monster in the night shadows.

Liz called back.

"Really, I can't do it," I told her. "I'm basically a shy person, and if you had been paying attention all these years you would know that."

I think she snorted. "You shy? Since when."

"Since Ethan got sick."

"Delainie, sweetie, think of it as a cozy little chat with a woman friend."

"I don't even know Jordana Baker, except on TV."

"You will. She's easy to talk to."

"Has anybody ever fainted on the show?"

"She's never lost a guest yet."

I suddenly remembered something I'd read in the newspaper. "What about the mayor? Didn't he have a heart attack while she was interviewing him?"

"It was a very mild one that happened after the cameras were off. It had nothing to do with Jordana or the interview." The deep breath she drew in was audible. "Delainie, this is your opportunity to tell people they need to become organ donors, that children don't have to die from illnesses like Ethan's."

"I know that. I want to do it, but I'm afraid I'll open my mouth and only the butterflies in my stomach will fly out."

"Okay, let's try a little rehearsal here. What is it that you would like to say?"

I thought of the information I'd gathered. "I want to tell about the thousands of people who die each year waiting for an organ."

"That's good. What else?"

"Um… I want them to know that about eighty percent of transplant recipients survive, even if they were near death before the operation? So they can see these lives really can be saved."

"That's great. Now, see, I've never heard those statistics before, and I'll bet our viewers haven't either. So choose four points you want to make and focus on them, and pretend you're talking to just one person on the other side of the camera, not a huge audience. Delainie, you have a mission here to help Ethan and a lot of other people. You can help save lives, and that's all that counts."

"Yes," I said, feeling the passion rise within me. Maybe I could pull it off after all.

Chapter 27

Three days later, I was in the bedroom, dressing for the television interview with Jordana Baker when Joel surprised me by coming home early from work and announcing he was going with us.

I felt a swell of hope. "To be on camera?"

"No, but I'll do whatever else I can to help."

I studied him. "Liz called you, didn't she?"

His shoulders lifted almost imperceptibly, a lame acknowledgment.

"Well, of course she did. She's worried I'll back out, so she asked you to make sure I got there. But you don't need to look after me. I'm fine."

Of course, that wasn't the least bit true. I'd already thrown up, and now my mouth was dry, and I had drenched the armpits of my favorite navy blue dress because my internal hydration system had gone berserk. I walked into the bathroom and shut the door.

Holding up my left palm, I examined it closely. I had written four numbers on it in blue ink, the statistics I most wanted to emphasize during the television taping. It was a juvenile thing to do, but I wouldn't feel that way when panic struck.

I rounded up Ethan, who was dressed in his only pair of slacks that weren't jeans or droopy cargo pants and a light blue shirt with its collar askew. They were too big but we cinched them with a belt. I'd heard that blue was a flattering color for the camera, and I hoped it would offset his jaundiced skin. I straightened his collar and combed and gelled his cowlicks into submission.

He gave me a worried look. "Do you think they're going me

to ask any hard questions?"

"Whatever they ask, I'm sure you'll know the answers."

We all three piled into the car. I pretended to be on civil terms with Joel, even speaking directly to him once or twice. It might have been a normal family outing if Ethan and I hadn't looked like condemned prisoners.

Liz met us in the busy Channel 3 lobby and led us through the swarm of visitors, delivery people, and staff down a hall to a studio, which she said the station was allowing us to use, whether or not they would broadcast the show. In the center of the room was a platform with a medium blue backdrop, a horseshoe-shaped desk, computers, and monitors. She took us to an interview set located off to the side.

Not one camera but three plus a phalanx of lights pointed toward two maroon easy chairs and a small black lacquered table that sat in front of a Japanese folding screen. Two cups decorated with the station's logo and bottles of water were placed on the table. The coffee emanating from the cups smelled strong enough to prop up any unreliable guest.

Jordana Baker swept in, wearing a pale blue summer suit and looking more petite than she did on TV. She tossed a cheery hello toward no one specific, then walked over to Liz and spoke to her. Despite her small size, she dominated the room with her energy and sugary beauty. Ethan, Joel, and the cameraman all stared at her.

When Liz brought her over and introduced us, she bent down and said to Ethan, "You're a brave boy, and we're going to show everyone how special you are."

Ethan nodded, although I suspected he had no idea what he was agreeing to. Liz hustled him off, and a few minutes later, he was sitting in one of the maroon chairs on the stage. Jordana took her place, and the interview began.

Despite her sympathetic manner, Ethan sat as stiff as a stick and answered her questions in monosyllables. He looked so scared, I ached for him.

My gel job on his hair backfired, and with each passing minute another spike shot straight out. Adding to all that was my fear that at any moment his nose might start bleeding.

After a few more failed attempts at drawing him out, Jordana looked uneasy. "What kind of things do you like to do, Ethan?"

He suddenly came to life. "I like to make monsters."

"Is that right? What sort of monsters do you make?"

"Oh, I make corpses — lots of them — and people with severed arms and legs," he said cheerfully. "Right now, I'm making a giant fly head. It's shiny black with big eyes and sores all over it, and I'm going to spray paint it and stick on pipe cleaners for its feelers. That was my dad's idea, because if you look at a fly under a microscope you can see them poking out. And it's all hairy so I'm going to use broom straws for that."

Jordana blinked and murmured, "Well, that's interesting," but it was obvious she had no plans to peer through any microscope. Nor would she continue this line of questioning.

She shifted in her chair. "Tell me, Ethan, what do you think is going to happen to you?"

"Well, my mom told my grandma...." He paused for breath.

Oh, no, what was he going to say?

"She told her that if I don't get a new liver I could die, but then later she said I would be okay if I worked at getting well."

Now, there was a mother to love. I closed my eyes.

"And are you working at it?" Jordana said softly.

"Yes."

"What kinds of things are you doing?"

"Well, I take a lot of medicine, but the worst thing is I have to eat food like green beans and tomatoes and bananas, which I don't like."

She leaned forward, conveying the message, there are just the two of us here. "Ethan, what's the hardest thing about being sick?"

I figured he would say the bleeds, the stomachaches, or the fatigue, maybe even the teasing from other kids.

He thought for a moment and seemed to forget the camera. His mouth trembled and his eyes glistened. "I hate seeing my mom and dad so unhappy." He paused. "They don't have any other kids, so I'm the only one who can make them feel better. And I don't know how to do that, except to get a new liver."

There was a moment of weighted silence. Then I heard Liz catch her breath. Tears sprang to Jordana's eyes, and she patted Ethan's knee.

I looked at Joel. He was staring at the black ceiling.

———

After a break in the taping, I was suddenly sitting across from Jordana, although I couldn't recall how I got there. Joel had taken Ethan to the cafeteria to get a soft drink. I stared at her unblinkingly, afraid that if I looked at the camera I would break into a thousand insignificant pieces.

She gave me a reassuring smile. "Delainie, tell me how you discovered Ethan's illness?"

Was the camera on already?

I thought she would tell me when we were starting. Maybe she did, and I simply hadn't heard her. I stared at her blankly. What had she asked me?

"How did you discover Ethan's illness?" she prompted.

The memory of the nurse's office at his school kicked in, and I managed to give a mangled description of those early days.

She asked a string of questions then. What caused his disease? What were his symptoms? How far had it progressed? Why couldn't Joel or I be the donors?

I stumbled through the answers.

She leaned forward. "Why don't more people donate their organs after their deaths?"

Now I was safe.

"I don't know why," I told Jordana. "Eighty per cent of Americans say they believe in organ donation, but only forty-two percent of them actually sign up to be donors." I stopped. I had said something wrong, but I couldn't immediately target it. Then it clicked in. "Ninety percent. That's it. Not eighty percent. Approximately, eighty percent is the survival rate if they get transplants. It's ninety percent who say they'll donate organs, but then most of them don't."

Jordana was staring at me, her mouth slightly open. My eloquence must have stunned her.

She sat back in her chair, maybe thinking if she relaxed, I would too.

I straightened up. "One hundred and nineteen thousand people are waiting for organs that would save their lives. More than fourteen thousand of them need livers."

"That's tragic, Delainie. What is it you would most like to tell people about Ethan's illness?"

I wanted to tell about the people who died while waiting for transplants, but now I couldn't remember if it was four or six thousand. I opened my hand and squinted at my sweaty palm, at the blue blur of figures. I couldn't make out any of them. I looked up, straight into the dreadful dark eye of the camera.

"Delainie?" Jordana said.

My breath came faster. Suddenly, a heart attack seemed like a reprieve.

She leaned closer and put her hand on mine. "Tell us what will happen if your son doesn't get a transplant?"

"He will die." It came out on a ragged, shallow breath.

"And there's no question about that?"

"None." I was glad Ethan wasn't in the room to hear me.

"What will it take to save him?"

My heart was beating so hard I felt sure everyone could hear it.

I gulped a few mouthfuls of air. "He could be saved tomorrow if he got a new liver."

I stopped to breathe again. I remembered what Liz had said about pretending I was talking to only one person, not a huge audience. I braced myself and faced the camera. "I don't even know you, but I'm asking for your help. I wish you could see what a gift you or a loved one can give after you die. Can you imagine having the ability to save someone else's life? And it's not just with a liver. The healthy organs from one deceased person can save the lives of as many as eight people."

"Is there such a thing as a living donor?"

I brightened.

"Yes. In the case of a liver, a living person can donate a small portion of it and go on to live a healthy life. It's one of the few organs that will regenerate." I wasn't sure about the small part, but I didn't want to scare anyone.

"I didn't realize there was such a terrible need for organ donation," Jordana said. "Why haven't we heard more about it?"

I began to relax, absorbed with my subject. "Maybe it's because it doesn't have the kind of drama that makes a good story. On the news, you hear a child has fallen into a deep hole. The whole community rushes to help. His photo is shown on every TV station in America. His parents talk about what a wonderful child he is, and tears run down their cheeks. People call in, offering ideas on saving the boy and pledging enough money to send him through Harvard if he survives. They mail him a menagerie of stuffed animals. They wait by the television, holding their breath, during the twenty-four or thirty-six hours it takes to bring him up. They cheer as if this child were one of their own, as if they all had a part in saving him.

"Well, I've got a child who has fallen into a hole. What's happening to Ethan is just as devastating, but hardly anyone knows about it. The doctors are doing a wonderful job, but it feels like some other people are throwing more dirt in the hole. His drugs cost a fortune. The insurance company has a limit on how much they'll pay. We're worried that we won't be able to afford the operation and, even if we can, no one's got an organ to give him anyway." I turned to the camera again. "I felt that if you knew about Ethan and all these other people who need organs, you would care."

I sat back, letting my hands fall to my sides.

Jordana was momentarily silent. Finally, she said, "Is the generosity of strangers your only hope now, Delainie."

"Yes, it will have to be that." I looked at her. "Are you a mother, Jordana?"

The question seemed to startle her. "I have a four-year-old daughter."

214

"Then you can understand how I feel."

Her eyes filled. "I can't imagine losing her."

For the first time in weeks, tears burned my eyes. I reached out and put my hand over hers. "I'm sure she'll live a long and healthy life."

For a moment, Jordana seemed unable to speak. Then she straightened, composing herself. "There must be times when you feel overwhelmed, when you think you can't cope."

I recalled my scuffle with Barbara over the rag. I suddenly understood what she had been trying to tell me.

"We control what we can," I said to Jordana, " even if it's only a scrap of cloth."

She looked puzzled but didn't ask me to explain.

"How has this crisis affected your marriage?" she asked.

I stared at her, realizing this was my opportunity to tell the world about Joel's infidelity. I could say my husband had an affair with a woman who wore a silver jumpsuit and smoked long, brown cigarettes, but I was refusing to play the disgraced little wife. I wasn't going to be Hillary Clinton, standing by her man.

It should be his humiliation, not mine.

I could say how unfair it was that he chose this inconvenient time to abandon us, a time when a sick child needs a strong, intact family. I looked at the darkness behind the lights and saw Joel's shadowy form. I wanted to ask him in front of everyone, how could you do this?

But then I felt my anger slowly drain away. I turned to Jordana. "My husband and I are both frightened. Sometimes we do and say things that hurt each other. That's not how we would like it to be, though. We're still very much in love and we only want what's best for Ethan."

I leaned back against the chair. I had said what I wanted to say.

Chapter 28

That evening, I stood in my old cotton nightgown at the open window of my bedroom. The room was so stuffy I couldn't get comfortable. It wasn't often that Seattle had ninety-degree temperatures in September.

Joel and I didn't speak much on the way home from the taping, but clearly the temperature had shifted in that respect.

Through the open screen, I could smell the fragrance of freshly mown grass and hear someone's sprinkler watering the lawn. How many times had I lingered here, gazing out at the neat rows of houses with their tidy yards and blossoming plants, loving everything I saw?

I closed my eyes. We'd had so many good times together. They flashed through my mind now like a stack of photos.

I wondered how other people managed to walk away from the history of their marriages because, as hurt as I was, I still trusted the goodness in Joel's heart.

I wanted to will myself back to a year ago when life at least seemed sweeter, but then I would have to go through the early stages of Ethan's illness all over again. Perhaps a year from now would be better—but only if Ethan lived. I didn't know where I would be then, but I couldn't be alone.

In the middle of the night, I woke up hot and thirsty, my nightgown feeling like a drenched wool blanket. I opened the bedroom door, intending to go downstairs and get a glass of ice water.

Joel stood in the hall, a dark shadow in the dim light.

"Oh!" I said, startled.

"Sorry, but it's so hot I can't sleep. I thought if I opened the door to the office and you opened this one, we could get a cross breeze."

"All right."

We stood in silence for a few moments.

Finally, I asked, "Do you want to stay married?"

"Of course. I never wanted a divorce in the first place."

I felt comforted that he didn't take any time to think about it.

He took a few steps toward me, into the light from our bedroom. He was wearing his black running shorts and no shirt, and I realized I wanted to touch his arms and chest.

"You're the one who said you wanted a divorce," he said.

"I've changed my mind."

His face looked awash with relief.

"We can't go back, though," I said quickly. "We need to patch up this marriage or—no, that's not what I meant to say. I don't want a patched-up marriage. I want a real one, where people stay together because they love each other, not because they're trapped or doing it for the kids. I don't want a reluctant husband, so if that's what—"

"I love you, Delainie."

The words surprised me. He didn't use them often, so they seemed to come from some other part of the room, from some other man.

"But love wasn't enough, was it? And I'm not buying your whizette as a simple distraction. What was it?"

He didn't answer for a few moments. Finally, he said, "I think I was lost. Or maybe you were lost, and I couldn't find you."

"Did you try hard enough?"

He thought about that for several seconds. "Probably not."

"If you wanted something, why didn't you ask for it?"

He shook his head slowly. "Maybe because I thought Ethan needed everything you had to give. Even if I had known what to ask for, I didn't want to take anything away from him."

He was right. We were both needy, and neither of us had anything left to give the other.

He pushed his hair back with his hand. There were little

grains of sweat on his forehead. "Every time I walked into this house, I couldn't breathe. I felt numb."

And, here, I had felt every single sensation, as if I'd been stripped of my skin.

"Do you miss her?" I asked.

"No. It wasn't how I thought it would be. I wanted it to be simple and uncomplicated. I had this idea I wouldn't have to think. I could just feel. It didn't work out that way. It turned out to be a tangled mess and I never stopped thinking the whole time."

"Does she know why you broke things off?"

"Yes."

"Has she accepted it?"

"She wasn't interested in a long-term relationship, Lainie. She's a free spirit, like we were when we were in our twenties."

He hadn't called me Lainie since the early days of our marriage. I loved the sound of it. He put his arms around me and we kissed. We didn't make passionate love on the nearest flat surface, the way we would once have, but I found myself leaning into him, craving the familiarity of his body.

Chapter 29

E vents happened quickly over the next week. Liz called to say
she'd shown a rough-cut to her boss. She was smacking her
gum at the other end of the line, feeling cocky, I could tell.

"He loved it," she said. "He tried to act as if it was his idea all
along, the bastard."

I started to ask when it would run, but she was already saying, "It's scheduled for next week. I told him that, considering
Ethan's condition, we couldn't wait long."

The following evening, as if to emphasize the need for ur-
gency, Ethan had a nosebleed that gushed interminably. He and
Joel were in the office sitting on the sofa and watching the
video of "Galaxy Quest" for the third time. I wasn't in the room,
but I heard Joel yell, "Oh, God."

Barbara and I were passing each other at the base of the
stairs. Our eyes met, and she said, "I'll get the towels."

I ran up the steps and into the office. Joel was holding a
plastic bowl littered with dead popcorn kernels under Ethan's
chin and trying to pinch the bridge of his nose, while blood
spurted into the container. Barbara came running in with the
towels. It took several minutes to stop the bleeding, and once it
was over, Ethan looked scared and exhausted. Joel's face was
the color of chalk, and I was inhaling as deeply as I could, trying
to find my next breath. Barbara wordlessly gathered up the
messy remains in her trembling arms and carried them off.

I looked at Joel. "Thank goodness you were sitting right
here." I didn't want to say what else I was thinking. What if
Ethan had passed out and bled to death alone in his bedroom

in the middle of the night?

I could tell by his face that he was thinking the same thing. I wiped up a spot of blood on the hardwood floor with my sock-clad toe. "Ethan, sweetheart, maybe we should have you sleep in our bed. Your daddy and I can take turns sleeping with you."

"That's a good idea," Joel said.

"I wish it had room for all of us to sleep in," Ethan said.

He looked expectantly at us, and I realized he was waiting for a response. He knew his father and I weren't currently occupying the same bed, but we're weren't going to acknowledge it.

"My goodness," I said, cheerfully, "I don't think they even make beds that big."

Chapter 30

After we tucked Ethan into our bed, Joel went back to our office. I found him there, rifling through a stack of bills on his desk. The pile was steadily growing.

"We have two hundred dollars left in our account." He sounded defeated. "I don't know where we can cut back, unless we eliminate some basics like shampoo and toilet paper and hot running water. My parents are paying for most of our food."

"The last time your mother went to the store she also bought toilet paper and shampoo, bless her heart."

"Well, then, I don't think we can trim our daily expenses any more than we have.

"Can't we get a loan?"

"Not as long as we have two mortgages on the house. We'll have to sell one of the cars."

"But we can't do that. I need a car to take Ethan to the hospital and clinic. You know the bus system in this city. It would probably require an hour and three transfers to get to—"

"I wasn't thinking of the Buick, Delainie. The only car that's worth selling is the Explorer. I figure we can get eight or nine thousand out of it, and we'd also be saving the cost of maintenance, license tabs, insurance, and repairs. Those things really add up."

"But how will you get to work?"

"Public transportation. I checked the bus schedule, and I can make it to the office with only one transfer."

"But Jaya is organizing a benefit drive for Ethan, and Liz thinks the interview may bring in some donations. Can't we wait and see what happens? Maybe we won't need to sell anything."

He tapped his pencil on the yellow pad. "We have eight hundred dollars in pharmacy bills alone, and that's after insurance has paid its share. We need some money now."

I picked up Ethan's medications at the drugstore so I knew how much they cost. The price on one drug alone was three dollars a pill, and he took three of those a day.

Joel laid his pencil down. "It won't hurt us to sell the car. A lot of people rely completely on public transportation."

"I know," I said, without any enthusiasm.

I also knew that any money we got from selling the car would staunch the flow of expenses about as well as a Band-Aid on a leaking roof. I left Joel sitting there, wearily hunched over the bills.

On the way to our bedroom, I passed a satinwood games table in the hall. I stopped and ran my hand over its surface. Among the antiques I owned, it was one of my favorites.

The frail, white-haired woman I'd bought it from had lived in the same house for her entire married life, all sixty-eight years. Her husband had died six months before, and she was moving to a smaller, more manageable place.

"So the kids won't ship me off to a nursing home," she said, only half-jokingly.

Most of her furniture was modest, but she owned a few exquisite pieces that her grandfather, a sailor, had fashioned entirely by hand without nails. It had precisely notched joints and an inlaid border of contrasting woods and jade he'd collected on his travels. On the underside of the drawer, he had signed his name, Jacob Marshall, and dated it September 4, 1882.

"I wanted to give it to our son," the woman said, "but he and his wife don't like old things. Their home is modern."

Just touching the wood, I could feel the sailor's rough hands sanding it smooth. It was something to cherish, not because of the value it would accrue over time but because of the love that had been rubbed into its very grain. The woman knew the table's worth, and I was happy to pay it.

As I left with the table, I said, "I promise I'll appreciate it as much as if I were your daughter."

That was ten years ago and she'd probably passed away by now. If I sold the table, she would never know. But suppose somehow she did find out. I felt certain she would understand.

———

That night, I woke up and wandered through the house, moving sluggishly, like one of those nocturnal animals you see at the zoo. Oscar trailed me, occasionally attacking my feet.

As I walked from room to room, I ran my hand along our antique furniture: the walnut sideboard in the dining room, the heavy round table that could seat fourteen at Christmas, the matching straight chairs. I didn't need to see them in the light and, in truth, I didn't even need to feel them. I'd long ago memorized every nick and groove.

I ran my hand across the rim of an eighteenth century silver bowl that had been one of my early purchases. I knew its cool, smooth metal by heart and would always know it whether I was able to touch it or not.

Maybe my father was right. You need to start fresh once in a while. After Joel left for work the next morning, I called Jaya. "I have to move some things. Could I borrow your van for the day?"

"Sure. Want to borrow me too?"

"Yeah, I'd like that."

She pulled up to our curb forty-five minutes later, wearing jeans, an old University of Hawaii sweatshirt, and a scarf to hold back her hair. I was waiting on the front porch.

She hopped out of the van. "So what are we moving?"

"Just some smaller antiques today. I'll see if I can get some dealers to pick up the larger ones. I figure it's faster and easier to sell them to individual shop owners than to try to arrange an auction. Besides, I know which dealers I can trust to pay a fair price."

She actually turned pale. "Why are you selling your antiques?"

"Because we need the money."

"But Rob and I are organizing a benefit drive for you. I'm almost finished drafting the letter, and Rob's going to look it over this weekend. We're asking for donations from everyone we know, and that's a lot of people, Delainie."

"And we will be eternally grateful, but we need some money right now."

"We'll loan it to you."

"Thank you, but no. We might never be in a position to pay it back."

"That's not a problem. We can afford it."

"I know but we can't. I'm afraid it would take something away from us that we need right now."

I tried to think what that was and finally decided it was our pride.

She looked at me sideways. "How does Joel feel about selling the antiques?"

I pondered her question for a moment, then managed a weak smile. "He doesn't know."

"Oh, Delainie."

"Actually, this has nothing to do with Joel. I'm doing this for Ethan—and for my father."

She gave me a puzzled look. "But your father passed away."

"Well, I know that, but I'm a slow learner about some of the things he tried to teach me."

Barbara watched in shock as Jaya and I carted the items from the house to the van. A few minutes later, Hal came out to help.

At one point, he was carrying a sewing basket that was more than two hundred years old when I passed him in the front yard.

He held up the basket and examined it. "My mother had one that looked a lot like this. Came from her aunt." He shifted his gaze to me. "Are you really sure you want to sell all these things? I mean, if you're doing it for the money, we could help out a bit."

I stopped to look at him and realized he had a small scar at the corner of his mouth and another alongside his nose. I'd never noticed them before. I laid my hand on his arm. "Thanks, Hal, but you've already done plenty, and we appreciate it."

Although I left Ethan's room intact, all the activity roused him from his lethargy.

"What are you doing?"

"Cleaning house," I said cheerfully. "Now I know why your grandma likes to do it so much."

He stared at the nearly empty dining room. We'd moved the furniture into the living room, closer to the front door.

"What are we going to use for a table?" he asked.

"We have an old door in the basement that we can put on some sawhorses. We'll throw a tablecloth on it, and it'll work just fine."

———

After Jaya left, I sat on the front steps to drink a glass of lemonade and rest. The sun had warmed things up, and I was damp and sticky. Although it was almost six o'clock, the temperature was close to eighty degrees. Up and down the street, roses were blooming. I could smell the heavy sweetness of an especially fragrant bush under our living room window. It reminded me of sachets my grandmother used to make out of lace and dried rose petals.

I looked up and saw Joel, carrying his suit coat over his shoulder and his briefcase and walking rapidly down the sidewalk toward our house. He stopped a few feet from me. His face was flushed from the brisk walk, but he appeared far more relaxed than he had the night before.

"I guess you sold the car, huh?" I asked.

"I took it to a dealer on Aurora Avenue, a friend of Jin's. He gave me ninety-five hundred for it. That's actually very good. That's the first time a dealer's paid me what I thought my car was worth."

He set down his briefcase. I scooted over, and he lowered

himself onto the step. "Walking up that hill from the bus stop is good exercise."

"You're going to miss the car when it rains."

"I'll get used to it. If I need a car at the office, I can borrow Jin's." He reached over, plucked a string from my hair, and shook if off his fingers. "What have you been doing, knitting dental floss?"

"I was moving furniture."

He gave me a puzzled look. "Why?"

"Two antique dealers are picking up some of our larger pieces of furniture tomorrow. That's why they're sitting in the middle of the living room." I grinned. "The furniture, not the dealers."

He stood, walked to the door, which was ajar, and opened it. I'd emptied the drawers from the china cabinet and the bureaus and piled our personal belongings in boxes. The whole place looked as if we might be moving out for good any day. He looked inside for several moments and then came back to where I was.

"Are you selling all of them?"

"No, only the more valuable pieces — and as many of the smaller antiques as I can get rid of. Jaya and I drove from shop to shop today, and I managed to unload a lot of those. We used her van."

"But that looks like almost all of them."

"We still have the beds and the lumpy sofa upstairs, and I kept your grandparents' dresser in the guest room."

He sat beside me again and took my hand, stroking it tenderly. "I can't believe you've done this," he said in a low voice. Those antiques were going to be for your shop. Selling them was a last resort."

I looked at him. "It's strange. I feel like I don't need them anymore. Maybe I'll try my hand at gardening after Ethan's well. I've always loved plants."

"After Ethan's well, you're going to wish you hadn't done this."

I thought about that. He was wrong, though. I knew I would have no regrets whatsoever.

I leaned over and kissed his cheek.

There were some things that didn't sell and some I let go below their value, but there were a few surprises too. Years ago, I'd bought a framed painting for fifteen dollars at a garage sale. Only eighteen-by-twenty-four inches, it showed a prim young woman sitting stiffly on a blanket near a pale blue lake. Her clothing and hairstyle told me the period was the nineteen thirties, but otherwise I knew nothing about it and very little about art in general. I bought it because I felt sorry for the young woman, who looked repressed and miserable. It turned out that some well-known artist (although I didn't recognize his name) had painted her. She brought in two thousand dollars.

After two frenzied weeks, I deposited $38,260.00 into our checking account, far more than I'd ever expected. The Pairpoint lamp sold for thirty-five hundred dollars.

Chapter 31

I was scared to look at Ethan now. His skin had taken on a greenish hue. I forced a cheerfulness I didn't feel, and the worst thing was he knew. Once, after I'd babbled breezily for several minutes, just to fill the air with sound, he looked at me with eyes that seemed suddenly old.

"It's all right, Mom," he said. "You don't have to try so hard."

No, it wasn't. It wasn't the least bit all right, but I didn't argue.

The television interview was scheduled to air the following evening, but he was so exhausted he didn't show any interest in it. Jaya, Rob, Cappy, and Jin were coming over to watch it with us. Liz had to be at the station but said she would call immediately afterward.

Joel set the TV set on the floor in the living room and switched it to Channel 3. The story would come at the end of the six-thirty-to-seven-o'clock time slot — three million viewers, more or less, Liz said.

Cappy arrived with Port and several bottles of wine. Oscar, who was sacked out on top of the TV, took one look at the three-legged dog and went back to sleep. Jin came bearing some fancy-labeled cognac called Remy Martin XO and a chocolate and raspberry torte he'd picked up at the Linger Longer Bakery. Jaya and Rob brought a basket filled with deli pasta salads, grilled chicken breasts, cheese, and bread. Joel's parents joined us, and we sat on blankets as if we were on a picnic.

Joel bundled Ethan in a sleeping bag and pillow, and Jin popped a gold paper crown on Ethan's head, saying, "You're the king, my man."

Ethan grinned and snuggled in. By the time we'd returned to the living room with our filled plates, his eyes were closed and he was breathing with a light wheeze.

"Should we wake him?" Jin said.

Joel and I said "no" at the same time. I was glad he'd fallen asleep. I didn't want him to hear some of the things I'd said during the interview.

When Jordana Baker appeared on the screen, everyone stopped eating. The interview flowed smooth and seamless, although they'd cut most of what we'd said. I noticed they'd left out the part where I'd babbled incoherently. Jordana wore her sunny beauty and interviewing skills well, and Ethan radiated sweetness, although it was clear he was ill and fatigued. When he answered Jordana's question, "What's the hardest thing about being sick?" I could hear Jaya sniffling. After the program ended, we remained where we were, hushed, the way people are after a movie in a darkened theater. Finally, Joel got up and switched off the TV.

Cappy struggled to her feet and leaned on her cane. "If that doesn't do something, I don't know what will."

Jin looked at me. "You were terrific. I know Joel's proud of you."

"Thanks." From the corner of my eye, I saw Joel pick up Ethan and carry him upstairs to our bedroom. My husband had changed in the last few days. He moved easier and his face looked more relaxed. I leaned closer to Jin and asked in a low voice, "How much did you give your car dealer friend to over-pay Joel for the Explorer?"

"You know I'd never do that."

I gave his hand a squeeze. "You're a good person, Jin."

I joined Jaya and Cappy, who were in the kitchen cutting the torte and laying the slices onto my chipped and scarred every-day plates. I'd sold my good china. I had used it only for weddings, funeral receptions, and the turn of each century anyway. As I reached for the paper napkins, I glanced at the clock. Fifteen minutes had passed since the program had ended.

Cappy followed my gaze. "Liz will call any minute. She probably got caught up in whatever they do after a program."

We ate our dessert on the living room floor and were drinking Jin's brandy from juice glasses when the phone rang. I picked it up and heard Liz's breathless voice. "Sorry I couldn't call earlier. The phones haven't stopped ringing."

"That's okay. I know it's busy there."

"No, Delainie, you're not getting it. We're being flooded with phone calls about the program. We have six people with Ethan's blood type who want to donate parts of their livers to him. We actually had one woman who wanted to donate part of her husband's although she hadn't asked him yet. Other people are asking where they can send money for Ethan's transplant."

"Oh, my God."

Jaya was poking me. "What's she saying?"

"Six people want to be donors for Ethan."

She turned and repeated what I'd said to the others. Soon they were making so much noise I was having trouble hearing Liz. I caught the tail end of "...people are asking how they can donate their organs for transplantation when they die."

I could tell she was crying, but then so was I. I heard her turn away from the phone and thank somebody. When she came back, she said, "We'll start sorting out the volunteers tomorrow. In a few weeks, Ethan should have his transplant."

I wondered if it could possibly be that easy.

———

After everyone else had gone to bed that evening, I closed up the house and walked up the stairs. As I neared the top landing, I heard a squeak on the floorboards. Joel was standing in the dark outside our bedroom door, his hands jammed in his terrycloth robe. I could barely make out his face in the dim glow of the Tasmanian devil nightlight.

"I turned everything off downstairs," I whispered. "Are you going to get something?"

"No. I was waiting for you."

He took a few steps toward me and pulled me into his arms. I moved willingly.

I suppose I'd been waiting too.

"You are the smartest, bravest, most generous woman I know." He ran his hands down my nightgown and kissed the curve of my neck.

I gestured toward the bedroom. "Ethan's asleep in our bed."

"Uh-huh." He cupped my breasts in his hands. "Let's go into the office."

"It has that sunken sofa."

"Yes, I know, but it doesn't have Ethan on it."

Chapter 32

The days after the interview surged in a way that reminded me of the surreal time in the hospital when Ethan was diagnosed. We were on one of those inflatable rubber boats hurtling through churning rapids on an unfamiliar river. Before the TV appearance, things weren't happening fast enough; now they moved too fast.

Channel 3 received more calls over the next few days. They even ran a little spot on the evening news, telling people where they could send contributions. The manager at our local grocery store shook Joel's hand and said he'd received permission to put little donation containers at each checkout counter. *The Seattle Times* called, asking if they could interview us and take photos. They ran a feature on Ethan, which brought even more contributions to his fund. Afterward, one of his classmates from school stopped by, asking if Ethan would autograph the newspaper clipping.

Liz said a few more people called to offer segments of their livers, but some of them were obviously wacky. Oprah never did contact us, but one of the networks ran the interview, bringing in more contributions and potential living donors. We decided to limit potential transplant donors to the Pacific Northwest region so that we could arrange for proper screening. My God, we suddenly had hope.

Liz was sailing high. She called twice a day, updating me. "We've got all the physical information and health histories on the prime candidates like your transplant coordinator suggested. Do you think we can get her to sort through these with us and narrow down the list?"

"I'll call Taylor Buchanan this afternoon."

Taylor was happy to help. Three days later, Liz and I were in her office watching as she pared the list. Most of them had to be turned down for reasons ranging from old age to medical concerns of their own. One young woman who took a bucketful of pills for diabetes applied, bless her heart. She apparently hadn't heard what I'd said about perfect health. Taylor narrowed the list down to four.

"How often does a stranger become a living donor?" Liz asked her.

"It's rare. There are a couple of cases where unrelated donors have stepped forward. A few years ago, a middle-aged man gave part of his liver to a young mother he'd never met before. She survived and is doing well. Most transplant organs still come from cadavers or family members or people taken off life support because they're in a vegetative state. For a whole liver to be extracted, the donor must be brain dead."

"So that's another way a liver might come through for Ethan," I said.

"Don't get your hopes up quite yet," Taylor said gently. "As you've already learned, there are so many things a donor has to have."

"Such as?" Liz asked.

"Such as the position of the donor's vasculature, which is why Delainie couldn't be a candidate. And there can be psychological concerns. The psychiatrist who interviews the living donor may find he or she has an idealized vision of what's going to happen. They may not recognize the dangers and long-term consequences to their health."

"Can we have more people examined if none of these candidates work out?" Liz asked.

"It costs thousands of dollars to put someone through the full workup. Delainie's insurance covered her, but I would be surprised if it will pay for the others."

I looked at Liz. "It's this one chance or nothing. We'll need the rest of the money for Ethan's care."

"Don't worry. This will work."

⸺

I sent a personal thank you note to all those people who had offered my son a part of themselves, careful not to let my tears drop on the writing paper. I couldn't possibly answer all the letters that came with contributions. There were even a few hand-scrawled missives from children, along with nickels, dimes, and dollars. Liz said I could express our appreciation on a follow-up program.

The four potential donors we chose had near-spotless medical histories, limited to such problems as broken bones, childhood ear infections, and athlete's foot. I wanted to be that healthy.

Taylor stacked the various materials we'd acquired. "Have them call for appointments with their own doctors for preliminary exams. When we have those results, we'll choose the best candidate and do a complete workup here."

Taylor gave me a reassuring look, and I felt a rush of excitement. "We'll contact the donors this evening."

⸺

Joel helped make the calls, managing to conclude his two within a few minutes, while mine lasted almost an hour. One of the men told me in agonizing detail how his daughter took three years to die of leukemia at the age of nine. I knew he needed to pour out his own grief, but I was shaking by the end of our conversation. The second person I spoke to was a young woman who worked at a preschool. She was twenty-three, unmarried, and childless. I glanced at the photo she sent with her medical history — a guileless face surrounded by a halo of pale curls, born a natural blonde, I was sure.

"I love children," she bubbled along. "Someday I'll find the right man and we'll have our own."

"Is that why you want to do this? Because you love

children..." I glanced at the name on the paperwork. "Sotalia Johnson." Unusual first name.

"Oh, yes. And because healthy people have to help those less fortunate, don't you think?" Her voice was sweet and suffused with youthful idealism.

"You do realize this is major surgery with serious risks?"

"I certainly do. I've done some research on it."

I was glad to hear her tone turn solemn. Maybe she wasn't as flighty as she had originally sounded.

"But," Sotalia continued, "I have to live with myself. I wouldn't be able to do that if I could save Ethan and didn't."

I had to restrain myself from immediately inviting her to our home for dinner. I already felt connected to her, and if she became the donor, I would ask her to join our family, maybe even become a member of my gourmet group.

If a part of Sotalia were inside Ethan, how could we not adore this young woman? After I hung up, I looked at her picture again, at her fine ivory skin and hazy filaments of golden hair, at the muted rust shade of her blouse. Perhaps I had been wrong about God not answering my prayers. I'd expected a direct, hands-on approach, but maybe he'd sent an angel instead.

Liz sat across from us in our living room. I was in one corner of the sofa we'd brought down from the office. Joel sat on the floor with Ethan, who held a grubby yellow, stuffed Pikachu with pink flashing cheeks, a remnant of his early childhood.

Along with a splashy orange dress, Liz was wearing her eager, high-energy look. "Martin wants to follow your story all the way through Ethan's transplant."

Joel raised an eyebrow. "Like an ongoing soap opera?"

"With more action though." If she'd detected any criticism in his remark, she didn't show it. "People want to know what happens next."

"How many appearances will it take?" I asked.

"Oh, four or five maybe," she said cheerily.

"Doing what exactly?"

Liz brushed back a sheaf of her blonde hair. "On this next one, we want all three of you."

I looked at Joel.

"It's up to you," he said. I decided it was a gesture of repentance.

"I would like you to be there."

Liz's head swiveled back and forth between us.

"All right," he said.

Liz leaned back with a satisfied smile. "Well, good. We're also bringing in the four finalists and—"

"You make it sound like a contest," Joel said.

She grinned, her gaze flicking toward Ethan. "They are winners, aren't they, big guy? After all, we chose them to help you. Anyway, we'll have you and the wannabe donors, and Jordana's going to conduct a group conversation, inquiring about their motivations and asking Ethan how he feels about — about various things."

I wondered if she would ask how he feels about living with a piece of someone else's body. I suppose it was our own little taboo, but we'd avoided that subject. I don't think Ethan wanted to talk about it either, because he moved his Pikachu across Joel's arm, the stuffed creature making strange little squeaking sounds and with Ethan engrossed as if he hadn't heard a word we'd said.

Joel pulled Ethan in tighter. "What about these other people? Has anybody asked them if they want to be on TV?"

"We have, and we've gotten a generally positive response from them."

"But not universal?"

"Well, no," she conceded. "One of the men said he didn't like the idea of it."

"Why not?"

Liz made a flighty little gesture. "Oh, he said he wasn't doing it for the publicity, but we said we weren't either."

I looked at Joel and he smiled back. So what if that was an outrageous lie.

Chapter 33

For the next interview, seven of us formed a semi-circle on the stage. Ethan, Joel, and I sat to Jordana Baker's left. The others, two men and two women, were at her right. Liz was giving them instructions on where to look and how to relax. This time we were taping in a cavernous studio, rimmed by cameras, cables and lights.

I studied the transplantation candidates, who all had type B blood and appeared glowingly healthy. Next to Jordana sat Rick Andover, thirty, a big, brawny machinist who looked as if a pinch of his liver would be enough to save Ethan. Joy Glaze, a twenty-nine-year-old software programmer whose serious personality reminded me of Cappy, sat beside Rick. Then came Sotalia, the effervescent preschool teacher, and Bob Unger, the owner of a landscaping business. Bob, the oldest at forty-one, was the one who didn't want to be on TV. He'd told Liz he would participate only if he didn't have to talk much.

The camera started rolling. Jordana introduced all of us, then turned to Ethan, who was looking uncomfortable. I understood completely because I felt nervous about going before the camera again.

"And what do you think of these wonderful people offering to give you a part of their livers?" Jordana asked.

He opened his mouth and promptly coughed up his meal, along with a spattering of blood. The only fortunate thing was the contents landed mostly in his lap, with just one spot on Jordana's celery-colored suit. The others stared at him in horror while he looked at me with wide, desperate eyes. I reached for him, but Liz intercepted me and scooped him up. And this was a woman who'd boasted she had never changed a baby's diaper and never would.

"It's all right, honey," she said, bustling him off the stage.

Joel rushed after her and took Ethan into his arms.

Liz stood there, her hands at her sides, her silk blouse now streaked multi-color. "Should we get a doctor, Delainie?"

"I'm okay," came Ethan's weak voice.

Joel sat on a chair and pulled Ethan on his lap. "Is your stomach cramping?"

"No."

"Maybe you should take him home," I said.

Ethan vigorously shook his head. "I want to watch."

There hadn't been much blood. Or maybe I was just getting used to these periodic ruptures.

"If he throws up again or starts to cramp, I'll drive him to the hospital," Joel said.

I looked at Liz.

"Whatever you want, Delainie."

"We'll see how it goes. Ethan, promise you'll let us know if you feel sick again."

He nodded, and I walked back to the stage and sat down. The transplantation candidates eyed me uneasily.

"I'm sorry, but it's part of the disease," I told them.

A shaken Jordana cleared her throat. "Okay, let's start again."

She had thrown a lovely scarf over the upchuck spot. She turned a brilliant smile on me and launched a series of questions: How did I feel about this munificent outpouring from strangers? What was the next step? Update our audience on Ethan's condition. How would the doctors determine who was the best possible donor?

So many friends had made these same inquiries that I could rattle off my responses without thinking. Ethan sat on his chair hunched over, not looking at the camera.

"All this must be so tiring," Jordana said.

"We're tired but grateful."

She turned to the transplantation candidates. "And, you incredible people. This goes way beyond common generosity. What made you do it?"

Each recounted some variation of feeling a compulsion to help Ethan. Bob, the one who had lost his daughter to cancer, identified with our fear and anguish. Rick stammered something about a religious commitment and his need to rise above his sins.

Jordana shifted uncomfortably. "I see."

I worried that Rick wouldn't make it past the psychological interview.

The quietest person turned out to be Joy, who had no children of her own but couldn't sleep the night of the broadcast until she had volunteered to be a donor.

"And have you had any trouble sleeping since then?"

"None," she said with a gentle smile.

Although Sotalia's motives for helping weren't much different from the others, she was the star. Vibrant, eloquent, and attractive, she competed with Jordana attention — to the extent that Jordana seemed reluctant to call on her after the first round of questions. No problem. Sotalia slipped into the conversation through such openings as, "Interesting you should ask that because...." More than once, I saw Jordana frown at her, but Sotalia's warmth and enthusiasm were so infectious she had most of us mesmerized.

Later, as we left the studio, Liz said, "The camera loves Sotalia. Jordana doesn't, but you wait and see. The TV audience will be rooting for her to be the donor."

I almost reminded Liz it wasn't a contest, but I didn't want her to think we didn't appreciate all she had done.

On the way home in the car, Ethan was unusually quiet.

I sat in the back seat with him while Joel drove. "Feel like you're going to throw up again, sweetie?"

"No."

"Tired then?"

"No."

I hesitated. "You're worried, aren't you?"

He fixed his attention on people walking past the shops at

the base of Queen Anne Avenue. Finally, he said, "I guess."

"About the price of tea in China?"

He gave me a quizzical look. "What tea?"

Joel said, "It's an expression that means we want you to tell us why you're worried."

"Oh." He looked out the side window again.

I worked myself up to a smile. "What's bothering you, Ethan Skywalker?"

After chewing on his lower lip for a time, he said, "I was thinking about those people who want to give me their livers. I'm scared it's going to make them sick."

"Has anybody ever told you that you're the kindest, most compassionate son two parents could have?"

"Just you. Except you don't usually say that funny word."

"Compassionate?"

"Yeah."

"That means you care about other people," Joel said.

"Like now," I added. "Only someone who is compassionate would be worried about others when he's having his own problems."

He looked down at his hands. "Is it bad to worry about me too?"

"No," I said gently, "it isn't the least bit bad."

Chapter 34

A few weeks after the transplant candidates had their preliminary medical examinations, Taylor called to tell me Sotalia Johnson had been chosen to go through the entire workup. Our insurance company wouldn't pay for it. The thousands of dollars would have to come from the fund Jaya and Rob had set up for Ethan.

After I hung up with Taylor, I phoned Joel. "The doctors chose Sotalia Johnson."

"Oh, her." He sounded disappointed.

"You don't like her, do you?"

"She's annoying, but then it's not a popularity contest. Did you tell Ethan yet?"

"He's sleeping, but I will, the moment he opens his eyes."

"Delainie, let's go out and celebrate tonight, just the three of us."

"Where?"

"Morningtown Pizza?"

That had been the place in the University District we frequented when we were young and broke and Ethan was a baby. I wasn't sure I wanted to return to a place with such strong memories of better times.

"Is the restaurant still there?" I almost hoped it wasn't.

"I passed it last week."

"Okay, then," I said reluctantly.

I should have been happy. Finally there was hope for Ethan, and our marriage was recovering. But I couldn't bring myself to trust happiness anymore.

After I hung up the phone, I went to Ethan's room and sat on the edge of his bed. I watched his eyelids flutter as though he were fighting some dream battle. His skin still had an ashen undertone. He had lived with this illness five months now — more, if you counted the time before his diagnosis. It was already the second week in October and school had started. We didn't send him, of course, and he hadn't protested. He would turn eleven in a few weeks, but he wasn't interested in having friends over for a party.

I looked around his room. Barbara had agreed to stay out of it, but it was nowhere near its usual condition. He no longer had the energy to mess it up. The Fly sat in the center of his workbench, but its grotesque form had barely changed. I told myself that if he finished it — when he finished it, I would display it in the living room. I stared at the creature now, wondering if I would someday cherish it the way I did his preschool works of art.

I laid my hand on his forehead and his eyes opened.

"Good morning," I said softly.

"Hi." His throat sounded dry and scratchy.

"I have something exciting to tell you. Remember Sotalia Johnson, the pretty lady who offered to be a donor?"

"Uh-huh."

"She's going to give you some of her liver? Isn't that nice of her?"

"Uh-huh." His eyelids dropped like window shades, then opened a few seconds later. He gave me a startled look. "I wasn't dreaming, was I?"

I kissed his forehead. "No, baby, you weren't dreaming."

He smiled and turned on his side. Tears slipped from his eyes.

I couldn't reach Liz or Jaya to give them the news about Sotalia, so I left phone messages. When I told Cappy, she suggested we get together that night and celebrate. For the thousandth time in my life, I wanted to be two people: the wife and mother who would spend the evening rejoicing with her husband and son. And the woman who could rejoice with her friends.

"Joel and I were thinking of taking Ethan to one of our old haunts we used to frequent when he was a baby and we were poverty-stricken," I said.

"Go, then. That will be good for you," she replied softly.

If her feelings were hurt, she didn't sound like it.

A few days later, we learned that Sotalia had skated through the workup. Her vasculature was exemplary, her test scores worthy of a Rhodes Scholar. That night, I celebrated with the group.

27

Ethan's transplant operation would involve two hospitals. One lobe of Sotalia's liver would be removed at University Medical Center and transported the six miles to Ethan at Children's Memorial, where another medical team would take out his diseased liver and replace it with Sotalia's healthy lobe. For both of them, the partial livers would regenerate to normal size.

Liz, Sotalia, and I were seated around a small conference table in Taylor's office, discussing the surgery date.

"We're going to have to schedule this a little further out because of the arrangements with University Hospital," Taylor said. She scanned the wall calendar. "How does the first week in November sound?"

Sotalia studied her iPhone calendar and then looked up. "I want to go back to Ohio for Thanksgiving. Will that give me enough time to recuperate?" She was subdued and soft-spoken compared to the animated woman she'd been in front of the camera.

"You should be able to travel by then."

"And my birthday is on November 6th."

"Okay," Taylor said. "How does November 7th sound to you?"

I looked across the conference table at Sotalia.

"Excuse me?" she said.

"November 7th for the operation. That's a little less than three weeks from now."

"Oh, yes. As soon as possible." I said.

Sotalia was still perusing her calendar. "I suppose that's okay although I won't have much of a birthday celebration."

After entering some notes in her phone, she and Liz talked about television coverage of the surgery. Liz was lobbying for filming the entire operation. Sotalia and I had given our permission, but Taylor wanted only minimal coverage in the operating room. They were going back and forth on various points and making little progress from what I could tell.

I stared out the window at the clay-colored sky and the rain streaking the glass. Ethan had awakened today with a skin rash, probably a reaction to an increase in one of his medications, although it had become difficult to sort out the cause of any new symptom. He was taking a medley of drugs now, some of this, a little of that with frequent changes and additional medication to control the side effects.

When it came to drugs, I felt I wasn't taking enough of them. The last time I was at the hospital, I had taken Taylor aside.

"Um, do you think you could get someone to prescribe me a few sleeping pills?"

"You should go to your own doctor, Delainie."

"I plan to do that, but in the meantime—"

"Make an appointment this afternoon," she said gently.

"Okay," I said, knowing I wouldn't.

Sotalia shifted in her chair. "When will we have our next newscast?" In her crisp, polka dot navy blue dress with a crocheted collar, she looked as if she'd stepped right out of a convent.

There was an awkward silence.

"Not sure yet. I'll have to talk to the news director about that," Liz said.

After studying the dates on her calendar, Sotalia gave Liz a generous smile. "Well, we should schedule it soon. I need to get it on my calendar. Will you let me know within a day or so?"

"As soon as I know," Liz said breezily.

Liz and I glanced at each other, and she raised her eyebrows.

A few days later, Ethan was so sick with stomach cramps and periodic bouts of throwing up that he never made it out of bed. We didn't take him to the hospital because times like this were becoming almost routine. We dosed him with as much medicine as he was permitted and hovered over him. By evening, he was feeling better, but he was so depleted he sank into sleep as if he were falling into a mountain of feathers.

Joel went downstairs to get something to eat, while I stayed with Ethan. I pushed the hair back from his forehead and whispered our mantra, "It won't be long now, sweetheart." His eyelids fluttered, s if he were tracking the frames of an action movie. Not even the jangle of the phone woke him. When I picked it up, Liz was on the line.

"Everything okay?" she said. "You sound exhausted."

"Ethan had a marathon vomiting episode, but he's sleeping now. You have no idea how reassuring it is to know this will be over soon."

"Yes, well...that's why I'm calling you."

"Is there a problem?" I could barely utter the words. It didn't take much to trigger my anxiety these days.

"Now, don't worry. It's nothing serious. I talked with Martin about doing another program before the transplant, and he thought it was a great idea. Except he wants me to do a segment at the hospital, with Jordana interviewing Taylor and the doctors, maybe showing them with Ethan. We haven't done any of that yet."

"It's all right with me if Ethan's up for it."

"I didn't think it would be a problem for you, but it is for Sotalia."

"Sotalia? Why? She wouldn't be involved, would she?"

"Well, that's the problem. Martin says everyone already knows she's going to be the donor, so there's nothing new there. Besides, she's so vibrant in front of a camera that she becomes the focus of attention, and this piece would be about

Ethan, the doctors, and the hospital, not her."

"That makes sense."

"Not to Sotalia. She's upset because we're not including her."

"How did she find out?"

"She called me this afternoon to ask about the next program. I couldn't lie. She would have found out later anyway."

I looked at Ethan. He lay with his hand curled against his chin, his mouth slightly open. I didn't want Sotalia angry, not for any reason. "Would it help if I phoned her?"

"Maybe. What would you say to her?"

I thought for a moment. "I would tell her how grateful we all are and how people are saying they saw her on TV and admire her for doing this and—" I hesitated. "And how it may even make her a celebrity."

"That's a good idea. It'll reassure her that we're not trying to leave her out of anything."

"She's means well, Liz."

"Yes, I can see that."

———

I waited until late afternoon the next day to call Sotalia, thinking it would be about the time she arrived home from school. I dialed her number from the kitchen phone. When she answered and I asked if she had time to talk, she sighed heavily. "Oh, I suppose."

I dredged up my resolve and repeated the little spiel I'd reeled off to Liz. Sotalia listened without comment until I'd finished.

"I know Liz is your friend, but she's very controlling." Her tone was apologetic, as if she hated to break this news to me. "It's her way or nothing. I question whether she's really thinking about what's best for Ethan."

"Oh, I'm sure she is."

"Well, could you talk with her then? Maybe you could impress upon her that we should be helping each other, not working against each other."

"How is Liz working against you?

"I thought she would do more for me than she has."

"I'm a little confused. Was something promised you that I'm not aware of?"

"It was certainly implicit in the arrangement."

"Um...what was implicit?"

"I help Ethan, and you and Liz help me."

I felt the panic that hits when the airplane I'm in suddenly drops altitude several hundred feet.

"I'm sorry, Sotalia. I didn't realize you thought that. What is it you would like Liz and me to do?"

"Well, this is a big story. I mean, other media are paying attention to it now, so I would think Channel 3 would want to get as much mileage out of it as they can."

"And exactly how would that help you?" I closed my eyes, hoping she wouldn't give the answer I feared she would.

"I don't want to be a preschool teacher all my life."

"You mean you want to work for a television station?"

"No. I want a better job than that."

I rubbed my hand across my forehead, trying to think what I could possibly say to her. Without her, we had no other hope. It would take too much money and more time to vet one of the other candidates. Even then, the other volunteers might not have the right vasculature.

"You'll have to forgive me, Sotalia, but my main concern is saving my son." I sounded too apologetic, too self-effacing. I didn't want her to think I was weak and desperate, although of course I was.

"I'm concerned about your son too."

I felt a spike of relief.

"But," she added, "it's not going to kill anybody to consider my circumstances."

I thought "kill anybody" was a poor choice of words, but I didn't point it out.

"If the television station isn't going to do this right, then maybe I should contact some national magazines."

"Magazines?"

"That's right." Her voice brightened, reviving some of that enthusiasm I'd heard six weeks before. "They pay for good stories, don't they?"

"No sense ignoring the advantages of the situation."

"Absolutely. I'm so glad you understand, Delainie."

"Yes, me too." I hung up the phone and lowered my head onto my hands.

"She's not going to do it, is she?" asked Barbara.

I looked up in surprise. She stood in the kitchen doorway.

"That woman, Sotalia," she said. "Has she changed her mind?"

"No, but she wants something we can't give her."

"You mean the money people sent in?"

"Thank God she can't touch that. But she wants more publicity. She's talking about selling her story."

Barbara reached up to tuck a wisp of hair under one of the dozen or so bobby pins she was wearing. I was beginning to think of that unruly thatch as a barometer of her distress. When she lowered her hand, it was shaking.

She stuffed her hands into the pockets of her brown print housedress, perhaps embarrassed by her display of emotion, and stared at some indeterminate point on the kitchen stove. "What if she doesn't get what she wants?"

"I don't know. I don't think she'll back out. She likes the limelight too much, but I hope she doesn't get any more demanding."

"I don't like that woman. She's too flighty."

"I don't either, but if she helps Ethan she can be as flighty as she wants."

I wondered if life had a law that said we must pay a price for everything.

I'd taken to waking at three o'clock in the morning. I'm not sure if there was any significance to the time. Maybe that's when the valerian wore off, or perhaps it was a form of self-preservation, allowing me to ward off nightmares. The closer we came to Ethan's surgery date, the more my bad dreams intensified. I saw Sotalia auctioning off slivers of her liver and people fighting each other to buy them. I saw Ethan being wheeled out from the operating room with a gaping, empty abdomen.

One night I dreamed I was attending someone's funeral, although it wasn't clear who was in the casket. I woke up shaking. Ethan lay squished between Joel and me, snoring lightly and sounding congested. I worried that he might have caught a cold or the flu. Secondary infection was a constant concern, because it meant the transplantation would be postponed. But, then, I worried just as much when I didn't hear his breathing.

I remember the day he took his first steps alone, toddling across the hardwood floor of our living room and scaring the bejesus out of me because he looked as if he was going to crash at any moment. I hovered nearby, ready to catch him. That was the worst part, knowing a time would come when I wouldn't be there when he fell.

———

The next morning I didn't hear Joel leave for work, and I didn't awaken until Ethan moaned.

I shot straight up in bed. "Oh, no, what's wrong?"

He eased onto his back and struggled to a sitting position. His hair stuck out and his pajamas were twisted around his arms and legs. He blinked at me with sleepy eyes. "Nothing. I was hot."

I looked at the beads of perspiration on his forehead. "You must have had a fever."

"No, I'm just hot."

"I'll get the thermometer." I jumped out of bed and headed for the bathroom.

"Mo-om."

I stuck my head out from the bathroom. "What?"

"I don't want you to take my temperature."

"Why not, baby? It'll only take a few seconds." I found the

thermometer under a box of Q-tips and hurried toward the bedroom.

"I'm not a baby," he shouted.

"Well, of course, you're not but--"

He slumped against the headboard. "Mom, I don't want my temperature taken. They did it a hundred times at the hospital."

"Okay. Could I at least put my hand on your forehead?"

He rolled his eyes and groaned, "I guess."

I sat down next to him and rested my hand on his brow. It was damp but not unduly warm. He smelled slightly sour though, and his skin seemed more jaundiced, his fingernails slick and rounded on the ends and faint rings around his corneas, a sign that more copper was building up in his system. Kayser-Fleischer rings, Taylor had called them. Joel said he couldn't see them, but I knew they were there.

I slid my arms around Ethan and clasped him against me. "I know you're tired of being sick, sweetie."

He made a face. "How come you call me things like that?"

"You mean sweetie?"

"Yeah, and honey and baby and pudding pie and other sappy names."

"I've always called you those things."

"No, you haven't."

"Yes, I have." Was his memory getting that bad?

His lower lip slid out far enough to hang a hook on it. "You used to call me Spiderman and Superman and Ethan Skywalker. Why don't you call me those anymore?"

I searched my weary brain. "I don't know. It's nothing intentional."

Tears slipped from his eyes and slid down his cheeks.

"Oh, sweetheart," I said, reaching for him. There, I'd done it again.

He squirmed away. "You're treating me like I'm younger, not older."

"I know you're growing up, but—"

Or would be, if this illness hadn't stopped his growth. Krishna, it seemed, was vaulting out of his clothes. Watching his friend look down on him, Ethan had to realize he wasn't growing at all.

"You act like I'm a baby," he said grumpily.

"Well, you are my—"

Fierceness glittered in his eyes. "And don't say I'm your baby."

I raised my hands in a feeble gesture. "But you are."

He flopped over onto his stomach and dove into his pillow. "I don't want to talk about it anymore. I'm going back to sleep."

I leaned closer. "It's going to be all right, Ethan Skywalker," I whispered. "You wait and see."

"You don't really believe that woman is going to give me part of her liver, do you?"

To say my heart sank wouldn't be doing the sensation justice. "Oh, sweet...Captain Marvel, why would you think that?"

"I hear things." The pillow muffled his voice.

I thought of my conversation with Sotalia a few days earlier and then of my talk with Barbara. "What things?"

"I'm not stupid, Mom." He turned over on his side. "I'm tired. I want to sleep."

He wasn't pretending because, in less than two minutes, his breathing eased into a light wheeze. I, of course, would never sleep again.

Chapter 35

Less than a week away from the surgery, Sotalia called, saying she wanted to postpone it.

"The *Globe* is interested in my story, and they want to fly me to New York to talk about it. I can't do that if I'm strapped to a hospital gurney."

I leaned against the kitchen wall for support. "Isn't the *Globe* one of those tabloids you buy at the grocery?"

"That's right. They pay better than a women's magazine."

I could see the near future. It would be this tabloid story first and then what? Some other reason to delay it? I frantically pieced together my rebuttal. "Taylor may not be able to reschedule the operation before Christmas."

"Yes, that could be a problem, especially since I'm going back to Ohio for Christmas."

"And she's leaving on vacation the day after Christmas. I would feel so much better if she were here for the surgery. She's so knowledgeable and experienced, and I know she would—"

"Well, we can't schedule everything around Taylor now, can we?"

I wanted to point out that we seemed to be scheduling everything around her, but I didn't.

"Sotalia, we can't wait. Ethan is getting worse everyday. If a secondary infection sets in, the doctors will postpone the surgery until he recovers." Why was I saying this? She'd heard it all from Taylor. I shifted directions. "Once the transplant's over, you'll have so much more to offer the *Globe*."

"But they want to be in on the arrangements. In fact, they said they would send a reporter here for the surgery."

I don't know what she was doing on the other end of the phone, but I could almost see her filing and painting her nails while saying all this.

"Sotalia," I said cautiously, "I'm concerned. I mean, Ethan's life is more important than any demands a tabloid might have. You do want to help him, don't you?"

"Of course, but Taylor said he isn't that sick yet."

My palm had gone so sweaty that I had to grip the receiver tight to keep it from falling. "What Taylor meant was that livers from deceased or dying donors are given to the most severely ill patients on the list: people who are close to dying. We don't want to wait until our son is near death."

"I understand that, but the point is we have some time. I want to get the terms settled with the *Globe* before the actual transplant."

Because, otherwise, she would have no lever-age with us. I closed my eyes. "And what will you do if they don't pay you enough?"

She was silent for a moment.

I heard a beep and saw Liz's name on my phone screen. She would have to wait.

"Sotalia?"

"I'm thinking."

I had hoped to embarrass her, but she gave no indication that I had.

"If the *Globe* won't give me enough," she said, "you could supplement it. You have all those contributions people sent in."

Well, there it was, and she wasn't even aware of the sizable amount Jaya and Rob had collected from their wealthy friends. I tried to keep my tone calm. "Legally, that money can be used only for Ethan."

"But this whole thing is for Ethan. What I'm doing is strictly for him. I found out what the statistics are on a living-donor transplant, and I have a five percent chance of dying. That's a huge risk for me, Delainie."

"And we will be eternally grateful to you for taking it, but we can pay only for the surgery, nothing more."

"Now, see, that doesn't make sense. The doctors performing the operation are going to be compensated, aren't they?"

"Yes, but—"

"Then why shouldn't I?"

"Because it's illegal to buy or sell an organ." Why was I arguing with her? She'd been told from the very beginning that her only reward would be knowing she'd saved a child's life.

Liz's name appeared on the phone screen again.

"Well," Sotalia said, "I'm going to have to give up my sick leave so that's money out of my pocket, and who knows how long it will take me to recover from the operation or what problems it will cause years from now? I could end up with liver problems of my own. I need to have some compensation just in case."

I leaned against the wall and closed my eyes. "We can't give you any."

"I guess I'll have to see how these arrangements go with the *Globe* then. I want to help, but I have to consider my own future too."

I had barely hung up the phone and taken a few desperate breaths when it rang again. It was Liz on the other end of the line, complaining, "I have been trying to reach you for the last fifteen minutes."

"I know but I was talking with Sotalia."

"You know then."

"I know she wants to delay the transplant and what she really wants is money and fame."

"I feel awful about this. I should have seen it coming, because I've certainly run into enough of people like her. Sotalia Johnson is what we in the business call a media whore. She loves the face time and will do her best to make money off it. If we had asked her what her career aspirations were, I'll bet she would have said she wanted to be an actress."

I was thinking of a black-and-white drawing that morphs from a beautiful woman into a witch when you shift your gaze slightly. I was so blinded by the one image, I hadn't seen the other.

"It's no one's fault," I told Liz. "I thought she was some kind of angel, put on Earth to save Ethan and I'm not even religious."

We were silent for several moments.

"What now?" Liz said. "Should we wait to see if she comes through in a few weeks — or months?"

"I don't know. He's getting weaker each day. Everything seems to be moving faster now. I'm really scared, Liz."

"I wish we could see if one of the other donors would cooperate, but I know the station won't agree to it. Martin is already trying to figure out how to tell our vast television audience that we've lost Sotalia. She's an embarrassment. We dredged her up, and now she's our responsibility and shame. The sad thing is the people who run the station care more about our ratings than about Ethan."

"It's okay. Even if they agreed to another search for a donor, I don't think we would have the time or money. Look at how long it's taken and how much it has cost to go through this process with Sotalia."

"I'm sorry, Delainie. I'm so sorry." Her voice was suddenly congested, thick with tears.

"Don't you dare blame yourself. You've done more than anyone could ask of a friend."

After I hung up the receiver, I continued sitting on the floor in the corner of the kitchen where our small table and chairs had been. I thought about staying right there and never getting up.

Chapter 36

I perched on the edge of the bed. Joel sat on a rickety folding chair he'd bought at Goodwill for two dollars. We now had five mismatched metal chairs, so that we each had one we could carry from room to room. The operation had been postponed because Sotalia had gone to New York to meet editors at the *Globe*.

"You're not surprised about her, are you?" I asked Joel.

"No."

"Why not?"

"Nothing surprises me anymore. Sotalia will do what she's going to do, and we're not going to be able to change that." He shifted slightly and the chair creaked like an old truck spring.

"Aren't you at least angry at her?"

He shook his head.

"Well, I am. She's ruined his chances for a living donor. If it hadn't been for her, we might have chosen someone who would follow through with it and Ethan would have his transplant by now. What she did was evil, and I hope she steps out of her house someday and a tree falls on her head."

He shrugged.

I stood and walked over to the window, feeling a tad guilty but not remorseful enough to take the words back. Although it was more than a week before Thanksgiving, one of the neighbors had already strung his Christmas lights, little white ones that hung from the eaves like glowing icicles.

I turned back to our dreary room, almost wishing I hadn't

sold all the furniture and lamps — not because I cared about them any longer, but because their absence left the room so empty and forlorn. Our only illumination came from an over-head fixture, a single bulb enclosed in a pink glass clamshell. I looked at Joel. Maybe it was the dim light, but it seemed as if all his worry lines had been ironed out. I looked again. Not only was the tension gone from his face, but the fire was missing too.

"You've given up, haven't you? You think he's going to die, and there's nothing we can do."

"No."

The anger he'd shown in the hospital was almost preferable to this new passiveness.

"Why won't you try to do something then? It's better than sitting here and hoping a liver will drop from Heaven — if there actually is a Heaven."

"I have this feeling of inevitability. If the UNOS system works the way it's supposed to, he'll get his transplant."

"Well, it certainly didn't work for Sarah Spencer, did it?"

"If you can come up with anything else, I'll do it."

"Well," I said, with a confidence I didn't feel, "there's sup-posed to be a black market for vital organs in third-world coun-tries. Maybe we should explore that possibility." I knew I was reaching but I'd run out of credible ideas.

He rested his elbows on his knees and pressed his palms together. "Do you really believe it exists?"

"I can't say that it doesn't. Can you?"

"No," he said. "Okay, let's suppose it does. Which country would you go to? How would you find these sellers of precious goods?"

I saw myself slinking down dark foreign alleys, questioning sinister-looking men, asking if they knew where I might buy a healthy liver. So what if it was ludicrous? If it were possible, I would do it. Now that I'd discovered right and wrong no longer had much significance, I would try anything.

I paced the floor, then sat on the edge of the bed again. "Don't mock me, Joel."

He rose from the chair and eased himself down next to me. "I swear I am not mocking you." He pulled me into his arms and stroked the back of my neck soothingly. I wanted him to hold me, but I didn't like the idea of his using affection to defuse my frustration.

"If you really believe this is a way to help Ethan," he said, "I'll get on a plane tomorrow to fly to Turkey or China or wherever this black market is."

I didn't believe him, of course. I leaned against him. There was something about him I couldn't identify right away. Then I realized what it was. He smelled different than he had a few weeks ago. He'd lost that tangy smell that seemed to come from his anxiety.

"You were right about the television program," he said. "I didn't believe it would work, but it did."

"No, it didn't work."

"Yes, it did. It brought in the money we need for his transplant operation, and it brought in donors. The rest wasn't your fault."

Although I'd told myself the same thing, I wasn't sure I believed it.

"What bothers me," I said, " is that you don't have faith there's anything more we can do."

"Faith? Strange that you should use that word because I suppose in a way I do have faith."

"In what? God?"

He thought for a moment. "Not exactly, at least not in the traditional, organized-religion sort of way. I'm still trying to find some wisdom, maybe even some holiness in all this, but I can't."

"Holiness?" The word seemed outrageous. "If you're going to get all Pentecostal on me, I won't be able to stand it. There is no holiness and certainly no mercy in a child dying."

"That's probably true, but I have to believe there's some reason for it."

I pulled away from him. "No, there is no good reason, and I won't accept that it's preordained or that we can't do anything about it. I won't give up so easily."

Chapter 37

Ethan was supposed to keep active, but he didn't have much stamina. Occasionally he worked on the Fly, but for only a few minutes at a time. One afternoon, I found him in his room, staring at it, his shoulders in a slump. The cat had chewed a hole in the papier-mâché, a crater-shaped bite, directly in the middle of the forehead. Oscar still sat on the workbench, serenely grooming himself.

I put my arm around Ethan and pulled him down beside me on the bed. "You can fix it. You could stick a plug in there."

He shook his head. "I'll have to patch it in layers. Otherwise it'll take too long to dry."

"How about this? You could make the hole another wound. That's what it really is anyway, a cat wound."

He gave me his what-a-stupid-idea look. "It's a hole, not a wound. Flies don't have big holes in their foreheads."

I hadn't seen any running around with oozing lesions either, but I didn't point that out.

"Well, okay," I said cheerfully, "maybe that wouldn't work, but you can still fix it. A new layer every day or two."

"I don't have time," he said in a low voice.

My breath caught at the back of my throat. "Of course you do. And, once you have your transplant, you'll have more time. You can build a whole collection of fly heads. How about one that looks like Vincent Price?"

He didn't answer but he leaned his head against my shoulder. I let my body go slack. I couldn't let him feel my fear.

I reached around to give his head a gentle noogie and came away with a small clutch of hair between my fingers. I must

261

have gasped because he looked up at me. "What?"

"Oh, nothing" I tucked my hand under my jeans-clad thigh. My God, he was losing his hair.

"Why did you make that noise then?"

"I was thinking about Oscar. I'd better call the veterinarian and see if the papier-mâché will harden inside him and turn him into a statue."

A year ago, he would have known I was joking. Now, he gave me a puzzled look. "Oscar's not a statue."

Still in my nightgown, I waited for the toast to pop up. I hadn't had much sleep. Ethan awoke in the middle of the night, almost writhing in torment from itchy skin. I called Children's Memorial and talked to a doctor, who prescribed a medication called Ursodial to soothe it. Joel put him in a cool bath and slathered him with baking soda, while I drove to an all-night pharmacy to pick it up. Then we took turns holding him in our arms until the medicine took effect.

Thanksgiving had come and gone. All week, I kept thinking Sotalia might phone, that she'd say there had been a misunderstanding and she was ready to set the date as soon as possible for the surgery. I even tried a little prayer, a plea for divine intervention. She never called.

I must have stared at the toaster for an entire minute before I realized smoke was curling from its elements. There was a bing, and a blackened slice shot up. I looked at the square of charcoal for a long moment, then tossed it into the wastebasket under the sink. I wasn't hungry anymore. I wasn't even sure that I had been hungry to begin with.

I climbed the stairs, determined to coax Ethan into eating enough breakfast for both of us. His eyelids were half-closed, but I knew he understood what I was asking.

"A bowl of cereal. I'll put some honey on it. Now, won't that taste good, Captain Marvel?"

He made a face. "I don't want any."

"A few slices of apple then."

"I'm not hungry."

I tugged on his arm. "Got to get up anyway. You need to move around so you won't get those muscle cramps in your legs. We certainly don't want those again, do we?"

He wriggled away from me. "You didn't have them. I did."

"I was using the royal 'we.' You know, like I'm the Queen Mum and you're Prince Ethan." I reached under his arms and managed to raise him to a standing position. It wasn't that he couldn't stand; he just balked at doing it. "And since I'm the Queen Mum, I get to give all kinds of orders, like 'You have to eat something' and 'You have to walk around.'"

In the kitchen, he sat on one of the folding chairs, while I cut up an apple and fixed him a slice of toast after turning the setting down. I set the plate and a glass of juice in front of him on a metal TV tray (another Goodwill find), then leaned back against the counter, and watched while he nibbled at the toast.

"Maybe we should go to the park this morning," I said.

He glanced out the window without much interest. "It's cloudy."

"That's never stopped us before."

"Well, I don't want to go outside."

He was turning obstinate, even slightly belligerent, and he looked at me with accusing eyes. Taylor said irritability was a symptom of the ammonia building up in his system, poisoning his brain, but there was more to it than that. He didn't trust me any longer. He probably believed I had lied to him. Hadn't he been a good kid? Hadn't he tried hard? None of that seemed to make any difference. No wonder he seemed angry all the time.

"Come on, let's you and me work on the Fly?" I said. "That's a good activity."

He rose sluggishly from his chair. "I'm going to my bed to sleep."

After he left, I took the remains of the apple and the toast and tossed them outside for the birds. As I closed the door, I remembered I needed to remind him about his doctor's appointment at three o'clock. We visited Children's Memorial at least once a week for new tests, ones that routinely gave us more bad news.

I walked out into the hall, expecting to see Ethan trudging toward his room. Instead, he was at the top of the stairs. Either, he'd changed his mind or he'd already forgotten what he'd intended to do. I didn't call after him. He wandered around a bit, then came back down the stairs.

A few minutes later, I was loading the dishwasher when Barbara came into the kitchen. She had Joel's freshly ironed khaki slacks draped over her left arm as if she were a walking clothes hanger. The deserted robin's nest in the tree outside our kitchen window was tidier than her hair. She tried to say something, but she couldn't seem to get the words out. The slacks slid right off her arm onto the floor.

It's her heart, I thought. "You sit right here on this chair, Barbara. I'll call 911."

"No."

"You don't look well. "

She shook her head, almost violently. "I'm not sick."

There was a clinic only a few miles away. I wouldn't feel comfortable until she'd had her heart checked out. Hal had taken off for Jackson's Hardware. I would have to bundle Ethan into the car because I couldn't leave him home. I was feeling torn, uncertain about that, when Barbara insisted again that she didn't need a doctor.

"There's nothing wrong with me," she said, although I found that hard to believe, considering her ashen face.

"It's Ethan," she said. "When I passed him on the stairs, I asked him a question. He looked at me, but he didn't answer."

"He gets confused. That's part of his illness."

"When is he going to get his new liver?"

"I don't know. I wish I did."

She clamped her arms across her bosom, as if holding something in. "At first I thought you would be the donor. When that didn't work out, I was counting on that woman you found through the television program."

"I was too." I reached for Joel's slacks puddled at her feet, but she waved me away.

"I'll do it," she said, her lips drawn tight.

But she didn't touch them.

There seemed to be an epidemic of confusion. I pointed at the slacks. "I was just going to hang them up."

"I'll do it." Her blue eyes blinked at me. "I've made the decision. I'll be the donor."

I suddenly realized what she was saying. "My God, you want to give Ethan part of your liver?"

Her features went all soft, as if the sharp bones under them had collapsed. "He's my grandchild, my son's only son. I should have offered earlier."

"Oh, Barbara, that is so kind and good of you but—"

"I've got good organs, except for my heart."

Organs degenerated after the age of seventy. She was too old to be a donor, but I said, "I'm afraid your heart wouldn't withstand the operation."

"I don't care about that."

I was stunned. She intended to give up her life for him.

As if reading my mind, she gave me a moist-eyed look. "It makes no difference. I'm an old woman."

"No, you're not." I rushed to her side and took her damp hand, regretting all the times I had thoroughly disliked her.

I patted her hand. "Ethan would be heartbroken if he lost you. You're his only grandmother."

She looked haggard, defeated. "I don't know how else to help."

I gave her a hug, something I hadn't done since my wedding day. "You are helping. You can't imagine how wonderful it is to have you here, cleaning and organizing things, buying and fixing our meals, and looking after Ethan. You're a comfort to us all."

She drew back and looked at me, her eyes awash with tears. "Do you really think so?"

"Yes, I do and I should have told you long ago."

"I worry I'm a bother."

"No, no. I couldn't have a better mother-in-law." I kissed her soft cheek.

Chapter 38

Ethan went into Children's Memorial the following week. The medications had done all they could for him. The copper was building up in his system, and there was no way to stop it. His liver was failing now, and he would need continuous monitoring.

Signs of the holidays were everywhere in the hospital, tiny white lights adorning the entrance, festive poinsettias and potted evergreens at the nurses' stations, children's brightly colored drawings in the lobby. A trio of madrigal singers drifted through the hall outside Ethan's room, crooning old English Christmas songs. Joel and I looked at each other over Ethan's bed, and he touched my hand. I gazed at Ethan's sleeping form, feeling the urge to grab his hand and not let go.

A few hours later, I left Joel with Ethan and went to buy us soft drinks at the hospital cafeteria. Rounding a corner in the L-shaped hall, I slowed my pace. Dr. Alan Sidon stood about thirty feet away, his back to me. I felt a tug in my chest, like someone yanking on a line. I hadn't seen him since that night I'd invited him into my fantasy.

There was another person with him, a woman, although her face was tilted so that I couldn't see it. She wore a white turtleneck shirt and a maroon jumper that hit her trim legs at mid-shin. They huddled against the wall, and he spoke to her in a low tone. I couldn't make out the words, but they had a soothing murmur.

Suddenly, she pulled back from him, and I saw her tear-streaked face, splotchy red against an arc of stringy blond hair. She appeared to be in her mid-thirties and might have been attractive under other circumstances. As it was, her eyes looked

267

dazed and the skin around them had been rubbed raw.

"It's not fair," she said through clenched teeth. "He wants to know why I won't make the pain go away. How do you explain to a five-year-old his mother can't do that?"

I couldn't make out what Alan said to her, but she shook her head vehemently. He told her something else in a low voice, and she gripped the dark green sweater he wore under his lab coat and pushed her face into it, sobbing audibly. He continued speaking quietly to her, his strong hand wrapped around her.

There was no lust in his touch, not even anything that you might call affection. The woman might have been anyone. She might have been me.

An adjustment in Ethan's medicine brought him out of his subterranean sleep by the next morning. We'd learned some time ago that administering drugs was an art form, a delicate balance between keeping a patient comfortable and over-sedating him.

Joel took the bus to his office after reassuring Ethan that he would return as soon as possible. I spent the next hour reading *Huckleberry Finn* to Ethan. We'd started it at home and were now at the part where Huck attends his own funeral. I suppose I could have omitted it, but I didn't have enough sense to think that far ahead.

"I'd like to do that," Ethan said.

"Do what?"

"Go to my funeral."

I didn't know how to answer. He was talking more and more that way. If I protested, he set his mouth resolutely and turned away. Our conversations became repetitive little dances, where he said something about death and I gave him ineffective little lectures on the power of positive thinking.

As I turned the page, I heard a jingling noise behind me. I smelled her Coco Mademoiselle before I looked toward the door. Sotalia stood there, wearing a dark green skirt, a green-

and-white Christmas sweater with a dozen or so gold bells dangling from sparkly ribbons, and a determined expression. When Ethan saw her, he wordlessly shifted to his side and fixed his gaze on the window, but I'll admit hope rose like a phoenix in my breast.

I said a polite hello, but when she stepped into the room, I rushed over, took her arm and guided her out. "Let's talk in the lounge."

In the hall we passed Ethan's gastroenterologist, Dr. Baxter. We greeted each other but I didn't slow down. I didn't want Sotalia to try to involve him in our conversation.

"What's going on?" she asked petulantly. "Everyone's acting like I'm some sort of pariah. Liz won't take my phone calls, and believe me I've left her dozens."

"I don't think you're a pariah. I'm glad to see you." I practically dragged her toward the lounge. "Let's step right in here where we can discuss this in private."

"And your transplant coordinator—I can't reach her either."

Poor Taylor. No wonder she'd gone to the opposite end of the country on vacation.

"How did you know we were here?" I asked Sotalia.

"When I couldn't get you at your house, I figured there weren't too many other places you would go."

I intended to sit by the window, but Sotalia walked over to the same small table where I had learned the horrors of transplantation from Alice Spencer seven months before, plopped down on a chair and gave an exaggerated sigh. "I don't know what the problem is. I ask for a little consideration, and everyone goes ballistic."

I was right then. She had come to express regret and reassure us she did want to donate part of her liver to Ethan. She would commit to a date, and Ethan could have his surgery within a few weeks, maybe right after the first of the new year. I clasped my sweaty hands together. "Then you'll do the transplant?"

She gave me a warm smile. "I want to, Delainie, as soon as we clear up these other matters."

"What other matters?"

She gave a little huff of exasperation as if she'd taught preschoolers who caught on quicker than I did. "The financial part of it."

"What about your deal with the tabloid?"

"We haven't reached an agreement yet. Their offer is much too low."

Even if we could buy her liver, anything we could pay would also be too low. I studied her clear blue eyes, her small nose with its slight upward tilt, and the halo of berry-tinted blond hair, trying to get a grasp on what offer she would accept. "How much money do you want, Sotalia?"

"Like I said before, it depends on a few things."

"No. It depends only on your willingness to be the donor. I want your price, no other conditions attached."

I'd surprised myself with my firmness, but I couldn't continue with this push-pull game any longer. We either had to give her what she wanted: compensation beyond her medical expenses, or we had to end it. Maybe we could pay her on some kind of installment plan. Never mind that it was illegal.

She pondered her answer, although I had the feeling she knew how much she wanted before she'd walked through the door. "I believe a reasonable amount would be one million dollars. I thought the *Globe* would give me two million, but they came up with only five hundred thousand. I still don't think it's enough, but I would accept their offer if you made up the difference."

My fuzzy brain calculated that it would take twenty years to pay off a debt like that. We'd taken care of what medical debts we could with money from the antiques and the TV donors. We couldn't possibly commit any future income (we would need it for Ethan's post-transplant care), and we couldn't have another fundraiser because any money we gave her would have to be hidden. I envisioned sneaking her thousand dollar bills on a dark street corner. Then it occurred to me if we agreed to pay her an initial sum and then reneged, she couldn't do anything about it. She couldn't sue because what she was doing was illegal.

"We couldn't pay you all at once," I said.

She frowned as if I were intentionally making things difficult. "Why not? I know you have the money."

"Not half a million dollars. Besides, I've already told you we can't give you anything from the donations. It's in a trust. We have to account for how it's spent. I swear to you we don't have any other money.""You have your house."

"It takes time—weeks, sometimes months to sell a house. Besides, we have two mortgages on it."

I would have given anything for her to say, *Well, of course you don't have the money. I'm sorry I asked.*

A burst of wintry sunlight splashed the room, and Sotalia focused her gaze on the breaking clouds outside the window.

She sighed. "What *can* you give me?"

"Right now?"

She nodded.

I tallied what was left from the antiques. "Five thousand." Even that was a stretch.

"How long would it be before you could compensate me with the full amount?"

Compensate? I loved her little euphemism.

"Four or five years."

I was fudging and I knew it, but I would deal with that after Ethan was safe. Maybe Joel's business would be making a million a year by that time. Maybe I would go back to antiquing and find that elusive treasure. Maybe I'd sue her for selling a chunk of her liver. Maybe I could get her arrested.

"I'm afraid that's too long." She seemed to regret having to deliver the news to me. She looked at me with the same clear-eyed expression that had snared me in the beginning. "I really want this gift to go to Ethan but..."

Gift? What was she talking about? She didn't know the meaning of the word.

She stood, and a thousand tiny bugs crawled across my flesh.

"Two years. We'll pay it back in two years."

I could see she didn't believe me.

I clasped my hands together to keep from grabbing her sleeve. "If you leave, you will get no money, not from us or the tabloids. Surely you realize that."

"I'm sorry but I can't do it without payment. I don't think you recognize the risks I would be taking."

I realized then it was over. She might actually believe what she was saying. She might be one of those people who thought a generous gesture deserved a commensurate return. Or she might just be a greedy woman. It made no difference. The result was the same.

Although there was no one else in the lounge to hear me, I spoke in a raised voice. "Gifts don't require compensation, Sotalia. And, now that I think about it, I don't want Ethan to have part of your liver. He might get some of your monstrous qualities along with it."

Her expression went cold. "You're going to regret you said that." She turned and walked out of the lounge.

She was right. I regretted it before the click of her heels on the hall floor faded away, but I would never have called her back.

31

If it were not for the hospital routine, I would have lost track of time. I calculated it now by meals served, vital signs measured, pills dispensed. The days were tediously uneventful, but it was the closest I had felt to Ethan since he was an infant. I sat at his side as much as possible, reading to him, and occasionally coaxing him to sit up and move around.

Joel divided his time now between the hospital and his office.

One evening, when Ethan seemed to be feeling better, he gestured toward the high-rise across the street. "See the Space Needle between those two buildings. It's all litted-up."

I almost didn't correct him. What difference did his grammar make now? Then, the force of that thought hit me. I might as well have said he didn't have a future beyond this Mother-Goose-style hospital.

"Lighted or lit, but not litted-up," I said.

"Lighted," he repeated out of habit. He fell asleep within seconds.

Later, when I was digging in my purse for a nail file, my hand slid across Ethan's binky. I pulled it out and held it against my cheek. He might not need his binky but I did. I slept with it clutched against my heart that night.

The next morning, I sat on the edge of his bed and slid my

fingers over Ethan's puffy hand, swollen from the poisonous fluids beneath his skin. His skin felt much too warm against my own.

"I've got this great idea," I said. "How about we ask your dad to stop by the house today and pick up the Fly? Then you could work on it here when you feel up to it."

He bent forward, suppressing a groan, and I knew his insides were cramping. After the spasm passed, he said in a low voice, "I'm not ever going to feel like it again."

"Sure you will. When you get well—"

"I'm not going to get well."

"Don't say that, Ethan Skywalker. Don't even think it."

He looked away from me. "I've been working at it like you said I should, but I'm still sick."

I smoothed the top of his hospital gown and layered the sheet across his chest the way you might fold a napkin. "I know you've been trying hard, sweet…uh, Ethan Skywalker, and I want you to keep doing that. But there are a lot of things about your illness you can't control. Not even the doctors with all their medicine can do that."

"Otherwise, people wouldn't die, right?"

I braced myself. "That's not something you have to worry about right now. Look how much stronger you feel today."

He also seemed more lucid, but I didn't say that. I wondered if he was aware that he often slipped into confusion.

"You're going to get a new liver, but we have to wait our turn. After that, you'll feel so good you'll want to build a whole new collection of gory creatures."

He pressed his lips together in a straight line. "Did Dr. Coe say he's getting me a liver?"

Dr. John Coe was the transplant surgeon who had visited him the day before.

"He's doing what he can, Superman."

"But he hasn't got one for me yet, has he?"

"That's not exactly how it works."

He slid down so that his head rested on the bottom edge of the pillow. "I know how it works." He turned on his side, away from me. "He can't get me a new liver any more than you can."

His tone wasn't accusatory, but if he had stabbed me in the heart, I could not have been more hurt.

"We have to give it more time," I said.

He was quiet for several seconds. Then he turned to look at me. "It's okay, Mom. You did your best."

How many times had I said that to him through the years? You don't have to be perfect, Ethan. Just do your best.

———————

One morning, Joel emerged from the hospital bathroom, the dark stubble scraped clean from his face, his business suit wrinkled but passable for a man who was living in a hospital. He strode to Ethan's bedside, leaned over, and kissed his forehead. Ethan's eyes opened slightly, and he murmured something.

Joel tucked the hospital sheet under his chin. "I've got to go to work, but I'll be back as soon as I can."

He walked over and kissed me on the mouth, lingering a little longer than he would have in the past. I slid my arms over his shoulders, and he pulled me against him, stroking my hair.

"I love you," he whispered. "I wish I'd told you that more often."

I kissed him back, then withdrew a little to look at him, noting the frown lines that had settled into trenches over the last few years. They were still there, but they'd eased in recent weeks and now a calm kind of sorrow altered his face.

"Tomorrow evening Jin and I have to take a new client from Chicago to dinner," he said in a low voice, "but I'll be here during the day."

I nodded. I knew he was spending as much time with Ethan as he could. The sicker Ethan became, the tighter we clung to each other. Every minute we weren't together as a family was time wrenched away from us.

A few hours later, Jaya called. She and the rest of the group had been phoning and visiting the hospital almost daily.

They must have set up some sort of schedule and then traded information. Jaya brought food every time she came — a bakery bag filled with cookies, a tray of pastries, a bowl of fresh fruit. I couldn't bring myself to tell her we had no appetite for sweets and little interest in food in general. I gave most of it to the nurses.

Now she was phoning to say the group wanted to bring dinner the next evening.

"Here?" I tried to envision us clustered around Ethan's bed, eating a pizza.

"We thought we could set up the meal in that lounge near Ethan's room."

"A meal?" I was genuinely surprised. "Well, sure, that would be great. Joel and Jin are entertaining their new investor tomorrow night, so it's just Ethan and me."

"Is there anything he can't eat?"

The question would have struck me as funny if it hadn't been so tragic. "Jaya, sweetie, it doesn't make any difference what you bring. He would love to see all of you."

They arrived at six o'clock the next evening, carrying cardboard boxes covered by dishtowels. They put down their cartons and hugged me with the kind of affection friends give when their hearts are breaking along with yours.

They gathered around Ethan, who looked at them through glazed eyes and managed a smile. I could almost measure his decline by the expressions on their faces. They tried to be upbeat and reassuring, but they couldn't hide their thoughts. They were thinking they couldn't possibly endure what we were going through. I didn't resent that. In their place, that's how I would have felt.

Jaya rubbed cream onto his chapped knuckles. "We've fixed a nice dinner for you and your mom, and we're going to eat it at the lounge just down the hall. Is that all right with you?"

"Uh-huh," Ethan said drowsily.

She asked if he was hungry. He wasn't, and he didn't think he could walk to the lounge either.

Liz turned away so that he wouldn't see her. "Oh,

Delainie," she said, her eyes pooling.

"How much longer will he have to wait?" Cappy asked quietly. "Have you heard anything at all?"

I motioned toward the door, and we all stepped into the hall.

"We've been told that when it's Ethan's turn and UNOS gets a donor that matches his blood type and size, they'll contact the hospital."

"Who provides UNOS with information on Ethan's condition?" Cappy asked.

I hadn't thought about that until now. "I suppose Dr. Coe, the transplant surgeon, updates UNOS periodically."

"Does that mean he can ask them to change Ethan's status on the transplant list?"

"Well, yes, I would think so."

I considered the implication of what she was saying. Joel and I had asked detailed questions about Ethan's condition, but we had never urged Dr. Coe to change our son's status. It suddenly seemed like an opportunity we had nearly missed. I would talk with him in the morning.

While the group set up the meal, I stayed with Ethan. Half an hour later, they called me into the lounge, where they had laid out Jaya's Wedgwood china, Waterford goblets, and sterling silver on a white linen cloth over two small tables shoved together. Dinner consisted of boneless chicken breasts topped by an orange sauce and pine nuts, steamed broccoli, rice, and freshly baked rolls, served by three women whose faces looked as if they'd been buffed to a shine.

I stood there, stunned. "You made this?"

"We've been practicing," Jaya said. "Liz did the centerpiece."

It was a simple, Japanese-style arrangement of two bird-of-paradise flowers and some grassy stalks rising from a bed of white rocks in a black dish. It looked very classy, very Liz. We sat at the table, and Jaya passed the basket of rolls.

I sniffed them. "These are amazing. You made these too?"

Liz nodded. "Used bread dough from the grocery freezer."

Cappy sent around her contribution, which she described as plain old white rice with some breath-freshener, aka parsley, sprinkled over it. The only slightly incongruous note was the assortment of black plastic cups that I remembered from Cappy's over-the-hill, fortieth birthday party, but when I saw her glance around, withdraw a bottle from a box on the floor, and pour wine into the cups, I understood.

I ate a bite of chicken and laid down my fork. Looking at their expectant faces, I felt my eyes go moist. "This is the finest meal our gourmet group has ever prepared."

32

"I have to talk with Dr. Coe," I said.

The tall, slim, white-haired woman at the desk in the outer office looked up. "I'm sorry, but he's not available right now."

Her no-nonsense manner made me think she had occupied this space, or others like it, for a century or more. She reminded me of my high school teacher, Miss Mona Dodge, maybe because they both seemed caught in a time warp of "White Shoulders" and dove gray cardigan sweaters.

This part of the office was no bigger than Ethan's bedroom, and file cabinets occupied most of it. It appeared it was part of Dr. Coe's personal office rather than a reception room for patients. He usually met with family members in their child's hospital room.

I planted myself beside the woman's desk. "I'll wait for him. My son is one of his patients."

"It's going to be a while. He just went into surgery."

I suddenly felt wistful. "Did someone else get a transplant?"

She gave me an understanding smile, making me think she wasn't so dour and stuffy after all. I didn't know who the patient was, that lucky person who had won the lottery, but I felt a sharp and bitter envy, a terrible and unforgivable resentment. Why couldn't it be my son?

She glanced at the clock on the wall. "Come back this afternoon around four. Maybe he can talk to you then."

My spirits fell. I had stayed up half the night thinking of all the things I wanted to say to him, and now I would have to wait. I shouldn't have gone directly back to Ethan's room, feeling as I did, but I didn't like the idea of his waking up without Joel or me there. When I walked in, his eyes were closed. I sat on the cot near the window and cried silently.

"Mom?"

I scrubbed my eyes and nose with a crumpled, disintegrating tissue, then walked over to his bed and planted an audible kiss on his cheek. "Good morning, Ethan Skywalker."

He opened his eyelids to half-mast and gazed at me. "You okay?"

"I'm fine. How about you? Is the old tummy better?"

"Uh-huh."

Greenish half moons underscored his eyes, and his lips were grayish purple. He seemed to be aging a terrible year each day.

"Where's Dad?" he asked groggily.

"He went to work really early so that he can come back as soon as possible. He should be here around noon."

He tried to sit up but winced in pain. He turned his face away from me.

I reached over and stroked his forehead. "Have I ever told you that you're the bravest person I know, Captain Marvel?"

He looked back at me. "Who's Captain Marvel?"

"Don't you remember? He's Genis, son of the legendary intergalactic hero Mar-Vell."

"You've never called me Captain Marvel before."

"Sure I have. Lots of times." Had he forgotten that too? There seemed to be these little black holes in his brain. "Captain Marvel is this muscle-bound dude who's been given cosmic awareness so that he can ferret out and battle evil forces in the universe. You always liked him because his blond hair turns white when he's cosmically aware."

"Superheroes never lose a fight, do they?"

"Sometimes they're struck down temporarily by the evil one or something that takes away their powers. Remember how Superman gets weak whenever he's near kryptonite?

"Yeah, but he tries to keep away from it."

"That's right. He always comes back and wins the battle."

"Always?" He was slurring his words, the way a sleepy drunk might do.

"Always." If only he could hold onto that thought. "Have you ever seen a funeral for a superhero?"

"I guess not."

"Well, there you go."

⸻

In the afternoon, the hospital pace picked up. Doctors and nurses strode the halls, their shoes squeaking on the waxed floors. I passed a group of three spry, purple-haired women carrying Get Well helium balloons and a teenaged boy wearing leg braces.

In Dr. Coe's office, I faced his gatekeeper again. She hunched over a leather-bound ledger on her desk. Although I couldn't read what she was writing, I could see the letters were small and precise and they rested on the thin blue lines like a row of birds on a telephone wire. When she looked up and saw me, the way she slid her arm over the pages made me wonder if she was penning her memoirs.

"Oh, Mrs. Franklin, you're back. I'm sorry but you won't be able to see him today after all."

I felt a surge of frustration. While I'd been waiting, I'd refined my arguments, and now they were building up inside me, ready to explode. I looked past her at the door with the fuzzy glass window. "He's in there, isn't he?"

She stiffened. "He's had a long day. He was in surgery for eight hours."

"It'll take only a minute."

"Maybe I can make an appointment for you two weeks from Monday." She reached in a side drawer and pulled out another leather-bound binder that opened into a calendar.

"Two weeks plus this weekend? My son is dying, and maybe

For the Love of Ethan

I can have an appointment seventeen days from now?"

Her mouth tightened. "Actually, it would be nineteen days, counting the first and last weekend. Dr. Coe is going on vacation for two weeks."

I settled my hands on her desk and bent over to look at her. "Vacation? Vacation?" I realized my voice was shrill. "How can a doctor go on vacation while children are dying?"

She didn't lose her patience and tell me to get the hell out of there, bless her heart, but she did tense up. "If you can stop by Monday morning around eight o'clock, maybe he can talk with you for a few minutes."

"No, no, my son is dying right now. We're talking minutes, not days."

At that moment, Dr. Coe opened the glass-windowed door behind her and walked out, carrying a raincoat, a briefcase, and a set of jangling car keys. He gently rubbed the skin near his receding hairline with his fingertips.

I rushed toward him. "I need to talk with you."

He frowned slightly. "Ethan's mother, right?"
I nodded. "My son needs a new liver immediately. He should be Status 1."

His assistant or secretary or whatever she was stood. "I told her this wasn't a good time."

"It's all right, Janice." He put the keys back in his pocket and gave me a weary but polite smile.

I eased myself between him and the door. "You have the authority to change my son's status with UNOS, don't you?"

"I'm involved in that decision, but it's not one I make unilaterally or arbitrarily." The words sounded rote, as if he'd said them many times before. "I'm sure Taylor has talked with you about—"

"Ethan can't wait any longer. He's too sick." The muscles in my neck and shoulders felt as if they were holding up a six-story building.

"I know this period is difficult, Mrs. Franklin, but he isn't at that point yet where we can request a change in his status."

"And what point is that?"

"We have very specific criteria. There are people on the UNOS list who have liver diseases more advanced than your son's, and many of them have waited longer."

I raised my voice a little higher. "Could you please explain to me how those people have managed to hold on then?"

He looked weary. "People have an amazing will to survive. We monitor our patients closely to determine if —"

"I'm not referring to liver function tests and other measurements like that. I'm talking about a little boy who is not going to make it if you don't do something right now. He can't remember things. His skin is green. His belly's swollen. He wakes up in the middle of the night with cramps, but he won't cry out because he doesn't want us to know. His skin itches. His hair's falling out. I worry that sometime he's going to have a nosebleed that won't stop."

I straightened to make myself as tall as I could. I realized five foot two wasn't exactly intimidating. "And you're going on vacation?"

My tone must have gone even shriller because Janice started making little soothing sounds.

"I'm sorry, Mrs. Franklin," Dr. Coe said, "but there are other very competent doctors here who can do the surgery, and there are people who have waited longer than your son. We try to be fair with the distribution."

I thought of what Alice Spencer had said all those months ago about Sarah and Ethan competing with alcoholics, rickety old politicians, and rock stars.

"But some on the UNOS list have ruined their own livers with alcohol. My son got his illness because he was unlucky enough to be born with it, and yet they'll get their transplants first.

Now, does that seem fair?"

Janice was giving him distressed looks, apologizing for not handling this problem herself, I suppose, but the doctor seemed caught up in our conversation now.

"Keep in mind that alcoholism is a disease too, and they have families who love them. Should we tell them that they don't count as much?"

"If I could, I would save every one of them, but I am a mother. My job is to protect my child." I remained rooted directly in front of him. "Can you tell me you've never transplanted a liver into a person who has waited so long he's too sick to recover?"

The color rose to his face. "Every time I do a transplant, Mrs. Franklin, I'm taking the chance I've waited too long. Sometimes, I make the wrong decision, and a liver that could have gone into someone healthier dies with the patient. That's something I have to live with."

"You play God then."

Janice gave a little gasp.

Dr. Coe looked at me for a long moment. "I wouldn't call it that—it's a terrible responsibility."

"You play God," I said more sharply.

He glanced at Janice, and I saw some wordless message pass between them. She immediately sat down at her desk, picked up the phone and dialed a four-digit number. Security, I thought. Well, fine, let them cart me off.

"Mrs. Franklin, if I could transplant a healthy liver into your son today, I would."

"But you won't."

The muscles in his face tensed. "I know you're under a tremendous amount of stress and you believe things couldn't look any worse but this won't help—"

I grabbed his raincoat-draped arm. "Tell me what will help then."

He backed up, leaving me holding the coat.

"Please, please," I whispered. "Tell me what to do."

I felt a hand on my shoulder and turned to see the powder-dusted face of Villardi, the social worker with the office full of lacy hearts and silk flowers. I'd managed to avoid her during the last few months.

She gave me a practiced smile. "Let's go to my office and talk, Mrs. Franklin."

"No, I don't want to talk with you. I want to finish my conversation with Dr. Coe." I handed him his raincoat.

"Actually, Dr. Coe is not the person to talk with about this," she said, trying to steer me toward the door.

I refused to move. "That's not true. He already told me he makes the life-and-death decisions here."

Her voice softened even more. "Do you feel you're having difficulty understanding the transplantation process?"

"No, I understand it perfectly."

"You can see the reasons for how it's done then."

"No, I can't."

"You're distraught, Mrs. Franklin."

"Well, of course, I'm distraught. My son is down the hall dying, and you're acting as if your main concern is I've gone crazy."

"Not crazy. That's not a word we use."

"Well, it should be, because I am going crazy. I hear strange voices speaking to me in an incomprehensible language. For example, Dr. Coe here is telling me he can't give my son a new liver until he's two minutes from death, and you're spouting social worker platitudes. And you want to know what else is crazy? Organ failure is the only medical condition I've ever heard of where a person has to almost die before they'll save him. I want someone to do something now!"

———————

"I suppose you're lucky they didn't haul you upstairs to the psych ward," Joel said.

"As it was, spending time with Miss Congeniality was more punishment than I deserved." I patted my mouth with a napkin to hide the tremor in my lips. I felt bad about my histrionics and I felt worse that I hadn't accomplished anything by it, and maybe I had even damaged Ethan's chances.

Joel and I were sitting in the hospital cafeteria drinking Cokes and nibbling cold French fries. By five in the afternoon, all the decent food was gone and the place was almost deserted. Joel had taken the news of my sudden lack of control rather well, I thought.

Eleanor Villardi called us to her office, and the three of us had a soulful little therapy session. A year ago, Joel would have been mortified, and he would have let me know it. Now, when he heard I'd dropped a few bubbles off plumb in Dr. Coe's office, he just gave me a sad, mellow smile.

I dipped a limp French fry into a puddle of ketchup, chewed on the end of it, and then laid it down. For some reason, every morsel I ate seemed like one less for Ethan. Some days I couldn't eat at all. My clothes hung on me like window drapes.

"Have we done everything we could, Joel?"

"I don't know. I would like to think so."

"I worry that someday we'll discover we didn't."

"His illness isn't our fault."

"I feel like it is. It was the combination of our genes that gave him the disease."

He made a little gesture I didn't know how to interpret.

"Are you angry with me?" I asked.

"Good Lord, no. You're doing the best you can."

There it was again. It's okay, Mom. You did your best. This time I didn't bother to hide my trembling lips. "There's something I've never mentioned before. I always thought I should have been able to save my parents."

He raised his eyebrows in surprise. "You weren't anywhere near that plane."

"Yes, but I should have been. I shouldn't have let them step onto it. As they walked toward the ramp, I remember having this weird little feeling, like a tarantula crawling across my skin. So what did I do? I blithely waved goodbye."

"And you blame yourself for not interpreting this feeling correctly?"

"Well, sure."

"Lainie, that's not rational."

"I know, but that's the point, don't you see? I can't find the rationality in any of this. Are our lives suppose to mean something, or is it only about getting through each day, whether it happens to be an ordinary one or the day our son dies?"

"I don't know, Lainie. You want me to come up with some explanation, but I can't."

"I envy you, though. You seem so serene."

His eyes filled with pain. "My God, I wish that were true. He pressed his hand to his chest. "I have this terrible, crushing pressure right here all the time now. I feel like I'm a failure as a father because I can't save my son, and I've failed you too. So I'm working on acceptance. I'm just trying to figure out how to live with this."

"I can't live without you and Ethan." My voice broke. "I can't even imagine life without him. I barely survived my parents' deaths. I'll never be able to laugh again, and I certainly wouldn't be able to love the way I did before. I couldn't risk that. Anything that used to make me feel good would hurt too much."

He took my hand and stroked it with his thumb until I thought he might wear a hole in my skin.

After a time, he said, "I'm sorry you had to sell the antiques."

"Don't be. I didn't need them."

"I'm sorry about the adul...my straying, too."

I thought about how long ago that seemed. "Strange how none of that is important anymore."

In Ethan's hospital room that night, I listened to his fitful breathing, and I stared at the windup clock on the bedside stand. I made a neat little pile of the dozen or so comic books I'd bought him at the secondhand store, and on the windowsill, I propped photos Joel had brought from home. I tried to sleep.

Occasionally, Ethan groaned or made little lip-smacking sounds. I watched midnight pass, then one o'clock. At two o'clock I got up and hovered over him, wishing I had never given birth to him so that he wouldn't have had to suffer. And then

I cursed myself for even thinking that.

33

The next morning, Cappy called and said she wanted to see me. I met her in the hospital lobby so that she wouldn't have to walk any farther than necessary. Even if she used a handi-capped parking space (I could never be quite sure that she would), the walk from the car to the entrance would take her ten minutes.

She'd made the concession of trading her old Volvo station wagon in for a new car with hand controls, but she steadfastly refused to use a wheelchair. Instead, she preferred to stagger and lurch from place to place. It was her way of controlling what little she could. She fit so well into the crowd of people with canes, walkers, and crutches that I almost didn't spot her leaning against the wooden column.

When I got closer, she grasped her canes and straightened.

I walked over and gave her a one-armed hug. "Thanks for coming. There's an espresso stand right over there. We could sit at one of those tables and have something to drink."

She looked around at the activity in the lobby. "Is there a more quiet place where we can talk?"

"There's a little garden with benches near the hospital en-trance, if you don't mind the cold and the extra distance."

"Good exercise," she said and painstakingly moved in the direction of the doors. Although there were wheelchairs at the entrance for patient use, I didn't dare suggest we borrow one.

I walked slowly beside her. The flowerless, leafless garden, which was tucked into a sheltered alcove, was deserted. Cappy arranged herself on a bench and laid her canes near her feet. I eased down beside her, feeling the damp chill shoot right through my blue jeans, the air so fresh and crisp it tasted almost lemony. We had an unclouded, stunning view of downtown Seattle, Puget Sound, and the snow-swept Olympic Mountains. Although it was only three in the afternoon, the sun was already turning the sky pink, the days so short now that we were cast into darkness by four.

I pulled my rain jacket tight around me. "You said on the phone that you wanted to talk privately."

"Yes, and you'll understand why in a minute. I have an idea that could get Ethan his transplant sooner than he might otherwise, but it's not without its problems."

"My God," I whispered.

"You did hear the problems part, didn't you?"

"I don't care. Whatever it is, I'll agree to it."

She seemed to ignore my answer. "Hmm," she said. "The first problem is that I'm not absolutely positive I can do it, although I'd say the chances are about ninety percent. The idea came to me that night that our group had dinner here. I remembered you talking about the United Network of Organ Sharing and how Ethan couldn't get his transplant until he worked his way to the top of the national list."

"Yes, but I don't know what we can do if Dr. Coe won't recommend a change. And he's on vacation for two weeks. Can you believe that?"

"That actually helps us. Some other surgeon will be filling in, someone who probably doesn't have the UNOS list memorized."

"I don't understand."

She stared at the mountains, but I don't think she was really focusing on them. "It occurred to me that with sixty-eight thousand people waiting for new organs, it's not likely UNOS keeps their names on three-by-five cards and stashes them in a drawer." She turned to look at me. "They use computers, of course."

"Computers? So?"

"Yes, the one thing I'm very good at. After our dinner, I went home and looked at the UNOS website. Their offices are located in Richmond, Virginia. Since then, I've managed to get inside their network, and now I'm trying to find out everything I can about it. I'm fairly sure I can access their database and put Ethan at the top of the list."

If she had said she planned to break into Fort Knox and pick up a few bars of gold, I could not have been more surprised. My entire body was trembling but not from the cold. "Can you really do that?"

"Well, it's been a few years since I've tried hacking a system, but of course it's possible to do. If a fifteen-year-old can manage it, I should be able to." The light was fading, but I could see her brown eyes, magnified by thick glasses, staring at me. "I want to make sure you'd be okay with that."

"It's a felony, isn't it?"

"Two-hundred-and-fifty-thousand-dollar fine and five years in prison, the last I heard, but there would be barely any risk in it for you, although there is a chance that if I were caught the federal authorities could track down my connection to you and Joel, and since Joel is in the computer business— well, they couldn't prove anything, of course, but they could make things difficult for both of you."

My hope dropped as rapidly as it had shot up. "I can't let you do it. You could go to prison."

She shifted on the bench, dragging her leaden legs a few inches, and stared directly into my eyes. "Delainie, you have a family—a wonderful family. What do I have? You three twits in our gourmet group and—" She patted her thighs. "And these worthless sticks. I hardly get out anymore, and what other friends I did have went off and found someone who could walk faster."

"Don't talk like that."

"I'm not feeling sorry for myself, but I'm not fooling myself either. At the rate I'm going, I'll be in a wheelchair by summer, and who knows how long it'll be before I lose the use of my upper body. Hell, I'd shoot myself in the head and give him my liver if I could. I don't have any kids. The gourmet group is the closest thing I have to a family. I mean, I'm going to die here pretty soon and I won't have done a damned thing."

I shook my head. "That's not true."

"But, don't you see? It makes me feel alive to do this. Can you imagine how it would be if I could help Ethan? And, for me, what's the risk? They're not going to throw me in prison. Even if they do, I'll have someone to take care of me."

"But UNOS must have some sort of security system, doesn't it?"

"Of course. I immediately ran into a firewall, but I got around it without much problem."

"Cappy, I don't know what a firewall is."

"It contains the software and hardware that block remote computers from illegal entry into a system or network."

"How can you be sure someone at UNOS won't figure out what you're doing and track you down?"

"So far, they don't even know I'm there. I'm using pirated accounts from different locations."

I drew the cold twilight air deep into my lungs and watched the downtown street lamps flicker on. My hands felt frozen. "He would be taking another person's place on the list."

"Yes, but one could argue it's not a fair system. A child should have priority."

"We can rationalize it any way we want, but it means someone else would die instead of him. I don't know if I can live with that."

"Delainie, which can you live with more? Dropping someone else down one position or losing Ethan?"

I covered my face with my hands. "It's like *Sophie's Choice*, an impossible choice."

"Is it?"

I slowly shook my head. "No."

I sat on the ledge that ran under the hospital windows in Ethan's room, the morning sun warming me through the glass. Ethan, his eyes still closed, moaned and turned on his side. The severity of his stomachaches was increasing. He was sleeping for longer periods, sometimes waking for only five to ten minutes each hour. He scratched furiously at his arm, leaving crimson marks on his gray-green skin. The medicine the doctor had given him for the itching wasn't working.

Joel came out of the bathroom, dressed for the office. His eyes were red-rimmed and the skin around them looked bruised. He had been in there crying. He strode to Ethan's bedside, leaned over, and kissed his forehead.

Ethan murmured something.

"Be back in a few hours, pal," Joel said. "I love you."

Although he'd always been affectionate with Ethan, he rarely said that.

He turned to me. "I love you too."

I could barely swallow, much less speak.

I hadn't told him about my conversation with Cappy. I was afraid he would disapprove, that he was a better person than I was. I feared everything now. After he left, Ethan made a little waking-up sound as he dug at his rash with his fingernails. His eyes were open, and I realized he was watching me.

"Let's try putting more salve on that," I said. Even if it didn't work well, it was better than nothing.

As I rubbed it onto his arm, he asked drowsily, "What are you thinking, Mom?"

I hesitated, then said. "About how much fun we'll have when you come home."

He looked away. "Yeah, me too."

I picked up the tube of salve.

He scooted toward me. "I'm scared, though." He gave me a regretful look. "I wasn't supposed to say that, was I?"

"You can say anything you want."

"I was scared you would cry if I told you."

"What's scaring you, sweetheart?"

He chewed on his chapped lower lip, working a tiny shred of skin there. "I'm afraid when I get old like Grandpa and die, I'll go to Hell."

I couldn't have been more startled. I didn't know he believed in Heaven and Hell. I had never pushed my agnostic inclinations on him, but I'd assumed he would absorb them over time.

I slowly twisted the cap on the tube of salve and laid it on his tray table. "Did someone say you would go to Hell?"

"No." His voice dipped lower and he was slurring his words now. "Krishna said I would probably go to Heaven, but he doesn't know I took Blake Barker's wall-climbing car and hid it in the bushes at school."

"A wall-climbing car?" I was trying to visualize it.

"Yeah, it's a really cool remote vehicle that has a suction fan." He looked over at me. "I bet you're thinking Blake found it later, but he didn't and the rain's probably wrecked it by now." He was struggling to get the words out.

"And that's it? That's why you're worried."

"Yeah. I don't suppose it makes any difference that Blake's a jerk, does it?"

"No. You shouldn't have stolen Blake's car, but I'm positive it won't keep you out of Heaven. People do far worse things, believe me." I thought of my own Faustian pact. "When you're feeling better, you can buy him a wall-climbing car with your allowance and apologize to him. You don't have to believe in Heaven or Hell to do the right thing."

He didn't answer immediately.

"How does that sound?" I asked.

"Okay, but if I don't go to Heaven or Hell, what will happen to me?"

I wanted to promise him all kinds of things. I wanted to tell him he would never hurt again, he would be rewarded for all the good things he'd done in his life, and our family would soon be safe and warm and together. I was supposed to think positively, but I didn't know what was true, and I couldn't lie to him.

All that was tight and sorrowful inside me rose to my throat. My chest hurt from trying to hold it back. When I opened my mouth, the words slipped between my lips more easily than I would have expected, as if they were waiting to be said. "You're afraid you're going to die, aren't you?"

He shook his head. "Huh-uh, because you promised I wouldn't."

His words hit me with a thud. I remembered our conversation in the car three months ago, a week or two after this nightmare began.

"You pr-promised," Ethan said.

I moved from the chair to the edge of his bed and slid my fingers over his puffy, warm hand, swollen from the fluids beneath his skin.

He lifted his hand to my face. "Don't cry, Mom."

"It's just something I have to do to keep me strong. Will you let me cry as long and hard as I want? Because maybe my chest won't hurt so much."

He hesitated, then said, "I guess so."

"You shouldn't be upset and you shouldn't think it's your fault."

"It's b-better if your chest d-doesn't hurt, isn't it?"

"Much better."

Ethan fell asleep again, and I walked down the hall to the lounge for a cup of tea. When I came back, Joel was sitting in the chair next to the hospital bed, stroking Ethan's chapped hand with a rhythmic motion. I'd left my cell phone on the windowsill.

"You just missed Cappy's phone call," he said. "I told her you would call her right back."

"Is that what she asked?"

He looked puzzled. "I assumed you'd want to. Was I wrong?"

"No, that's fine."

Was it possible she could have slain all those demons and found the magic passwords already? The process sounded so frivolous, like playing one of those elaborate, super-realistic computer games with such names as Doom and Conquerors. I didn't want to call her. I wished she had done it without me, that she'd never asked for my approval. She knew we might be taking someone's life.

Maybe she couldn't face that responsibility alone. Maybe she hoped I would say no, leaving her to feel she had done what she could for Ethan.

I looked at the tethered phone on the stand beside Ethan's bed. "I'll call her in the lounge on my cell. I don't want to wake him up."

Joel gave me an odd look but didn't say anything. He knew that made no sense. The way Ethan slept these days, it would take more than softly spoken words to rouse him. I walked to a nearby lounge, sat on the cloud bench, and dug out my phone from my pocket. I told Siri to contact Cappy. She answered on the first ring.

"Hi, Joel said you called." Could she hear the reluctance in my voice? I didn't want to sound ungrateful.

"I'm looking at the UNOS list right now. Actually, there are several lists, but they're categorized by blood type, location and status. I put him at the top of the matching one."

"How many people were above him before you put him there?"

"Only two. Both status one."

"Were they children?"

"You don't want to know that, Delainie."

A woman, about thirty years old, walked into the lounge. She wore black jeans and a wrinkled white blouse, and her eyes looked glassy with fatigue. She must have a child here, I thought, and was probably looking for privacy like I had. After glancing at me, she sat on a blue vinyl bench and picked up a magazine, fingering the edges but not opening it. Instead, she fixed her gaze on a blank section of the wall above two frolicking sheep.

I lowered my voice. "Whose place did Ethan take, Cappy?"

"There's no reason for you to know. Would it make any difference who it was?"

"No...yes. Yes, it would make a difference. Is it a man or a woman?"

"A woman."

"Does it say anything about her, like how old she is or where she lives?"

"She's thirty-seven and she lives in Pendleton, Oregon."

"What else does it say? Does she have any children?"

"Delainie, don't do this."

"Does she have children?" I asked firmly.

"Possibly."

"My God," I whispered, "a thirty-seven-year-old mother with children." I looked at the woman across the room. It could have been her, a mother with problems like mine.

I was suddenly silent.

"Delainie? Don't think about it. Just don't think about it."

The woman glanced at me, then cleared her throat.

"I don't know if I can do it, Cappy."

"Okay," she said quietly.

"I'll call you later."

"Sure. I'll be here, waiting."

———

Joel and I were in the hospital cafeteria at seven that evening eating Chinese chicken salads for dinner. The only Asian influence I could detect in the salad was that the chicken chunks had been dipped in some soy sauce and a few crisp noodles had been scattered across it. It smelled old, as if it'd been yesterday's meal, but that didn't matter because I wasn't hungry anyway. I laid my fork aside.

Joel poked at a piece of lettuce. "Ethan had a bad day, huh?"

"Did he say that?"

"No, I was thinking that if you got any tenser, your bones would snap."

I rubbed my forehead with my fingertips. "I have a headache."

Joel balled up his napkin and dropped it on his plate. "Did you—?"

"Yes, I took a handful of aspirin but it didn't help."

I watched a waitress clear a nearby table, scooping up the cardboard plates, the plastic cups, and the straw covers that were scattered here and there like pickup sticks.

"You need to get out of this hospital and breathe some fresh air. Maybe you're coming down with the flu. You've been cooped up here for two straight weeks, absorbing all these germs."

"I don't want to leave Ethan."

"Nothing is going to happen in the next few hours. He's been sleeping comfortably, and I'll sit right next to him until you come back."

"I don't know where to go."

"Visit Cappy."

Strange that he should suggest her when he knew Jaya was the great comforter in our group.

"I don't feel like seeing anyone."

"Then go downtown and walk through the stores. You need to get out. You need to do something for yourself, even if it's just for an hour or two."

I winced. I was doing something completely selfish, but I couldn't tell him about it.

He must have sensed something because he reached over and covered my wrist with his hand. "You know, Lainie, I didn't think there was anything now that we couldn't talk about."

I looked up at the perforated white plasterboard squares on the ceiling. There shouldn't have been any secrets between us.

Chapter 39

I walked down the hill from the hospital, past the stores with all their cheery Christmas decorations, and continued toward the waterfront. Most of the boats in the harbor had colored lights strung along their masts, but the state ferries looked like sanctuaries from the pain of happy holidays. The ferry from Bainbridge was just arriving. It was on a whim that I decided to take the ferry to Bainbridge Island.

I purchased my ticket and waited for the boat to unload. Once it was empty, walk-on passengers were allowed to board first. I walked across the ramp and climbed the stairs to the passenger deck and sat in a booth near a window.

Soon I felt the ship moving. It was past peak time for the commuters, so the passenger deck wasn't crowded. A few people sat here and there nursing cups of coffee, reading newspapers and books, or working on laptops. I bought some hot tea at the snack bar and walked through the doors to the front deck. The night was cloudless. The frigid wind made my head throb. No one with any sense was out here, but then I didn't want to be around anyone. I could barely tolerate myself at the moment.

A gust of air hit me, wrapping my hair around my face, and spraying me with salt water. The coat I wore was warm enough on land but not on an open ship, and it wasn't waterproof. I retreated to the outdoor smoking area, with its rows of slatted wood benches behind a Plexiglas window. I thought I was alone there too, but I heard a light cough and smelled smoke. The orange tip of a cigarette skipped through the air.

"Miserable, isn't it?" a woman's voice said.

"Sure is," I said. So much for isolation.

I moved further into the shelter. In the dim light from the ferry's interior shining through the window behind us, I could see that she was about my age. She was tall and thin and wore a navy blue trench coat, one that looked like it might have come from an expensive shop. Her streaked ash blond hair, styled to curve under at her jaw line, had the marks of an excellent hairdresser.

I sat on the bench about eight feet from her and patted my own wild hair into place. "I have this romantic view of boats, but every time I get on one I become a target for Mother Nature."

She scooted closer to me, then laughed, the smoke deep in her lungs rattling her voice. "It's funny. I make this trip so often I forget I'm on a boat. I wouldn't even come up here if I didn't need a cigarette. It's not allowed on ferries, of course, but I don't think they'll catch me here. I don't smoke in my car or inside my house."

I buried my hands in my pockets to keep them warm. "That's a good policy."

"You'd think it would be. You'd think it would help me cut back, but it doesn't. I just end up leaping out of the car at regular intervals." She looked at the cigarette and made a face. "I hate these things."

I didn't respond. She didn't need any criticism from me.

She crushed the cigarette in a metal canister near her. "Yesterday, I came home from work and found my eleven-year-old daughter in her bedroom crying. She'd seen a documentary at school about the effects of tobacco. The scene that bothered her most showed a woman smoking a cigarette through a hole in her throat. She wanted to know how soon I would have to do that."

"A child that age makes a wonderful conscience."

"She sure does. I told her she's a stronger person than I am." She tucked the pack of cigarettes back into her purse. Do you have children?"

"An eleven-year-old son."

"Aren't eleven year olds wonderful? Is he a stronger person than you are?"

"Oh, yes. Although, I may be expecting too much of him." I pulled my jacket closer around me. "Not that I'm perfect. Right now, I'm about as imperfect as I have ever been."

"That's the way I feel. On the one hand I have this sweet daughter who's breaking my heart, and then I have this seventeen-year-old son who thinks I'm pond scum on the surface of his tortured life. He smokes, of course."

"How many times have you tried to quit?"

"About twenty, and that's just since my kids were born. Once I lasted three months. I went to a treatment center that time. They gave me patches and pills, and I could call them whenever I lost willpower. I lasted three long, excruciating months, and then I went back to smoking a pack a day."

I nodded.

"I really don't have many symptoms from smoking yet, but I get sick to my stomach every time I buy a carton of cigarettes. I guess that should tell me something, shouldn't it?"

"I would say there's a message in there." I thought of the unrelenting headache I'd had since Cappy told me she could manipulate the UNOS status list.

She laughed. "Yeah, like my body telling me I'm making the wrong choice."

"Uh-huh."

We turned to look at the approaching lights of the ferry dock.

"Now arriving Bainbridge," a voice said over the loudspeaker.

The woman stood and gathered up her purse and briefcase. When I didn't move, she gave me a questioning look. "Aren't you getting off?"

"No, I'm making this a round trip. It was nice talking with you." I held out my hand. "I'm Delainie."

She shook it. "I'm Cindy. I enjoyed the conversation too. The regulars don't usually like to talk."

Inside, people were hurrying toward the stairs to the car

deck.

"Have to go," she said. "The cars will be moving soon."

She turned to go..

"Cindy?"

She looked back.

"Try again, okay?" I said. "You're stronger than you realize."

She nodded.

After she left, I walked to the railing, leaned over and stared at the pure dark water. I saw something under the surface move — maybe a sea lion or one of those little pilot whales that populate Puget Sound. I swear there's something about being on the water at night that makes you see clearer. Maybe it's left over from times when your life depended on your night vision.

When I arrived at Lake Union, I walked down the long pier to

Cappy's houseboat. Little wisps of steam were rising from the lake into the cold night air. Most of her home was dark, but the light from her office window cast a warm glow over the black water, making it look as if it had been enameled.

I knocked quietly. I could hear Port barking, charging the door, and then panting noisily, but Cappy didn't answer until I banged on a window. After a few minutes, she opened the door and, leaning on her canes, gazed at me through bloodshot eyes. "Tell me Ethan is okay."

"He's the same. But I'm not. I feel like I'm rotting inside. I can't do it."

She opened the door wider, and I followed her into the living room, where she switched on a floor lamp and then turned to look at me. "Why?"

"Why?" I asked in surprise. "Because it's wrong. I appreciate everything you've done, but I can't get around the fact that we're killing someone, maybe not directly and maybe not right away but somewhere along that UNOS list. Even if we kept Ethan at the top of it, that doesn't mean this will work. The surgeon who is filling in for Coe might question it. He'll say, 'Somebody screwed up here,' and not do the operation."

"Suppose he doesn't question it, though. Wouldn't it be worth taking the chance?"

"No. If he did the transplant and that woman in Oregon died because she doesn't get a new liver in time, it would be my fault. This is a mother with children, Cappy, not some has-been, alcoholic actor or filthy rich ballplayer who massacred their own livers. How can I do that to a mother who's just like me, who's an ordinary woman trying to do her best?"

Cappy eased herself down on the sofa. "If that's what you want."

"You know I'm not religious, but I've always had moral standards. I really believe that whatever you do will come back to you. I know my lame version of the golden rule isn't all that reliable when you look at what some people get away with, but it's what I've based my life on."

She didn't say anything.

"Cappy, you're my dearest friend, but I don't want you to sacrifice yourself and I don't want to steal life from someone else."

What little light that was left in her eyes went out, and I realized how much her ability to save Ethan had meant to her. I hurt for her too.

The weight on my shoulders felt as though it would crush me. "I'm sorry," I whispered.

She lifted her hands slightly, then dropped them onto her lap again. "Don't be. It is wrong, of course."

As if someone else were acknowledging my decision, a wave smacked the houseboat, knocking it against its moorings. Across the lake, the festive, Christmas decorated Space Needle appeared to teeter like a saucer on a stick.

Chapter 40

We spent Christmas at the hospital, and I suppose in its own way it was the best one we'd ever had. Ethan rallied a bit, even sitting up for a time and talking to us.

Barbara and Hal arrived precisely at nine in the morning, and Ethan opened the gifts we'd set under his miniature plastic tree — a chemistry set, a watch that looked like it could tap into outer space, a book on special effects —things we feared he would never have the opportunity to use. Joel gave him an envelope filled with photographs of Ethan's monsters, fake road kill, severed limbs, and other creations he'd made through the years. They huddled over the pictures until Ethan's eyelids drooped and he had to rest a bit.

Hal brought his own present for Ethan, wrapped in a page from the Sunday comics and tied with green twine. It contained a pocketknife (contraband in the children's ward), a chunk of alder to practice carving on, and sandpaper in various grades. Hall showed him how to use the knife safely, cutting the wood with small, smooth movements. The nurses saw what he was doing but didn't say a word. We should have encouraged Ethan to spend more time with his grandfather.

Cappy and Liz came to the hospital around three in the afternoon, shortly after a cheery veteran nurse gave Ethan his medications, and Jaya, Rob, and Krishna arrived half an hour later. The room soon filled. Barbara and Liz sat in one corner, talking about knitting. Barbara, who was working on a brown sweater for Hal, showed Liz how to hold the needles. With her tongue firmly in the corner of her mouth, Liz managed to knit an entire row— something I never thought I would see.

Krishna was describing his own chemistry set to Ethan, telling him they could use it blow up Washington State. Joel stood there, touching Ethan's shoulder — always touching him and smiling at all of us. When Liz left, she hugged Barbara and thanked her for the knitting lesson.

As much as Ethan seemed to enjoy the holiday, he suffered for it. By evening, he could barely focus his eyes. His muscles began cramping, and he coughed up blood. Nurses ran in and out of his room, checking his vital signs, dispensing medicine, frowning with concern.

Ethan didn't bounce back to his pre-Christmas condition. He no longer had the strength to sit up. He slept fitfully, only a few hours at a time, and often woke up with cramps in his legs. We hardly left his side now. My friends took turns bringing us take-out meals. Ethan looked at them through glazed eyes.

At times, he flailed his arms and yelled things like "Stop doing that!" and "That's no way to behave!" at the walls, and I wondered what battles he was fighting. The only thing that kept me sane was that he didn't appear afraid.

Occasionally, his eyes cleared, and he strained to look at us. I believe he understood everything at those moments.

Three days after Christmas, Dr. Sidon came to check on him. He looked at all the nurses' notes on Ethan's chart.

He bent over him. "How are you feeling, Ethan?"

Ethan shifted uncomfortably but didn't answer. Dr. Sidon listened to his heart and palpated his belly. Ethan groaned.

After he'd finished, he took Joel and me aside. "I'll ask UNOS to move him up to Status 1."

I cried then. Joel put his arm around me, and I leaned against him. I had waited for this moment. I had even begged Dr. Coe for it, but now it seemed unbearable.

"Oh, God," Joel said, "I don't know how to thank you."

I nodded, unable to speak.

Dr. Sidon said, "This doesn't mean he's at the top of the list. There are people ahead of him, but he's getting closer. UNOS works very hard to keep it fair."

I winced because I had tried to do something very unfair. I grabbed the arm of Dr. Sidon's jacket. He didn't pull away. He actually smiled. I guess he was getting used to me now.

"Please tell me he'll get the liver in time," I murmured.

His smile softened. "I can't tell you that but we always hope."

After the doctor left the room, Joel took in a deep breath and said, "I can't believe I'm praying someone else will die so our son can live."

I didn't know if I could ever tell him what I had almost done.

———————

Three days before New Year's, the candy stripers went from room to room, removing the red-and-white felt Christmas stockings from the patients' doors and taping up silver paper starbursts instead.

Ethan didn't see the one with his name on it. Even if he wanted to leave his bed, we would never have been able to un-tangle the network of tubes running in and out of him. His face shone with a film of perspiration, and he couldn't keep his eyes open for more than a few seconds. Sometimes, he tried to speak, but his tongue got in the way of his words.

I heard a flurry of sirens outside and saw nurses in the hall rushing toward the sounds.

Dr. Sidon stopped by every few hours. Every time he walked in, I gave a start. But he'd only come to check Ethan and reassure us that UNOS would contact the hospital as soon as the appropriate donor liver became available.

I stood and grabbed the bed rail to keep from wobbling.

"There was an accident," I said. "I heard the sirens."

"Yes, a motorcyclist. He's alive but has severe brain damage."

"Oh." I didn't want to ask the question.

Dr. Sidon saved me. "His blood type is A. I'm sorry."

His voice seemed to be coming from very far away.

The next day, Ethan drifted in and out of awareness. He no longer spoke at all, but I could feel when his muscles cramped or his breathing changed. I could sense fluctuations in his body temperature and his blood pressure. I felt attuned to him, the way I had during the last months of my pregnancy. I tried to open myself to his pain and absorb what I could of it. I hurt so much that I convinced myself my methods were working.

I sat beside him, clutching his hand and whispering, "I love you, Ethan Skywalker," over and over. Once, his eyes fluttered open, and he looked directly at me. I knew he had heard. I said, "I love you, Ethan Skywalker," again so that he could hold that in his mind. An instant later, he retreated into whatever dark cave protected him now.

All the things they say about death and dying are true, especially the part about not wanting the person you love to suffer any longer. It seems to rise unbidden as a plea to whomever would listen. Don't let him suffer anymore. Please just give me that.

I walked over and eased myself onto the cot next to Joel.

That night, I stayed on my cot beside Ethan's hospital bed, occasionally leaning my forehead against the mattress and dozing off. Joel was on the other side of me. Sometime in the next few hours, he crawled over the inch that separated our cots and folded me in his arms, his breath moist on my temple. There was barely room for me, much less him, but I felt secure in the curve of his body.

Sometime during the night, someone tapped my shoulder. I looked up and saw a nurse with hair like spun gold hovering above me. "It's here," she said in the sweetest voice I'd ever heard. Relief and joy surged through my body and tears came like the waters from a flood, but my excitement jolted me awake. There were only three of us in the room, and Ethan lay just as he had.

Chapter 41

In the early morning, I heard a soft voice.

"Mr. And Mrs. Franklin?"

I awoke abruptly, immediately regretting that I had spent so much time sleeping. I couldn't bear the loss of even a minute now. Joel stirred then too, and we stiffly untangled ourselves from the cot.

I blinked at the silhouette, the light from the hall backlighting him, and recognized his form.

"Doctor Sidon?" I asked eagerly.

"...A car accident...Tacoma." I could barely understand what he was saying. "Three teenage boys. One dead. Two have sustained severe brain injuries. They won't recover."

"And their blood types?" I whispered.

"They're identical twins and their type is O."

I fell back onto the pillow. Ethan was type B. "I can't imagine their parents' pain."

I thought about the woman with type B in Oregon. She wouldn't get a liver either.

"I don't understand," Joel murmured. "Why are you telling us this? It seems so cruel because it can't help Ethan."

"I guess Doctor Coe didn't fully explain about the blood types."

I shook my head. At least my headache was gone. "Tell us what?"

He smiled down at me. "Type O works with all other blood types. It's a universal donor."

Maybe Dr. Coe had told us, but we were so swamped with

information, I continually felt underwater.

"One of the livers is being airlifted here. Should arrive in half an hour. The other is going to a woman in Oregon."

I tasted the tears running down my cheeks. I had thought there would be a brass band, cymbals and drums at the very least, but the room was utterly quiet. I couldn't trust myself to speak—or to believe.

<hr />

The doctor and nurses took Ethan directly into surgery. I floated in and out of time, but I was dimly aware it was the last day of the year. Outside, the city had come out from under its veil of winter rain. The sky spread out, still and satiny, with a sun so bright it seemed phosphorescent. Steamy billows rose from roof vents on other buildings. People passed on the sidewalks below, their breath spinning frosty puffs, their coats tightly clutched around them.

The day passed hypnotically as we waited. I tried not to breathe in case Fate might notice me and crush my hopes.

I don't know how long the surgery took. I couldn't have said whether it was morning or afternoon, but I remember Dr. Sidon standing in the doorway in his rumpled, blood-stained scrubs, his paper mask dangling, his mouth forming a tired smile.

I knew the transplant was successful before he said it.

<hr />

That night in the recovery room, Joel leaned over Ethan and kissed his forehead. "It's New Year's Eve, buddy. They'll be shooting off firecrackers soon. Next year, we'll do that, okay?"

I think Ethan heard him because his eyes fluttered. Perspiration matted his hair, finally subduing his cowlicks, but he didn't seem to be in pain. I held his hand, the one that didn't have a needle stuck into it, and savored its warmth.

Joel looked at me. "You need to get some rest, Lainie."

I shook my head. "I have to be able to hold onto him."

He arranged our cots so that they lined up parallel on each

side of Ethan's bed. I laid close enough so I could reach up and touch him. We looked like the Three Bears.

Once we'd settled in, I glanced at Joel. He stared at the ceiling, his eyes shiny with reflected light from the lamp over Ethan's bed. He was weeping.

I wish I could say I understand now how the world works. But I don't. After all these months of anguish, it occurred to me that "liver" has the word "live" in it. Why hadn't I thought of that before?

I wish I could explain why Ethan managed to get a transplant and others can't. I wanted to console the family, but they asked to remain anonymous. We would never be able to thank them enough or ease their terrible pain. We could only be grateful.

I wish I could say the rest of our lives would be blissful, but I didn't believe that either. I decided I wouldn't think beyond each day. I knew I wouldn't be able to protect Ethan, that a mother can do only so much, that wishes and caution and strength aren't enough, but I heard Ethan saying, *Just do your best, Mom.* I also knew I'd never stop worrying about him. His life would always be fragile but then so were ours. Loving can be painful but having no one to love is worse.

We must have dozed because the next thing I remember was the sound of horns blasting on the street outside. I jumped up from the cot and looked at Ethan. His eyes were open and he smiled. Maybe it was my imagination but his color already looked better.

"Hi, Ethan Skywalker," I said. "How are you feeling?"

"Okay, I guess," he said drowsily.

In seconds, Joel was beside me. "Hi, buddy."

"Hi, Dad." He glanced around the room. "I didn't die, did I?"

"No," Joel said, tears in his eyes. "You have a new liver. You're going to get well now."

Firecrackers sizzled and popped, and a sequence of four booms rattled the hospital windows.

"What's all that noise?" Ethan asked.

"Fireworks," Joel said. "They're shooting them off from the

Space Needle. It's New Year's Eve."

I turned and stared out the window at the darkness. Rockets boomed, better than a brass band.

Hazy ribbons of light in red and blue and gold and green shot from the Space Needle and soared and twirled and spiraled down, breaking into a thousand tiny points that rained like confetti.

A giant burst of silver illuminated the cotton sky. It must have been the grand finale because afterward all was quiet.

ABOUT ME

It's unlikely I would have ever written a novel if I hadn't lost my job. I was Cineplex Odeon's advertising director for the Northwest region, and life was good.

Then, the company shut down the entire Seattle office, and I was suddenly out of work. I hated getting up each morning to look for a new job, so I decided to write a novel instead. How difficult could that be? I was a journalist. I knew how to write. Uh-huh.

I cloistered myself in a room all day and wrote and wrote and wrote. I was sure I'd written the great American novel, but when I sent it out, I couldn't find an agent or an editor to agree with me. In despair, I spent three days in bed, during which I got pretty sick of myself.

Eventually, I crawled out and wrote another novel. I knew the movie business, drive-in theaters and Indiana, where I'd grown up. Writing *The Starlite Drive-in* was like opening a spigot.

Shortly after finishing it, I acquired an agent and, a few months later, a major New York publisher, William Morrow & Co.

I sent an advance copy to my parents. My mother wrote back, "It is a good book. If all the cussing and some of the sex were out of it, it would be a very good book. Love, Mom."

My life changed dramatically. I was now a published writer and people treated me differently. They acted like I was a smarter, more interesting person than I'd been just a few months before.

I received an invitation to attend a Literary Guild party in the New York Waldorf Astoria's Starlight Room, which coincidentally occurred on my birthday. It was one of those evenings when all the stars, planets and moons moved into alignment.

Another highlight was the avalanche of notes and letters I received from readers. Many told me about their nostalgic memories of childhood and drive-in theatres. I wrote back to as many as I could and thanked them.

Life was good again.

ACKNOWLEDGMENTS

I appreciate the information and help the doctors and staff at the University of Washington Medical Center and the United Network of Organ Sharing (UNOS) gave me in writing this book. They save lives and I can think of no higher contribution to humanity.

Manufactured by Amazon.ca
Bolton, ON

43637101R00182